PENGUIN BOOKS

MY SISTER VICTORIA

Charlotte Moore was born in 1959. She read English at St Anne's College, Oxford, and History of Art at Birkbeck College, London. She was a teacher for twelve years before taking up writing full-time. She has published two other novels, *Promises Past* and *Martha's Ark*. Her journalism has appeared in *The Times*, the *Independent on Sunday*, the *Daily Telegraph*, *Tatler* and the *Spectator*. She lives in Sussex with her three young sons.

My Sister, Victoria

CHARLOTTE MOORE

PENGUIN BOOKS

PENGUIN BOOKS

Published by the Penguin Group
Penguin Books Ltd, 27 Wrights Lane, London W8 5TZ, England
Penguin Putnam Inc., 375 Hudson Street, New York, New York 10014, USA
Penguin Books Australia Ltd, Ringwood, Victoria, Australia
Penguin Books Canada Ltd, 10 Alcorn Avenue, Toronto, Ontario, Canada M4V 3B2
Penguin Books (NZ) Ltd, Private Bag 102902, NSMC, Auckland, New Zealand

Penguin Books Ltd, Registered Offices: Harmondsworth, Middlesex, England

First published 2000
1 3 5 7 9 10 8 6 4 2

Set in 11/15pt Bembo
Phototypeset by Intype London Ltd
Printed in England by Clays Ltd, St Ives plc

In memory of Hilary Mary Moore, 1927–96

Acknowledgements

Special thanks are due to Sarah Molloy, Louise Moore and Harriet Evans; to Tom and Sarah Norris; and particularly to Eva Littna.

I

It's been years since I paid much attention to my birthday. Even when I was a child, the celebrations never really seemed to fizz. The date had something to do with the somewhat muted atmosphere – I was born in the middle of January, too close to Christmas to be exciting, not close enough to be interesting. Mine was a birthday that people found easy to forget, not like Victoria's. Victoria was born on the first of May. When else?

But I wasn't thinking about Victoria as I battled my way home from the underground station. Birthdays bring back memories, and for several years after she left they were painful occasions for me, but I had trained myself so rigorously to suppress all thoughts of her that at last I seemed to have succeeded. No, this birthday felt different. My legs ached as I toiled up the steep hill that led to my flat, and I had to scrunch up my eyes against the gritty North London wind, but my hopes were high. I would be spending this birthday evening as half of a couple, for the first time since . . . it would be quite difficult to work out when. I'd met Alex Malone six months earlier at a dinner party given by our mutual friends Maddy and Ned, and we'd been seeing each other ever since. Maddy had been supplying me with introductions to what she regarded as suitable spare men since the early eighties; it had become a standing joke between us. But at this particular dinner party on that steamy July evening six months before, something had just gone right for once, and now Alex Malone and I were spending most of our nights together, at his place or at mine. We'd even embarked on a little gentle house-hunting at weekends. At (just) thirty-seven and with an unspec-tacular romantic history, I was far too cautious to count on retaining the affections of a newly divorced, childless, intel-ligent man with an interesting job – he's the political editor for one of the broadsheets – who seemed to share a significant number of my tastes and interests, and who could easily pass as handsome if you didn't mind skinny men. So I wasn't announcing anything to the world at large, was hardly daring to reckon the number of potentially childbearing years I had left, though a child was what I wanted above all else. But the fact remained that we had spent a couple of Saturday mornings inspecting flats in the more affordable parts of Kilburn and North Kensington, at his instigation, not mine. And tonight Maddy was giving another dinner, ostensibly to celebrate my birthday, but really, I knew without asking, as an act of consolation, to nudge our coupledom a little further down the road of certainty and public recognition.

Even as a child I had trained myself not to look forward to things too much, because quiet disappointments were easier to cope with than clamorous ones, so now, as I struggled back from the tube, I allowed myself only five minutes to dwell on my hopes before I folded them up and tidied them away. In those five minutes I gloated on what the coming year might bring. A wedding? Nice, but not essential. A flat – the most likely outcome. And Alex only picked up the details of two-bedroomed flats. A baby, then. I knew Alex had always wanted children, it was his ex-wife who had demurred. Thank goodness she had! A baby. My next year's birthday present, to Alex and to myself.

A lot can happen in five minutes. My baby — a boy, chubby and rosy with blond hair — was almost out of toddlerhood by the time I reached my ground-floor flat. But so efficient had my mental discipline become that he was quite packed away before I'd even turned the key in the lock, and when I stood in the communal entrance hall and out of old habit scrutinized my appearance in the mirror that the landlord had installed in an attempt to create space and light where there was none, my main feeling was simple relief to be out of that dirty, bullying wind.

I pulled off my hat and fluffed up the springy brown hair that always looked so sad and squashed after having a hat on it. My hat annoyed me. It was a lovely hat, like something out of *Anna Karenina*, suede the colour of cigars with a brim of thick brown fur flecked with black. Fake fur, of course, but a very good fake. When I wore it, I liked to imagine my face below it, fragile and flower-like on the slender stem of my neck. But when I actually caught sight of my reflection, there was that same earnest, pleasant-looking bun of a face that had been looking back at me for thirty-seven years, nothing remotely haunting or vulnerable about it. The hat annoyed me because it had no transforming powers. I would never look like a tragic heroine, even though you could say that there has been tragedy in my life.

My pile of birthday post lay on the hall table, bound by a thick rubber band. I picked it up and unlocked my own front door, which had three different kinds of lock. Not my paranoia; the previous tenant had been pestered by a stalker. I do not feel that I am the sort of person who would get stalked.

I set the post aside untouched and filled the kettle. I'm always starving when I get back from work, and gasping for a cup of tea. Whether I've had an expense-account lunch in pursuit of a story – I'm a journalist – or a peanut-butter sandwich on a park bench, it doesn't make any difference. The minute I'm through the front door I head straight for the fridge. I took out a polystyrene tub of taramasalata and dunked Ritz biscuits into it. Some of them broke, leaving ugly crumbs.

I licked my fingers and pressed the replay button on my answerphone. Children's voices giggled their way through 'Happy Birthday To You' – that was Rose, my god-daughter, and her little sister, Imogen. Maddy's children – and so far, the most important children in my life. The song was followed by their mother's rich, laughing voice, shooing them off the telephone and adding that she'd expect Alex and me at half past eight. The next message was from my friend Katie, who's one of the least organized people I know – even her voice sounds dishevelled – ringing to say Happy Birthday and she'd see me at Maddy's but she might be a little late because she'd forgotten the date and had promised to pop in to a private view which was really important because Milo Whatsisname, the artist in question, was terribly sweet but didn't have a lot of confidence and – here the tape ran out, leaving the highly coloured but inexhaustible skein of Katie's monologue dangling. I smiled. There would be no chance of an early night – we wouldn't be seeing Katie before eleven, if at all. I somehow doubted her ability to get from Soho to Highgate in one piece, after a few drinks. Katie is the only friend I've got left whose behaviour hasn't changed at all since she was nineteen. Like me, she's childless and – I was about to say single. She is. I keep forgetting I'm not.

No more messages, then. I pricked the little bubble of disappointment that threatened to well up at the absence of Alex's soft, humorous voice, but then there came a thump at the door. My spirits dipped; I knew that thump. It was the hallmark of Mrs Curtin, who was eighty-three and lived alone in the flat above. Her thumps were usually motivated by the need to lodge a complaint – not necessarily against me, the world at large would do. I briefly considered pretending to be out, but that kind of pretence isn't really an option for a vicar's daughter like me. And in any case, I had been feeling vaguely uncomfortable about Mrs Curtin ever since Alex had called her Mrs Cushion by mistake. I don't think she heard, but still . . . I opened the door.

Mrs Curtin was looking rather as if Birnam Wood had come to Dunsinane. Her arms were full of one of the largest bouquets I'd ever seen. It was a state-of-the-art bouquet, with curly twigs and interesting berries and a shock of foliage as well as flowers. She pushed the bundle into my arms. 'These came for you dinnertime,' she said. 'They should of known you'd be out. Here, take 'em, they don't do my asthma no good.' I burbled apologies and thanks. 'A bit messy,' she opined, 'all them leaves. Still, it's the thought that counts. He'll be wanting to put a ring on your finger one of these days. Watch out for them lilies,' – jabbing one – 'them lilies stain.' And she stumped off upstairs.

The bouquet was much too big for any of my three rather humble vases. I propped it in the sink and opened the miniature envelope that came with it. 'Will you marry me?' said the little card, in backwards-sloping florist's handwriting. The room span. I hugged myself and danced a little jig. 'Do you know,' I told the little card, 'I rather think I will.'

I ran a bath, washed my hair, and wrapped myself in the worn, plaid dressing-gown, faded to a colour that had no name, that had once been my father's. Since his last stroke he'd had to spend so much more of his time in a dressing-gown that Aunt Marigold and I had together chosen him a new one in a washable flannel, and I'd carted the old one off, claiming that I was going to throw it away; but in the event I didn't have the heart. I had forced myself, over the years, not to be sentimental about objects, and the dressing-gown was one of the very few items in my flat that had any link with the past. It was not a garment that I would wear when Alex was around. I had a silky kimono-type thing as well, but I'd never really enjoyed wearing it much. The trouble with me and clothes is that in the last analysis I lack conviction. I'm a successful career journalist and I try to look the part. My clothes are well cut, as is my hair, my jewellery is minimal but of good quality, my make-up is carefully understated. I've trained myself to throw away cloggy mascara and laddered tights. I even went to an image consultant once – I was forced to by Maddy – so now I know what shapes and colours to avoid, and I stick to the rules. But I can never concentrate quite hard enough to get all the details right, and it's the details that give you away. My hair will spring out of the most expensively achieved shape; I have never been able to suppress its desire to do its own thing. And a truly smart woman would not give houseroom to a dressing-gown like mine even for the best of sentimental reasons.

It wasn't until after the bath that I remembered my post. I sat bundled up in that dressing-gown on the edge of my bed, opening birthday cards and waiting for my skin to stop feeling clammy so that I could put on my tights. My bedroom was a mess – books and magazines strewn over the bed, tufts of cotton wool floating like dolls' icebergs on the glass top of the dressing-table, a scrap of paper screaming DUSTBINS stuck in the frame of the mirror where I wouldn't miss it in the morning. In our early days I'd have made tidying the bedroom a priority if Alex was coming round. Was it a good or a bad thing that, in relation to tidying up, we no longer seemed to be in our 'early days'?

There were quite a few cards – I've got good friends – including a postcard from my brother Simon, who is working for a relief agency in the Sudan. It was pure luck, surely, that this arrived actually on my birthday. Simon had always only the haziest idea about other people's birthdays, though he usually managed to narrow mine down to the right month. The postcard, blurred photographs of different kinds of Sudanese wildlife set in separate, jauntily angled frames, was curiously floppy. Simon had covered it with cramped handwriting in blotchy biro. I laid it aside, to decipher at leisure.

I left the most boring-looking letter till last. My name and address were typed on to a brown envelope. I did just notice, though, that it said Ruthie Rampling, which was a little odd because anyone remotely official would put Ruth, or Ms R. And when I opened it and saw the handwriting – I can hardly describe the effect it had on me. I felt as if I had been chopped down the middle by a giant cleaver, and as the two halves of my body fell tidily asunder I glimpsed a gully, a chasm, pointed rocks and tangled trees and dark birds wheeling overhead on ragged wings. And above all, the thunder of rushing water.

That was all over in a second or less, and it left me trembling and alone on the edge of my bed, pale and naked beneath a looming shadow. I tried to shake it off; I stepped back into my strong grown woman's body and tied my big bunchy dressing-gown more tightly round myself. I couldn't read Victoria's letter. I mean I physically couldn't. When I tried to look at it my eyes fizzed black and bottle-green, as they do when you enter a dark interior from a sunny garden. I couldn't even touch it. I threw it on to the middle of my bed and slapped a magazine on top of it, and then something automatic took over and I did my hair and face and put on a short black skirt and a rust-coloured velvet jacket that made my eyes look bluer, because there was still a normal and reassuring voice inside me telling me that it really wouldn't be a good idea to answer the door to Alex wearing that dressing-gown.

I tried sitting on the living-room sofa with a newspaper, but that was useless. I flicked through my birthday cards again and arranged them on the mantelpiece. I wandered back into the kitchen and saw the flowers in the sink, touched the lilies' staining tips, and thought, He wants to marry me. I mustn't forget that. I opened the fridge and took out a half-empty bottle of white Rioja and poured myself a glass. I raised my glass to the light and twirled the straw-coloured liquid and said it aloud: 'Alex wants to marry me.'

But meanwhile, on my bed – our bed, almost – Victoria's letter festered like a wound. And I knew I had to read it before Alex arrived. So I swallowed my drink in one gulp and braced myself. The address at the top said Edinburgh. Why Edinburgh? Victoria had nothing to do with Edinburgh. The only fact I'd known about her in the last sixteen years was that at some point she'd gone to live in America. I have a feeling that our Aunt Marigold always knew roughly where she was, but I made a point of never asking. And my father – well, these days it was difficult enough for him to talk about the weather. There was never any need to talk to him about Victoria.

I read the letter. It was not very long. It did not attempt to summarize the last sixteen years. What it did say was this:

I've been through some difficult times, Ruthie, and I'm coming to the end. To tell you straight: I've got cancer. I lost a breast – careless, eh? – and now it's spreading to my lymph glands. It's only a matter of months. We're living here with my friend Maisie Nicholls – you may know of her, she's quite a well-known potter – and this is all right for the time being, but – there's quite a big 'but'.

Ruthie, I want you to look after my daughter for me. Her name is Isobel Ruth Rampling, and she's eight years old. People say she looks like me. I'd far rather she looked like you.

I got your address from Westaby. I'd imagined you'd be baking

9

cakes for a great big bouncy family by now, like Aunt Sarah, but it
doesn't sound like it. But please, whatever your circumstances, take
Isobel for me. You don't owe me anything. No one could be more
aware of that than I am. But do you remember, the things we said
by the sea, all those years ago?

There's no one else. Be brave, Ruthie, be brave enough for both of
us. Remember, we belong together.

There followed some practical details, the names and addresses of doctors and schools and solicitors. There was no mention of the child's father.

I folded the letter and put it into the drawer of my dressing-table. Then I withdrew it again and put it into my jacket pocket. It seemed safer to carry it with me. The blood drummed in my head. I didn't know what to do, but my instinct said, carry on with this as if nothing has happened. I rinsed out my wine glass and retouched my lipstick and then the doorbell rang because Alex had come to claim me as his bride.

He didn't hold out his arms to me. He stood on the doorstep grinning, and said, 'Well?'

'Well what?' I said, affecting insouciance, trying to play a teasing game.

'Well – has it been a good birthday so far?'

'Pretty good,' I said. 'Above average.' I could see doubt flicker across his face. Had the flowers arrived? Had the card fallen off, unnoticed? Had the florist got the message wrong? But there wasn't any real uncertainty about the eventual outcome. 'You can come in,' I said, going ahead of him into the kitchen.

'Any – surprises?' he asked. 'Oh! I see your sink is full of flowers.'

'Mrs Curtin brought them down,' I said, smirking. 'I can't imagine who they're from.'

'Can't you?' he said, and now he did hold out his arms, and I fell into them. 'Oh Alex, they're fantastic,' I whispered as he buried his face in my neck.

'Does that mean Yes?'

'I rather think it does.'

He began to manoeuvre me towards the bedroom. 'We've got time,' he said, 'haven't we?' But Victoria's letter crackled in my pocket, and I pushed him gently away. 'Not really,' I said. 'Later.'

'All right,' said Alex. 'Later will be even better.'

In the taxi he chattered on about when and how and where we'd live, and then as we rumbled into the tree-filled Highgate square where Ned and Maddy lived, he said, 'You're very quiet, Ruthie. Are you sure – '

'Of course I'm sure,' I said. 'But Alex, don't let's announce it tonight. I need some time to get used to it. Please.'

It was obvious he minded, obvious that this evening had taken shape in his mind as the perfect backdrop for the announcement of our engagement – Alex is naturally greg-arious, and the delighted response of our friends would have added considerably to his own delight. But he just said, 'Whatever you say, Ruthie. Whatever it takes.' He squeezed my hand, and for the first time ever the pressure of his was unwelcome, like an itchy glove on a warm day. I endured it because we were nearly there, and I thought, damn you, Victoria.

There were ten of us at dinner, all well known to each other. We happily guzzled Maddy's bold, vibrant food and swilled Ned's adventurously chosen wine and exchanged gossip and in-jokes. If I was a little distracted it was not so anyone would notice. Alex was seated down the other end of the table, which was almost a relief.

Imogen and Rose, clean and sweet in white lawn nighties sprinkled with rosebuds, their dark curls burnished by the candlelight, leaned against our chairs and demanded titbits and sips of wine. They had to be shooed off to bed three times. The third time I offered to accompany them, glad of the space to think. I let them tell me – not for by any means the first time – the names of all their stuffed animals. I read them one story each, then waited in the rocking chair in their darkened room listening to the slowing of their breathing. This, I thought, is the texture of their childhood, the sighing creak of the rocking chair, car headlights making watery arcs across the ceiling, spicy smells and adult laughter drifting up the stairs. I thought of Ned's dark stubbly chin making them giggle when he kissed them goodnight, of Maddy's amber beads bumping their noses as she bent over them. I thought of the pair of them, only eighteen months between them, Imogen already the leader despite being younger, dreamy Rose the creative force in their elaborate, conspiratorial games. Impossible to imagine that there was anything in the world to do them harm. And yet, what had become of my childhood, the sounds, the scents, the rituals that had nourished the furthest recesses of my mind? There had been a time, once, when for me, too, all had been as sweet and calm and safe as it now seemed to be for these two sleeping girls. But that time had been gone for thirty years.

And what of Victoria's child, this Isobel Ruth – my mail-order daughter, if Victoria had her way. If she had her way! When had Victoria ever not had her way? In her days of life and health I had never found the strength to thwart her. Now that she was dying, how could I possibly resist?

I thought of Alex downstairs, bright, kind, ordinary Alex, who loved me just in the good and comfortable way that most people understand. I knew that if I took Victoria's daughter, my future with Alex would be lost. 'I won't do it,' I told myself, 'dying or not.' And then I thought, You fool, she doesn't have to be dying. Why, why, after all these years, do you still automatically believe her?

I heard the doorbell and the sound of Katie's voice in the hall, that breathy, laughing voice that had become part of the comfort of my adult world. I raised myself from the rocking chair, trying not to let it creak, and slipped downstairs to greet her. 'God, honestly,' she exclaimed as we embraced, 'the things I do for you, Ruthie Rampling. *Everyone* was at this private view – and I mean, *everyone*.' She reeled off the names of some fashionable actors, artists, models and the like. 'Such a sacrifice! And I bet you've scoffed all the risotto, too.'

'No, no,' called Maddy from the kitchen. She came out with a covered plate and hustled us to the dining table. 'Here,

Katie. Pepper, olive oil, Parmesan. Everything your heart could desire.'

'Not exactly my heart. My stomach is a far more important organ – or at least, it gets a lot more use.' Katie scattered Parmesan shavings over her portion with a liberal hand. She continued her account of the private view. 'Lily McBain was there – Oh yes, you *do* know, Ruthie. That skinny model there was all that fuss about.'

'Lily McBain?' asked Ned. 'What's she like, in the flesh?'

'In the flesh doesn't really describe it, Ned. "In the bone", more like. I've never seen anyone so tiny in my entire life. She's this wide' – Katie held up a fork – 'and her arms are like – not sticks, something softer than sticks. Like thongs.'

'But is she beautiful?'

'Oh yes, she's beautiful all right. It's rubbish, the papers saying she'll turn little girls anorexic. She looks healthy enough. You can see she's just meant to be like that.'

'But that won't stop plump little girls from starving themselves – '

'Well, maybe not, but that's not Lily McBain's fault. What's she supposed to do, take the veil? To have beauty like that, it's a kind of genius.'

'You sound very taken with her, Katie,' put in Maddy as she ladled out tiramisu.

'Oh, I am, I am. I'm a great sucker for beauty. I love the way it doesn't need any further justification.'

'I wonder,' said Alex, 'whether someone can be that beautiful and still be human. I don't think I've ever properly known anyone like that.'

14

'I certainly haven't,' said Elizabeth, who was sitting on his left. 'I mean, lots of pretty people, obviously. In fact, if I like someone enough I nearly always think they're pretty.'

'How sweet you are, Lizzy,' teased James.

'Yes, aren't I! But a real beauty – I mean, you never see them in the street, even. Surely they don't exist, outside magazines?'

Oh, they do, I thought. I let the conversation swirl away from me, and I concentrated on my pudding and struggled for mastery over the pricking in my eyes. Oh, Victoria, I thought, what will this cancer make of your beauty, my lost sister, my secret twin? If it hadn't been for that great beauty, would any of it have happened? And there I was back believing in her again, because when you feel great love for someone, you have to believe in them. And I knew that if I was to understand my own future as well as my own past, Victoria's was the story that would have to be told.

2

'Run,' whispered Victoria, touching my arm. 'Just run. He won't be able to keep up.'

I obeyed. I heard Simon calling 'Ruthie, Ruthie, wait for me,' and I didn't like to hear his gruff little voice growing fainter and more forlorn, but of course I had to follow Victoria – the flash of her thin brown legs, the snaky streamers of her long black hair – as she ran just ahead of me, down the path that led to the sea.

We scrambled, panting, over the rocks. Victoria knew just where to place each sandalled foot. I was larger, and I knew the cottage, the beach, the whole place, so much better than she, but I was the one who skidded on seaweed, fell flat against a barnacle colony and raised a red weal on my arm, splatted the palm of my hand into a globule of sticky tar when I reached out to break my fall. But I didn't care, once I was safe with Victoria behind the big Watch Rock.

We sat on the Throne Stones, a pair of humps, smooth and dark like the backs of seals. The Throne Stones could only be reached when the tide was low. My grazed arm throbbed pleasantly in the hot sun. I couldn't hear Simon's calling any more. All I could hear was the greasy squeal of gulls and the slap and sigh of the waves as they broke in lacy ruffs on the sand.

I took off my sandals and wove dark emerald strands of

seaweed in and out of my toes, but I couldn't quite put Simon out of my mind. Ever since I was born, my mother had drummed into me a sense of responsibility for him; more than that, she had insisted that I love him too. Doing your duty isn't enough if you don't have love, she said. Love suffereth long, and is kind. Love seeketh not her own. St Paul's words to the Corinthians were the cornerstone of my mother's philosophy, I now realize, and she did a pretty good job of sticking to them, too. But as for me at ten years old – well, I thought I knew about suffering long, and I was sometimes kind. But Simon could be very annoying.

Victoria, as so often, seemed to read my thoughts. 'He'll be all right,' she said. 'He won't get lost. He'll give up, and go back to the crabs. He prefers them. Really.'

I allowed my conscience to be calmed. It was true that Simon loved his crabs. He kept them in an aquarium on the wooden bench in the porch and spent hours with them, not doing anything, just watching and muttering. I thought of him crouched there, twiddling a feather or a twig in front of their feebly snapping claws, and felt better. I opened my tarry hand, remembering just in time not to rub it on my shorts. I scraped at the stain with a splinter of driftwood, then ground my palm into the sand. The beach was covered by a hot dry crust, but my hand squirmed down, into the cold, slow ooze beneath. I looked up at my cousin, sitting with her legs tucked under her on the higher of the two stones, looking like the statue of the Little Mermaid in Copenhagen. I had not been to Copenhagen – at ten I had never yet left England – but someone had sent a postcard of the Little Mermaid to my mother and she'd given it to me to stick on the side of my wardrobe. Victoria was envious of that. She said her mother, my Aunt Angela, never let her stick things up with Sellotape because it left marks. I had never seen Victoria's bedroom because Uncle Jeremy worked for an oil company and they always lived abroad; I only saw Victoria when they had home leave, which in my opinion wasn't nearly often enough.

Though I hadn't ever seen her bedroom, I thought about Victoria a lot; far more, I'm sure, than she ever thought about me. In my head I had a picture of her room – large, white, with a fan whirring on the ceiling and slatted green shutters at the windows, because Uncle Jeremy had been posted to a hot country, a country in Africa beginning with M. There was a gauzy white curtain that would billow like a ghost when the hot dry wind crept through the shutters. That much, Victoria had described to me. The rest I made up for myself. I never thought of toys in her room, just whorled, pink-lipped shells and painted beads and garlands of exotic flowers. Fruit, too; pineapples, and mangoes, which I imagined were bright orange, and little red bananas, heaped in a wooden bowl. I don't know why I thought Victoria would have fruit in her bedroom. I didn't know anybody who did. I never did; just a plain digestive biscuit and water in a plastic beaker, to keep me going before breakfast, because I always woke at dawn.

When I lay in my own bed at home, which was the Rectory, Gadham, Oxfordshire, I could see the Little Mermaid postcard on the side of my wardrobe. I often lay and looked at it and made up stories about it. And now, here sat Victoria like the statue come to life, with her black hair falling about her shoulders in waves that dwindled into points and her dark eyes fixed on the distant, glittering horizon. Already, Victoria seemed to belong to this seaside place. The old coastguard cottage was owned jointly by our two families, but inevitably my family had used it far more, because of Uncle Jeremy being abroad. But this summer we were spending virtually the whole holiday there together, and it was Victoria who had established precedence. It was she who gave names to trees and rocks and walks, who shared her magic realm with her clumsy vicarage cousin with a dreamy and generous grace. I was in awe of the pull and power of the sea, I feared it almost as much as I loved it; but to Victoria the sea was a kindred spirit. Even the cotton frock she wore, once blue, had faded to a soft sea-colour that intensified the even brown of her skin. That frock had once been mine – my mother lent Aunt Angela things so that they wouldn't have to bring so much luggage from Africa – but it had never looked like that on me. It was years old. You could only see the bright blue it had once been if you pulled at the cracks in the seams, or peeped into the tunnel of the hem.

I drilled holes in the sand with my piece of driftwood and watched the water well slowly up. 'What are you thinking about, Vicky?' I asked, shy and curious.

Victoria kept her eyes on the bright distance. 'I was thinking', she replied at last, 'about how people would say these stones are for a king and queen, but they're not. They're twin thrones, for twin queens.'

My cheeks burned with glad hope. 'Us, you mean?'

'Ruthie,' said Victoria, turning her head, 'do you know

about the twin – the real twin?' Her voice was deep with portent – her eyes, now that she turned her gaze on me, glowed with mournful mystery. I shook my head and swallowed. I knew that I was about to be taken further into Victoria's confidence than I had ever been before, and I didn't trust myself to speak.

'Oh yes,' Victoria went on, 'I was never meant to be alone. I had a twin sister. She was born one minute after me, and her name was' – there was a tiny hesitation – 'Eleanora. But she died when she was only three days old.' Her voice tailed off, leaving me brimming with the sense of an elusive, haunted past.

'Oh, Vicky!' I yearned to touch her, but I didn't dare. 'How awful! I never knew.'

'Never tell!' Now Victoria's gaze seemed to blaze with something frightening, like anger, only not quite anger. 'On your honour, Ruth Rampling, you must tell no one. My mother has never, never got over it. To hear it talked of would kill her!'

'Vicky, I swear, I'll never tell a single person. I'll – ' I struggled to echo my cousin's story-book delivery – 'I'll bear the secret with me to the grave.'

Victoria's gaze relaxed. She seemed satisfied. 'Ruthie,' she said, more levelly, 'do you understand, now, why I've brought you to the twin thrones today? Do you understand why we had to get away from Simon? Ruthie, there is something that you must do.'

I would have done anything. I opened my mouth to say so, but Victoria didn't seem to expect an answer. She reached out and gripped my shoulders. 'You must become my twin, Ruth

Rampling. You must take her place. Can you do it, Ruthie? Look into my eyes.'

I looked, though it was as hard as looking into the sun. 'Oh Vicky, I'll do it,' I whispered.

Victoria dropped her arms. 'Good. Now for the blood.'

'Blood?'

'The mingling of the blood. When we've done that we'll truly be twins. I'll be in you and you'll be in me. Your children will be my children, and mine will be yours. And we'll be loyal to each other, for ever and ever.'

I wasn't usually keen on blood, but at that moment, fired by gratitude, I would have lacerated my flesh in any way Victoria wanted. I was almost disappointed when she pointed to the dark beads that embroidered my barnacle scrape. 'Squeeze those,' she commanded. 'That'll be enough.' She peeled a strip of Elastoplast from her own knee and began to reactivate a two-day-old injury.

We chose a limpet shell to act as a crucible but we couldn't really squeeze enough blood out, so in the end we just used our fingertips. Victoria found another ripe scab and pulled it off, and produced enough blood to make the sign of the cross on my forehead, high up under my bouncy fringe. 'From henceforth,' she intoned, 'be thou Ruth Eleanora Mary Rampling, for all eternity.'

I'll never wash it off, I said to myself, as we returned to the cottage with linked arms. It'll be there under my fringe for as long as I live. But when I looked the next morning, the cross had already gone.

★

21

When we got back from the beach we were hailed by our mothers, who had been picking raspberries. At the back of the cottage was a tangly, jungly area too small to be an orchard, too disorderly to be a kitchen garden. Here the raspberry bushes grew, haphazard, draped in green nets to keep the birds out; there were also gooseberries and currants, red and black. A white rose, half wild, wove its way through the currant bushes. I remember gazing at the jewelled globes of fruit dangling next to the frilly white flowers and wondering if anything could be more beautiful. There were apple trees, too, the fruit still small and green at this time of year, and two cherry trees with a hammock strung between them. You couldn't eat the cherries, they had big stones and thin, brilliant-red skins, but Victoria and I piled them high on ivy-leaf platters for the fairy feasts we loved preparing.

The raspberry season was almost over, and some of the berries fell apart at a touch. My mother and Aunt Angela had been working hard; it would irk my mother to let the fruit go to waste. Everything was bottled or made into chutney and jam. I didn't like bottled fruit much, it was often sour and watery, but in winter we had it for pudding nearly every day. In those days you weren't necessarily expected to like what you ate – at least, not in a vicarage family like ours.

We waded through the long grass that was full of knapweed and purple vetch. My pulse was racing, because of abandoning Simon; in my mother's eyes there could be no greater crime. She beamed, as she always did when she saw us, but immediately she asked, 'Where's Simon, Ruthie? You haven't left him on the beach?'

I opened my mouth to answer but Victoria got in first. 'He didn't come to the beach, Aunt Frances. He wanted to play with his crabs.' That explanation was typical of Victoria. It wasn't exactly true, but it wasn't exactly untrue either. I would have blurted something out – either the truth, or a clumsy, oversized lie that would have been instantly detected.

My mother sighed, and rubbed her forehead, leaving a raspberry smear like a tiny ruby comet. The gesture was entirely characteristic. No one else ever rubs their forehead quite like that. When someone dies, a little world dies with them – a language, a culture, a whole system in miniature. I've never seen anyone, say, peel potatoes quite like she did – potato at chest height, knife pointing away from her, skimming the peel off in quick little flicks. But on this day in high summer in 1969 my mother was very much alive, her broad, square face hardly lined. 'Girls, girls,' she said wearily, 'I did tell you to keep him with you. The world is still a dangerous place when you're six. If he wouldn't come with you then you should have told us. You've been gone for ages. Ruth,' – she handed me her basket – 'take those into the kitchen. I'll have to go and look for him.'

Aunt Angela added words of admonishment, but we didn't take much heed. Aunt Angela scolded us, particularly Victoria, quite a lot, but a word of reproof from my mother hurt much more. I seated myself with the basket on the kitchen doorstep, its worn bricks warmed by the sun, and atoned by picking out bits of leaf and twig and rescuing the little white maggots that were humping their way in panic to the top of the raspberry mound.

'He's not in the porch,' called my mother, 'and nor are the crabs. I'll go down to the shore.'

'He can't have gone far if he was carrying the crabs,' said Aunt Angela. 'Victoria, help me lay the tea, and please apologize to Aunt Frances when she gets back. Really, the one thing you girls are asked to do . . .'

This wasn't accurate. We girls were asked to do many more things than one. I saw Victoria's mouth go tight, but she followed her mother into the house with an air of crestfallen obedience. Victoria was wise, and knew when to say nothing.

Aunt Angela always looked immaculate, even if she was only picking raspberries for jam. She wouldn't have looked out of place, that afternoon, at the Queen's garden party. She had on a dress of shiny cotton-poplin, I think it's called – broad stripes of lemon and white, with a close-fitting sleeveless bodice and full skirt with big patch pockets. Her sleek hair, dark like Victoria's, was held back by a band made of the same material. My own mother never had anything that matched, and her light brown hair, like mine, twisted its way out of anything that was supposed to confine it. A raspberry had exploded against the back of Aunt Angela's skirt; the juice was spreading in rays. She would be irritated by that. It was hard to wash anything at the cottage. It all had to be done by hand, of course, and usually in cold water – the boiler was a family joke. Noticing the squashed raspberry and realizing that Aunt Angela had not noticed it gave me a queasy, guilty feeling I could not account for. The enormous superiority of my mother over Victoria's always bothered me, because I assumed it bothered Victoria too, and I hated to think of clouds on her horizon.

We rarely discussed our mothers. That was tact on my part, but on Victoria's it was probably a simple lack of interest.

Aunt Angela was only my aunt by marriage. My real aunt now joined us in the kitchen. Aunt Marigold was an Oxford don, a lecturer in history at one of the women's colleges. She was our father's unmarried elder sister and she spent much of the summer with us. She always seemed to have a pile of papers to work through, but she approved of her nieces – she liked clever girls, and assumed we were clever, because we were related to her – and when she turned the beam of her attention on us we rather enjoyed it. She had a dry wit, a sense of the ridiculous, and a talent for reading aloud. She now took over the preparations for tea, cutting bread, grating cheese, slicing tomatoes, her actions firm and sure. I know Angela winced at the way Marigold did things, but I admired her swift, strong movements, even if she did make things look rough and ragged and she never remembered to lay the tea strainer or the butter knife. Aunt Angela apprised her of the disappearance of Simon, including our culpable negligence. 'It's quarter past now,' she said. 'Perhaps I ought to go and help Frances look. What *can* he have been doing with those crabs?'

'Who knows?' said Marigold, slooshing water round in the big brown teapot. 'Simon is a law unto himself. Sit down, girls.'

'What's a lorruntoo?' asked a husky little voice from the door, and there stood Simon, naked and streaked with grime, and my mother, radiant with relief, his shorts and T-shirt limp in her hand. Simon was holding a bucket. A black-tipped pincer waved above the rim.

'He'd taken the crabs for a holiday,' my mother explained. 'Put them back in the porch now, Simon, and then come and have your tea.'

'Simon, why are you naked?' Aunt Marigold enquired when he'd returned the crabs.

Simon looked puzzled. 'Can't remember,' he said. He wriggled into his place, took a slice of bread and butter, and asked again, 'What's a lorruntoo?'

Mum, too delighted at his safe return to notice the state of his hands, gave him her vague, sweet smile. 'I don't know, darling. Is it a kind of animal? I have a feeling it might be a bit like a bush baby. Shall we ask daddy when he gets home?' She sprinkled cheese on top of his bread and butter; he blew on the surface to dislodge it.

'It's what Aunt Marigold said I was.' His hands were so dirty that when he picked up his mug of milk he left smudges on the sides.

'Aha!' Marigold let out a shout of laughter. 'A lorruntoo! Frances, what I said was that Simon is a law unto himself.'

'He's certainly that,' said my mother, and Victoria and I shared in the general mirth. Victoria tapped my ankle under the table, and I knew what she meant. We were safe from any further interrogation; the protean mystery that was Simon's mind had wandered miles from the subject of our defection now.

3

When my father and Uncle Jeremy returned that evening, the 'lorruntoo' story made them roar with laughter. It was a sweet-scented evening. Simon was already in bed, but the rest of us sat in the fading garden to watch the sun set over the bay. My mother sat on the bench, stringing beans for supper, the colander lodged in her broad lap. Aunt Angela, ever the hostess, brought out sherry glasses on a tray. Victoria and I sat on the cooling grass in our nighties, our arms wrapped around our knees, and watched the sun's fiery colours seep and dissolve into the sea.

Victoria's father and my father were twins. There was a theory that they were identical twins. It seemed strange to me then – it still seems strange now – that a pair of twins could reach adulthood and still not be sure whether they were identical, but such was the case. Victoria and I used to spend a lot of time discussing the matter. Their choice of profession and their choice of wives were very far from identical; Uncle Jeremy was an executive for a multinational oil company while Julian, my father, was an Anglican clergyman. They looked quite different, too. You could never get them muddled up. My father's hair stood up in two wiry wings above his ears; he had a small bald patch – a clearing, my mother used to call it – which turned pink in the sun and then peeled. Uncle Jeremy had a similar patch, but he did his best to minimize it with close, careful haircuts and some kind of lotion that smelt (I thought) of lemons mixed with fireworks. My father wore glasses, with sensible unbecoming black plastic frames. If his glasses fell apart, which happened quite often, he would mend them with Bandaid cut off the reel in the bathroom cabinet. He had no idea about clothes whatsoever. I suppose an indifference to such things is part of the job description if you're a clergyman, and my mother wasn't much better. Dad wore his dog-collar nearly all the time, mainly because he forgot to take it off, and it looked terrible with the trousers he called jeans, though they weren't jeans at all. They were made of some stiff, light-blue fabric with an almost metallic sheen and they had pretend stitching painted down the seams in white. They flared suddenly at midcalf and then stopped, abruptly, too many inches above his inevitable Jesus sandals (desert boots in winter). The 'jeans' loomed large in my young consciousness, but perhaps they didn't appear until later than 1969. More like 1972, probably. It would surely have taken several years for my father to catch up with flares. I do remember my mother liked them because they didn't have to be ironed, so they certainly predate her last illness.

Uncle Jeremy would never have worn 'jeans', not even the real sort. He wore trousers that were tailored and pressed, even on holiday. Aunt Angela brought a travel iron with her to the cottage; I remember my mother laughing about it. Despite living in Africa, both Jeremy and Angela had a horror of shorts, and I must admit the baggy khaki numbers my father wore for hiking over the hills did make his legs look as if they could be snapped in two, like twigs. Uncle Jeremy favoured cravats; my father used to tease him about them and call him Mr Toad. Jeremy had glasses too, but they had narrow gold frames and, he claimed, were 'strictly for reading and driving'. The glasses were a great teasing-point because we all knew that he should have worn them all the time. 'I have an astigmatism,' he used to say, because it sounded more manly and interesting than being short-sighted. He was a vain man, but endearingly obviously so. My father had his share of vanity, too, though I didn't realize it at the time. His was intellectual vanity, nothing to do with appearances. I don't know if that makes it any better. Or worse.

If you looked close enough, though, you could see that in their details the two brothers were identical. Victoria and I had a list. Ears, nostrils, way of walking (lollopy). Fingers – not fingernails, because Uncle Jeremy wielded the clippers with considerably more frequency and skill. Their handwriting was very, very similar, though you could tell whose was whose because Uncle Jeremy used a fat fountain pen with a snouty gold nib, while my father used pencils, Biros, any old thing. They laughed in exactly the same way, and at that time they laughed often. Quite recently I watched a repeat of *Hancock's Half Hour* with my father, the one about giving blood, and he laughed and laughed. It was an eerily nostalgic sound.

The brothers had an excellent understanding of one another. There were loud discussions at mealtimes, but underneath there was a high degree of mutual tolerance. Faces could redden, fists could thump the table about Vietnam or Biafra or the death penalty, but when the plates had been cleared away one of them would say to the other, 'Fancy a walk, old man?' and the other would reply, 'Good idea. What about Dunmore Point?' (or Lollard's Gap, or the Great Barrow, or any other of the landmarks on the stretch of Dorset coastline that we considered to be peculiarly ours). Then they would cast hopeful, spaniel glances at my mother and Aunt Ange, who would exchange a look and smile indulgently and send them on their way with a blessing, for both women were wise enough to acknowledge that Julian and Jeremy had a very particular need to be alone together.

Most of the table-thumping happened because at some point during the 1960s Uncle Jeremy changed allegiances politically. My parents were Labour. They both came from families where a principled, Fabian, Welfare-State socialism was taken for granted. Everyone we knew voted Labour, I assumed, or would have assumed if I'd been of an age to give the matter much thought. I knew that a lot of people were Conservatives, just as I knew that a lot of people were Roman Catholics, but I felt as if they all lived a long way away. I understood about choice; at my state primary school play-ground life was all about making choices based on instinct and ignorance. You had to be oranges or lemons, cowboys or Indians, Wall's ice-cream or Lyons Maid, mods or rockers, and (a little later) Beatles or Stones. Once you had chosen that was it, that was what you were. I was lemons, Indians, Lyons Maid, mods and Beatles. I just was. I could only have given the haziest reasons why.

When I was about eight, Grandma and Grandpa Rampling died within a few months of each other − leaving the Dorset cottage to their three children to share – and not long after that Uncle Jeremy declared that he had become a Conservative, even that he hoped one day to be a Conservative MP. Looking back, the connection of events is obvious. I wonder whether it was weak or kind of him not to reveal his convictions to his parents before they died. My own parents had made sure that I was more politically aware than most eight-year-olds, and I remember asking my mother whether Aunt Ange would have to be a Conservative now as well. My mother bit off her thread – she was mending something, as she so often did – and replied with a kind of laugh, 'Oh, darling, Aunt Angela comes from a Conservative family!' And then I realized that Aunt Angela always wearing lipstick and having more than one handbag was something to do with coming from a Conservative family, and I understood that though my mother really was fond of her, it was good of her to be fond of her, because Aunt Angela must by definition be a tiny bit limited, a tiny bit inferior. Though of course my mother would never, ever have said so.

On that balmy evening in the summer of 1969, the evening of the day when Victoria and I became twins, Uncle Jeremy's future was the topic the grown-ups were arguing about. They started arguing as they drank their sherry in the garden, and they were arguing so hard that they missed the moment when the hard red rim of the sun slipped out of sight below the horizon, even though I tugged my father's trouser leg to draw his attention to it. My mother had gone in to cook the beans and check that the shepherd's pie wasn't burning, and her departure seemed to make way for Aunt Marigold to work herself up into a genuine rage. Jeremy had been making

31

enquiries about standing for parliament, and Aunt Marigold was livid because he was thinking about standing in the manufacturing town in the north Midlands where they had all grown up. Grandpa Rampling, like my father, had been a clergyman – an archdeacon, eventually. He was much admired for his loyalty to this drab and godless urban community; he had always eschewed easier options. Aunt Marigold felt strongly that her parents' decades of labour among the poor would be belittled if Jeremy became a Conservative MP. He thought, I suppose, that it would be an advantage to have some knowledge of the area he was trying to represent. My mother popped her head out and called 'Supper!' and she and Aunt Ange tried to deflect the conversation on to a different tack, but when they were all seated hostilities broke out again.

Victoria and I had been sent to bed, but we sat at the top of the stairs, as we often did, and nobody noticed. We were fascinated by the adult world, known only in part; we had also gleaned much useful information on the way about plans that were being laid for ourselves. On this occasion Marigold told Jeremy that if he insisted on standing for this particular seat he might as well 'spit on Father's grave'. I expect I remember this because as she pronounced 'spit' she actually did spit, inadvertently. Just a little fleck; it landed in the green beans. None of the adults noticed. My mother scooped up a spoonful and said, 'More beans, anyone?' and Uncle Jeremy ate them. Victoria and I nudged each other and shook with silent giggles. 'More beans, anyone?' became one of our private jokes. I've avoided eating green beans ever since.

'Marigold, do try not to be so melodramatic.' I can still hear

Jeremy's deep, modulated voice. He had a soothing kind of charm. 'It's a safe Labour seat, as you well know. The majority was at least ten thousand in '66. It would just be a good place for me to cut my teeth.' We didn't take in Aunt Marigold's reply because the phrase 'cut my teeth' was new to us and therefore comical, and Victoria pretended to saw her teeth with an imaginary knife which threw us into such paroxysms of mirth that we were discovered and chased off to bed. We had bunks at the cottage; Victoria lay in the top one and whispered a story to me about twin mer-princesses who tamed and rode sea horses, and I looked at the moon whose face filled the curtainless window until I felt as though I only had to close my eyes and I could fly to its very heart.

Uncle Jeremy never did stand for parliament. Events got in the way. Perhaps he wouldn't have been a very good MP; he was rather easily swayed. But there's no doubt about it, Aunt Angela would have made the most perfect Tory wife, if only she'd had her chance.

That summer, the summer of 1969, was the last before Victoria went to boarding school. The reasons given were all sound ones: the International School she had attended in Edwards-town, the capital of the newly independent state to which they had been posted, just wasn't academic enough; the climate was unhealthy; terrorist outrages were on the increase as the nation struggled to establish its new political identity. Victoria herself seemed to think all these reasons were acceptable. I think she was rather looking forward to boarding school, of which she had a highly coloured view based on the fat, mildewed volumes of Angela Brazil that we found in the cottage – relics, presumably, of Aunt Marigold's unimaginable girlhood. In these yarns girls called Magsie and Tattie and Gwethyn formed secret societies and discovered missing fortunes and German spies. These girls never 'said' anything; they declared, they mourned, they twinkled, they bubbled, and for some time they had a deleterious effect on our prose style. We even tried to introduce some of their expressions into our conversation, but our fathers laughed immoderately and crushingly when we exclaimed 'O kafloozalum!' or claimed to be having 'ripping fun'.

I did not fully share my cousin's vision of boarding-school life as a continuous series of adventures. The high jinks were, for me, undercut by the shocking understanding that what it all meant was that Uncle Jeremy and Aunt Angela could bear to be parted from their only child. I had never spent a single night away from my mother, not even when Simon arrived; he was born at home, which in those days was the rectory in my father's first parish in Lincolnshire, and the midwife gave my father the afterbirth to burn on the garden bonfire. I was four years old; I remember the midwife arriving on her bicycle, and Grandma Cole – my mother's mother – taking me out to feed the ducks on the village pond. I don't remember my first sight of my brother at all.

Boarding school had never been an issue for me. I was reasonably content at the village primary school; I had three good friends, as well as a few enemies, mainly boys, who teased me because I 'spoke posh' and wore fawn socks instead of white. But now a worm of doubt burrowed in my mind. My parents couldn't afford boarding school, but if they could, would they . . .? I knew they loved me. They often told me so. But anyone would have thought Uncle Jeremy and Aunt Angela (especially Uncle Jeremy) loved Victoria, and yet . . . I resolved to broach the subject with Aunt Marigold, as a truthful and reasonably independent witness. Aunt Ange took Victoria to London for two days to buy school uniform at John Lewis; the coast was relatively clear. I remember hovering round Marigold as she sat writing letters in a deckchair in the shade of the cherry tree. Her angular profile was set in concentration, her thin mouth turned downwards, which gave her a forbidding look. Her short, bobbed hair was already more grey than brown. A drunken wasp landed on the top of her head, maintaining an unsteady balance on one wiry, wayward lock. She looked up and saw me, but it didn't dislodge.

'Ruthie,' she said, laying down her pen, 'you look as if you've something to tell.'

This was a promising opening, but I couldn't ask my question because I was afraid of what the answer might be, so I said, 'There's a wasp in your hair, Aunt Marigold,' and the moment passed.

4

My father was – is – a historian (I nearly wrote 'an' historian, but why should I? It's not what anyone says). His area of special interest was the Victorian period, perhaps because people got so excited then about religion and church politics. What gets people going now, with an equivalent degree of fervour? Nothing ideological, that's for sure. Perhaps matters that might broadly be termed 'psychosexual', I don't know. Anyway, my father felt more comfortable with the nineteenth century than with the twentieth. He had a sense of the fabric of Victorian thought and behaviour that sometimes seemed to obscure his apprehension of the here and now, like a curtain. His *magnum opus* was to be a life of Gilbert Rampling, a Liberal MP and social reformer, who was some kind of ancestor of ours. He had been a follower of Gladstone's and had been keen to set up special hospitals for the treatment of pregnant women and very young babies. A surprising interest for a Victorian man, perhaps, and as in the case of Gladstone and his prostitutes there were detractors who cast doubt on Gilbert Rampling's motives, but still, he was an interesting ancestor to have. My grandparents had a trunkload of his letters and papers, and after they died my father set to work sorting and cataloguing them – that was his chief leisure occupation. Not everyone's idea of leisure, but that's what it was for him. Neither of my parents found frivolity at all relaxing.

Once I was old enough, my father trained me to act as a kind of secretary. He worked through the letters calling out names and dates for me to write down in a series of little red notebooks. He had drawn up from his research tangled family trees dotted with arrows and question marks, and these I drew up neatly using rulers and coloured pencils and thick creamy paper that had a vanilla-ish smell. These family trees stretched beyond the Ramplings themselves. My father was interested in all Gilbert's friends and colleagues, and we ended up with enough trees for a small forest. Gilbert Rampling was a well-connected man, and I now realize that at the age of ten or eleven I was drawing up a network that involved just about every eminent late Victorian. They seemed to be intellectual tourists, these people. If Gilbert Rampling found himself in Cambridge, or Manchester, or Edinburgh, or virtually anywhere, he would call on the most distinguished resident churchmen or writers or physicians, much as one might nowadays seek out the best shops or restaurants or make a detour for something belonging to the National Trust.

I loved being my father's secretary, even though I didn't understand much of what was going on. I pretended that I understood more than I did, because my father often forgot that I was only a child and would read out extracts that particularly amused or excited him, and I became adept at supplying the appropriate responses. Our labours in his cluttered study felt close and cosy and important. And I came to enjoy the letters themselves, the physical fact of them, their

37

sweet, musty smell, the faded brown handwriting that scuttled across and across, the occasional delicate enclosure, a pressed plant or the lock of a child's hair folded in tissue and enfolded in time. Some envelopes were edged with a band of black; that was for mourning. Some correspondents still used sealing wax, others gummed flaps. I imagined the fingers of the dead folding the papers, their tongues licking the stamps. I absorbed all this, and though I could tell you shamefully little now about the life and achievements of Gilbert Wenham Rampling, what became strong in me was a sense of the elusive glamour of the past. The details of lives long since lived had a powerful allure, which made it all the more painful for me when my own past let me down. But that didn't happen for years and years to come.

Even at seven or eight I was interested in the history of my own family and would ask numerous questions, to which Aunt Marigold supplied the most satisfactory answers. Aunt Marigold lived in North Oxford during term times in a cocoa-coloured flat that belonged to her college, but during the vacations she spent a lot of time with us. With her help I built up a mental gallery of pictures of her childhood, of her parents' childhood, and even beyond, that seemed at times more solid and satisfying than my own present. Perhaps this was just a way of fleshing out my rather uneventful vicarage existence. Not that the young Marigold and her twin brothers had had a very much more adventurous time, but over all their doings was cast the exotic veil of the past. And it fascinated me, the idea of legacies, not financial ones particularly, but the impact one life has on another, the knock-on effect, if you like. If you want to think about it, on your shoulder you can always feel the touch of the hands of the dead. When I was a child I thought of that touch as a caress. Now I feel it more as a weight, I think. Or a grip.

My grandparents had, of course, been living history to me. Peter Rampling, my father's father, had to retire quite early – he developed Parkinson's disease – so I never knew them when they were living in the large redbrick rectory darkened by sooty laurels that stood in the middle of Colborough, though I felt as if I'd known it because I had made Marigold describe it to me in such painstaking detail. By the time I knew them they lived in a modern bungalow in a dull dormitory village a few miles outside the city. Neither grandparent had felt equal to the task of sorting through the contents of the high-ceilinged, seven-bedroomed rectory, so they had simply left behind everything over a certain size and brought the rest, unsorted, with them. As a result the bungalow was crammed with trunks and packing-cases and every cupboard and bookshelf was overstuffed, and it was hard to find anywhere comfortable to sit. Whatever could not be crammed into the house was piled in the garage, leaving no room for my grandmother's Robin Reliant which stood in the lane in all weathers. It was always dappled with bird droppings and sticky from the little bits that fell off the trees. What kind of trees could they have been? Limes? Or is it just an association of ideas that makes me think limes would cast down stickiness?

My grandfather's illness had frozen him. He trembled only slightly, but every movement had to be planned in advance, and his voice was no more than a whisper. His skull was like a badly wrapped parcel, the skin of his face was folded and very, very grey. 'He is quite literally', said Marigold, 'a shadow of his former self.' I was very fond of him. To me the whispering was a sort of game, and I used to decorate him with daisy chains and feathers and strings of cut-out paper dolls. I think he enjoyed it. I hope he did. I treated him as a kind of toy ghost, and I have had friendly feelings about ghosts ever since.

My grandmother, Joan, I was less fond of. She was not a cuddly person and she put no one at their ease; Marigold said that she had a way of asking for the milk which made it seem as if the whole table was in a conspiracy to keep it from her. She had spent her whole life being a tower of strength; she had been at least as active in the parish as her husband, and crises were her speciality. The times she lived through provided her with plenty. High unemployment, wartime bombing raids, measles epidemics and the like had brought out the fighter in her, and she had very sincerely done her best to alleviate suffering, even to save lives. I recognize her now as a frustrated career woman. She worked hard all her life, and what soured her was not, I think, the lack of financial reward or the ungovernable tide of human wickedness and folly, but rather the inevitable need, as archdeacon's wife, to play second fiddle. Even in retirement, her husband's illness directed sympathy and attention towards him and away from valiant, unyielding Joan. Chronic invalids do have status, even if it's status of a kind they would gladly relinquish. It was always said that Joan coped marvellously, but she wore a martyred air.

It was thanks to Grandma Joan, though, that we had the Dorset cottage, and that was one legacy that worked entirely for good. She was a resourceful woman and she could be imaginative too. In the summer of 1935 the Ramplings took their three small children to Dorset for a change of air. They stayed in a boarding house near Lulworth Cove, the kind which had notices saying things like 'No sand in the bedrooms' in minute, cursive script. A little further along the coast they came across a pair of half-derelict coastguard cottages tucked into a cleft in the crumbling, snub-nosed cliffs that were studded with fossils like sixpences in a Christmas pudding. The cottages were parcelled up with what could have been an orchard and a rough lawn with a surrounding fringe of trees. The way the whitebeams turned their leaves silver side out echoed the metallic glints on the surface of the bite-shaped bay that glimmered at the end of the path that led from the garden gate. Life in Colborough during the 1930s was grim; Joan Rampling had seen that daily contact with sickness of soul and body, with want that nudged the edge of starvation, had stretched her husband's nerves taut and brittle, so she decided to use a small legacy from a maiden aunt to buy and maintain the cottages as a family refuge. Peter balked at first – was it right to spend the money on property when they were surrounded by so much need? – but Joan insisted.

'Aunt Lilian would have wanted the children to have proper summer holidays,' she declared. 'What she would not have wanted would be to have her money lost in mopping up after the mistakes this Government has made.' Her firmness carried the day, and for a few short weeks each year the Ramplings worked at putting the cottages to rights. The two were converted into one – drawing up the plans for that was exactly the kind of thing my grandfather most enjoyed – and the troubles of Colborough could be temporarily lost in the rhythms of sanding and painting, digging and planting, while Julian and Jeremy and Marigold netted shrimps and hunted for fossils and assembled safe little fires.

Even in the war years, when there was no petrol to spare, they sometimes managed to get down there, packing the barest of necessities into knapsacks and piling bicycles on to the train. They talked, at first, of Joan and the children weathering out the war there; though on the coast, it was quite far west, and much safer than Colborough, which as an industrial town would be targeted by the Germans. But the plan was never seriously formulated. Twelve-year-old Marigold, an ardent royalist for a brief but intense period, insisted on staying put and doing her duty just as the young princesses had done, and her mood chimed with the rest of her family. The idea of seeking protection for his own children when the vast majority of his flock would be unable to follow suit went against my grandfather's grain even more than the idea of being parted from them. When the vicarage windows were cracked by a 500-pounder that droned over the rooftops only to sink into a nearby public garden, causing devastation to no more than a tulip bed, it felt as if their courage had been vindicated.

So the beloved cottage had – has – never been properly lived in, at least not since the days of the coastguards. That's what gives it its special character. Its holiday simplicity remains untouched by the taint of everyday life. Whenever we stayed at the cottage, time would hang in suspension and all consider-ations of work and money and duty were packed away out of sight. One could behave so much better when one was there, because nothing was expected save that one should live in the moment. There were few neighbours and no telephone, nothing to shape and organize life except the weather and the changing moods of the sea. That cottage was an anchor for me, for all of us. I never wanted anything in it to change. Even the old privy at the end of the garden with its dank odour and roof of flaking corrugated iron – when my father and Uncle Jeremy knocked that down and built a (not terribly successful) barbecue out of the bricks, I minded. I wanted roots, and a clergyman's family isn't allowed to put down roots. You're packing up and moving off to a new parish every few years. It always strikes me as odd that in the popular imagination – of city dwellers, at any rate – the vicar is a central character in the fantasy drama of close-knit, rose-scented rural life, up there as a symbol of continuity along with the red-faced farmer and the spinsterly schoolmarm and the bosomy type who runs the village shop, when in fact most vicars are up and off after five years or less, severing ties at a stroke. Nothing permanent about them.

But I digress. I set out to give a brief history of my father's family, and have made my way back to my own childhood and that forlorn feeling of not belonging which was why the cottage was so important. This is really Victoria's story. Victoria felt that way about the cottage, too. Poor Victoria. If I, who spent a considerable chunk of my childhood in the same house in the same Oxfordshire village, felt deracinated, how much worse it must have been for her. By the age of ten she'd lived in four different countries, and none of them was England.

I suppose family history always leads back to one's self. That's what makes it interesting – each glimpse of your family's past gives you a new angle on yourself, like catching sight of your reflection unexpectedly in a shop window. And I was, and am, excessively interested in my own story. That was such an important difference between me and my brother when we were children. I don't think Simon ever thought about himself at all, whereas I never seemed to think about anyone else.

My strange little brother's more bizarre behaviours were often dismissed with the comment, 'He'll grow out of it.' All the adults seemed to think that, except for my mother, but it was Aunt Angela who most often took refuge in the idea. Simon presented a challenge to Aunt Angela, who had many preconceived notions about what children were Really Like. According to her, children were driven by three powerful impulses: they wanted to win, they wanted to acquire, and they wanted to eat things that weren't good for them. The best thing that could happen to a child would be to get a prize or a present or an ice-cream. The positive side of her assessment was that they were Eager to Please, they Responded to Praise, and that through an elaborate system of rewards and punishment they could be trained out of their Bad Habits.

Not all of Aunt Angela's doctrine applied to her own daughter, but this was unbeknownst to her because Victoria, when occasion demanded, could always provide what was expected of her. My Victoria, my lovely gypsy, showed herself only in glimpses to the adult world. No, it was Simon who stood athwart. Simon had no more competitive instinct than his crabs – probably less, as they at least clambered on top of each other in search of some better deal. Attempts to teach Simon to play football or cricket withered in the face of his utter indifference. It was discovered, later, that he was short-sighted; spectacles made him better able to see the ball, but they did nothing to make him want to do anything with it. Chess did eventually become a passion, but it was an abstracted sort of a passion – I don't believe he really noticed whether he won or lost at chess. Simon had Interests and Theories, and he only cared about buying things that would further these. If a birthday or Christmas present did not accord with his current preoccupations he would set it quietly aside and forget about it. Teaching him new skills was almost impossible if he didn't want to learn – I wonder if he knows how to tie a tie, even now – but his concentration on his chosen subject was absolute. He was the most fully occupied child I've ever met.

My father called him Brother Juniper. Brother Juniper was a follower of Francis of Assisi – always my father's favourite saint, but isn't he everybody's? – who took everything literally. A sick man desired a pig's foot above anything, so Brother Juniper just went and cut the foot off a pig and gave it to the man. 'Oh, poor pig!' I exclaimed when my father told me this story as he sat on the edge of my bed one evening. 'Yes, and poor swineherd,' he continued, 'left with a hobbledy pig. But Brother Juniper never understood the consequences of his actions. He was amazed when people got angry with him. He was always giving things away, including his own clothes. Once he cut the bells off an altar cloth and gave them to a poor woman.'

He seems to have liked cutting things, I thought. He sounded like a bit of a nuisance to me, but my father seemed to regard him with a kind of admiration, just like the rest of the monks. 'The others revered Juniper,' he went on, 'because he was pure in heart. St Francis said he wished he had a forest of such Junipers! Don't you think that's nice, Ruthie? I'm sure God's saving a special place for Simon.'

Such talk always embarrassed me. I rolled myself up in my bedclothes and grunted assent. Young as I was, I understood that my father was placing a particular kind of trust in me by talking to me in this way. St Francis's attitude towards Brother Jumper's eccentricities was, I knew, the only right response; my father was helping me to see that. But it was difficult, sometimes, with Victoria.

Simon had a puppy – this was some years later – called Emma, a floppy little mongrel with silky spaniel ears. He was given the puppy because at the age of nine or whatever he was he still had no friends. That was not, of course, stated, but it was obvious. Victoria and I were jealous; our many requests for a puppy had always been rebuffed.

Soft, sweet Emma came with us to the Dorset cottage and we all three of us lavished her with attention. One afternoon Simon had to stay in bed because he had cracked his head on a low-hanging branch and my mother suspected concussion, so we took Emma for a walk without him. 'But don't go up the cliffs,' called my mother. 'She's too little to understand heights.'

Victoria waited until my mother was fully occupied in the garden. Then 'Emma, Emma,' she called, setting off up the cliff path.

I ran after her. 'Hey, you can't take her up there. Mum said.'

Victoria's nose wrinkled in scorn. 'Don't be ridiculous. She'll never know. I don't know why she thinks we can't look after a puppy properly, for God's sake.'

I didn't argue. The steep, crumbly path was too much for Emma's scrabbly paws, so we took it in turns to carry her. At the top of the cliff, on the warm, close-bitten grass, Victoria put her down. She gambolled away, faster than we had ever seen her go before, and she didn't stop when she came to the edge. One moment she was there, the next she wasn't. The most horrible thing was the silence.

There was no question of apportioning blame. We went back and told the story together and both received equal punishment. It would not have crossed my mind to doubt the justice of that. When I think of that incident now, the tingling blue sky and the surging sea and the bumbling puppy who just disappeared, I almost wonder if I didn't dream the whole thing.

5

What do the words 'Oxfordshire village' mean to you? Golden stone, nodding hollyhocks, honey for tea, bobby on a bicycle, that kind of thing? And a river curling through it all, not too big, no intrusive gushing, just a pleasing babble and an ancient bridge and a few well-placed ducks, I expect. When I tell people, 'My father was the rector of an Oxfordshire village,' they're off on the communal fantasy I mentioned earlier, and they don't really seem to believe me when I tell them that our village wasn't quite like that. Gadham was large. About three-quarters of it had been built since the war, in the fifties and early sixties, before planning restrictions had any force. There was nothing planned about it; it had simply swelled to accommodate people employed in light industry in Oxford or Thame or High Wycombe. There was a patch in the middle that was pretty, or would have been if the front gardens hadn't been sheared as close to the cottages as possible to make room for the juggernauts that groaned and rumbled through, taking corners too fast and rattling the pint glasses on the bar of the Moon and Stars, the pub that still aimed to be the centre of village life.

Our rectory was near the church, of course – St Michael and All Angels, nice solid fourteenth-century bell tower but appalling Victorian windows – in a quiet road on the edge of a big new estate. The Old Rectory was one of the prettiest houses in the village; Georgian, big windows, huge copper beech, stable yard . . . It was owned by a man who worked in television; he kept his two Bentleys in the stables. By the 1960s very few Church of England rectors lived in Old Rectories. Most of them, my father included, lived in serviceable rect-angles of brick and raw tile, with metal window-frames that corroded easily and tiny token chimneys. They're not bad, those New Rectories; four bedrooms plus a study, sliding picture windows, a purpose-built garage – you can't complain. But they're not houses you can get fond of. I know; I tried hard, and I couldn't. Maybe that's deliberate, to keep clergymen flowing round the country, like healthy blood.

Simon and I had a bedroom each, and then there was the spare room which we called Aunt Marigold's room because she was by far the most frequent guest. My mother had a sister, too, Sarah, who was three years older than her. Aunt Sarah was physically very like my mother, only more so; broader, with thicker wrists and ankles, her hair even frizzier, her face even more freckled. She was a schoolteacher, and was a sensible, good-hearted woman, possessed of many of my mother's qual-ities but more prosaic, lacking my mother's sympathetic imagination and – the word that springs to mind is grace. Not physical grace. That was Aunt Angela's department. It's very hard to describe what made my mother special, but it was a quality that seemed to have been bestowed on her from outside, like a gift. It's something rare. For a long while I believed that Victoria had it too, but it turned out that she didn't. Quite the reverse.

Aunt Sarah had married Uncle Roger Wintle and they and their labradors and their three sturdy sons, my big boy cousins, lived in Cumberland, about as far north as you can go and still be in England, so although we were on perfectly cordial terms they didn't play a very big part in my life. I liked their noisy, out-of-doors good humour, but they existed on the periphery of my consciousness. For the first ten years of my life I didn't see so very much more of Victoria either, but when I did it was so much more . . . intense.

I've got a very good memory. I can always date things, too. Perhaps that's due to my historian father, or perhaps it's because there are certain dates in my life that are so momentous that all the rest of the memories resolve themselves round them in coherent order. At the end of that summer of '69 I thought that Victoria's departure for boarding school would be one such date, but of course that event was well and truly eclipsed, later. Anyway, I remember perfectly us packing up the cottage and Uncle Jeremy setting off for London because his leave had ended and he had to fly back to his job in that African country beginning with M, while Aunt Ange and Victoria came back to Gadham with us so that Ange could finish getting all Victoria's things ready and take her to boarding school from there, because it was only thirty-five miles away.

Victoria didn't like saying goodbye to Uncle Jeremy. She really was very fond of him. Victoria never cried, but she did hide her face in his shoulder for a few moments before he got in the car. He rumpled her dark hair and told her not to worry about boarding school and said he'd write to her very soon. She shook her face free and said, 'Oh Dad, it's not school I'm worried about. I just don't want your plane to crash.'

Dad and Aunt Marigold took the train back because there was no room in the Mini, and Simon fell asleep on top of me and Victoria which was very annoying but we just had to put up with it. We broke the journey halfway for our picnic, which was what it always was when Mum made it: Marmite sandwiches, bananas, a KitKat to share, and lemon barley water in a screw-top jam jar. We ate this in a little wood where there was a bank with lovely twisted roots sticking out, and Victoria and I pretended it was a castle for elves. Even though we were ten we still liked anything to do with magic – we even pretended we believed in it, sometimes. Simon wandered a little way into the wood and came back holding a toad almost as big as a kitten. After a bit of arguing, Mum agreed that he could take it home, so he put it in the lemon barley jar with leaves and grass and a few blackberries. I said, 'Toads don't eat blackberries, Simon,' and he said, 'I know that. They're just for him to look at.' Mum and Aunt Ange laughed. Grown-ups always liked it when Simon said things like that.

Back at home, Aunt Angela shared a bedroom with Aunt Marigold – their nightwear must have provided an interesting contrast in styles – and Victoria shared my bedroom with me, and Simon shared his with his toad, now more commodiously housed. The Z-bed was made up for Victoria, but once our lights were out she always got into my bed because the mothers got cross if they heard us talking. And we would whisper until we stopped making sense, then fall asleep together in my bed with both our heads on one pillow, which was as it should be since we were now secret twins.

We spent our last week of the holidays in the house and garden, mainly, because I didn't want to bump into any of the children I knew from school. It would be difficult to refuse if they asked us to play, and I didn't want to share Victoria with anyone. Even more than that, I dreaded the exposure of my real, home self, towards which I felt at once tender and ashamed. It was bad enough in ordinary times, being the vicar's daughter, and eating brown bread not white, and having real candles instead of fairy lights on the Christmas tree. I had learnt to circumvent some of the problems, even – I mistakenly believed – conceal the more glaring points of contrast, but Victoria was not aware of my morbid sensitivity on this subject, and her faintly exotic otherness would highlight the flimsiness of my artificially constructed primary-school identity. It would not be long before my other life started again; soon I would be buying new things for my pencil case and finding out whether Debbie Driver was still my best friend now that we'd gone up into Mrs Myatt's class. My school life, or at least my playground life, had its own kind of excitement. The girls were segregated from the boys at playtime; sometimes a group from one side or the other would organize a raid and drag a hostage of the opposite sex across the painted yellow line that divided us as strong as a force field. But more often the boys would get on with their football, and we would chant our rhymes – 'Twiggy, Twiggy, little star, how I wonder what you are, underneath that mass of hair, like a beetle in despair . . .'. We skipped a lot, a girl at each end of a long rope, and as we skipped we sang:

'There's somebody under the bed,
Whoever can it be?
I felt shock-a-nervous,
Debbie come in with me.
Debbie lit the candle,
Under the bed she looks,
Ruthie go out, Ruthie go out,
There's nobody under the bed.'

But I never played these games when I was with Victoria.

How did we spend our time? We drew pictures a lot, of beautiful women going to balls. They had tiny waists and bunches of ringlets tied with gigantic bows; their eyelashes reached up to their hairlines. Victoria could draw people in profile, but when I tried I always seemed to give them huge lantern jaws. So I drew my flat, full-fronted beauties, scattered at intervals over the paper, and Victoria would position her more delicately featured profiles in between. The style was, broadly, mid Victorian; we were influenced by a costume drama on television and by the *Illustrated Dickens* (complete works) in my father's study. Their crinolines billowed out, ruched and furbelowed. Satin, taffeta, watered silk; trimmings of swansdown and Honiton lace and tinkly jet. It was beyond the power of our felt-tips to convey the richness of their imagined attire, but we would discuss it, languorously. Then we would write their names next to each bug-eyed belle, in special curly writing – Annabella, Marianna, Esmeralda, Gloriana. By the two prettiest we would write Victoria and Eleanora, but those names we wrote in mirror writing. We wrote stories, too, in tandem, like a junior Somerville and Ross. Victoria had most of the ideas, and I did most of the writing. I felt like a humble – willing – scribe at the time; looking back, I realize that the arrangement was engineered because in terms of technical accuracy I was much the better writer. Most things occurred to Victoria before they occurred to me.

Then there was dressing up. We loved to play at weddings, but neither of us wanted to be the groom so we were usually bride and bridesmaid. Sometimes we roped Simon in, but he was the most hopeless groom – he was always so dirty, and his attention wandered. Aunt Angela would sometimes set aside whatever useful adult activity she was engaged on and help us to dress. I remember once she coiled Victoria's hair on top of her head and wove cornflowers into it. My hair wasn't long enough to put up.

We liked Aunt Ange to help us, but then we liked her to go away again too. This wasn't a problem; there were plenty of things for her to do. The clothes list sent by Victoria's school was a formidable document. My mother would read bits out, gasping in amazement. 'Twelve white handkerchiefs, named! Brown sandals, outdoor lace-up, indoor strap. Black plimsolls, bedroom slippers (plain), hockey boots. Anyone would think the poor girl was an octopus. Should we tell them she's only got one pair of feet?'

Even more daunting was the school's List of Rules, sent out in advance for each newcomer to commit to heart. Letters home were to be written on Saturday afternoons. Additional letters midweek should only be written in cases of emergency.

Pocket money, not to exceed ten shillings per term, was to be handed in to the matron on arrival. Her gin money, suggested Aunt Marigold, which we thought very humorous and daring. Comics – comics were not allowed, unless they were *Look and Learn* or *Tell Me Why*, which were the sort of things Simon liked. Confectionery was discouraged. Any confectionery given to any girl was to be passed on to matron, who would share it out. 'When I was at boarding school,' said my mother consolingly to Victoria, 'my mother used to send me vests with sweets sewn into the insides.' 'Oh Frances, don't give her ideas!' Aunt Angela complained, but she would be smiling, too.

When she wasn't out buying things in Oxford or sewing on name tapes – even face flannels had to be named – Aunt Angela would help my mother with the myriad tasks that occupy the clergy wife's time, each one a stitch in the busy and rather formless tapestry of her existence. Cooking, mending, sweeping, dusting, typing up the *Parish News* and, later, copying and distributing it; making tea for the rural dean, flapjacks for the boy scouts, posters for the jumble sale; sharpening crayons for Sunday School, sticking the bindings back on to decrepit hymn books, keeping us children out of the way while my mother comforted weeping parishioners – and that happened really quite often. With hindsight, I'm impressed by elegant, narrow-minded, Conservative Aunt Angela. She'd always had servants to do things for her, and yet when she was staying with us she worked ceaselessly at the most menial tasks without complaint. The truth is, she was fond of my mother, and the affection was reciprocated despite their vast differences. They could be critical of one another – I once overheard a snippet of conversation between my parents on the (to me) fascinating topic of why Aunt Angela had never had any more babies, and my mother said, with untypical sarcasm, that Angela wouldn't want to spoil her figure for anything as insignificant as a baby – but such moments were rare. They had, after all, married twin brothers, so they must have had something in common. I liked it when they were together in the house. They generated a kind of cosy hum.

So that last holiday week passed, and became, as such weeks do, a way of life. Then suddenly it was the Last Night, and Aunt Angela was writing out labels to tie on Victoria's trunk, and Victoria and I were staying up to have supper with the grown-ups, and Aunt Marigold was slipping the Hamish Hamilton *Book of Princesses* into Victoria's overnight bag as a surprise for her to find when she got to school. Victoria crept into my bed for the last time that night, and we didn't talk about school at all, but whispered a long story to each other about twin babies, girls of course, who were put to sea in a basket and landed on an island and grew up and ruled over all the speaking animals there. Victoria fell asleep first and I lay feeling the flutter of her breath and the scratch of the lace edge of her nightdress, and I thought I wouldn't sleep at all that night. But of course I did.

Next day, after lunch – baked potatoes and cauliflower cheese, with Victoria's choice of pudding which was Raspberry Ripple, and she was allowed to scrape the cardboard wrapper – Aunt Ange drove her away, and we all waved until the car was out of sight, but nobody except me knew that Victoria was waving with two fingers crossed, because that was our secret twin sign.

Then my mother told me that she had telephoned Debbie Driver's mum and that I was to have tea with Debbie that afternoon, and I was very angry at first and said I wouldn't go, but of course I did. Debbie Driver had Cindy and Ken and Cindy's horse which I think was called Patch – or was that her little sister? – so we played with those and she showed me her new Baby Doll nightie which was bubblegum pink and there were special knickers which you wore with it. So it was established that we were still going to be friends even though we were going up into Mrs Myatt's class. And I was glad that my mother had made me go. I didn't forget Victoria, but I slipped into my second skin and settled quite comfortably back into my new, old life.

6

The five o'clock news on Radio 4 gave us the information that changed everything, for all of us, for ever. Or at least, that's how we would have heard about it, if we had been listening properly, but how often are people listening properly when the really important things happen? That afternoon, that April teatime, could not have been more ordinary, and we could not have been less prepared.

It must have been a Tuesday because my mother was folding copies of the *Parish News* ready for distribution, and that was the day the *Parish News* got folded, the second Tuesday in every month. That was the kind of thing that paced our lives, like Sunday School happening in our living-room every fortnight, and the committee of the Mother's Union having coffee in the kitchen once a month. Simon and I were eating our tea in the kitchen. My mother usually stopped whatever she was doing to talk to us – mainly to me, because Simon didn't say much – while we ate our tea. But on this particular Tuesday she was extra busy because Uncle Jeremy, Aunt Angela and Victoria were due to arrive the next day and she had to get things ready for them. They were going to stay with us for the few days that were left before Victoria's boarding school re-opened for the summer term.

We were eating eggy bread. That was what we often had

when Mum was busy. Eggy bread was slices of bread dipped in beaten egg, and then fried. I think other people call it French toast. Simon liked to smear his with jam, which was disgusting. When we had finished that we were allowed three sweet biscuits, but only one of them could be chocolate. On my way home from school I would plan what biscuits I would choose, and in what order I would eat them. Ginger nut, custard cream, and then chocolate digestive – something like that. We used to argue about Bourbons a lot, about whether they counted as chocolate. We insisted that they didn't. My mother used to get so sick of the argument that she would threaten to stop buying them, but she never did. There were few luxuries in our house, but there were always several varieties of biscuit, because our kitchen was a thoroughfare for all sorts of parishioners, bossy or helpful or lonely or miserable, and tea and biscuits were constantly dispensed. My mother tried to keep the teatime hour sacrosanct for us and she didn't invite people to call at that time, but there were many, many people who needed no invitation. My mother excelled at tea and sympathy. She was too careless over details to be a perfect clergy wife. Her flower arrangements sprawled, her sponge cakes failed to rise, she would let my father celebrate Communion in a crumpled cassock or odd socks, but she had a limitless capacity for listening to, and remembering, the stories that people wanted to tell.

The pips sounded for the start of the radio news and somebody rang the doorbell at the same time. My mother and I were halfway through a conversation about the flowers I was to pick to welcome Aunt Angela and Victoria. 'Oh, botheration,' said my mother, getting up. I put two spoonfuls of sugar in my tea; I liked to drink the tea without stirring it, so that the last inch would be purely sweet, like a reward. I would tip my mug up and let the wet sugar run down into my mouth in one delicious rush. Then I would scoop up whatever was left with my forefinger. That was what I was doing when it dawned on me that the newsreader was talking about Edwardstown, the capital city of the African country where Victoria lived.

My mother came back into the kitchen with the verger's wife, who often helped her with the *Parish News*. 'Mum,' I said, forgetting to greet Mrs Pockney, 'I think he said there's been a plane crash in Edwardstown. The flight was going to London.'

Mum looked distracted. She stroked my shoulder on her way to refill the teapot for Mrs Pockney's benefit. She switched off the radio in passing. 'There must be lots of flights out of Edwardstown,' she said. 'Don't worry about it, Ruthie.'

'Quite right,' chimed Mrs Pockney. 'Never trouble trouble till trouble troubles you.'

My mother smiled, but I could tell she was a little worried, because Simon helped himself to two chocolate wafers out of the Huntley and Palmer's assortment and she never even noticed. 'I'll get those flowers, shall I?' I said, siding the plates as I had been trained to do.

'Good idea, darling.'

Aunt Angela liked the little Lent Lilies that grew in the long grass under the hawthorn hedge. I ran my fingers down their frail stalks, snapping them off as close to the ground as I could. I liked picking flowers. It was a chilly evening; the raw air made me sniff, but the pinkish light that swelled behind the gun-metal clouds seemed full of April promise. I heard an aeroplane overhead and could just see its tail light winking through a parting in the clouds. I thought, perhaps that's the plane Victoria's on, and said a quick prayer. Please God, I said, let it not be her plane that crashed. Or if some people have to die, let it not be Victoria. Let it be Uncle Jeremy and Aunt Ange, even, but please, please not Victoria. Thy Will Be Done.

The broken daffodil stalks bled trails of colourless slime across my hands that burned in the cold dew. I had enough daffodils, so I started to look for primroses for Victoria. In the shaggy margins of our garden could be found primroses of several colours besides pale yellow. I wanted ten, all different, one for each year of her life. I found white, pale mauve, mid pink, magenta, and a dirty purple that was almost brown. I couldn't get enough for her age, so I cheated and added primulas from the flowerbed, but their hot, bright colours and furry heads looked wrong next to the wild ones, like imposters in poor disguise. Lights winked on in the housing estate; mothers stood at their doors calling their children home. 'Co-lin! Tee-na!' It was a melancholy sound.

When I got back in I found my mother had already put the Z-bed up, next to my bed. I put the flowers in water, cleared out a drawer for Vicky's things, helped my mother with the sheets. I thought of the news again, tried to listen to the echoes of the newsreader's voice before they faded from my memory. 'Mum,' I said, plumping the pillow, 'do you know what time their flight was supposed to be? Because there definitely was a crash.'

'I don't know exactly what time, darling. They're going to spend the night with Angela's parents in London. There must be lots of planes, Ruthie.'

'You could ring Aunt Angela's parents.'

'I wouldn't want to worry them if there's no need. Listen, Daddy and I will watch the news on television tonight and we'll tell you about it in the morning.'

'Tell me tonight! Come in and tell me straight afterwards. I won't be asleep, I swear.'

My mother smiled. 'You know Daddy doesn't like you to say that, darling. And I very much hope you will be asleep, but I'll look in to check.'

'Promise?'

'Promise.'

I tried to keep myself awake by reading with a torch, but it had the opposite effect. So it wasn't until the next morning that I found my torch battery was flat and that the jet leaving Edwardstown for Heathrow never left the ground, that when fire broke out they let the children off first, and that as a consequence Victoria was now an orphan.

My nightmares were precise, repetitive, boringly realistic. My subconscious didn't seem to bother to edit or transform or find equivalents for what happened, or what I thought had happened. Over and over again I saw my aunt and uncle running, flames shooting from their heads like huge hair, and I woke, several times a night, to find myself sitting bolt upright in bed, my fists clenched, my mouth open as if to scream. My mother came in sometimes – it seemed as if she didn't go to bed at all for at least a week, though I suppose she must have done – and put her arms round me, but her comforting couldn't make it go away. For the first time in my life, nightmares could not dispel horrors, only intensify them. It was exhausting.

The adults tried to prevent the details from trickling down to Simon and me, but the accident was big news. Newspapers disappeared from our house for a few days, but I scanned them furtively in the village shop where I was sent on an abnormally large number of errands. Term began, for which we were all thankful, and my father went to London to sort out funeral arrangements and to meet Marigold, who had flown straight out to see to Victoria. I was glad when my father went. When I saw slow tears roll down his cheeks at times when he thought nobody was watching it frightened me, as if he was made of wax and might melt.

Sixty-nine people died, of whom thirteen were British. One of them was an MP who'd been on a fact-finding mission; it was his death that kept the accident in the news for so long. I remember the list of the dead, like guests at a rather grand party – Miss Venetia Kenn-Weston, Sir Arthur Mainwood MP, Mr Jocelyn Percival, Mr and Mrs Jeremy Rampling. And then others.

The aircraft had trundled along the runway for a bit, looking quite normal, and then in a matter of seconds the people waving their loved ones off had to watch as fire spurted first from one wing and then from the other, and the plane rolled off the end of the runway and collapsed in the scrub like a shot gamebird. The crew were very gallant, said the survivors. They helped all the children out to safety and some of the adults too.

None of the crew survived. My mother told me that when people died in fires they were usually overcome by smoke first, which didn't sound as bad as being burned, but I wasn't wholly convinced. I knew that some of the people who had escaped from the plane were on fire. They ran across the rough grass and tried to scramble over the barbed-wire fence. Victoria was standing on the other side of that fence, waiting. What she was waiting for never came.

Victoria stood by that barbed wire as still as a stone until somebody led her away to hospital. What did she hear, what did she see? She never told me. But when I imagined her there, when I tried to become her so that I could share and understand, the hot, howling wind was what filled my ears, louder than the roar of the burning plane, louder than the cries of the dying.

Some of the survivors were badly burned. Victoria had only one small injury: the top joint of the little finger of her left hand was severed. Several years afterwards, Simon, apparently noticing it for the first time, asked her how it happened. She just said, 'My hand was trapped,' and the subject was closed. It was a clean and simple injury, but they kept her in hospital until Aunt Marigold reached her. I suppose there was nowhere else to put her. I overheard my mother say to my father, 'How can that poor child ever board another plane?', but when Aunt Marigold brought her back, Victoria seemed not so very different; pale, with a bandage on her hand and her hair cut short because, as she told us in an impassive way, 'It smelt of bonfires.' She was quiet and calm. I lay awake at first, listening, because I yearned to comfort her, but I never heard her cry.

All the luggage was burnt, so Victoria had no clothes, except for the extraordinary ill-assorted garments that Aunt Marigold had bought in a hurry to take out to her. All she had left behind in the Edwardstown house were flimsy sundresses, nothing suitable for the rigours of an English spring. So we shared more than ever, because we shared all our clothes, including underwear, until my mother got organized enough to buy her some more. They went to Oxford together on the bus on a day when I was at school, because Victoria wasn't to go back to her school for several weeks. They arrived back with lots of carrier bags and an iced fruit ring for tea and a sense − on my mother's part at least − of smiling relief that some sort of hurdle had been crossed. That was their first trip as mother and daughter − because, of course, we adopted Victoria. My father, typically, explained it to us in a way that he hoped would accentuate the positive. When Simon asked, as he inevitably did, 'Why did God let Uncle Jeremy and Aunt Ange die?' my father said, 'We can't answer that, Simon. But now we have Victoria. Victoria is God's gift to us.' His voice wobbled, and I slipped away because I couldn't bear it, but I did hear Simon say, 'Well, I think that's pretty stupid of God. Nearly as stupid as killing all the cows.' This was a reference to the Seven Plagues of Egypt, an episode that fair-minded Simon had always found particularly irksome. I didn't comment, but I didn't think it was so stupid. God had made us a wonderful gift, and if that was the only way he could do it, well . . . I shied away from the tangle of feelings into which such thoughts would lead me.

It turned out that Uncle Jeremy had made arrangements

with my parents, long before. It was all written down. Victoria was to continue at her boarding school, but she would spend her holidays with us, and she would legally become my parents' daughter. I wondered what she would call them, but she settled that question for herself. She chose 'Papa' and 'Mama', Victorian style, which fitted, I suppose, with the sense of drama with which she had always run her life. We went on sharing a bedroom – a proper bed for Victoria was one of the first things that was bought – and my mother would come in to kiss us goodnight, one night me first, the next night Victoria. That seemed fine to me, but I think I was relieved that she hadn't wanted to call them Mum and Dad.

7

'Why doesn't your cousin go to our school?' Debbie Driver asked. We were in our first term at secondary school, an ex-grammar school in the throes of becoming a comprehensive, and Debbie Driver was still technically my best friend. We walked about, arms linked, at break times, and Linda Willis and Susan Pitt walked with us. Debbie and I sat next to each other in class, but there was an unease in her; she inclined towards Linda Willis like a plant yearning towards the light. I wouldn't have minded a split. Debbie and I had little in common beyond habit and a stock of stale in-jokes, and my heart misgave me at the thought of spending the next five years glued to each other's side, but the trouble was, if Debbie and Linda became an item then I would be left with drippy Susan Pitt. The boys called her Spit or Spitty, and however often they did it tears never failed to spring to her eyes. I didn't mind Susan; she bred gerbils, which was a plus point, but there was no spark between us, and I lived in fear of calling her Spitty by accident, because it did seem quite appropriate.

Debbie Driver's conversation was mainly about television programmes that I wasn't allowed to watch, but at least she had a bit of go about her, a sense of mischief that Spitty conspicuously lacked. When she asked me why Victoria didn't go to our school we weren't actually in school, we were in the transport café round the corner from the school, which was absolutely out of bounds. The expedition was Debbie's initiative, but I gladly concurred. When you're a vicar's daughter you have to make a few gestures to prove that you're something else as well, even though you know, and everybody else knows, really, that the flavour of the vicarage curls all the way through you like jam in a Swiss roll. But I had to try. So Debbie and I squeezed through the gap in the wire netting at the top end of the playground where nobody ever went, because the boys always played football at break and the girls hung around the toilets, and then we cut across the field to where the newly widened main road swept round a dangerous corner, and there we sat in the smoke and steam of the transport café drinking Coke and sharing a doughnut. Debbie had more pocket money than me, naturally – no one had less – so she paid for the doughnut and I just paid for one Coke. It didn't bother her; she was good like that.

We had made several expeditions of this nature, and it was a mark of the fact that we were still best friends that we never asked Linda and Susan to join us. Linda would have been on for it. Linda was already about five foot six; she claimed to have been wearing a bra for two years, and she had an eyeshadow palette, peacock hues arranged in the shape of a fan. She used it at weekends – we'd all had a go, one Saturday afternoon at Linda's house. But while the rest of us rubbed at our eyelids hard when it was time to go home, Linda's mother actively encouraged her to wear it for special occasions; she put Linda's hair in heated rollers, too. Linda wore her school skirt very short and pulled her white socks right up so that they lapped her smooth knees. Linda and her long pale thighs would have cut a dash at the transport café. But Spitty – no, poor old Spitty would not have been able to cope. So here I was with Debbie, sipping Coke and being best friends, and Debbie had to start asking me about Victoria.

I said, 'She's not my cousin, she's my sister.'

Debbie said, 'She can't be. Your mum and dad aren't her mum and dad. She's your cousin.'

'She's adopted,' I said firmly. 'She's my sister now.'

Debbie licked the tip of her forefinger and dabbed it in the sugar bowl. 'Well, if she's your sister, how come she's not at school with you?'

'She doesn't have to be.'

'They usually are,' said Debbie. That was true. Debbie's sister Mandy was in the year above. Linda had two sisters, three and four years ahead of us, who were objects of great admiration for me, as for most of the girls in our year. To me they were indistinguishable from adults. And Simon, my own brother, had been with me at primary school, where indeed he still was, struggling along somewhere in a world of his own but officially in Mrs Dougary's class.

'She's at boarding school,' I countered lamely.

'I know.' A grain of sugar trembled in the corner of Debbie's mouth, caught on one of the tiny golden hairs that grew there. 'Don't your parents like her, then? Sending her away like that. It's not surprising if they don't like her much, seeing as she's not really theirs.'

Debbie's thin, fair hair was parted straight down the middle and tied below her ears into bunches. The bunches were secured with turquoise plastic bobbles threaded on elastic. I looked at the white road of her parting that went all the way from the front to the back of her head and I thought, I don't like you very much. I said nothing, because my chest was tightening as it always did when anyone said anything remotely critical of Victoria, and it was desperately important that I did not cry. Debbie would not see that there was anything to cry about.

'If my mum died, my Auntie Norah would come and live with us,' said Debbie. 'My mum told me that. You know, some days I think I wouldn't mind.'

'Oh, you shouldn't say that!' I exclaimed. 'Of course you'd mind.'

'Why? You know my mum. She can be a real pain in the you-know-where.'

'Yes, but if she . . .' I couldn't bring myself to say the word.

'Died – yeah, I know. It would be bad, really. Shouldn't tempt fate.' Debbie crossed her fingers for luck, and looked round for some wood to tap. 'But your cousin – she doesn't care, does she? You always make it sound like she don't really care.'

'She does care,' I retorted, but even as I said it it set me wondering. 'But – well, she's brave.'

Debbie said, 'Why don't you ever bring her round? You say she's your sister, but no one sees her. You ashamed of her, or something?'

I dug my nails into the fatty plastic of the banquette and tried to think of something that would shut her up. I said,

'She's ill. She can't go out.' It was a mad thing to say, because now I would have to back it up, but I had the satisfaction of having caught Debbie on the hop. Her lips parted slightly in a doll-like expression of surprise. I improvised, something I had never been any good at. 'She's got an illness and she's not allowed to talk about it. She gets special treatment at the boarding school she goes to. She – '

'Oh!' cried Debbie, pleased. 'You mean she's handicapped!'

'No!' I spoke so loudly that some of the lorry drivers turned round. Debbie kicked me, harder than she needed to, and we both buried our faces in what remained of our Cokes. 'We better go,' I whispered. 'We've only got five minutes.' On the way out I took Debbie's arm, as usual. 'Don't tell anybody,' I begged. 'My mum will kill me if she knows I've told.'

Debbie seemed convinced by this unlikely scenario, and she promised. I knew she would tell at least Linda – Debbie loved a bit of gloom and mystery – but she would tell Linda not to let it get back to me, so that would be all right. I was frightened of my own lying, because I would never be able to keep track of it, but this was the best I could do. We ran back to school, flapping our arms to get the smell of smoke out of our clothes, but we needn't have bothered. Mr Lapworth was waiting for us, and his face was like thunder. Stephen Morris, the school sneak, had watched us go; we must never, ever set foot in the café again, the management would be warned to look out for us, and we were to miss swimming for the rest of term. Of course, our parents would have to be informed. Debbie was pink and defiant, but I was glad on all counts. I didn't care about the café, I didn't like swimming, and it would be a relief if my parents tried to discourage my friendship with Debbie Driver.

Victoria came home every fourth weekend, which was all the school allowed, apart from half-terms and holidays. It was understood between us that our two worlds of school should not intersect. Victoria told me stories about boarding school, stories of grotesque matrons and cruel teachers and girls whose home lives touched vivid extremes of tragedy or eccentricity, but she and I both knew that all this was less than half true. They were stories, and we both understood the nature and function of stories. Victoria was a storyteller, I was a listener. Actually, I was more than a listener. I was someone who could absorb her ideas and mould them into sense and shape.

She asked me very little about my own school life, and I wove no colourful fancies for her entertainment, because it had never been my job to entertain Victoria. She knew enough; the names of my friends and chief enemies, and the hideousness of the lunches – food at her school was awful too, of course, but awful in a more dramatic and potentially life-threatening way – but we shared a sense that my school experiences were in some sense peripheral. Living in the middle of Gadham as we did, we could not wholly avoid encounters with its inhabitants, but if Victoria and I, out walking or riding our bikes, were greeted by one of my classmates, we would just grin and wave and carry on. The separateness of vicarage life was a help, for once. No one really expected the vicar's daughters to join in with anything properly, and the aura of tragedy that hung over Victoria had a deterrent effect.

It is hard to say exactly why I laboured so strenuously to keep Victoria-life and school-life apart. I was proud of my sister-cousin; too proud – my pride squeezed my chest and hurt me. My excitement in her company left me exposed and vulnerable. I was selfish, too. I could bear her to have friends at her school, girls I'd never met, but I could not have borne for her to make friends with anyone I knew. It had been a fact of my whole life to date that she was more important to me than I was to her, and I had no expectation that this would change. I could do nothing but strive to contain as much of her as I had got – which was as much as anyone had, now that Uncle Jeremy was dead.

My mother, who had had to make a career out of noticing things, worried. She interpreted our insularity as a fear of the world, and indeed it would have made sense if the plane crash had made us fearful, only that wasn't really the case. She urged me to ask friends round, wrote to Victoria's school to emphasize that any child would be welcome at the Rectory on an exeat weekend. I had been a Brownie – you had to be, if you were a vicar's daughter – and now my mother wanted both of us to be Girl Guides. But being a gentle, liberal, civilized woman, she talked everything through with us, never forced anything on us that we didn't want, so she carried on making the suggestion and we went on thinking of different ways of saying No, and nothing ever happened.

We did agree to ride. That was our one 'hobby'. Victoria had learned to ride in Africa; it was the only aspect of her past life that I ever heard her say she missed. In bed at night she would murmur fantastic tales of her exploits, and I loved to

73

picture her bareback on a white Arab stallion, sinewy legs gripping its flanks as if they'd grown there, horse and rider eating up the burnt brown miles as one being, black hair and white mane rippling in the scorching wind. I dare say it wasn't quite like that; certainly, it wasn't remotely like that at the Horse and Pony Rescue Centre a couple of miles out of Gadham to which we cycled on Saturday afternoons. No Arab steeds ever needed rescuing, apparently; there were no thoroughbreds at all, just a collection of shaggy ponies in various stages of decrepitude, who had been rescued from – where? Fairgrounds, seaside resorts, child-owners who had lost interest? – to spend the rest of their days in relative ease at the Rescue Centre. We could not afford riding lessons, nor did the Centre offer them. The manager, a tiny woman with a crinkly walnut face and a streaky grey ponytail secured by a rubber band, was supremely indifferent to human needs, but she did let us take the less decrepit ponies out hacking, for a very small sum.

I couldn't ride when we first went. Victoria taught me. We were supposed to wear hats, of course, but they made our heads itchy and hot so we took them off as soon as we were out of sight. Loose hair fed our fantasies. We wanted as much romance as possible. The ponies were called things like Sooty and Dalek and Mister Mischief, but Victoria could weave romance out of the most unpromising material. We were Red Indians, last survivors of our tribe, seeking a new homeland where we could nurture the ancient secrets of our race. We were highwaywomen, outlawed from society, robbing the rich to give succour to the poor. We were warrior maidens armed

74

with elven swords on a quest to overpower the dark lord who threatened our realm. (My father read Tolkien aloud to us, when he had time.) Sometimes we were plucky little Britain going for showjumping gold in the Olympics, but that one was something of a last resort.

I wasn't a good rider. My timid nature got the better of me. If Sooty (or Dalek, or Mister Mischief) put his head down to crop grass, down I would go too, rolling in what felt like slow motion over the pony's shoulder to land on the grass with a jarring thud. Victoria would call out, 'It takes seven falls to make a horsewoman,' but she never fell. Perhaps she had got all her seven falls behind her, in Africa, but I don't think so. I have never seen Victoria at a physical disadvantage.

She had no fear of danger. The plane crash seemed to have made no difference to that. If, in our rambles through woods and farmland, we came across an obstacle like a stream or a fallen tree, she would point out to me the safe and easy route, then, calling, 'Keep your head and your heart high and your hands and your heels low!' she would set off in search of the most difficult and dangerous way for herself. She would have cleared five-barred gates if her mounts had been up to it. I admired her. It was impossible not to.

The only thing that bothered her was barbed wire. She never tried to jump anything that involved barbed wire, and once when she set poor old Dalek at a gap in a hedge and he stumbled and ripped his foreleg on some wire she hadn't seen, she slipped quietly off his back and was sick into the ditch. She looked up at me; I was dithering as usual, and Dalek was balancing his leg on the rim of his hoof, pushing at the wound with his soft, whiskery nose. The colour had leaked out of her face and her eyes looked black. She wiped her mouth on her sleeve and gave me a grin and said, 'I thought those sausages tasted a bit funny at lunch,' and I took her explanation whole, as I always did. It was a long, long time later that I remembered something I overheard Aunt Marigold tell my mother, when I'd come down for a drink of water after I was supposed to be asleep. 'Francie,' Aunt Marigold had said, 'she saw them hanging, burning, on the wire. I don't think we can expect her to forget that.'

8

Unease wriggled, maggoty, inside all of us that year, my first year at secondary school. I told myself I could manage my divided life, no problem. I could be an ordinary girl at an ordinary school, quite good at English but useless at netball, Debbie Driver's best friend and the person most often chosen to take the registers round in the morning. I could be all of that when Victoria was away at school, and when she was back I could unzip that seamless disguise, roll it up, pack it away and live my true life as the secret twin of Victoria the bold, Victoria the beautiful, Victoria the strong. At this time I had no doubt that my twin self was my true self.

Of course I can do it, I said, as I told myself the story of my own life, that ceaselessly fascinating saga that was playing in my head through all the in-between-times – dressing, church, waiting for the bus. But in truth, with every day that passed it was getting harder to hold everything together. Stopping myself from flying apart became such hard work that it even affected my breathing. At meals I ate fast, hardly chewing, letting out my breath in little grunts. My mother noticed. 'Ruthie, relax,' she would say, massaging my shoulders. 'No hurry, darling. I can write a note to Mr Cumberlege to say you didn't understand that maths.' And sometimes I would agree that it was indeed the maths – or whatever – that was worrying me, just to keep things simple. Simon found a golf ball, once, on a patch of wasteland where we used to play. He took it home and cut it open with a razor blade – typical of Simon to want to do that – and inside were rubber bands, thousands of them, wrapped round and round each other like some weird insect's nest. He sliced through the bands and a bullet of white lead shot out and nearly hit him in the eye. He had to go to hospital to have the stuff taken off his face, but I could see he thought it was worth it. Anyway, like that golf ball – that's how I felt.

My father was restless. This was nothing new. Before Jeremy and Angela's deaths he had been making noises about moving on, but then the business of adopting Victoria had put all other considerations to one side. But six months later – only six months! It was extraordinary how quickly we assimilated the unthinkable – he applied for the post of chaplain at Westaby College, a boys' public school, mainly for boarders, about forty miles north of Gadham. I can see now that this was both predictable and sensible, despite the fact that my mother hated the idea. My father wasn't really cut out to be a vicar. He was genuinely a spiritual man, but he lacked the common touch. A lot of people bored him, and as a rule the less educated they were, the more they bored him. (With my mother it almost worked the other way round.) Poor Dad, he never realized that he bored them, too. Preparing the weekly sermon was probably his favourite part of the job, but on Sundays his lengthy expositions of the knottier parts of Galatians or St John were but languorously received.

My father was – still is, when he has a chance to be – a deeply kind man, and he masked his boredom and irritation from those who caused it, so far as he was able. This mainly took the form of retreat. He withdrew into his study, into his books, into his thoughts – into his prayers, probably. When going about on parish business, he went on foot whenever it was feasible, to save on petrol, ostensibly, but really to stretch the minutes of precious solitude and to blow sorrows and cares out of his head. The more he walked, the more my mother worried. The car was one of the few things I remember them arguing about. 'Take the car, Julian, please. Even you can't walk to Oversham in twenty minutes, and you really must *not* be late for the ordinands.' 'Julian, it's going to *pelt*. If you must walk then *please* let me pick you up.' 'Darling, it's no use telling me you're leaving the car so that I can use it because *I don't want it*.' But he always won. He always walked.

The school chaplaincy was like – sorry, was – the answer to a prayer. The teaching of history and divinity as well as the usual duties of a chaplain, good accommodation, intelligent pupils, proper holidays ... I know that my father, casting round for a shelter from the bleak chaos into which he had been hurled by the loss of his twin, saw Westaby College as a little grove of academe where matters of the mind and of the spirit were gently disputed amongst gifted, sensitive souls, adults guiding their tender charges towards peaceful living and enlarged understanding. My mother took a different view. She disliked moving house – 'I'm like a cat,' she would say, 'I like to curl up in one warm place.' She didn't realize that the warmth to be found in a place was for the most part generated by her. She was one of those people who made sense of a place just by being in it. I suppose cats are a bit like that, too.

She dreaded the cloistered society of a public school as much as my father longed for it. Aunt Marigold's tales of life in her Senior Common Room had always given her the horrors. My mother liked tramps and children, and old women who lived on tea and sardines and refused to be rehoused by the council. She wasn't attracted by the 'like-minded' masters' wives whose companionship was held out as a lure. But she did not stand in my father's way. I'm sure she thought that the chaplaincy was a soft option, that being a parish priest was the only real thing, but she also recognized that a soft option was what my father needed. Jeremy's death had diminished him. He needed a haven, he needed time to rebuild. It was ironic, given her well-concealed reluctance, that she was one of the main reasons he was given the job. They interviewed him on his own first, then both of them together, and she shone. I learned this years later, when the Rampling family had become a part of the texture of life at Westaby College.

Simon and I were in the bathroom when we were told that the move would definitely happen. We were too old to share a bath, but in the interests of economy I was made to use his water. It still gives me a little buzz that now, as an adult of independent means, I can have deep, hot baths as often as I like. Dry towels, too. In my childhood the towels were always soggy, because of Simon going first.

My mother was sitting next to the bath, swathed in one of her many enormous aprons. Simon was pushing a couple of lengths of stick up and down the side of the bath and emitting the kind of high-pitched drone that meant he was lost in some endlessly complex and private game. I was saying,

'Oh, hurry *up*, Simon. Oh, Mum, *please* hurry him up,' but they weren't paying any attention, and then my father came in with a twitchy look round his mouth and said, 'Ruthie, Simon, I have a letter here that I think might interest you.' Then he explained, and I looked round the narrow, steamy little bathroom with its unshaded sixty-watt bulb, and its slippery brown lino floor that never looked clean, and I thought how terribly I would miss it. I felt a pang of affection for the curtains, which were made of pale green towelling with a kind of stylized seahorse design, and I said in a small voice, 'Will we be allowed to take those curtains?' and my mother smiled and said, 'Of course, if you're fond of them.' Simon's droning noise had stopped. His head appeared over the rim of the bath, his rough, dusty-looking hair streaked darker with splashes, and he said, 'Will Victoria come too?'

'Yes, darling,' said my mother, still smiling, 'Victoria will always come with us.'

'Oh,' said Simon. 'Does she have to? Because I think it would be better if we left her behind.'

I don't remember how my parents replied. I stole a glance at them, and what I do remember is the look that they exchanged, a look almost of panic that made my scalp crinkle.

'Will there be room for the guinea pigs?' asked Simon. I turned to the misted window-pane and drew goblin faces on the darkened glass.

This happened in the spring of 1971, though we weren't actually moving until the summer. I put off telling people until it felt too much like lying not to. I was round at Debbie Driver's when that moment came; we were sitting cross-legged on her lilac satin eiderdown and I was plaiting the cone of orange hair that spurted from the head of one of her plastic trolls. She had trolls and gonks and Snoopys, but she never played with them, just rearranged them in the various cushiony recesses of her pink and mauve bedroom. Debbie was counting her money, sorting the new decimal coins from the old. 'Horrible little things,' she said, jingling the tiny, bright coppers. 'Toy Town money, if you ask me.' That was just the kind of remark her mother would have made. She poured the coins into a beaded purse and zipped it up. 'When we're second-years, are you going to do French or DS?' she asked, apropos of not much, and I said, 'I'm not. Neither. I'm not going to be a second-year,' and explained. There was a little pause, and then Debbie said, 'So you won't be living in Gadham no more.' I concurred. 'And you won't be a vicar's daughter no more,' she added, and the idea excited me then; but now, of course, I know that you can never stop being a vicar's daughter, no matter what happens to you.

9

'She's old enough to be told,' said Aunt Marigold. 'If you keep it from her, it'll only be worse for her in the long run.'

My father made a reply, but I heard his words only as a vibrating mumble. Marigold's voice had a carrying quality that my father's lacked. Marigold and my father were in the kitchen, which was directly below my bedroom. I was lying on my bed with *Wuthering Heights*; I was nearly sixteen, about to take my mock O levels. Our accommodation at Westaby College was a former lodge, early-nineteenth-century Gothic, all gables and pointed windows. The garden was a bite taken out of the woods; just below us ran the River Sale, the broad curve of which formed the boundary of the school's grounds. The Chaplain's Lodge was considerably more picturesque than the Rectory at Gadham, but it was also more cramped, and the low ceilings were thin. In the mornings I could lie in bed and breathe in aromas of coffee and toast and bacon, so that it almost felt as if I'd eaten breakfast before I actually had.

The adults knew I could hear things, because I'd often complained about noise from the kitchen when I was supposed to be working and wanted an excuse not to. But on this occasion it was late, and they probably thought I was asleep. It had escaped their notice that my habits and routines had altered over the past few years; my father adhered to quaint old-fashioned notions about bedtime and pocket money and Ruthie-I-don't-think-you-should-be-watching-that. My mother was a little more realistic, but my mother was ill.

I turned *Wuthering Heights* face down on the pillow and listened. Marigold again, 'You're going to have to rely on her quite heavily over the coming months, Julian. Don't you think it would be wise to take her into your confidence?' Another mumble from my father. I lay, ears straining, holding my breath. A couple of years earlier I might have banged on the floor and called out gaily, 'Hey! I can hear you!', but a couple of years ago they would have been discussing birthday presents or a school report – safe secrets. Not like now.

I eased myself over the edge of my bed and hung, bat-like, the blood humming in my head. I wanted to put my ear to the floorboards, but I didn't think I could get myself on to the floor without some kind of thud. I caught sight of my reflection in the mirror on the wardrobe door, the other side of my high iron bed. The pull of gravity made my face dusky, pouchy; my hair fanned out like a snaky halo and my upper lip hung down leaving my teeth bared. I could seriously spook myself if I looked long enough. I thought of Mr Rochester's mad wife, her dark, bloated face, and pulled myself up in a hurry, catching my chin on the iron rim of the bed frame. The jolt made me feel sick and angry, out of control; as I nursed my jarred face I heard the click of the latch on the kitchen door and Aunt Marigold's feet on the stairs, then the familiar creaks and knocks of my father locking up. There would be nothing more to listen to, that night.

It seems odd to me, now, but I really wasn't sure what Aunt

Marigold was talking about, despite the quietness of our just-over Christmas, despite the fact that my mother took a rest on the sofa every afternoon and went to bed at seven most evenings. The previous summer my mother had gone into hospital to have a lump removed from her armpit – 'Just a cyst, I expect. Nothing serious.' 'Why don't they leave it in, then?' 'Well, they have to have a look, to be on the safe side.' I had never been very interested in health. Doctors and hospitals had never formed part of my childhood game-cycle. A lump in the armpit sounded neither serious nor interesting, just ugly. The operation meant we couldn't go to Dorset, which was a pain, and for a couple of weeks Victoria and I tried to be a bit more helpful round the house and were duly praised for it. Then school began again and my mother was back in the kitchen and we thought no more about it.

Mum had paid frequent visits to the doctor since then, but these had become part of the pattern of existence. 'Where's Mum?' 'At the clinic' – it seemed as unnewsworthy as Dad running the Debating Society on Wednesday evenings, or Simon going out with his binoculars at weekends. I was fifteen, and like most fifteen-year-olds I was fully occupied with doing almost nothing. I wrote letters, to Victoria, to my French penfriend, to my schoolfriends whom I saw every day – we would give each other great screeds to read during double chemistry. I wrote a diary, too; page after page chronicling the minutest variations in emotional temperature. Adolescent girls treat their hearts as mothers used to treat new infants, weighing them after every feed.

I was generally considered an unselfish girl. This meant that

I wasn't too surly about washing up and wasn't as awful to Simon as I suppose I could have been. Of course, there's no such thing, really, as an unselfish fifteen-year-old. I loved my mother very dearly, but I don't believe I expended one second's thought on whatever she might have been going through. When I heard Aunt Marigold talking about me that night it felt quite exciting, quite momentous. There was only the tiniest cold current of fear.

There was no immediate chance of going to sleep. I read another chapter, but it was a chapter containing more than its fair share of old Joseph's impenetrable Yorkshire dialect, and I took in nothing. I got up and lifted the curtain; the bare trees cast their black nets at a shrunken winter moon. I opened the door a crack, and listened; no sound but the whirr of the blow-heater in Aunt Marigold's room. She was still up, then. Yes, there was a line of weak light along the bottom of her door. On the landing I hesitated, my bare feet chill on the moonlit floorboards. Downstairs, the clock on the mantelpiece chimed midnight. I jumped, then knocked.

'Come in, Ruth.' Aunt Marigold seemed unsurprised. She sat in the wicker armchair, a pad of A4 propped on her knee, the blow-heater directed towards her lean shins. She was still fully clothed in her fawn jersey and no-colour tweed skirt, despite the lateness of the hour. She held a cigarette, a tottering tower of ash. She often lit a cigarette and then forgot to smoke it. 'Oh,' I said, 'you're working.' But she flicked the ash-column into a saucer just in time, and laid her pad and pen aside.

There was no second chair in our tiny spare room so I sat

on the bed, which was high and lumpy, like all our beds. Aunt Marigold was not a cuddly person, but Victoria and I had often climbed into bed with her because she was so very good at reading aloud. She read us lovely Victorian books like *The Runaway, Black Beauty, The Rose and the Ring*. I wished she'd read to me still, though I was too old and awkward to ask. I'm sure she was the only person who could have made sense of Joseph's wearisome dialect.

I pulled my nightgown down over my knees and wrapped my cold feet in its hem. 'Aunt Marigold,' I ventured, 'I heard you talking about me.' Vicars' daughters are trained to speak the truth. Sometimes that can be quite useful.

'Oh,' said Aunt Marigold. Then a pause. She raised an enquiring eyebrow at me. 'Tell me what you heard.'

'I could only hear your voice. Dad was mumbling.'

She laughed her short laugh, a kind of amused shout or bark. Then her beaky face folded into solemnity. 'Ruth,' she said, speaking slowly, 'you are fortunate in having parents who love you very much indeed.'

I was embarrassed. I blew hot breath down into the neck of my nightie, where it was stretched taut over my knees. If I said anything, it was only 'Mm.'

'I go back to Oxford tomorrow,' she went on, 'as you know. I've offered to stay, but your father says not to, and it would be quite difficult to rearrange tutorials, and so on. Difficult, but not impossible. I'm not lecturing this term. Ruth, I want you to telephone me at once if you think there is any need. I have an extension in the room where I teach. Let me write down the number for you.'

Aunt Marigold seemed to think that I knew something I didn't. I tried to conceal both my bewilderment and my ignorance. I nodded, and took the piece of paper. She fixed me with her hooded eyes. 'The next few months will be very hard for you,' she said. 'For all of us, but perhaps particularly for you. People will come to rely on you, my dear, and you are quite young to be put in that position. But you will cope, because you are strong. Rampling women are strong.'

I had never heard Aunt Marigold talk like that before. I listened, but I asked nothing, because any question I had would sound like the question of a child. And I wanted so much to be a 'Rampling woman,' strong, a coper. I said, 'I'll manage, Aunt Marigold,' and she gave an approving nod and grunt.

'It's your birthday on Saturday, isn't it?' She opened a drawer. 'I was going to leave this behind for you, but I think I'll give it to you now instead. I don't expect you to wear it.' She handed me a flat black box, battered at the edges, fastened with a metal clasp. A jewellery box. I was astonished. Marigold had never before given any of us a present that wasn't books.

'It was my mother's,' said Marigold, 'and her mother's, before that. My grandmother, Edith Gurney. Distantly connected to one of the great Quaker families, and endowed with their sense of public service.'

I pushed up the catch. Inside lay a band of black velvet on to which was stitched a twist of silver set with dozens of tiny – 'Diamonds?' I whispered.

'Yes, they're real. Surprisingly enough. It's late Victorian, I should think. 1880s. You wear it round your neck – originally for mourning, but – ' Marigold stumbled, flustered, though I didn't then see why. 'But now, of course, it's just a thing that's quite fun to have. And a little piece of family history.'

'I love it,' I said. 'I think it's beautiful.' I fastened it round my neck. It fitted quite well, just a shade too slack. My aunt inserted an investigative finger.

'Hm. Nearly. You'll fill out to fit it. People do. If you want to wear it, that is. No need, you know.'

'Who was she mourning?' I asked, my fingertips exploring the velvet that managed to feel soft and brittle at the same time.

'Who? Edith Gurney? Good question – her father, I would imagine. An interesting man – made quite a lot of money through patenting a new technique of copper plating, and spent most of it setting up schools for pauper children. And Edith carried on his work. They both deserve to be written about, one day.'

'We seem to have had a lot of people like that in our family.'

'Indeed. Investigating them all would make a most interesting study. Perhaps you'll be the one to do it, Ruth.'

'Me?'

'Why not? I could see you as a family historian. You've a sound sense of the past, and you already write well.'

My heart beat faster at this unexpected and unlooked-for praise. 'But they're not very famous, are they? I mean, to write about – '

'Not very. But they're quite remarkable in their own way. And the way they all connect up – families are such interesting organisms. I sometimes think everyone should have their history written.'

I warmed to the theme, emboldened by Aunt Marigold's expansiveness. 'Do you think, some day, someone will write a book about Victoria? Because I'm sure she's going to be the one.' I felt my cheeks turn pink as I spoke.

'The great one? Possibly. Yes, Victoria certainly stands out. But Ruth, never underestimate yourself. Or young Simon, for that matter. There's enormous potential in all of you – ' I thought I detected the hint of a tremor in her voice. She circled the room, shifting papers, switching off the fire.

I took the hint. I kissed her thank-you and good night, received the usual dry peck in return, and went back to my room, still tingling with the thrill of feeling my past behind me and my future before me. Where the two met they crackled like electric wires, and that meeting point was somewhere in the middle of me.

I drew back the curtains. The moon, now clear of the snatching twigs, sailed high in the windy, littered sky. I held the collar up in the moonlight and the diamonds winked blue and white. I fastened it round my neck again and brushed my hair till it crackled and stood right out, and then I stared and stared at my reflection in the wardrobe mirror until my body felt as if it was floating, and my head seemed severed from my shoulders by that black mourning band.

Tim Bryant started visiting when my mother was in hospital after her second operation. The reason for his visits was to play chess with Simon, which was part of the general rallying-round that happened once the school community had cottoned on to the seriousness of my mother's condition. Some of the help I would rather have done without – Mrs Pedlow, for instance, the wife of one of the housemasters, 'blew in' to make us beastly meals: corned-beef loaf and gritty salads and mashed potato that was more lump than not. We would rather have lived on cheese on toast, but turning people away, whether well- or ill-intentioned, was not a skill possessed by either my father or me. But Tim and the chess was a good thing for all concerned.

Tim was the son of one of the science masters. He was seventeen and was supposed to be in the lower sixth, but he was having a term off to get over glandular fever. 'They call it the kissing disease,' he said to me, almost the first time he came to the house, 'but it can't be in my case because I've never kissed anyone. Not properly.' I turned my face away, mortified for him, and thankful that Victoria wasn't there to make me laugh – there was only Simon in the room, and he wasn't listening – but when I looked back, Tim seemed entirely composed, not remotely aware of having said something that would make any right-minded person want to crawl away and die of shame. Tim liked folk music and looking at old churches. His family lived in a school house right on the far side of the grounds. He had cycled over to see us and had forgotten to unstuff his corduroy trousers from his schooly grey socks. That evening I wrote a satirical letter about him to Victoria, including a drawing, but it wasn't long before I wished I hadn't.

Chess was one of the things Simon was good at. Simon had certain specific skills, like reading maps, but there were lots of things he couldn't do at all. He was twelve years old but he could barely swim or ride a bicycle and he could never remember to say things to people like hello and please and thank-you. He got on well with Tim, who didn't mind whether or not such things were said. At chess they were evenly matched, despite the discrepancy in their ages. The games were rarely finished in one session; Tim started calling three times a week, even four. They would play for a couple of hours while Dad was at the hospital – I went with him, though not every day – and then Dad would call a halt and make us sit down for supper together, which was something Mum had always insisted on. Tim would help us out with Mrs Pedlow's offerings – he didn't notice what he ate – and then Dad would disappear into his study, reminding Simon to go and do his homework as he went. Tim and I washed up, and drank Nescafé. Tim was surprisingly good about doing things like emptying bins. I suppose his mother, who had no daughters, had put some effort into training him. Once, as he carried a load of logs from the shed into the living-room, I said, 'Aren't you too tired? You're supposed to be ill, don't forget.'

Tim said, 'It's OK. I feel really wiped out in the morning, but I'm all right now.' He piled the logs next to the fire, and added in a matter-of-fact way, 'Sometimes I just start crying for no reason. That's the illness.'

I said, 'I do, too, sometimes. Just start crying.'

'But you've got a reason,' said Tim. His pale greenish eyes looked so kind and concerned that I knelt down on the hearthrug which was peppered with splinters and cinders and I cried and cried. Tim knelt beside me and laid an arm stiffly across my shoulders. 'People do get better,' he said. 'They do.'

I wanted to believe it, so I did. Sometimes people saying something like that when things are bad feels almost as good as if it were true. So I came to associate Tim with comfort. He started bringing me things, after that – books, mainly, and records, and photographs he'd taken of bits of churches. He wasn't interested in God. 'I'm an atheist,' he would say, not belligerently, but just as one might say, 'I do Physics A level,' or, 'I'm lefthanded,' as if it was just a fact about him that didn't have to affect anybody else. He liked the physical presence of churches, not their spiritual or even their historical significance. I think the reason he liked them so much is because they are the same but different. Different types of spires, or buttresses, or misericords – infinite variations within a recognizable pattern. He felt comfortable with that. Like chess, a bit.

I couldn't bring myself to listen to the records, which were mainly folk with a few medievally ones featuring crumhorns and the like, but I did like the books. *Narziss and Goldmund* was one of them. 'Narziss is all mind – he's austere, he controls himself,' Tim explained, his eyes shining behind his glasses. 'Goldmund's the sensualist, he travels, he has experiences. Put them together, and what do you get? Human nature!' He clapped his hands together and clasped them to demonstrate. Tim loved things that yielded to exposition.

In mid March my mother came home, and Aunt Marigold too. Aunt Marigold put a stop to Mrs Pedlow's culinary activities – not a complete halt, the odd batch of Eccles cakes still got through, but Marigold and I did suppers between us, and thanked God for baked potatoes. We put the Eccles cakes on the bird table until Tim said it wasn't really fair on the baby birds, who might choke from being fed huge barbed flakes. We moved an armchair into the kitchen and my mother sat in that and took her food on a tray, because she wanted to be near us. She didn't eat very much. Everything had to be cut into small pieces before she could manage because her left arm didn't work properly any more.

People visited a lot and brought jam and flowers. Mum was too weak to arrange the flowers, even with her good hand, and she'd never been much good at it even though she loved them. Marigold and I were no great shakes at it either. Everything seemed to be the wrong length. 'It'll be lovely when Victoria comes back,' said my mother. 'She's so clever with flowers.' To her visitors she said how very lucky it was that it was only her left arm that was affected, and how excellent it was to be at home again, and how lovely it was to see everybody, and no, visitors didn't make her too tired. And she pretended not to notice the little start they gave when they first took in the yellow puffiness of her face and the fact that her hair was falling out. My mother's hair had been like mine, thick, wiry, springing out round her face. Now, when I helped Marigold make her bed in the morning, I found it lying on the pillow in skeins.

My mother's altered state threw me into a rictus of self-consciousness. Communication between us had always been easy, fluid; now, nothing felt right. To talk about ordinary things, like school, housework, family, neighbours, seemed like a callous disregard of her condition. To talk of the future – summer-holiday plans, A-level choices – was impossible; it was taking all our strength to deal with the present. To air my small problems and grievances as I had been wont to do seemed petty and selfish. To talk of her illness was unthinkable.

It was a horrible waste. I had been blessed with the easiest mother alive. She was tolerant, gentle, amused; there was no detail of my life – or Simon's, or Victoria's – that didn't interest her. Simon managed far better than I, because he carried on just as usual. It had never been possible to have a real conversation with Simon, but every now and then he came up and told you about things that interested him. His mind was a storeroom for Fascinating Facts. We developed a family term – Double-Fs – to describe the kind of things we knew he'd latch on to. At the time of my mother's illness there was a spate of astronomical Double-Fs. 'I'm looking forward to 1999,' he would announce, without preamble, 'because that's when the next solar eclipse will happen. But you'll only be able to see it from Cornwall so we'll have to go there for the holidays instead of Dorset. If we're still alive. The chances of a meteorite smashing into us are very small but you never know. There was one in Siberia in 1908 that devastated three thousand square miles.'

'How lucky', said my mother, smiling faintly, 'that it was Siberia.'

'Not so lucky if you happened to be a reindeer. Look, Mum, I've made a chart of all the constellations you can see from our garden at this time of year. Mum, do you think they'll find a way for humans to live on the moon? Because lots of people are going to need to soon, if there's a nuclear war.'

Nuclear war, and in particular the effects of radiation sickness, were new obsessions of Simon's. I didn't make the connection at the time, but this interest increased a hundredfold at the time when Mum became really, seriously ill.

My new awkwardness with my mother led me to wish, sometimes, that she could have stayed in hospital until she got properly better. That wish made me feel ashamed, and shame compounded the awkwardness. I can see, now, that it would have been much the best for me to witter on in the old way, moaning about my teachers, asking for help with homework. My mother tried to draw me out with questions, but her voice was so weak, so different, that I could only answer in monosyllables. Her stillness unnerved me. All my life my communication with her had taken place against a background of movement. Always as we talked she would lay tables, stitch up hems, answer the telephone; now she was propped on cushions, her cardigan buttoned over one great sausagey useless arm, her whole body motionless but for the flicker of her bright blue eyes that looked small now in her swollen face, and my remarks resonated uncomfortably in the stillness, naked and shivering in their banality. My mother, wise as always, sought a solution to the problem, and dictated her thank-you letters to me, letters to all the people who had sent her things while she was in hospital. There was a stained-glass window in the school chapel based on a design by Burne-Jones – I bought dozens of postcards of one of its details, an adenoidal angel with its head on one side and a dove aiming at its left shoulder, and on these I inscribed my mother's variations on a theme: feeling much better, doctors are pleased, looking forward to the summer. It was a soothing occupation. Writing the messages so many times helped me to believe them.

Then Victoria came home for the Easter holidays and everything changed. I had never felt shy about seeing her before. I didn't go with my father to collect her, because at my state school term didn't end for a few days more. I dawdled at the end of the school day. I hung about the gates chatting to Christine Wright and Jan Saunders. I even fell in with their suggestion and went along with them to Dino's, the steamy café behind the bus depot where the best of the boys from our year were wont to congregate because there was a particularly elaborate pinball machine. Christine smoked Number Six and Jan and I had banana milkshakes while we waited to see whether Paul Dalloway and his mates would turn up. Everybody fancied Paul Dalloway – even I did, in a theoretical kind of way – but Christine fancied him the most. She tattooed 'P. D.' on to her knee during maths, using a compass and biro ink. I had never fancied anyone enough to contemplate doing that.

We waited, and he didn't come, and I deliberately missed two buses, because I didn't want to be home before Victoria.

At last, even Christine showed signs of restlessness, saying that he was most likely out with that fat slag Sandra Sandeman who didn't have the word 'No' in her vocabulary, so I slung my bag over my shoulder, waved a jaunty goodbye, and set off to catch the next bus.

When I got home I saw the car, so I knew that Victoria was already home, and as soon as I opened the front door I sensed a difference. There was always a difference, with Victoria. You know when the clocks go forward and suddenly it's light in the evenings? That's how Victoria's return always felt to me.

They were all in the kitchen, except Simon. Victoria was on to the flowers already; they were laid out on the draining board. Her slender fingers moved quickly amongst them, stripping slimy leaves, snapping overlong stalks, tossing withered ones into the compost bucket beneath the sink. She didn't stop what she was doing when I came in – we were never effusive, especially not in public – but her dark eyes flashed a private smile at me and she said, 'Ruth! You've been ages.' I muttered something about the buses, slung my school bag in a corner, and began to rinse out vases, and soon Victoria and I were working on the flowers in rhythm while Aunt Marigold scraped carrots and my father laid the table very badly, and my mother lay back in her chair, watching, half smiling at everything and nothing.

I asked where Simon was. 'Playing chess,' replied Marigold. 'I expect young Tim will be staying for supper. He's become quite a fixture, Victoria. I must admit he's no trouble. Lay an extra place, would you, Julian? Someone will have to sit on the wobbly stool. Simon, I suppose.'

I looked at Victoria to see whether she'd met Tim yet. She grimaced and hung her mouth open with her head on one side, just as Tim did when he was really concentrating on something. I giggled. I didn't really like it, but being in cahoots with Victoria was more important than standing up for Tim. She laid two fingers against the palm of her other hand in a V-shape for me to see. This was a private sign; it meant 'virgin', which indicated scorn. The label wasn't to be taken too literally — Victoria and I were both virgins, for heaven's sakes — but it was a useful condemnation of those who, like Tim, could be regarded as naïve, unworldly, over-enthusiastic. I started sticking the trimmed and sorted flowers into vases. Victoria did the same; her arrangements soon achieved a springy, glowing coherence while mine just straggled and drooped.

I left her to it and went to help Aunt Marigold. We were having roast chicken in honour of Victoria's return; I saw a bottle of red wine, its cork drawn, standing by the warm element at the back of the fridge. My father knew little about wine but he had a vague idea that if it was red it should be 'chambré'; a bottle behind the fridge always denoted a sense of occasion on my father's part. I mashed the potatoes as carefully as I could, pushing each one through a sieve instead of just thrashing about with a fork. I grated nutmeg into them; my mother gave me a little nod of approval. Victoria, having finished the flowers and distributed them about the house, scanned the table to see what my father had missed. There was always something. Tumblers; salt and pepper; serving spoons; she ticked them off on her fingers. While we worked we talked. Victoria told us tales from school — the matron who hoarded used matches in case of a wood shortage, the busty captain of the hockey team who had flown her bra from the flag-pole on Founders' Day. My mother laughed aloud. Her eyes followed Victoria's quick movements, and her face glowed with something like gratitude. I turned away, because she never looked at me like that.

I summoned the chess players and my father, who had wandered off to his study the way he tended to when there were too many females in the kitchen. I had a book of Tim's to return; it was Larkin's *The Less Deceived*. It was the first book of poems that I had read from cover to cover. I handed it to Tim with some pertinent comment, but he slipped it into his bicycle bag with no display of interest. I was a little put out. I thought the poems were brilliant, and I thought I was a little bit brilliant, too, for understanding some of them. I had rehearsed a series of astute and sensitive remarks to make about them and had not expected to find myself short of an audience. But perhaps just before supper, with so many people around, was not the best moment. Tim and I could always find another chance.

My father said Grace. We all sat down, and Tim insisted on taking the wobbly stool. My father poured the wine with some ceremony; my mother even took a little, though she barely touched her lips with it. We raised a toast to the return of Victoria, which was our ritual beginning to every holiday. Victoria made some graceful and witty reply – I can't remember what she said, but I do remember that Tim laughed uproariously, far more loudly than the witticism warranted, and we all looked at him, and I realized in a flash that in future he wouldn't be interested in my opinions on Larkin or any other subject, because Victoria was beautiful, and that counted for more than anything else. For a piercing second I minded acutely, and then I thought, 'Oh, well,' and passed round the vegetables.

My father carved. There was not very much chicken between seven of us – Simon was a vegetarian of conscience, but not where roast chicken was concerned – and the plump golden dome was soon reduced to a crumbling white escarpment. Dad hacked off the wishbone to give to Victoria and we all saw something glistening in the black cavern of the interior. 'Hey!' said Simon in excitement. 'It might be a tape worm!' It wasn't a tapeworm, it was the plastic bag of giblets that Aunt Marigold had forgotten to remove.

'Oh my Lord,' said Marigold, 'I do hope plastic's not carcinogenic.' Then she covered her mouth with her hand and gave a kind of strangulated cough and started fussing people about whether they had enough gravy. But it was too late.

'What's carcinogenic?' asked Simon.

'I know,' said Tim, ever eager where facts were concerned. 'It's a substance that causes cancer.'

In the tiny silence that followed I felt dizzy, as I had when I first realized that my pupils were not patches of black pigment but thinly covered holes, like little wells dropping down into my head. My father said, 'I must say, Ruthie, these are the best mashed potatoes I've ever eaten,' and people clashed their knives and forks a lot. I stole a glance; poor Tim had dropped his mouth open in heavy dismay, while high on Victoria's cheek there burned a delicate flush of scorn.

11

'I won't be going back to school next term,' Victoria announced.

I was carrying an armful of my mother's clothes. Mum found the stairs very difficult, so for the time being she was to sleep in my father's study on the ground floor. For the time being. I laid the clothes on the divan. 'What do you mean, you won't be going back?' I asked, stupidly.

Victoria ran a hand through her fine, dark hair and shook it back from her face. 'Is what I said open to interpretation?'

We were both due to take our O levels in June, after which we would leave our respective schools. Westaby College took a few girls in the sixth form, and as daughters of the chaplain we would not have to pay fees. All this was already settled. But not to go back for that crucial O-level term? I said, 'Oh, Vicky, you haven't been expelled, have you?'

Victoria's pride was only visible in the twitch of a nostril. 'Not yet. But if they make me go back I'll get myself expelled.' She arranged herself cross-legged on the bed and pulled me down beside her. 'Ruthie, I'm needed here. Aunt Marigold's going to have to go back to Oxford at some point, and you just won't be able to cope alone. Admit it. You all need me.'

I didn't know what to say. I had assumed that we'd rub along somehow, that in a few weeks my mother would be on her feet again, that we would just put up with a dirtyish house and Mrs Pedlow's suppers until everything got back to normal. But I had never been able to resist Victoria's dramatic fervour. 'We'll manage,' I said, suddenly unconvinced. 'Don't do anything drastic, Vicky.'

Victoria took my hands, threading her fingers through mine. 'Sometimes, someone has to do something drastic. This family is very sweet, but you're like a bunch of ostriches at times.' The image of ostriches, bunched and tied with a bow, struck us both as funny. 'Well, you know what I mean,' Victoria went on when we'd stopped laughing. 'And I'll be sixteen next month. I can leave school if I want. I ought to be treated as an adult with reasonable opinions. I mean, you can get married at sixteen, for Christ's sake.'

'Only with your p–parents' permission.' I stumbled when I mentioned parents to Victoria because I was still not clear as to whether she thought she had any. She answered only with a silence which I took to be meaningful. I busied myself with my mother's clothes, smoothing them and folding them in ways that weren't really necessary.

Victoria uncurled herself and walked to the window. It had a deep sill, deep enough to serve as a seat. The window was small-paned, cottagey; it framed a square of our enclosed, untidy garden, which in its turn was framed by fine old trees, oak and hornbeam, sycamore and sweet chestnut. April green glowed luminous through a veil of fine rain. Victoria arranged herself on the seat, her silhouette dark. Against that aqueous background she reminded me once more of the mermaid, the sea-princess who had bewitched my childhood. 'You'll manage,' she said, her voice dreamy. 'But you'll need to do more than manage. I know what it's like, remember.'

Something icy spiralled through the hollows of my bones. 'It'll only be a few weeks,' I faltered, 'and then we'll be back to normal. It's not worth leaving school for.'

'Ruthie,' Victoria almost whispered, not turning her head, 'she isn't going to get better.'

I jumped up, flung open a drawer, shoved the clothes in. In a whirl of temper I made up the divan bed, thumping pillows, shaking open the sheets so they cracked in the dusty air. 'You can't say that.' I was almost shouting. 'You don't know. Nobody knows. She's had the operation. It's out – it's finished. It's just stupid to – ' I was crying, but my eyes were dry. My chest heaved, and I couldn't stop the sobs escaping, ugly and harsh like a difficult cough. 'You don't know everything, Victoria Rampling. You think you know it all – well, I'm telling you, you don't.'

She waited until my fury was spent, until I was sitting, crying properly now, on the immaculately made-up bed. She waited until I had just begun to be frightened, then she slipped down from the window seat, light as a fairy, and took me in her arms. 'Ruthie, don't blind yourself,' she murmured, smoothing my hair back from my wet face. 'It'll only make things worse.' She was smaller than me, but her rare embrace seemed all-enfolding.

'I want her,' I sobbed. 'I want her like she used to be.'

'I know, I know.' Victoria's voice was vibrant. She was whispering, but bee-like it filled the room. 'I know just how you feel. I'll take the pain away, Ruthie, because I'm the only

104

one who knows how. Whatever happens, you'll always have me.'

I allowed myself to be soothed, to sink into the soft cloud she seemed to be offering me. The chemistry of crying did its work; my tears mingled with the spring rain and the hard ache inside me began to melt. Then we heard a step on the stairs and sprang apart. With heads bowed we worked on setting the room to rights, plugging in a bedside lamp, clearing Dad's papers off the only comfortable chair. When Tim called half an hour later, I'm sure my face was still blotchy and my hair even more tangly than usual, but it wouldn't have mattered anyway. I don't think Tim had noticed one single thing about me since Victoria came home.

I never even tried to imagine my mother's suffering during this time. I was too afraid of it. I was still enough of a child to believe in magic thinking, to fear that concentrating on her pain would make it worse. Certainly, when Victoria said, 'Ruthie, she isn't going to get better,' the words rang in my head like a death knell sounding out my mother's doom.

There was the selfishness, too. There always is. I was selfish and lazy; I wanted things to stay as they were, or had been. To accept and understand my mother's condition would have required an emotional effort that I just wasn't prepared to make. I considered that I had had a happy childhood, and I didn't want to have to revise that opinion. I resented the mixture of upheaval and tedium that I sensed grief would bring. Children are always thinking 'It's not fair!' because they have so little control over their lives; adults, with their luxury of choice, can afford to think 'It's not fair!' on behalf of others. At sixteen, with a dying mother, I'm afraid that what I was most forcibly struck by was the wrong done to me.

Victoria got her way. She never went back to school. It was just about to become an issue between her and my father when my mother's condition worsened and she was taken back into hospital. Despite chemotherapy, the cancer had spread to her lymph glands. Aunt Marigold was given compassionate leave by her college, so there we all were, squeezed into that cottage, unable to admit to each other that hope was something that ought to be given up because it was just getting in the way.

Dear old Tim. He was a great help to us, because he was a diversion. He was a practical help, too. He went on keeping Simon occupied with interminable games of chess, and he patiently answered Simon's questions about nuclear weapons, which in their growing complexity defeated the rest of us. Tim knew quite a lot about nuclear weapons because he was a member of CND, and he read all their literature. Tim was a great joiner-upper.

But for Victoria and me, Tim was something we could laugh at. His adoration of Victoria was all too painfully apparent. He said very little directly to her, but he used me as a channel of communication. He still brought me books and records, out of politeness, I suppose, but when he handed them over he would often make off-hand remarks like, 'Victoria might be interested in that,' or, more daringly, 'The third track reminds me of Vicky, a bit. See what you think.' I couldn't risk getting properly interested in his offerings any more, much though I would have liked to, so I shared with Victoria the scope for mockery they provided, and found myself getting used to the pain of doing so.

We were no nastier about Tim than we had been about other characters from our shared acquaintance. It was our habit to construct a caricature made of details of behaviour and appearance, but these caricatures soon took on a life of their own which bore a decreasing resemblance to their originals. Aspects of Tim – the way he breathed, the way he said, 'Well, yeah, basically,' the way he tucked his trousers into his socks – were exaggerated and distilled by us until the humour of them worked like homeopathic medicine – first Tim's socks made us laugh, then socks in general, then something at one or two removes from socks. We thought we were merely keeping ourselves entertained, but, of course, we were also reinforcing the walls of our private realm, adding cosy furnishings to the snug little watchtower from which we were wont to look down on the world at large. There was only room for two in our fortress. We were still the secret twins.

12

'And what about you, Ruth?' asked my aunt. 'Have you made up your mind about France?'

We were eating breakfast in the kitchen about a month after my mother's death. Aunt Marigold insisted upon certain rules, and one was that we should all sit down together for regular meals, just as we always had. Breakfast was the most difficult, because some mornings it was hard to feel that there was anything worth getting up for, but we did what Aunt Marigold said. Acting on instructions made things easier.

It was my aunt's way to spring a new topic for discussion on us at breakfast time. It was all part of her disciplined approach to the period of mourning. It stopped my father from flicking unseeing through the newspaper and Simon from fixing his gaze on that corner of the kitchen where my mother used to move back and forth between the kettle and the toaster while we ate. Marigold had tried launching a few topical issues at us – the Common Market referendum, the adoption of Vietnamese orphans – but our responses were limp, and she found she did better with practical matters, things that needed sorting out. On this particular morning she was running through summer-holiday plans, in particular the French exchange visit that had been proposed for me. For some time I had been corresponding with Agnès Bertrand, who lived with her family on the outskirts of Paris. We had sent each other photographs. Agnès had a small, puckish face, not pretty, but smiley. She wore a brace on her teeth – so did I, and her brace looked even more offputting than mine. Her hair was plaited in clumps behind her ears. She looked young for her age, which was the same as mine. She wrote on mauve writing paper in strange, curly handwriting, claiming to enjoy music, art and sport. I didn't like sport, myself, but then you can't have everything. It had been intended that we would exchange visits the previous summer, but then my mother became ill for the first time and everything had to be cancelled.

I emptied my mouth of toast, and said, 'Yes, I'd like to go. I'd like to see Paris.' I had still never been abroad, so my images of Paris were of the most hackneyed tourist-brochure variety. The Eiffel Tower, long sticks of bread, mannequins on a catwalk – that kind of thing.

'Excellent!' Aunt Marigold loved decisions. 'I think it's a very sound scheme. Don't you think so, Julian? It should set Ruthie up nicely for French A level. Let me have the address, would you, Ruth dear, and I'll write to make all the arrangements.' By this I understood that I did not have to be the one to inform famille Bertrand of my mother's death, and I was grateful.

'We'll have to have her back, of course. We'd normally be at the cottage in August – well, she can come to the cottage. She'll probably enjoy the sea. Now, let's see . . . if you leave in mid July, say the eighteenth . . . three weeks each way would be about right, I think.'

Three weeks! I had only ever been away from my family for

109

four days, on a school camping expedition to South Wales. I ran my fingertip across the top of the table, collecting crumbs. Our kitchen table was Formica, the colour of crushed raspberries speckled with cream. That colour had always seemed to me the very essence of home.

Simon tipped his bowl to catch the last spoonful of Rice Krispies. He said, 'Why does it have to be Ruthie? Why can't Victoria go?' Simon's voice was always flat, lacking inflection. It wasn't clear whether he was objecting to my proposed absence, pointing out Victoria's equal right to a French exchange, or simply asking for factual information.

'Victoria is not going to do French A level,' explained my father. 'But if she wants to go . . .' Both my parents had always been scrupulously careful to be fair to their adopted daughter.

Victoria demurred. She, too, had once had a French girl to write to. But poor Monique's descriptions of her life in a dormitory village near Lille had filled Victoria with such horror that she had, she claimed, deliberately written a letter that would make it impossible for her ever to be invited to stay. I asked her what she had written; she just laughed, and said, 'I hinted at dark crimes.' Now she said to my – our – father, 'Oh no. It's much more important for Ruthie. I'm quite happy to go to the cottage with you.'

My father smiled. Victoria was the only person who could make him smile, just then. 'Come on, Simon,' I said, carrying my plate and mug to the draining board, 'get a move on.' Simon licked the butter and jam off his knife – a habit that no one had ever been able to break – and as usual we set off together to catch the bus. There had been talk of Victoria attending my school for this last, O-level term, but she'd managed to wriggle out of that unappealing little plan. There was no point, she said. It was only revision, and she could revise on her own. She would sit the exams in the school, but that was all. My father was in no mood to argue, so she stayed at home, helping him with his research and getting the occasional hour's coaching in maths and science from masters at the College. Marigold helped her with history, and Tim offered to set her revision tests. She went along with that with nonchalance, though to me she expressed exasperation, with which I affected sympathy.

'I don't want to go to the cottage if you're not coming,' said Simon unexpectedly. We didn't as a rule say much on the way to school, both occupied with our private thoughts.

My undernourished ego unfurled itself, warmed by any attention, even from so inconsiderable a quarter. 'Why not?' I asked.

'Without you and Mum there's no point going.' The hedgerow was bursting with the sweets of early summer, but Simon kept his eyes on his feet, scuffing along the lane.

I didn't want to show him how pleased I was. I put on a grown-up voice and said, 'Why don't you invite someone down with you? Perhaps that would be more fun.'

'Who?' demanded Simon. 'I haven't got any friends.'

This was true. He never had had any. He had shown no signs of minding before, and didn't now, not really. His tone was matter-of-fact, not plaintive. I thought, and came up with Caspian Margolis, son of the Head of Classics at the College. In theory, Caspian and Simon were friends, because they were the same age, and Caspian also wore glasses and liked collecting facts, but when I said, 'What about Caspian Margolis?' Simon just let out a kind of shuddering noise, and I did understand.

The bus drew up. We sat in our usual places, right at the back, and got our homework out. Mine was biology revision, learning parts of the skeleton for a test. The diagram swam before my eyes. 'Simon,' I said, 'it won't always be like this.' I put my arm round his shoulder. He said, 'Don't do that. Unless you want me to cry.'

He breathed a misty patch on to the window, scratched patterns in it with his fingernail. Then he said, 'Do you think Tim would come?'

'Where? To the cottage?'

'Yes. Then I could play chess with him. That wouldn't be so bad.'

Suddenly I knew that I really, really did not want Tim to be at the cottage when I was away in France. 'Well, maybe,' I said, searching for a reason for him not to go that wasn't actually a lie, 'but I expect he'll be too busy. He's bound to have other plans.'

'Busy? Tim?' said Simon.

It didn't seem likely. 'Shut up, now, will you?' I said. 'I've got to get this skeleton learnt.'

'Oh heavens!' my father said. 'You ought to take them a present.' My rucksack was packed and waiting in the hall, and the train that was to take me to London on the first leg of my solo voyage left in half an hour.

'There's no time,' cried Victoria. 'Get them something in London, Ruthie. You've got an hour's wait, haven't you?'

'Yes, but what? What shall I get? What can you buy at Waterloo? Dad?'

My father ran his fingers through his two wings of hair. 'Flowers?'

'They'll die before she gets there. Or get squashed. What about chocolates?'

'I'm sure they have better chocolates in France,' I said.

'They can't do,' said Simon. 'Maltesers are the best chocolates there are.'

I wanted to cry. I saw myself, a tiny figure bent double by my rucksack, toiling through a maze of alien city streets with a box of Maltesers in my outstretched hand, like alms. I looked imploringly at my father.

'Books,' he said. 'There's bound to be a bookstall open.'

'But they'll all be in English!' I wailed. 'I can't give them a book they can't read.'

'It could be one with pictures in.'

'Simon, they're not children.'

'They could be photographs of interesting things, like animals, or, or –'

'How am I supposed to know what they're interested in?'

'Jam,' said Marigold, coming in from the kitchen.

'Why on earth would they be interested in *jam*?'

'No, no. Real jam. Jars of it.'

'I can't give them *jam*.'

'Why not? It's very English. Look, don't waste any more time arguing, or you'll miss that train. Here – blackcurrant, raspberry, quince jelly. I bet you they don't have quince jelly in France.'

'They do,' said Victoria. 'It's called coings.'

Aunt Marigold wrapped each pot deftly in newspaper. 'Victoria, don't be difficult.'

Victoria rolled her eyes at me in a way that meant, 'Aunt Marigold is on another planet.' Aloud she said, 'I'll come with you to the station.' Marigold and Simon stood at the door, waving.

In the car, Victoria slipped her shoes off and rested her bare feet on the back of the driver's seat, either side of my father's head. If I had done that he'd have told me it was dangerous. 'You can ditch the jam at the station,' she suggested. 'Give it to a tramp or something. And you can buy them a book about the Royal Family. Frogs love the Royal Family, because they haven't got one.'

'You shouldn't call them frogs, but it's a good idea,' said my father, who wasn't supposed to be listening. 'I'll give you some cash when we get to the station, Ruthie. Five pounds should be plenty.'

But when we got to the station he found he had no money on him. Nor did Victoria. Nor did I; only travellers' cheques, and just enough cash to cross London.

'Jam, then,' said my father, kissing the top of my head. 'I'm sure Marigold's right.'

'I'm not,' said Victoria. 'Ditch it, and send them something when whatserface goes back. Or pretend you had something and it got left on the train.'

'I know you won't do that,' said my father, 'because it would be untrue.' But he gave Victoria an indulgent smile.

'Write to me!' she called as my train pulled out. 'We can always spring a rescue if it's really dire.' I leaned out of the window, waving for as long as I could still keep her small, gallant figure in sight.

I didn't feel homesick until I was on the ferry, and then I felt a tightness in my chest that at first I took to be seasickness, but the summer sea was like a mirror, and my whole being yearned for the chips that my neighbour was eating, so it couldn't have been. Surreptitiously I unrolled one of the jars of jam, because I wanted to see my mother's handwriting on the label. 'Quince Jelly '73.' Two summers ago. I thought of my mother's freckled hands, slicing the knobbly, unprepossessing fruit; the muslin bag bulging with fruit pulp hanging from a hook in the larder, juice dripping all night into a basin. My mother skimming the fluff off the boiling syrup with a little tin mug; the fluff in a saucer, cooling for our tea. Beneath that foamy, yellowish scum, amber jelly, honey-scented; Mum dividing it between the three of us, with perhaps just a little bit extra for Victoria. I shoved the jar back into my rucksack, but it was too late to halt the slide of hot, slow tears.

'Cheer up, pet,' said my neighbour. 'Have a chip.' I smeared the back of my hand across my face and took one. The owner of the chips was a middle-aged woman, hugely fat, her legs pushing each other wide apart, her puffed feet squashed into exercise sandals. 'I could say it might never happen,' she said, patting my arm, 'but by the look of you it already has. Here's a book – take your mind off it, whatever it is.'

She laid a magazine full of crossword puzzles and knitting patterns on my lap, and the thought of how nice English people were and how crazy it was to leave them behind and venture among our ancient enemies the French made me want to weep afresh.

My forebodings were confirmed when Agnès was not there to greet me at the station. I was met by Monsieur Bertrand and Agnès's younger sister Isabelle, who bore aloft a piece of cardboard with my name on it. M. Bertrand spoke no English at all, and my French had temporarily evaporated, but I managed to pick up something like 'Bien méchante' – enough to know that there was trouble afoot. Isabelle, who was about ten, shrugged, and gave me a rueful, sympathetic smile. She was as thin and bendy as a pipecleaner doll and she wore her hair in bumpy plaits, just as Agnès did in the photograph she sent me. It turned out that I would spend a lot of the next three weeks playing vingt-et-un with Isabelle, but naturally I could not foresee that.

M. Bertrand wore no seat-belt. He drove very fast, turning the steering wheel by slapping it with the palm of his hand, and swearing at other drivers. My French was too poor to allow me to judge the strength of his oaths, but Isabelle sometimes interjected a remonstrative 'Papa!' He spoke to me only to point out various tourist landmarks; the only response I could think of was 'Vraiment?' When we reached the apartment block in the banlieu where they lived, which was right at the end of one of the metro lines, I forget which, he heaved my rucksack out of the boot and set it down with a crack that made my heart sink. Sure enough, by the time the lift had reached the fifth floor, a dark stain was seeping across the canvas.

M. Bertrand didn't notice. Isabelle did. She pointed it out to me and made a gesture to imitate the cutting of someone's throat, and laughed. She was a strange girl, but my bag did look as if it might have contained a dismembered body.

The evening was beginning to resemble a murder played in reverse, for even through the front door of the apartment we could hear screaming. M. Bertrand affected not to notice, but Isabelle said, 'C'est normal, tu comprends?' and got ticked off for 'tutoying' me without permission. M. Bertrand failed to open his own front door; it appeared to be bolted from within. He rang the bell, and his wife, after fumbling with locks and chains, swept us all in as calmly as if there were not someone at the far end of the flat howling and hurling their weight against a door that bowed under the impact. Madame Bertrand was soignée, with upswept hair and a print silk dress, pleated and belted. She is the only person I have ever met who attached a bunch of keys to her belt.

She kissed me twice without making the slightest contact with my skin and then propelled me and my luggage across the vestibule into the bedroom I was to share with Isabelle. I was to have shared with Agnès, I gathered, but 'malheureusement, c'est pas possible.' I didn't care. All I could think about was my rucksack leaking crimson spots across the lino tiles. To my intense relief a little dog – a Yorkie, I think, one of those whitish ones that can't see out – followed us, obliterating each drop with a slap of its unfeasibly large tongue.

The bedroom was narrow, dominated by a high bed with a quilted satin headboard and a white crewel-work counterpane. There was barely room for the camp bed, hastily and imperfectly assembled, by its side. A small altercation followed, Madame informing Isabelle that she was to relinquish her own bed for the next three weeks, and Isabelle – understandably – raising objections. I explained, using feeble gestures, that I would be 'très contente' to use the camp bed, and as confirmation I sat on it, whereupon it collapsed. Isabelle uttered a cackle of simian mirth and had her ears boxed, so quickly that I hardly knew it was happening. When she hit her children Madame used the same neat and elegant movements that characterized all her activities.

The bed was re-erected, and then Madame withdrew, leaving me to unpack. Isabelle perched cross-legged on the proper bed, nursing her boxed ears, dry-eyed and curious. She jerked a thumb towards the room next door where the screams had given way to what I took to be growled threats. 'Agnès,' she said, unnecessarily.

The opening of my rucksack could no longer be avoided. I spread my hands in what I hoped was an authentically Gallic gesture of apologetic dismay. 'Ma confiture . . .' I faltered. Two pots had smashed, the blackcurrant and the raspberry. From the way it had oozed into every part of the sack I guessed that the raspberry had never set properly. 'Why don't you use pectin?' I heard a ghost voice say. Aunt Angela. And then my mother; 'I think it alters the taste rather, don't you?'

Isabelle was actually quite helpful. She fetched her mother and between them they cleared the mess. Travel-stained though I was, I now had nothing to change into. All my clothes had to go straight into the washing-machine. Monsieur Bertrand sat in the living-room with the door open, smoking his pipe. He chuckled at intervals, and when he next saw me he said, 'Mademoiselle, aimez-vous bien la confiture?'

He continued to sit and smoke while Isabelle set the table for supper. I tried to help but I wasn't much use because I didn't know where anything was, and when I was handed things I wasn't sure what they were or where they went. I put tumblers at the right-hand corner of each setting, as we did at home, but even that was wrong. Isabelle pushed each one back so that it stood midway between knife and fork.

When she had finished cooking, Madame unlocked Agnès's door, but Agnès didn't come out. There was now silence from within. We sat down to eat; Monsieur wished me 'Bon Appétit,' and as I drank my soup I wondered whether it was possible that Agnès had commited suicide. I rather hoped so, because then, surely, I would be allowed to go straight home. Conversation at table was spasmodic, and no attempt was made to involve me, which was one small good thing.

Agnès appeared after the clearing of the soup plates, driven out, perhaps, by hunger. She was tiny, not much bigger than Isabelle, and she bore not the faintest resemblance to her photograph. Her small eyes were circled with thick kohl so that they resembled targets. She wore a cheesecloth shirt knotted beneath her almost non-existent breasts. Her trousers, cut low on her hips and made of purple velvet, were ragged from trailing on the ground. Her feet were bare. A message, indecipherable to me, was written in Biro across her midriff. Her long hair, which hung down over her face, had bits of orange string plaited into it. Madame handed out plates bearing flat, pale meat shaped like the sole of a shoe. 'Escalope de veau,' she stated. I had never had veal before, but it smelled good. Agnès must have thought so too, for when her mother said with just a hint of menace, 'Tes chaussures, Agnès,' and withheld her portion, she left the room without a murmur and returned shod in a pair of cork-soled clogs made of dirty orange suede, of the kind that had been fashionable in England two summers before.

We all drank red wine with water in it, even Isabelle. When Agnès lifted her head to drink I saw that she no longer wore a brace. I saw also that she had painted a third eye in the centre of her forehead. My brace was still very much in place. Madame noticed it, and asked me how much longer it would be before it came off. Only another six weeks, I told her. It was coming off before I started the sixth form. She pointed at Agnès, and said something along the lines of, 'When she had her brace, we never had any trouble with her. Taking it off was a big mistake.'

I looked across at Agnès and then, quite out of character, I dropped her a wink. It was the sort of thing Victoria might just conceivably have done, but me – never. Agnès looked startled, then haughty, and then she allowed herself a very small, very sulky, smile.

13

Poor Agnès. She was in love, of course. Isabelle outlined the plot to me that first night, and its intricacies were later supplied by Agnès herself, by her mother – even Monsieur put in his two centimes' worth. I became, not exactly a repository for confidences, but a kind of flypaper for them. I had only to cross the field of vision of any member of the Bertrand family and, if no one else was within earshot, I would be bombarded with pellets of information that I was powerless to avoid.

It seemed that Agnès had no sooner shed her brace than she had welded herself to the first unsuitable young man in sight. She called him Coco – I never found out whether that was his real name. Whenever she said 'Coco' I found myself thinking of January evenings at home in front of the fire, of sipping the sweet pinky-brown drink from my turquoise Capricorn mug and draping the wrinkly skin over the chip in the rim. Coco the boy – or man, as Agnès considered him – was neither sweet nor homely. He had all the usual attributes of an undesirable boyfriend – motorbike, leather jacket, random facial hair – but what really got Madame Bertrand's goat was the fact that his parents were divorced.

The problem of chaperoning Agnès occupied Madame Bertrand for much of each day, and probably for a considerable part of each long, stuffy night, too. The flat was airless. At nightfall, the windows were locked as well as shuttered, though it was hard to see why. I don't think even Agnès would have escaped from a fifth-floor window. I used to wake in the small hours with my nightdress glued to my body. There was no room for restlessness on my narrow camp bed; I lay rigid, willing the hours to pass, thirsty for the sight of an oak tree in an English field. I would have slept naked but for the small, powerful presence of Isabelle lying barely a foot away from me, cool and composed despite her high-necked, tight-cuffed flannelette nightgown. She slept on her back, her hands folded on her chest, as if she had been embalmed. I did once try slipping into the living-room to read until dawn, but the following day Isabelle told me that she was a light sleeper, and after that I didn't dare.

I couldn't see how anyone could sleep in that atmosphere. I pictured Madame, glassy-eyed, hair coiled in a net, plotting and planning until the break of day. The days evolved a pattern, so that after a week I felt as though I knew no other life. Every morning Agnès, Isabelle and I would trail round after Madame through the local shops and markets, and while she prodded cheeses and sniffed melons and twanged the gill flaps of fish, Agnès would hang back and we would have murmured conversations about the perfections of Coco and the iniquities of her parents. After lunch – always three courses, and always delicious – we were supposed to go sightseeing for my benefit, but this did not happen for the first half of my stay, because over lunch some minor contention would blow up into an exchange of insults, and Agnès would be locked into her bedroom. Then

Isabelle and I would spend the slow afternoons playing vingt-et-un while Madame flicked through copies of *Paris Match* and *Vogue*. 'I adore your Royal Family,' she would say, yawning, 'but Her Majesty has no idea how to dress. All that money, and so little chic.'

I lived for the meals, which enticed and repelled me in almost equal measure. Madame was an excellent cook. I had never tasted really good food before, and I gobbled it with an alacrity that startled everyone, not least myself. There were so many dishes that were new to me – smoky artichokes, squatting like affronted animals in puddles of melted butter; tiny unnameable shellfish, each one repaying half a minute's work with one second of explosive deliciousness; boeuf en gelée, that looked like dogmeat but melted in the mouth; a pudding that seemed to be nothing but cream, coaxed into the shape of a plump and quivering heart. In direct contrast to Madame's elegant control, her meals seemed to be trying to burst their bounds. Salads curled their tentacles above the rim of the bowl, cheeses oozed their ripeness into their beds of straw. If I thought about it too hard, the food came to resemble alien life forms, so I ate it as quickly as I could, because otherwise I might not have been able to eat it at all. Agnès, who picked at her food, looked at me with no attempt to conceal her disdain; her father turned my appetite into one of his ponderous long-running jokes. Even Madame, at first gratified by my appreciation, grew twitchy. For the first few days, for breakfast we had home-made pain au chocolat as well as croissants and brioche, but by the end of my stay it was just bread and jam and café au lait. Perhaps she worried about sending me home in a swollen state; more likely she was shocked by the increase in her housekeeping bills.

And I did gain weight. I'd never been truly fat, though I wasn't slim like Victoria. My stomach jutted like a little shelf, and my thighs touched each other most of the way down. That was my normal state. But it didn't take long chez Bertrand before my jeans became impossibly tight and my cheeks filled out in a way that made me look even younger and less sophisticated. It bothered me; every day I told myself to slow down, but every day appeared some fresh display of Madame's culinary powers, and like one bewitched I was unable to stop myself as I chewed and swilled. The Bertrands all left a morsel on their plates; this was clearly etiquette, but I just couldn't make myself comply. I did wonder what Agnès would make of the staples of our diet at home, of macaroni cheese and tuna pie and Aunt Marigold's horrible curried eggs. But I found it difficult to believe that Agnès would be allowed to come to England at all, so closely guarded was she.

After a while, Agnès realized that if she modified her behaviour a little, I could provide a useful escape route. For three lunches in a row she kept her eyes lowered and refused to rise to her mother's coolly provocative remarks. Having no excuse to lock her up, Madame grudgingly agreed to take us into town. My first taste of Paris apart from the Gare St Lazare was an afternoon in the Galeries Lafayette looking at bedlinen, but at least it was a change from vingt-et-un. Mindful of the fact that I had not yet offered my hostess a gift – the surviving pot of jam sat in the bottom of the wardrobe, hidden by my spare towel and almost vibrating with pathos – I boldly steered the girls into the book department and bought a volume of photographs of the life and times of the Queen Mother. Madame was pleased, almost touched. The next day we were allowed to travel alone, though we were under strict instructions to be back by five.

Agnès wasted no time. As soon as we were round the corner from the apartment block she nipped into a telephone booth, from which she emerged almost staggering with excitement. We were to take the metro into town; Coco would be waiting outside Notre Dame in half an hour. At the station, Agnès bought mint chewing gum to freshen her breath. She scrutinized her appearance as best she could in the unsteady reflection provided by the carriage windows. She licked a fingertip and ran it over her eyebrows, which she had plucked so high that they formed arches which were positively Gothic. She ran her hands through her hair and pulled the out-growing fringe down over her face. She had no watch, so she kept grabbing her sister's thin wrist and twisting the watch face towards her. When Isabelle pulled her arm away in protest, Agnès turned to me and said, 'If you had a boyfriend, you would know that every second is an eternity.'

Nettled, I said, 'I do have a boyfriend.'

My lie was rewarded with the undivided attention of both sisters. 'He's called Tim,' I said, 'and he's seventeen.'

Agnès ran her eyes up and down my body, as if seeing me for the first time. She looked suspicious. 'Have you a photo?'

I had, actually. In my wallet I had a photograph of the whole family, crowded on to our front doorstep. Tim had been there at the time, so of course he was asked to be in it, too. Victoria had taken it with the camera she had been given for her sixteenth birthday. She had made me a present of the picture the night before I left for France. 'You might need it,' she had said, enigmatically; that comment now seemed eerily prescient. I passed the photograph to Agnès. She held it close to her face, scowling. Tim was standing behind Simon, so only his head and shoulders were visible. The worst aspects of him, like his socks, were hidden. All that could really be seen was a lot of curly fairish hair.

'He wears glasses,' said Agnès, shortly.

'Yes,' I replied, 'like John Lennon.' That would not have been a cool thing to say in England, but I had gathered that in such matters French youth lagged behind us rather. The comment seemed to strike home with Agnès.

'He likes music?'

'Oh yes. He plays in a band.' Tim and his tenor recorder were the prop and stay of the Westaby College Madrigal Society, so it wasn't technically a lie.

'What do you do with him, Root?' asked Isabelle. None of the Bertrands had mastered my Christian name.

'Do with him?'

'I mean, do you kiss him?'

I was spared from telling another out-and-out lie by the intervention of Agnès. 'Isabelle,' she screeched, 'tais-toi.' She gave her little sister's arm a sharp and unaffectionate pinch, and in the swift action I saw a flash of her mother's cool spite.

The train rattled to its destination and the discussion was closed. We emerged, squinting, into a world of fierce sun and bright stone, the air full of voices and the whirr and clap of pigeons' wings. Paris at last, I thought, as Notre Dame and the glitter of the Seine imprinted themselves upon my consciousness. I sniffed, hoping to catch the authentic French aromas I had read about, but it smelled the same as London really, just dustier.

Coco was where he had said he would be, with his motorbike. He said not a word to Isabelle or me, but enfolded Agnès in his arms and fastened his mouth on to hers.

'C'est dégoutant,' commented Isabelle, just out of earshot. She extended a dismissive hand towards the soaring façade of the great cathedral. 'Ça, c'est Notre Dame. Allons-y.'

Her eye had been caught by a row of souvenir shops the other side of the *place*. I said, 'I would like to see inside.' Isabelle's face puckered with astonishment. 'Tu veux?' she asked. 'Vraiment?' Then she shrugged resignedly and followed me in.

Great vaulting spaces always provide me with the expected frisson, and Notre Dame was balm to my fettered senses, despite the fact that Isabelle dogged my footsteps all the way round. I sat in front of one of the rose windows and tried to lose myself in the pulsing vortex of colour, but a dry little voice close to my ear said, 'C'est jolie, hien?' and then, 'J'ai bien faim.' So I gave up long before I was ready and we went and bought chips with mayonnaise on them and I bought a postcard of the Mona Lisa and Isabelle bought one of a little bug-eyed boy pissing against a wall. Agnès was ten minutes late, so we leaned on the parapet of the bridge and I wrote my postcard to Aunt Marigold. I wrote, 'I have not yet seen this' on the back of the Mona Lisa in extra large letters in the hope that Isabelle would see, but I doubted whether her English would be up to it. She wouldn't have been interested, anyway.

Agnès showed up at last. Her face looked blurred and rather pretty. She showed us her love bite, which was so far back on her neck that it was completely concealed by her hair. Isabelle thought that, too, was 'dégoutant,' and I must say I felt the same way. On the way home, Agnès kept stretching and sighing and allowing mysterious half-smiles to flicker across her face in a manner that she clearly considered befitted one who was A Real Woman, and I played Hangman with Isabelle on the back of the old metro tickets, and Isabelle kept winning because we had to play in French. We got back just in time. Madame sniffed Agnès and said she must have been smoking, and Agnès said, quite patiently, that the mètro had been full of smokers, so Madame sniffed Isabelle and me and seemed satisfied. Monsieur came home early from the porcelain factory where he was a manager and complained of a headache, so that created a diversion and I slipped off to write to Victoria. I told her that she had been right about the Royal Family, and gave her a lurid description of Agnès's love bite complete with illustration, but I didn't say anything about the use to which I had put her family photograph.

Victoria wrote to me twice weekly during my three-week exile, but the very regularity of her letters made me feel still more forlorn. I felt that she was writing because she was sorry for me, like a conscientious house mistress or a dutiful godmother. The letters were newsy, spritely, and of uniform length – four sides, plus illustrations. They were the kind of letters you would write to a convalescent, but I wasn't a convalescent; I had a long way to go before I could start to recover, and at that stage I didn't even know exactly what there was to be recovered from. One might have thought that the new parallel between Victoria and myself that the loss of my mother had created would have been of interest to both of us, but somehow it wasn't. Even when the facts encouraged it, I never compared myself with Victoria.

Victoria's letters contained no mention of my mother – our mother, indeed – and nor did my father's, or Aunt Marigold's. Silence was the way my family dealt with such matters – silence, and diversion. So my father wrote about things he'd read and things in the news that he thought might interest me, though they didn't, much, and Marigold wrote short notes about Paris, travel arrangements, and what was out in the garden. I was grateful for their reticence. Their letters did what they were supposed to do, which was convey a sense of continuity, and assure me of my place in the scheme of things. It was only Victoria's breeziness that troubled me, because it made me feel so very alone.

14

My rash announcement about Tim's significance in my life was made about halfway through my stay with the Bertrands. This meant that I spent most of the second half worrying about how to cover up or evade the lie when Agnès returned to England with me. The plan was that we should go straight to the Dorset cottage, returning to Westaby only for the last week of the holiday. I didn't know for certain where Tim would be. Simon had asked if he could join them all in Dorset, but the matter had still been unresolved when I left for France. In my letters I couldn't possibly ask.

So I pondered and agonized, and as my outward relations with Agnès became more cordial, inwardly I liked her less and less. I was not aware of having met anyone so self-absorbed in all my life. Her egotism was a blessing in a way, because she showed so little interest in me, except as a passive recipient of her longings and complaints, that I did not have to add much detail to my core lie. Isabelle asked questions, but because she was younger she didn't need to be answered, except with enigmatic hints. My communication with Agnès was mostly limited to our metro rides. Her exemplary behaviour at home continued, and therefore we were allowed into town most afternoons. Coco would always be waiting for us – for Agnès – at our destination; he and Agnès would disappear for two or three hours, and Isabelle and I would be left to our own devices. Isabelle was quietly obstructive about my sightseeing attempts, though I did get her into the Louvre, once, on the grounds that there would be a shop attached. There was, and Isabelle was happy. What she really liked doing was shoplifting – tiny things, things that could be hidden in the palm of her hand.

The days dragged, but the weeks whizzed by. When there were only four days to go, I realized that I had to act. A postcard arrived for me from Simon; it said, 'Dear Ruthie, I found two Miller's Thumbs near the waterfall. Dad thinks he saw a goshawk. Hope you are well. From Simon. P. S. Tim is coming tomorrow.' Emboldened by panic, I locked myself in the bathroom straight after breakfast and wrote to Tim himself. I adopted a bright-and-breezy, all-pals-together tone. 'Hi Tim!' I began, and then explained my predicament as the result of some kind of jocular misunderstanding. 'So pleeez,' I ended, 'do your stuff, and pretend you're going out with me. It would be a real laugh. See you, Ruthie. P. S. I do know you're not.'

I sealed and stamped this uncharacteristic missive before I could get cold feet, and I posted it that morning when we went to the market with Madame. I worried that Victoria would see it first and wonder what on earth I was doing writing to Tim, and I had thought about disguising my handwriting on the envelope, but the French postmark would be a give-away. And Tim would probably show it to her in any case. He was so candid and impulsive. 'Hey! A letter from Ruthie? Why's she writing to *me*?' I pictured him waving the letter about at breakfast, in front of all of them. I was just going to have to brazen it out as a rather odd joke.

Soon after that, everything changed. Perhaps Madame Bertrand became suspicious of Agnès's lamb-like demeanour, or perhaps she was bored with not having anyone to punish. Whatever the reason, we were sitting at the dinner table the night before our departure sipping the champagne that Monsieur had just opened – to celebrate getting rid of us, I supposed – when Madame, coming in from the kitchen, set down her steaming tureen and, with a silent aim worthy of any bird of prey, fell on Agnès, seized her tangled hair in both hands, and twisted it up above her head. Agnès's hands flew to her neck, but in vain; three large lovebites were revealed in various stages of decay, mauve and dirty yellow like flattened fungi. Madame emitted a shriek in which triumph and rage struggled for mastery. She yanked at the twist of hair and tried to drag her daughter away from the table. Agnès hung on to the tablecloth; Madame, mindful of her crockery and glassware even at such a moment, kept her grip on the hair with one hand, snatched up a pitcher of water with the other, and tipped it over Agnès's head. Spluttering and shaking, Agnès let go of the tablecloth, and was somehow bundled out of the room. 'Serve the soup,' Madame hissed over her shoulder at her husband before thrusting Agnès back into the solitary confinement with which she was so familiar.

Madame returned to the table within seconds; only the rapid rise and fall of her chest beneath its cream chiffon ruffle gave any indication of the scene we had just witnessed. My French was much improved, but I could not understand many of the insults that Agnès was yelling from the other side of the locked door. I could, however, understand the one remark her father called back at her. It was, 'Silence, or else – the whip.'

There seemed to be only one thing for it. I ate. I always ate, but this time I surpassed all previous records. Three platefuls of velvety, pale-brown soup; two entrecôtes, Agnès's as well as my own, with unctuous pommes dauphinoises and spinach darkly gleaming through a cloak of cream. What a beautifully extravagant thing to do to spinach, in our house always the Cinderella of vegetables! There was salad, piles of it, to be folded and subdued like crisp, green laundry, and the slick of dressing to be rounded up with hunks of bread. Cheese – I especially remember a Pont L'Evêque smelling deliciously of rotten cabbage, heaving through its cracking crust. And because it was our last night, Madame had made a chocolate mousse, as nearly black as it could be, an emulsion of richness only just held together, glistening on the plate, the sweetness of it slashed by the crème fraîche that I ladled on top with an unstinting hand. My champagne glass seemed bottomless, like an enchanted goblet in a fairy tale; every time I drew breath from my monstrous sucking-in of food it seemed to have refilled itself. My performance provided the Bertrands with a welcome diversion. Monsieur was able to take all his favourite jokes out for exercise – he even reverted to jam, and asked me, for by no means the first time, whether all English girls possessed such hearty appetites.

Madame encouraged me. She nodded and smiled her approval, and said that young girls who were too thin would never find a husband. This seemed odd when one considered her reaction to the behaviour of the slender Agnès, but then, Madame was odd. She watched me eat until it was as if she, not I, had had her fill, and then she leaned her elbows on the table and pressed her fingertips together and said with a thin-lipped smile, 'And now perhaps Root can tell us how Agnès has been meeting this – '

I think she used the word 'garçon' for Coco, but I can't tell you for sure, because the room was turning and something huge was swelling inside my chest and I could feel pricks of sweat breaking out along my hairline in an exact and most unpleasant manner. I opened my mouth to speak, but then I realized that it wasn't going to be words coming out, and I reeled away from the table and was sick, sicker than I'd ever been in my life before.

I didn't make it to the bedroom, or even out of the door. I tried to aim for the floor, which was covered in slippery lino printed to look like marble, but my vomiting was so gargantuan that I splashed the sofa and armchairs which were upholstered in a damask of very pale pearly pink. The Bertrands rose in alarm to rescue their possessions and I sank to my knees on the floor, but even as I heaved, out of the corner of my eye I saw Isabelle snatch her mother's keys where they had been left by the side of her plate – for once, not returned immediately to her belt – and slip unnoticed from the room. Madame was rolling up a heavy rug, Monsieur was holding the little dog by the hind legs in an attempt to prevent it from lapping up my sick. Its nails scrabbled on the shiny floor; Madame screeched at Monsieur not to let it make marks. During the short altercation that followed, I realized that Isabelle had released her sister not only from the bedroom but from the apartment, and had replaced the bunch of keys exactly as she'd found them. She had a mop and bucket in her hand. 'Good girl!' cried Madame, seizing them. 'At least I have one daughter who does not disgrace me.'

I struggled to my feet. I felt weak and shaky but incredibly, joyously well, as one does when one has been sick in such a thorough-going manner. I tried to apologize but I was ignored. I made feeble attempts to clear up but I was waved away by Madame, by now in full protective clothing of rubber gloves and wrap-around apron and galoshes. Yes, she really did put on galoshes to clean up my vomit.

Their utter lack of sympathetic interest was a relief. I murmured something about bed and retired to my room. I made my preparations hastily, shoved my bespattered clothes into the bottom of my rucksack where I hoped the smell would not offend Isabelle, and lay down on the camp bed for the last time. Isabelle did not appear for ages. I would not have been surprised to find that the Bertrands had redecorated the entire living-room. I lay tense, listening for the sounds of their discovery of Agnès's flight, but they were obviously far too busy to notice. I heard Isabelle's light tread, feigned sleep, and soon slipped into the real thing.

I woke at four with an ungovernable thirst. I could barely lick my sour lips with my stiff, dry tongue. I eased myself off the camp bed, which I had long since decided was about as comfortable to sleep on as a dead dinosaur, and crept into the bathroom. The water was said to be 'non potable', but I didn't care. I cupped my hands under the tap and gulped the water down, loving the way it trickled down my hot face. If it makes me ill, I thought, then at least I can be ill at home. Ill at home! What delightful visions of cosiness, of reading in bed and flowers in a jam jar and bread and butter with the crusts cut off! And oh, the bliss of earache, with a hot potato in a sock to hold against your ear! My mother's remedy. I wiped my dripping hands. What would being ill at home be like, now that my mother was gone?

On my way back to bed I paused, listening. Not a sound, save for the gentle snores of Monsieur and the wheezy snuffles of the little dog who slept by the front door but who never woke at the sound of footfalls. A thought struck me. Unless a miracle – or whatever the word was for a bad miracle – happened, Agnès would not be able to come back to England with me. I shuddered with joy and relief. On impulse, I tried the handle of Agnès's bedroom door. Too bad if it disturbed Madame – nothing mattered now.

The door opened. There wouldn't have been the time, or the need, for Isabelle to lock it behind her fleeing sister. The shutters had not been closed; the salmon-coloured dawn, struggling through the neon haze that haloed the city, brought plenty of light into the narrow, cell-like room. I moved about, touching Agnès's things – the hand mirror with a photograph of Marc Bolan Sellotaped to the back, the locked diary that lay on her dressing-table as a kind of dare to her mother, an Indian necklace of beads and tiny bells which she'd told her mother that she'd bought on one of our expeditions, but which Isabelle and I knew Coco had bought for her. Her high, white bed looked scarcely touched. On the wall above its head hung a rosary and a crucifix. I wondered if Madame had noticed that the crucifix was upside down.

I withdrew. The click of the door handle sounded like a gunshot to me, but still Madame didn't stir. My body felt cool at last, but I didn't sleep again. I lay in wait for the morning wide-eyed, counting the hours on my fingers – so many hours to Gare St Lazare, so many to Le Havre, so many to the cottage. And I thought about Madame, and what could have happened to her that would allow her to lock her child up for the night without food, without water, without even checking if she needed to go to the lavatory. I wondered if there was any crime any of us could have committed that would have made my mother consider treating us in such a way, but I didn't think about it for long, because no, of course there wasn't.

By breakfast time I was starving, but I kept myself in check. Buoyed up as I was by my imminent return, I still had no wish to listen to any more of Monsieur's jokes about my appetite. But I need not have worried, because the disappearance of Agnès was discovered while I was in the shower, and I breakfasted unnoticed, under cover of a brisk cross-fire of questions and recriminations. These flew exclusively between the parents; Isabelle sat dipping bits of baguette into her hot chocolate looking pure and uplifted as if she was on her way to First Communion. It was then that I realized that the Bertrand parents were quite stupid.

There was talk of the police, but there was more talk of what to do with the redundant ticket to England. 'It's far too late,' keened Madame, as near to grief as I ever saw her. 'They'll never give us a refund now.' Monsieur, who was working himself up into pompous, blustery mode, announced that he would ring the travel agent immediately; of course it was possible, if only those lazy so-and-sos had their wits about them . . . then Isabelle's small, dry voice broke in: 'I could go to England. I could go instead of Agnès.' Finding all eyes were on her, she shrugged. 'Then the ticket wouldn't be wasted.'

'Your passport?' I faltered, clutching at straws. But it turned out that Isabelle already had her own passport. She had paid a solo visit to a Swiss aunt, the year before.

Madame visibly brightened, and Monsieur, after a little huffing and puffing, decided to accept the idea. Isabelle's suitcase was packed in a trice; I saw some sumptuously wrapped parcels being transferred from Agnès's luggage to hers. Madame plundered the depths of the wardrobe for a kilt, a sort of felt bonnet, and a cardigan with a tartan trim. 'It's always cold in England,' she told her daughter. I said nothing. I rather liked the idea of Isabelle picking her way across the Dorset beach in full Highland rig.

Monsieur had taken the morning off work to take us to the station, as Madame did not drive. She pecked all of us twice, once on each cheek, with no perceptible increase in warmth for her own flesh and blood. The telephone rang as we were leaving; Monsieur did not linger to see whether it brought news of Agnès.

The journey seemed very long. I had finished the books I had brought with me from England, and Isabelle had packed no reading matter. I spent my last few francs on some chocolate and a comic for teenage girls containing photo-stories with speech balloons. My French still wasn't up to much, but I could manage the balloons. Each story ended with a photograph of the mouth of the hero clamping down on that of the young heroine. Isabelle pointed at one of these pictures. 'Sexy!' she exclaimed, puffing out her bubble gum. When we were well and truly out of Paris she startled me by stowing her gum in an ashtray – Monsieur hadn't appeared to notice that our seats were in a smoking compartment – and pulling a packet of cigarettes out of her bag. The cigarettes were long and thin and brown, a brand I was unfamiliar with. 'Tu veux?' she asked, holding out the packet. I shook my head. Isabelle flicked open her lighter with a practised air. She was ten.

She asked a few questions about my family; she had always shown more interest than Agnès. She said, between puffs – I don't think she inhaled – 'And he? Will he be there?'

'Who?'

'The boyfriend, of course! Who else?'

Who, indeed? Last night's drama had driven the problem of Tim out of my mind. But if my letter had arrived in time, then how would Tim behave? I affected insouciance. 'I don't know. He might be. It's not important.'

Isabelle leaned over and took my magazine. She took a Biro out of her bag, chose a story which featured a heroine who faintly resembled me (frizzy hair) and said, 'Root, it's you.' She cackled. 'And this,' – pointing at the male protagonist, who had a chiselled jaw and improbably wide lapels – 'this one is Tim.' And to reinforce the humour she wrote our names with arrows pointing to the faces in the frame that showed the final clinch.

★

My father met us at Southampton. Monsieur Bertrand had told me he would telephone to inform my family of the change of visitor; this clearly had not happened. I explained Isabelle's presence; my father looked bewildered, and I felt a little sympathetic ache for Aunt Marigold and Victoria, who would have spent all morning drilling him on salient facts about Agnès. My father hardly looked at Isabelle, anyhow; he fixed his eyes on me with a look of hungry delight. And 'me' was all he saw – he would never have noticed whether I looked unhappy, or ill, or fat, or well, in a million years. 'You look well,' he said, which was what he always said to everyone. It was the adult equivalent of 'You've grown.'

Isabelle perched primly in the front seat of the car, while I sprawled in the back, luxuriating in the coming of the dark. Our part of Dorset attracted thousands of summer tourists, but in the twilight the landscape seemed deserted, prehistoric; great humped bones of rock and chalk smoothed with a thin skin of earth and grass. The evening star hung in the purple air like a note in music, and I thought of Simon. Stars always made me think of him.

Our cottage was so lonely that you could hear any car coming from a long way off, so they were all at the door to meet us – Victoria, Simon, Aunt Marigold. And Tim. Just behind the others, but there. I could see from their faces that there had still been no call from France, and before I could explain Isabelle, Simon blurted, 'She's very small.' Isabelle took it in good part. She made a funny little bow, like the organ grinder's monkey that she was, and everybody laughed.

Marigold went to help my father with the luggage. Tim,

who had been shifting from foot to foot, stepped forward. 'I got your letter,' he said loudly. 'Welcome home, sweetheart.' And he kissed me on the lips.

'I've missed you,' I said, also loudly. Then Tim moved to relieve Aunt Marigold of my rucksack, and I swivelled my eyes round to see whether Isabelle had noticed. She had; she was looking impressed. In the same glance I took in Victoria. I had never before seen her look taken aback. She dropped her eyes to avoid mine, and leaned against the door-frame with folded arms.

15

Tim was with us in Dorset for only a week. It was an acute relief to me when he left. He had played his part so earnestly, grabbing my hand or hurling an arm round my shoulders when Isabelle was in sight, reverting to his normal indifferent fraternal mode when she was not. The whole thing worked as far as Isabelle was concerned. She was too young and too foreign to notice how very uncool Tim was, and as he was tall and had a deep voice and hair that was longer than most parents would like, he passed with her as a proper grown-up boyfriend. 'Sexy!'

But as for me, I hadn't been back on English soil for half an hour before I realized that what Isabelle thought didn't matter two hoots. Agnès, I was sure, was never going to be allowed to visit us, even if she wanted to. I was never, ever going back to the Bertrands – at that time I was never, ever going back to France at all, except possibly in disguise – and I knew no one was going to try to make me. Transplanted to foreign soil, Isabelle seemed a weak, withered little thing. The sea and the cliffs alarmed her and she stuck to the house when she could, making Simon play Hangman with her or fiddling with our ancient wireless, searching for Radio Luxembourg. I almost felt sorry for her. The only day she really enjoyed herself was when we went to Swanage and she stole some sticks of rock and a keyring.

So there was good old Tim, faithfully acting out the part I'd assigned to him, unaware that there was no longer any need. How could I tell him? I practised sentences – 'Oh, and by the way, Tim . . .', 'Tim, you know that letter? Well . . .' – but I knew none of them would make it out of my mouth without first throwing me into a disabling spasm of agonized embarrassment, so instead I just hung on till the end of the week. And besides, I half longed for, half dreaded, the possible moment when Tim's acting would turn into something real.

Once, it felt as if it was going to. We were sitting in the sun on the wooden bench in front of the cottage, and Tim, for Isabelle's benefit, twiddled a strand of my hair, winding it round his finger. No one else was there. Victoria was out riding. A rich landowning neighbour kept hunters, and he was pleased to have Victoria to exercise them from time to time. He liked a girl who knew what she was doing. His horses were out of my league; I had never been anything but a timid rider. It was rare for Tim and me to be alone together without Victoria. Isabelle sidled back to the house – she liked to help Aunt Marigold with the housework – and Tim's fingers stayed in my hair, and I thought, it's now or never, and my heart bumped against my ribs as if it were a dinghy cut loose from its moorings. My hair was warm and sweet in the sunshine; still he didn't take his hand away. Ever so slightly, I turned my face towards his. He looked into my eyes. Behind his glasses, his own eyes looked intent and kind. I could see little flecks of brown in his irises, which were a greenish-grey colour, changeable like water. 'I've never looked at your eyes before,' he said, scanning my face. 'They're very round, aren't they? They're not at all like Victoria's. No one would guess you were related.'

'I'd better go and check on Isabelle,' I said. Tim disentangled his fingers, and my heart slunk back to its proper place. I couldn't have admitted it at the time, but that was when I began to realize that it could be possible to hate Victoria.

Even after Tim left, things didn't feel right at the cottage. I had hungered for this place through those hot, trapped nights in France; I had walked my imagination round every inch of it, had summoned to my aid the spirits of wood and cliff and shore. But somehow I had not returned to the cradling haven of my dreams. Everyone was pleased to see me; it was I who didn't seem to fit. In my absence they had developed little rhythms and rituals which were mysterious to me. After supper, for instance, my father would scan the newspaper (*The Times*, in those pre-Murdoch days) until he found the article he wanted, then he would hand it to Victoria without a word, and she would read it aloud to him, sitting on the floor, her head leaning against his knee, while Marigold, half listening, cleared the table. 'Why are you doing that?' I asked the first time. 'Oh,' said Victoria, her voice distant and mystified, 'we always do.' Always? I had only been gone three weeks.

I understood what they were doing. For all of us, it was our first time at the cottage without my mother, but the others had had three weeks ahead of me to stretch flimsy coverings over the great dark gaps her absence made. The garden was the worst place for missing her. Nobody had the heart to pick the fruit, which bloomed and rotted and fell away into white fur or grey dust. I avoided the garden, preferring to take my solitary walks along the cliff top or the shore. There, the cries of wind and seabirds spoke a more general melancholy, more acceptable than the swift, gut-twisting pain that I felt at the sight of the neglected blackcurrants, the overburdened plums.

In the absence of other comforts, I carried on eating. Not quite in the heroic style of my French exploits, but seconds and thirds and picking between meals, oh yes. My father was the only person who failed to notice my gain in weight. Victoria commented freely. 'God, Ruthie,' she said, 'you've got a cleavage. I wish I had one.' But of course she wished no such thing. Aunt Marigold ladled out extra food whenever I asked for it, and refused to be worried, but she certainly noticed. 'It's just puppy fat,' she declared resolutely. 'She'll lose it soon enough. I was the same at her age. Absolute nonsense for a girl of sixteen to diet.'

'She might be pregnant,' suggested Simon, entirely without malice.

Victoria and I laughed with our hands over our mouths, and Isabelle copied us, though I don't think she understood. 'Don't be ridiculous, Simon,' said Aunt Marigold tartly. But I saw her cast a look at me that was both appraising and anxious.

I nearly said, 'Of course I'm not, Aunt Marigold,' to set her mind at rest, but then some instinct that I didn't know I had held me back. The instinct said, 'Go on. Let her worry about you.' And I finished off the crumble and scraped out the custard jug with a spoon.

So fat I had become, and fat is how I started my sixth-form career at Westaby College.

16

'I will if you will,' said Victoria.

We were standing by the pigeon-holes, scanning the notice-board. There were notices about sports fixtures, with lists of team members. Comments, not flattering, had been freely inscribed next to the more controversial choices. There were notices, yellowed with age, that were always there, about lost property and fire regulations. There was a handwritten notice that said SEX in big red letters, and then underneath, in black, it said, 'That made you look! The Christian Fellowship isn't just a bunch of squares. Come and find out, Weds at 5.30, Room 14.'

And then there was the notice that interested us, announcing auditions for a production of *A Streetcar Named Desire*, to be directed by one of the boys in the Upper Sixth. 'A gown-free production,' it said. 'Gowns' was the school slang for teachers. This play would be organized and performed entirely by pupils.

I was tempted. I had done no acting at all, but I'd always wanted to. I knew Victoria had done a fair bit at her boarding school, though I'd never seen her perform. She'd always banned the family from her school functions. I considered. I would never have the courage to audition on my own, but with Victoria by my side . . . 'OK, then,' I said, 'let's give it a try.'

We had both seen the film version, with Marlon Brando and Vivien Leigh, at FilmSoc a couple of weeks before. 'I can't remember,' I said, 'are there any really small female parts?' I was thinking of myself. I knew Victoria would settle for nothing less than Blanche du Bois.

'There's the sister,' said Victoria.

'That's huge.'

'Don't be pathetic. You'd be fine.'

'How do you know? I've never even been a shepherd in a nativity play before.'

'You *must* have been in *something*.'

'Well, I was supposed to be the Angel Gabriel once, but I got 'flu. That was when you were in . . . Africa.'

'Ruthie, I just know you'll be great.'

Warmed by her words and by the certainty that Victoria had only to open her mouth to be given the lead role, I followed her into tea. We had been pupils at the school for about a month, and we still did most things together. There were very few girls; several years of familiarity with the buildings, the grounds, some of the masters, even some of the pupils, had failed to prepare me for the shock of joining the sixth form. Frankly, the boys *en masse* frightened me, and going into tea was the most frightening thing of all. The College had been built in the latter half of the nineteenth century in a variety of architectural styles, all of them grandiose. The dining hall was modelled on somebody's idea of Scottish baronial living. Noise and steam and the fug of bodies all seemed to rise to the top of the vast, vaulted ceiling and swirl there. We came in from the bright October afternoon to be met with a blast of dark, roaring, sweaty warmth, as if we were stepping into a dragon's mouth.

Tea gave the sixth-form boys some of their best opportunities for showing off to the girls. They could run along the benches to get to their places at the massive carved oak tables – indeed, they could vault right over the tables. They could yell at the pale-faced thirteen-year-old fags to bring them toast – 'Oi! You! Two thick white! And get a bloody move on!' They could cajole the serving women into giving them extra doughnuts. And they could – and this was the worst bit – throw things at each other. Depending on which 'gown' was on duty, the meal degenerated into a confusion of pelted crusts and buns to a greater or lesser degree. My fear was of being caught in the crossfire. How could one retain one's dignity if struck full in the face by a piece of rock cake? It hadn't happened yet, but I knew it would, one day. Such a thing would never happen to Victoria, but it could happen to me.

As well as eating and yelling and chucking things, most of the older boys kept one eye on the door. Tea was informal; one could wander in at any time between four and half past, and the girls tended to come in late, so that they could choose the company they kept. The girls didn't go into tea to eat – teenage girls can't eat in front of boys unless they're very thin. They came in to see and be seen. The social shape of the evening to come was outlined at tea.

Victoria slipped a hand under my elbow as we entered the hall. Displays of physical affection between girls were common. When we kissed or squeezed or groomed each other we were like stallholders setting out our wares in front of the boys. The two of us were typical examples of the way the girls formed pairs – one pretty and sought-after, the other plainer, plumper, less assured. There were not enough of us for the beautiful ones to make friends with each other. Each beauty found a foil as a way of emphasizing her especial charms. The difference between Victoria and me and the other pairs, of course, was that we were sister-cousins. The uniqueness of this arrangement had so far prevented us from making close friends of either sex, though we had many interesting new acquaintances. Our blood tie gave us a faintly freakish aura which counterbalanced Victoria's obvious attractions, my gauche approachability. 'You're weird, you two, did you know that?' said one baffled swain early in our school career. Victoria had a trick of sliding her eyes sideways that gave people the feeling that she knew something they did not. 'And who wants to be normal?' she countered in a manner that stymied any response.

Now she scanned the tables with furtive ease. 'There, over there,' she whispered, 'by the urns. Rick Emerson.'

'Who's that with him?'

'With the hair? That's Sholto de Grey.'

'He can't be called that!'

'He can. Come on. Let's go.'

This was a career move on Victoria's part. Rick Emerson, reputedly one of the cleverest boys in the Upper Sixth, was the would-be director of *A Streetcar Named Desire*. Sholto de Grey, Victoria told me later, was one of the few genuine aristocrats on the school roll. He was far too languid to get involved in anything as energetic as a play, but he was Rick's best friend, and the sort of person Victoria would want to be noticed by. Not me. One glance, and I was terrified of him. But I followed Victoria without demur. The boys shuffled along the benches to indicate welcome.

'What's this I hear about a play, Rick?' asked Victoria, sipping tea. She had taken to wearing black lace mittens which accentuated the daintiness of her fingers. Unlike me, Victoria did not bite her nails.

'Are you interested?' asked Rick. 'Why don't you come to the audition? And you too, er – Ruth.'

'Maybe,' said Victoria, smiling her Mona Lisa smile. 'When are you auditioning?' Of course, she knew when, but it wasn't cool to read noticeboards.

I drank my tea, and wished that I had some toast, and stared at Sholto de Grey. I couldn't help staring, he looked so extraordinary. He was such an arrangement of limbs and white skin and fine, tight bones. It was hard to remember he was a schoolboy at all.

His long forefinger was stained with nicotine nearly all the way up. His hair, which poured out of his head in spirals, was almost the same colour – the colour of a beech hedge in autumn. On a girl it would have been beautiful hair, but coiling out as it did from the scalp of Sholto de Grey it reminded me of something I'd read somewhere, about how the hair of corpses goes on growing after they've been buried. Their nails, too. Sholto's nails were long and ridged, with ragged cuticles. He saw me staring and dropped me a slow wink. I could see the bulge of his eyeball through his thin eyelid, like a reptile's. 'Are you going to be in the play?' I stammered, because I couldn't think of anything else to say.

He laughed a laugh like a cartoon hyena, 'Har-har-har,' and let his friend answer for him. 'Sholto?' said Rick. 'Sholto doesn't need to act. His whole life's one big act – the Arts Council should give him a grant. I wouldn't have him in *Streetcar* if you paid me.'

'Tosser,' drawled Sholto, rearranging his long thin legs with a scissoring movement. Rick held forth about the play, his big, intelligent face alive with enthusiasm. He wanted so-and-so for this part, and so-and-so to design the set. 'And Tim Bryant to do the music. You know Tim?'

'We do,' said Victoria, noncommittal.

'He's a bit of a nim, but he knows about music. One good thing about nims is they're reliable. Not like the effete remnants of our clapped-out aristocracy.' He took hold of one of Sholto's ringlets, held it high above his head, then let it drop. 'Visual aid, girls – one effete remnant.'

Sholto's skull-face stretched into a grin. His teeth were chaotic, like his hair. 'Watch it, my old pal,' he hissed, 'or I'll make a bonfire of your nasal hair.' And he flicked a cigarette lighter under Rick's nose. The flame rose and fell so quickly that nobody noticed, except us. Rick laughed, unperturbed.

'So you'll audition, then?' he reiterated, trying to look as if he was including both of us but really looking at Victoria. I liked Rick, who seemed confident without arrogance, but I wished he hadn't called Tim a nim. 'Nim' was the school word for someone who was over-keen, a teacher's pet, sexually unappealing. It was the equivalent of 'virgin', as used by Victoria and me. I wished Rick hadn't said it, but I couldn't deny the justice of it, even to myself.

As we walked out of the hall we fell into two couples, Rick and Victoria in front, Sholto and me behind. 'You know,' said Sholto, his shoulders hunched vulture-like under his great black overcoat, 'if I was going to be interested in anyone, I could be interested in your cousin. Just a thought.' And he flicked his lighter again, and lit a banger that he had in his pocket, and cast it back into the middle of the hall with a twist of the hand so deft and carefree that he might have been skimming stones on a beach.

The banger went off like a bomb in the crowded hall. We didn't stay to witness the results; we moved quickly, and nobody saw who did it. 'Come back to my study,' said Rick. 'We'll talk about the play.' I followed. With the bang ringing in my ears, I was almost unsure that Sholto really had said that thing about Victoria.

We got the parts. I don't think that anyone else auditioned, actually. Victoria was a natural. I was not, but I liked the play and liked the part, and, because I knew nobody would be looking at me, I relaxed sufficiently not to make a complete fool of myself.

The production lurched from one crisis to another. Rick was adamant that no member of staff should be involved, which meant that we ran into endless problems about budgets and booking rooms for our rehearsals. Rick's air of maturity and control proved to be deceptive. He thrived on disorder. He engineered explosive arguments between various cast members, which resulted sometimes in more energetic acting, but more often in one of the performers walking out, to be either cajoled back or replaced. I was too scared to argue with anyone, but I was reduced to tears on a couple of occasions. Victoria was the only one who refused to be drawn. She remained enigmatic and coolly friendly, reserving all passion for the acting itself. All the male members of the cast were in love with her.

Sholto de Grey, true to his word, had no part in the play, but he took to hanging around rehearsals. 'Director's assistant,' he would declare, with his drawl and his slow wink. Our favourite place to rehearse in was a prefabricated building in the least scenic part of the grounds. It was not much more than a Nissen hut, with a couple of rooms for piano practice and one larger space which was grandly titled the 'drama studio'. It was freezing, ugly and ill-lit, but one could smoke there with very little fear of being caught. Sholto de Grey chain-smoked. He arranged his long body on top of a pile of gym mats and watched us, his head, that looked so fragile, like a porcelain skull, propped on one hand. In the other hand he held the cigarette that seemed to be an extension of his bony fingers. An earnest boy who had a minor role as one of the card-players dared to question the wisdom of allowing Sholto to be there. 'If they think we've been smoking in here, they could ban the whole production,' he pleaded. Sholto's eyes, which looked like amber marbles, rolled in their hollow sockets. 'Darling,' he said, like a theatrical dame, 'if they accuse you of smoking, just tell them it was me. I bear a charmed life.' Then he shifted his long bones inside the carapace of his overcoat and settled down to watch Victoria once again.

Victoria knew full well that she was being watched. She

loved it. To all the others she gave the impression of being utterly absorbed in her part, but I could see from some casually elegant gestures that were new to her repertoire that she felt herself to be the observed of all observers. The way she flexed the tendons in her slender neck, the way she twisted her hair back from her face . . . she was acting the part of an actress. At the end of each session, Rick would gather us all into a circle and dole out praise and criticism, and Victoria would smoke a single cigarette, fastidiously, sparingly. Rick turned the lights out, so that any passing gown would assume we'd locked up and gone. We leaned against each other in the gloom, feeling the warmth of flesh through clothing – it could be any arm pressing against yours, it didn't seem to matter whose. I only half listened to Rick, who was fond of the sound of his own voice. Victoria only smoked if it was Sholto who was offering. I remember her face, lit by the quick flare of his lighter, simplified and stylized into a beautiful mask, all cheekbones and slanting eyes.

Tim came to some of our rehearsals. Rick found it easy to persuade him to mastermind the music once he knew who was in the cast. We had seen less of Tim at home lately; now fully recovered from glandular fever, he had thrown himself back into A-level work with vigour, and Simon, who had also started at Westaby in the lowest form, had in theory less time for chess. I had been abrupt and awkward with Tim ever since the summer and the strange interlude of our non-relationship. I kept meaning to broach the subject with a few matey and flippant remarks, but the time had somehow never seemed right. So my contact with Tim had dwindled to the exchange of a falsely hearty 'wotcher' when we happened to encounter one another about the place, and for the first few weeks of rehearsals it seemed as if we were unlikely to get beyond that point.

I could see Tim watching the watchers. He didn't join in much with our discussions of the play – he was usually fiddling with some part of the sound system – but when he caught sight of Sholto or one of the others paying court to Victoria, his mild eyes would flash with pure dislike. My heart ached for him. He would never get Victoria in a million years. I just wished he could spare himself the humiliation of wanting her.

He could have had me, even though there were still things about him that made my scalp prickle with embarrassment. Almost anyone could have had me, actually, for the price of a few kind words. But it would not have occurred to anybody to make a play for me at that time, hedged in as I was by the double defence of my fat and Victoria's constant companionship. I wasn't quite as fat as I had been when I got back from France, but I might as well have been as far as the casual observer was concerned, because I took care that no one should see any of my body contours at all. We girls had no school uniform, just a few scarce-heeded restrictions on colour and skirt length. I shrouded myself from neck to ankle. I wore a woollen skirt, navy blue, over thick black tights – two pairs, sometimes. The skirt reached to the tops of my ankle boots, which were crêpe-soled and clumpy and laced up the front. I wore two T-shirts, both baggy and grey, then a vast black poloneck jersey that drooped well below my hips, and a grey cardigan with holes in the elbows that I had purloined from my father. Over all this went a giant donkey jacket that I'd found in an Oxfam shop. The jacket had a hole in the lining that was like a secret pocket, and into this I stowed biscuits. I wound two grey scarves round my neck, and stomped about like a Russian potato-picker, or like Queen Victoria in extreme old age.

Being a girl, albeit an almost invisible one, I couldn't be seen to do much more than toy with school lunch; the biscuits were my private sustenance. I ate them in the lavatory at breaktime. Even this was difficult to achieve, because the other girls used to retreat to the lavatory in gaggles and perch on the washbasins and smoke and laugh and cry; a locked cubicle was respected, but I had to keep the sounds of my chomping quiet. I developed a technique of sucking mouthfuls of biscuit. This made ingestion slow, but silent. I longed for school lunch – at home, cooking had all but stopped. My father said that he didn't want us bothering with cooking when we had so much school work to do, and for himself he was far too busy to mind. So we lived off toast, mainly, sometimes with something on it like cheese or beans, sometimes without. I heard Aunt Marigold remonstrate on the telephone. 'They get a proper cooked lunch, remember,' said my father. 'Surely no one needs more than one cooked meal a day?' Maybe Simon, lost to view in the unimaginable nether regions of Junior Lunch, forged his way unabashed through roast beef and mashed swede and apricot crumble with extra custard, but Victoria and I certainly didn't. I ate biscuits; Victoria ate (I think) nothing.

Even Victoria didn't know how fat I was. Even I didn't really know. We still shared a bedroom – separate rooms had been offered, and rejected – but I had taken to dressing and undressing in the bathroom, claiming it was warmer in there, which it was. It was also the only room in the house with a lock on the door. I hardly glanced at myself as I peeled off my woolly layers and pulled on my mother's old nighties, which were high-necked, warm, and floral. In the past, Victoria and I had often shared a bath, for companionship as much as for economy. Now, I always seemed to find a reason not to. 'I don't like baths,' I would say. 'They take up so much time. I'll just have a wash.' And I would shiveringly insert a sponge through the gaps in my floral tent.

And so I got out of the habit of looking at myself, or of having anyone look at me. And though in theory I would have liked Tim to be my boyfriend – or anyone else, really – the idea became more purely theoretical every day, because I was becoming a non-girl, a spreading, asexual mass. Sitting cross-legged in that draughty rehearsal room, feeling the warm bodies of my neighbours leaning against my sides and the chill of the dusty floor seeping through my many layers, I suddenly realized that Rick was talking about costumes, and that I, like everyone else, would have to wear one.

'Ruthie, you'll need one of those summer-frock things,' Rick was saying. 'You know, with buttons down the front, and short sleeves.'

'In the play I'm supposed to be pregnant,' I said, stupidly.

'That won't be too difficult to imagine,' quipped one of the card-players. He meant to be funny rather than spiteful. I don't think the remark got much of a reaction from the others, but I'm not sure, because the blood was humming in my head.

Rick, to his credit and my relief, ignored him and ploughed on. 'What shoes would Stella wear? Sandals of some sort, I guess. Have you got anything at home that might do?'

Victoria said, 'Oh yes. We've got everything we need for Ruth's costume at home. We've even got those hair slides, you know the ones I mean? Like combs.' I could tell that she had heard the remark about my looking pregnant and been stung by it on my behalf, but on Sholto de Grey's face I thought I caught the fading glimmer of a supercilious smile. That's it, I thought. Either I get thin, or I don't act. In my head I reckoned the number of days left until the first performance. Twenty-three. Just over three weeks.

The weight just fell away. This was hardly surprising, as for three weeks I almost stopped eating. Breakfast was a cup of tea, black, no sugar. I struggled through till lunchtime gulping water to fill my growling stomach. Before lunch I ate one biscuit – a cream cracker instead of a digestive – then pushed the cooked food round my plate in the approved disdainful manner. Tea was just that – tea, lots of it, black again, and another surreptitious cream cracker to get me through the evening's rehearsal. My stomach would pound and leap and gurgle, so I took to walking about hunched over it, arms folded as low down as they would go. I probably didn't look particularly odd. Teenage girls often wrap their arms round themselves, nursing something that aches, a womb or a heart.

Supper was my meal – a piece of toast and a satsuma. Nothing on the toast, of course, and each segment of satsuma had to be painstakingly stripped of its pith, because the soft whiteness of the stuff made me think it might be fattening. I cut the crusts off the toast, and each day I shaved a little more off the edges. My father, on the rare occasions when we ate together, did at last notice. 'You girls,' he would say, never distinguishing between us, 'you eat like sparrows.'

'We had a big lunch, Dad,' I would say, not growing even faintly warm from the lie. That was a peculiar side-effect of my crash diet. It made me able to lie as skilfully and naturally as . . . well, as Victoria, I suppose.

We'd never possessed any bathroom scales, but I didn't need them. Three times I had to reposition the button on the skirt I always wore to school, and my bra wrinkled uselessly over my deflated breasts. I can hardly believe, now, that I kept it up for three weeks – I, who can never skip breakfast, I, who spend all my idle moments daydreaming of culinary delights to come. But my sixteen-year-old self was focused on one goal for those three weeks. I was going to play the pregnant Stella Kowalski, and I was going to need a cushion stuffed up my dress.

Victoria soon had my costume sorted out – a cotton print dress of my mother's, pale blue sprigged with pink. It was a very old dress, one I could not remember her wearing. I used to sniff some of her clothes, sometimes, as a way of remembering her, but this one was too old to smell of anything but mothballs. Shoes were a problem, until we found some improbable white stilettos with slingbacks and long, pointed toes. I couldn't really imagine earthy Stella tripping round New Orleans in them, but they had what we considered to be a suitably old-fashioned look. I was puzzled by them; they were not the sort of shoe my mother would ever have owned, and besides, they fitted me, while her feet had been bigger than mine. I pondered aloud.

'They were my mother's,' said Victoria, almost with impatience. It made me jump. Why did the idea that Victoria had once had a mother of her own seem so incongruous? So few traces of Aunt Angela remained, in this house at any rate. There was a framed wedding photograph in the living-room, Angela's white-gloved hand hooked round Uncle Jeremy's elbow, her perfect dark lipstick making her mouth look detachable, like a sticker, her bouquet of roses black scrolls, as if they had been carved out of wood. But the black-and-whiteness of the photograph and the elegant formality of their wedding clothes conveyed little of their characters. Wedding photographs rarely conjure up a sense of the reality of the people getting married. Rather, they date-stamp them; the wedding is the moment when they become history.

There wasn't much else, apart from the photograph. I believe that such possessions as had been deemed worthy of salvage were being kept in storage by Ronald and Pamela Brooke, who were Aunt Angela's parents, until Victoria was twenty-one. At home, we hardly ever mentioned Aunt Angela. We rarely mentioned my mother either, but when we did, it was almost as if her return was expected. I wondered why.

I picked up the white stilettos, imagining Aunt Ange's elegant legs rising up out of them, the fragile ankle bones, the glossy shins. 'I don't think I should wear them,' I said, faltering.

'Why ever not?' said Victoria, tossing her hair. 'I don't care about them. They're only shoes. Now, what I need is a feather boa.' Victoria, as Blanche du Bois, needed several changes of costume. Plundering the school green-room as well as jumble sales and our cupboards at home was the best possible fun. Our star find was a silvery evening-gown made of some sort of clingy crêpe de chine; it was backless and virtually frontless, ruling out underwear. Victoria twirled in it on our bedroom floor; it ran from her small pointed breasts like water. 'Vicky!' I cried, aghast with admiration. 'You can't!'

Victoria drew on an imaginary cigarette. 'Why not? It'll get them going.'

'You've already got them going, my dear.'

Victoria laughed a short, secret laugh and ran her hands over the cold, supple stuff. 'The future Lady Sholto de Grey?' Then, seeing my look of horror, 'Only kidding, Ruthie, dear. I couldn't marry anyone who never cleans his fingernails.'

17

Rick Emerson told us that he wanted us all to forget the screen version of *Streetcar*, but in casting Stanley Kowalski he had, perhaps unwittingly, selected Westaby College's only answer to Marlon Brando. Charlie Bassett had big round shoulders like Action Man and thighs that looked as though they would at any moment burst through the shiny navy-blue trousers of his school suit. His dark hair fell in a thick flop across his forehead, he was a prop forward in the first XV, and it was rumoured that he shaved twice a day. His bluntly handsome countenance was unlit by any flicker of humour or intellectual fire; to me his beauty was as dead and dreary as that of a civic statue. Just looking at him bored me.

His acting bored me, too. He had a deep voice and a passable American accent, gleaned, no doubt, from much boyhood watching of Westerns. (We couldn't afford to be too particular about the regionality of our accents. Anything generally trans-atlantic had to do.) Charlie's movements were cumbersome, but that wasn't inappropriate. He managed to dominate a space, just because there was so much of him. Rick seemed satisfied with his performance, but I was not: a kind of dim bewilderment was the best equivalent he could manage to the character's acute emotional need.

He was, it goes without saying, in love with Victoria. In

rehearsals he had to touch her quite a lot, and whenever he did so his thick neck would turn a dusky plum colour and his mouth would hang open in a manner that I found particularly unappealing. He had a girlfriend, a small blonde person called Annabel who wore one of his rugby shirts over her skin-tight jeans. She watched our rehearsals sometimes. Charlie would hardly address two words to her and she would sit on the gym mats, uninvited by Sholto de Grey, trying to look interested and not cross. Poor girl, I thought, at least she can relax when he's doing his scenes with me. Charlie had to touch me, too, of course – I was his stage wife – but whenever this happened it was as if he'd been asked to shift an awkward piece of furniture. Through all my layers I could hardly feel his touch, and I was glad.

Victoria felt differently. She teased him and petted him in a way that made me think of a princess and a tame minotaur. She didn't like blonde Annabel, and I suspect she enjoyed her half-concealed discomfiture; she enjoyed, too, Charlie's dumb admiration, which was such an easy and constant warmth to bask in. But what she was really trying to do, when she crooned 'Char-lie' in her half-mocking way, and pushed his hair back out of his eyes, and tweaked his collar to suit her requirements – all this was truly aimed at riling Sholto de Grey. And he was unrileable. I was near Sholto once when, at the end of a rehearsal, Victoria had persuaded Charlie to let her play leap-frog over his broad, stooped back. Sholto watched through half-closed eyes. 'I love it,' he said, not necessarily to me. 'Beauty and the Beast.' His upper lip was so thin that you could see the humps of his long teeth beneath.

The play was to go on in the last week of term, which was the week before Christmas. There were to be three performances. My father was to attend the last one with Aunt Marigold, who was, as usual, joining us for the Christmas holidays. I didn't want Marigold to see the play. I hadn't seen her since early September, which felt like another lifetime. I almost wondered if I would recognize her.

What I should have wondered about was whether she would recognize me. My face had changed more than my body. My naturally round cheeks were now flat planes, and my nose and chin looked prominent and pointed. My eyes seemed to have receded into my skull; my untrimmed hair circled my face, dull and dry like a discarded nest. I was always cold, despite my layers, and my lips were chapped and blue. When I caught sight of my reflection I was pleased with what I saw. The gaunt girl who stared back at me did not look beautiful to me, but she did look older, alien, tragically wise.

My body, though, was not behaving itself. The weight slipped off my limbs and shoulders like melting snow; you could have counted my ribs and the knobbles of my spine. But my stomach was a tight, bloated ball, larger than ever now in comparison with the rest of me. When I made a quick sideways movement it swung with me like a sack.

I wanted to exercise, but that was hard. There were so few girls at the College that no team sports could be organized. Some girls swam or played squash, but you could opt for social services instead. Victoria and I both had. Victoria dispensed tea and chat at the Day Centre of the local psychiatric hospital. I ran errands for a cross old woman with a dachshund who lived in Westaby village. The village was a short bus-ride away. This was my best chance of exercising unobserved – instead of taking the bus, I would walk. Or run.

The day of the dress rehearsal was a Monday, which was one of my days for visiting Mrs Bishop. The weather was bitter, the air full of a mizzling spray that was not snow or rain or even sleet; the only appropriate term I could think of was 'precipitation', that horrible word which reminded me of my Physical Geography O level. Even at two o'clock, the day showed signs of resigning itself to becoming evening. I walked to the top of Westaby Hill, my toes burning in my thin gym-shoes, then, once I was pretty sure that I was out of sight of anyone who might know me, I ran. Everything hurt. My feet hurt, from the cold and the pounding on the tarmac, my joints ground in their sockets like pestles in mortars, my chest heaved as though something very large was burrowing its way out of me, an ache sang through my teeth as they tried to jiggle themselves free of my gums. When I stopped I felt like a badly assembled jangling mechanical toy.

I walked the last stretch of the way, fighting to get my breath back. Mrs Bishop took little interest in me and I preferred it that way – to turn up gasping on her doorstep would be asking for unwelcome attention. By the time I reached her bungalow I believed myself to be perfectly composed and ready to receive her shopping list. But Mrs Bishop was not impressed. 'What's the matter with you?' she asked accusingly, lifting off the door chain. 'You look as if you've seen a ghost.'

I essayed a smile, though my ears were corkscrews of pain. 'Just a bit cold, Mrs Bishop. Any shopping need doing today?'

'You come right in, my girl, and sit yourself down. There'll be no shopping for you today, the state you're in.' I tried to protest, but without being rude I could not shake off Mrs Bishop's propelling hand, and quite suddenly I was in her living-room. The coal-effect electric fire was a shout of orange in that pastel room. The hot, dry air fell on me like a counterpane. I looked at my gym-shoes, spattered like a pair of Dalmatians, and I thought, I mustn't mess up her carpet. And then everything went silver and black, and I fainted.

'There, dear. Lie like that. Head to one side. I used to be a nurse, you know.' I didn't know. An active life for Mrs Bishop was not something I had ever imagined. 'Take a sip of this water, if you can, and I'll make you a nice cup of tea.' I lay on the thick, fawn carpet, my eyes so close to it that its tangle of hairs looked like a prehistoric forest. The clock on the mantelpiece ticked, the coal-effect fire sang. I had never felt so comfortable, not for weeks and weeks and weeks. I lay perfectly still, waiting to take my orders from Mrs B.

She came back in with an aluminium tray on which were tea things and a plate of toast. Her dachshund snorted at her heels. 'Leave, Rupert!' she commanded as she set the tray down, but Rupert and I were old enemies, and he was incensed to see me laid low on his good carpet. I jumped up to escape Rupert's growls, felt my legs buckle under me, and cast myself on to the sofa just in time.

'I'll put him out,' said Mrs Bishop, and did so. That was quite a concession for her. 'Now get this inside you.' The tea was sweet and soupy, its surface puckered with dusty scum.

'Just look at you.' Mrs B's chilly fingers circled my wrist.

'You're all skin and bone. What can your mother be thinking of?' My heart lurched, but it seemed there was no need to reply. 'Eat that toast, now. Chew it slowly, mind. Dry toast's the thing to settle your stomach.'

The toast was heavenly, each mouthful a warm wave of deliciousness. I felt the strength trickle back into my body, and I realized that I was going to be able to get away without weeping. Murmuring thanks, I embarked on the second slice.

'The state she's in! She could eat up the loaf.' Mrs Bishop shook her white head and clicked her dentures. Then a thought seemed to strike her. She leaned forward. 'You're not – are you?' she asked, peering. 'You haven't done anything you oughtn't?'

I didn't catch her drift. 'Everyone's on a diet,' I assured her. 'Perhaps I've just overdone it a bit, that's all.' It was only later, walking back up the hill with my damp gym-shoes wrapped in the *Daily Express* and a pair of too-tight zip-up sheepskin boots on my feet, that I understood what she had been hinting at. 'Pregnant!' I said aloud. 'Another one who thinks I'm pregnant! I wish I was.' And I ran again, as far as the bus stop, which was enough running to help me throw up the toast I'd eaten. I wasn't going to let two slices of toasted Sunblest stop me from being Stella, now.

'Now, will that stay?' Victoria gave my cushion stomach an experimental prod. 'It looks the right shape, but what about that bit when Charlie has to grab you? You don't want to have to give birth on stage.'

I patted the bump. 'Specially not to such a strange-looking

baby as this one. Though at least no one could say, "Darling, he's got your eyes."'

Victoria laughed. 'Jump up and down a bit,' she ordered.

'And drink gin and have a hot bath? All right.' I bounced up and down on the bedroom floor, hoping Victoria wouldn't notice what an effort I found it. Victoria's strapping was expert: there was no premature delivery.

'What about your boobs?' said Victoria.

I stopped bouncing. 'What about them?'

'Don't you think they need stuffing, too? They get bigger when you're pregnant.'

'Do they?'

'Oh yes. Everything does except your brain.' Victoria pulled a face to indicate disgust. 'They go all swollen and stripy, like melons, and then afterwards they collapse and go flat, like fried eggs. For God's sake, what a system! I'll never be pregnant.'

A memory stirred within me. My mother talking about Aunt Ange . . . 'She wouldn't want to spoil her beautiful figure . . .' 'I bet you will,' I said. 'You'll want children.'

'I won't. You can have the children. I'll just be their exotic aunt, who swoops down from time to time and gives them glamorous presents.'

'Like Aunt Marigold, you mean?' We laughed.

'But I don't believe you,' I went on. 'You will have children. Everyone does.'

'Ruthie, I'm not everyone.'

'No, but – ' I couldn't think what to say next, nor could I account for the aversion I felt for the idea of a barren Victoria.

'They tie you down,' she said. 'They make demands on you, and all I want is – ' She stopped.

'Is what? All you want is what?' My heart pounded. I was so close.

'Oh, to be free, I suppose. What a cliché.' Victoria shrugged.

'Well, if you have them – I mean, *when* you have them – and you want to go off somewhere, you can always leave them with me.'

'Thanks, Ruthie. I'll remember that.' Victoria rummaged in a drawer. 'Now, what about your stuffing?'

I was quite keen on the idea of stuffing. The deflating of my breasts over the last three weeks had somewhat alarmed me. I thought of our long-ago bridal games. 'Socks, d'you think?'

'Socks.'

I pushed a couple of pairs down the front of my dress. The effect made us both giggle. 'Maybe just one in each,' suggested Victoria. She unrolled the socks, folded them, reinserted them. That certainly looked a little more natural. She surveyed them with her head on one side, then for a brief, surprising moment she cupped my breasts in her hands and pushed them together. 'Pity,' she said. 'Until recently you had a perfectly good cleavage of your own. Still . . .' She turned away. 'I can understand it,' she said. 'I would have done the same, if I was you.' And that was the only reference she made to my altered shape.

The first night, it was hard not to feel disappointed. The audience looked tiny to me, we'd put out far too many chairs. The two front rows seemed to consist of nothing but first-year boys – first-years who went to a play or concert in the school were let off compulsory prep, so their presence was hardly a vote of confidence. 'It's always like this on the first night,' said Rick with the airy confidence of the seasoned professional. 'Most of them won't come back for the second half, either. The first night's just an extra dress rehearsal, really.' But several members of the Upper Sixth's glitterati who had sworn to come also seemed to have stayed away, and I could tell Rick was more rattled than he looked.

The little boys didn't leave after the interval, though; in fact, some of them came back with friends. Simon was there, on the end of the second row; I'd been trying not to look at the audience, but I saw light from an opened door catch his glasses, and I recognized the familiar shape of those suddenly opaque planes. Between scenes, we twittered backstage about the slight increase in numbers. 'At least some people must think it's good,' I said. Sholto smiled, his head, like the Cheshire Cat's, detached from his body in the half-light. 'Pubescent lust,' he murmured. 'Don't you just love them? Dear, spotty little things.' I thought about Victoria's costumes, and felt deflated.

'And the best is yet to come,' continued Sholto. 'That little grey number – mmm!' He kissed his fingertips, and released the kiss to the dark air. 'That'll give them all sweet dreams.' As he spoke, Charlie Bassett lumbered past, shining with fresh sweat. 'De Grey,' he growled, 'that's enough.'

Sholto contemplated him with his head on one side. 'What's eating you, Caveman? Woolly mammoth got away today?'

Charlie positioned himself in front of Sholto, squaring his

shoulders. 'If I hear you speak about her like that again, Faggot, I'll – '

'Is that Her with a capital H, Caveman? Oh, my poor little Neanderthal! You have got it bad. Let Nanny kiss it better.' And Sholto leaned over and placed a precise, dry kiss on his rival's cheek.

Charlie staggered back as if he'd been struck. If he had gathered his wits he would surely have attacked, but at that moment Rick appeared from the shadows gesticulating with some loss of his accustomed cool. 'Charlie, Charlie, you're on, for fuck's sake.' And I was on, too, very soon afterwards, and it seemed to me that this little confrontation had a galvanizing effect on poor Charlie's laborious acting.

When Victoria came on in the thin silvery dress a kind of shuffling sigh arose from the audience, and one brave soul whistled. At the final curtain the applause was prolonged. I saw Mr Falconbury, a biology gown on duty that week, summoning Rick aside for a word, and when we'd changed Rick called us together. He doled out much praise, of which he was usually sparing, and then he said, 'Oh, and by the way, Falconbury thinks the rape scene goes a bit too far. Just thought I'd let you know.' Victoria said nothing, but she coloured slightly and shook out her hair in a manner I knew to be defiant.

We walked home together through the frosty park. We laughed and laughed, and gave each other playful little shoves. I told Victoria about the spat between her two chief admirers. 'Oh, poor old Charlie!' she exclaimed. 'All those hormones – it's like an illness. Someone ought to apply leeches.'

'Annabel?'

'Annabel? She's gone. She got off with Garth Edmonds on Saturday night – you know, that rower? The one with the scar? She was standing on the river bank this afternoon, wrapped up in his scarf. Apparently.' And we were both lost in a fresh outburst of giggles.

My father was out, running Junior Debating, but Simon was at home. So, to our surprise, was Tim. He'd slipped off at the end of the performance, not waiting to listen to Rick's little homily. He and Simon were setting up the chessboard on the kitchen table. The kitchen was the only warm room in the house, unless anybody took the trouble to light the living-room fire, and most days nobody did.

We burst in like two ponies, stamping our cold feet and shaking out our hair. Tim and Simon said nothing beyond 'Hello,' and in the blankness of their response our mirth withered.

'Well?' demanded Victoria, filling the kettle. 'Some opinions, please, boys.'

'It was good,' said Simon, simply. 'Except the person who was the main person shouted too much. You could see his spit. And the one in the red shirt didn't have a very good accent. He sounded Asian to me.'

'Oh,' said Victoria. 'Tim?'

'I don't know,' said Tim, not looking up. 'I was concentrating on the music.'

'Oh, come on! I know you watched most of the second half. I saw you, standing at the back.'

Tim straightened his row of pawns. 'Well,' he said reluctantly, 'it was quite good. If you like that sort of thing. But I won't get involved with a play like that again.'

'Why not?'

Tim looked up. 'Too much showing off.'

Victoria dropped teabags into mugs. 'God,' she said, quite cheerfully, 'you're such a bloody killjoy. You're as bad as Fudge Falconbury.'

'What did he say?'

'That the rape scene was too – extreme.'

'Well,' said Tim, 'I think he was right.'

'Was that a rape scene?' asked Simon. 'Oh.'

'Jesus!' exclaimed Victoria. 'Come on, Ruthie. These two are about as exciting as a bowl of cold porridge. We should have gone down the pub.'

We huddled on my bed with our eiderdowns round our shoulders, drinking tea. I had eaten less than ever that day – only half a satsuma. But inside I felt so tight with excitement that I could not have forced down another thing.

'Ruthie,' said Victoria, half serious, 'which one would you go out with, if you were me?'

'None of them,' I said, 'unless Tim.'

'Tim? Be realistic!'

I wondered, afterwards, why I'd said that. I suppose it was because I knew she never would.

Word – of the brilliance of the production, or of the transparency of Victoria's silver dress – got round, and on the second night the audience more than doubled. At certain points there were catcalls and foot drumming, and I wished more than ever that my father and Aunt Marigold were not coming to see it on the last night. There was a chance – it was December, Aunt Marigold was arriving by train, and in the mid seventies trains could not have been said to operate with a Mussolini-like predictability. But the chance was a slim one, and I knew that I had to brace myself for a culture clash of the most toe-curling kind.

I was seized with a great affection for my part, and was mourning the loss of it even before it was over. The pangs of early-onset nostalgia were not the only pangs I was suffering. The cramps in my starved stomach almost prevented me from walking. All day I sipped warm water; it was all I could tolerate. Even toothpaste made me feel sick. But, like a miracle, the pains disappeared the minute I was on stage, and I felt warm, fed, blooming, like the pregnant Stella I was supposing myself to be.

I couldn't see my father or my aunt in the audience, but then, I was trying not to look. I had a dim sense that the hall was packed, that there were seatless figures leaning against the walls with folded arms. I remember the boys who were front of house complaining that they'd run out of programmes. (I remember, too, the muzzy smell of those programmes, cranked out on banda machines. Whatever happened to banda machines?) And then we were up and running and the audience was vocal – too vocal. We had to stop acting once or twice, to wait. Rick was exhilarated and annoyed. 'Jesus, what a bunch of jerks!' he muttered as the roars of approval peaked, but his face was twitching with pride.

Victoria changed her costumes behind a screen in the corner

of the green-room. I helped her, if I wasn't on stage. The changes were quite complicated – things had to happen to her hair and make-up, as well as her clothes. Victoria's hair was slippery, and we had lots of trouble with hats and kirby-grips. The moment came for her to put on the by now notorious silver gown. There was a skylight in the roof of the green-room; as she slipped out of the skirt and blouse she'd been wearing, the moon, almost full, rolled out from behind a bank of cloud and light poured down into our dark corner. Victoria stood, all but naked, as if frozen in the stony light. 'I can't,' she said. I held out the silver dress for her. 'I can't,' she said again, not moving. 'You heard them out there.'

I nodded. Her little naked body, so completely familiar to me, had become something else, something from another world. '*Those are pearls that were his eyes*' – that was what came into my head. I shook out the dress. 'You must,' I said. 'It's too late, now.' Then the moon rolled on, and Victoria unfroze. She slid into the icy material. 'Quick, quick,' she said. 'My hair.'

I shoved in the last grip just before she stepped back on stage. I tried to close my ears to the football-crowd reaction that greeted her. I leaned back against one of the unused flats, suddenly giddy. And there was Tim, bearing towards me. 'Ruthie,' he whispered, 'you look as if you're going to be sick.' He put an arm across my shoulders.

Whatever it was that had kept me together began to loosen. I couldn't afford to let that happen. So I moved away, with a gruff 'I'll be all right. It's just – '

'Vicky, out there, in that dress? I know. I hate it, too. Well, I mean I hate – '

'Tim, is my dad watching? And Aunt Marigold?'

'Third row, on the left. They had reserved seats.' He took off his glasses, wiped them on his T-shirt. The T-shirt said, 'Coggerton Folk Festival 1974'. It had once been black, but was now a greenish grey. Tim put his glasses back on. 'I told my parents not to come,' he said. 'I didn't want them to see her make an exhibition of herself.'

'What's wrong with you, Mary Bloody Whitehouse?' It was Rick, looming up from behind. He was holding something stiffly in front of him. Dark flowers, in Cellophane. A fan of red roses, the kind that have no scent and hang their heads as if they were seasick the minute you get them in water, but . . . well, they weren't for me.

'For the leading lady,' said Rick, without apology, 'at the curtain call.'

There was a cast party afterwards. It was held in a classroom that opened off the hall we'd been using. Desks and chairs were pushed to the edges, but no other steps had been taken to create an atmosphere of festivity, and it started off as an awkward affair. Victoria, back in her jeans, was almost extinguished by her roses; she didn't seem to want to let go of them. There were cans of shandy, which represented the huge concession the school authorities felt they made on such occasions, and some peanuts, and some big bags of crisps. We stood about holding our cans and talking to each other a bit and wondering how to proceed, when Sholto de Grey swept in, his greatcoat wrapped tightly round him.

'Come to me, sweethearts,' he gloated, his amber eyes

glinting. Having made sure that there were no gowns in sight, he spread his coat wide like a pair of black wings. Bottles clinked in the pockets. 'Take them, take them. See what Santa's brought for good little girls and boys.'

Giggling, we delved into his pockets. Vodka, rum, brandy, Scotch – mainly in the form of miniatures, but lots of them. I suppose they were all stolen, though I didn't think about that at the time. And then when we'd drawn out all the miniatures, Sholto fished out a paper bag, its neck tightly screwed. He held it up and shook it; there was a dry rattle. 'I do so enjoy my nature walks,' he said. 'So instructive.' He tapped the contents of the bag out on to a table top. There lay a pile of little dark-brown curly things, like stray punctuation marks. I had no idea what they were, but I found we were being urged to eat them. I took one. 'More than that,' Sholto sighed. 'Come on, Stella-for-Star. Break your diet. It's party time.' He opened my hand and placed several in my palm. I chewed. They tasted of nothing very much, but they were hard to swallow. 'A chaser', said Sholto, 'is what you need.' He unscrewed a miniature whisky and held it out to me. I took a mouthful. It exploded like a firework in my shrunken stomach.

'Magic mushrooms,' Victoria whispered. 'Completely natural. They can't hurt you.' The floor tipped a little. I sat on the edge of a table, swinging my legs and waiting for the magic to start. My little whisky bottle felt snug in my hand, and every now and then I sipped from it, as if it were a fairy flask, and I a traveller in a fantasy land.

My memory of the rest of the party comes back to me in patches. I remember laughing and laughing, as if I would never stop, but without any sense that it was fun. I felt like a tap that had been accidentally left on. The laughter ran out of me, and I wished somebody would come and make it stop. Someone – Tim? – had sorted some music out, and people were dancing, but whenever anyone asked me to dance I said, 'I'm laughing, not dancing,' and they drifted away. Victoria danced with Charlie first. She danced neatly and well, smiling to herself; he rolled round about her as if he was aboard a ship, and with each lurch I could see that he was trying to gain ground, but she kept stepping just out of reach. His actions reminded me of a certain make of doll, a round-bottomed doll that wouldn't fall over however much you pushed it: 'They wibble and they wobble but they won't fall down.' Nearby, Sholto lounged. He looked at me with new approval. 'I think it's time', he said, 'that I saw that Neanderthal off. The Ice Age cometh.' And he began to dance, a weird, writhing, flipping movement that made his long limbs shoot out like tentacles.

People kept coming up and saying things to me – I was female, after all, and that counted for something – and everything came to me in snatches, as if a switch inside my head was being flicked on and off. One moment everyone was dancing, and Victoria was smiling her you-can't-catch-me smile, and the next moment something shot up into the air, and I saw that it was an arm with a fist at the end of it. There was staggering and shouting, and I heard Sholto hiss, 'What are you going to do about it, Caveman? Drag her off by the hair?' He had dark lines running down from each nostril, and someone said, 'Jesus, Charlie, you've broken his nose.' Then suddenly Tim was there and Victoria gasped out his name like a Barbara Cartland heroine and fell into his arms. Though Tim is not the sort of name that Dame Barbara would ever give her heroes.

I just sat there. The only magic the mushrooms had worked was a kind of detachment, so that I could listen to the sound of my own laugh and look at the swinging of my own legs without much sense that they had anything to do with me. It may have been a long time later that Charlie Bassett lumbered up to me and said, 'Ruth, come over here.' All right, I thought, and let him tow me away to a shadowy corner. We slumped down with our backs against the wall. Charlie mumbled on and on about Victoria and blonde Annabel and prickteasers, and then he said, 'But you're not a pricktease, are you, Ruth?' and I let out a noise like a screech-owl and said 'I certainly am not.' Then Charlie lurched sideways and his damp face loomed up in front of mine, and I realized he was going to kiss me. I thought, 'Oh well,' and then I thought, 'I'm being kissed by the best-looking boy in the school,' and that thought made me laugh again so I turned my laugh into a sort of choke. Charlie unplugged his face from mine and said, 'Sorry, sorry.' I said, 'It's all right,' and he launched into it again. It seemed to go on for ages and ages. I started thinking about my homework and particularly my French because Monsieur Henri had made us swear to finish our proses by the end of term and the end of term was tomorrow. Then it dawned on me that Charlie had put his hand up my jumper and I wondered whether I ought to do something about it. Charlie said, 'I thought you had big tits,' with the aggrieved air of a child whose Christmas present didn't come complete with batteries, and I couldn't think what to say to that so I said nothing. Then the overhead strip lights juddered on, and Charlie said, 'Bugger it. Falconbury.' Everyone was shuffling and trying to hide things and adjusting their clothing, and Charlie said, 'This is it. This'll be one enormous bust.' I said, 'Isn't that what you wanted, an enormous bust?' and giggled, but Charlie just edged away as if I was the person on the bus who sits down next to you and talks to you too loudly about Jesus.

I don't remember leaving the room, though I do remember Mr Falconbury writing something in a notebook, and saying, 'The chaplain's daughter. You ought to be ashamed of yourself.' But I suppose he could have been saying that to Victoria. I don't remember how I got home, either. The next thing I remember is lying in my own bed with a faint smell of sick on my pillow and Aunt Marigold laying her dry palm on my forehead and saying, 'Oh Ruthie, just look at you. What on earth did you think you were doing?'

I spent most of the Christmas holidays in bed. The doctor came, and for the first four days I just had soup and cocoa, and spoonfuls of tonic out of a sticky bottle. The tonic was bright green, like cartoon poison, and it tasted of metal. Aunt Marigold sat with me quite a lot and read Nancy Mitford aloud. Then I moved on to toast and porridge and *Mansfield Park*, and on Christmas Day I ate most of the dinner downstairs with the others and started *To The Lighthouse*, which wasn't as involving as I thought it would be, but that didn't matter too much because by now I'd got used to the fact that Victoria and Tim were an established couple who smirked at little private jokes and sat on the sofa holding hands.

I put weight back on, but I didn't get fat again. I regained my real figure, the kind of figure of which people say, 'She looks quite nice but she could lose a pound or two.' My round thighs came back, and my little shelf of a tummy. And that is the shape I've been, give or take, ever since. I wasn't truly anorexic. I'm not the type. Just motherless. I think that was the only thing that was really wrong with me.

18

Victoria and Tim lasted, as a couple, for a year and two months. For the first few weeks people at school went around asking, 'What does she see in him?' I was a silent, suffering witness when Tim was jeered at *in absentia*, his physical shortcomings catalogued, his musical tastes reviled. Victoria's light, by contrast, shone all the brighter. Tim's critics were male. The girls tended to say he was 'sweet', and they warmed towards Victoria more now that she was safely bound up in the sixth-form equivalent of holy matrimony. A couple of them even became, up to a point, her friends.

When Victoria danced at parties, though, that's when a cat's-paw of trouble would stir up the smooth waters. Nearly every pupil at Westaby College boarded, so in term time the school's Entertainments Committee provided pseudo-parties for us – 'socials', they were called. They were held once a month in the gym, and they had to finish at half past ten. A loose cordon of matrons and duty masters surrounded the building, protecting the shrubbery from infiltration by smokers or drinkers or worse. Despite, or perhaps because of, these restrictions, a surprising amount was achieved at each social in terms of the reorganization of the sixth form's social and sexual hierarchy. In the (almost) complete absence of drink, drugs and cigarettes, the only entertainments were dancing and what the agony aunts of those days termed 'heavy petting'. Making conversation was uncool, and anyway the music was too loud. We knew how to converse, after a fashion, but it was embarrassing to do it in public. It was much worse for a girl to express an opinion in a crowd than for her to let a boy put his hand up her shirt in full public view. Conversation was something that happened in twos and threes, behind closed doors.

For most of us, these socials were about choosing and being chosen; for the already established couples, they were about showing off. This meant dancing only to certain 'special' records, giving blank stares to the girls who were bussed in from a neighbouring school to redress the imbalance in our own, and leaving, together, early. Tim hated the socials. He was a useless dancer, and after a couple of goes he wouldn't even try. He would break the rule of cool and talk to people – to me, often – or lean against the wall and watch Victoria, or just not bother to turn up at all. But Victoria was always there, Tim or no Tim, because she loved to dance. Her black hair would whip across her face like bootlaces and her eyes would snap and shine, and if I chose to look I would see the old Victoria, my secret twin, the princess of the seashore. There were two or three records that were 'hers', and when these were playing the other dancers would melt away leaving only Victoria, upheld by the music; the whirling centre of a circle of uneasy admiration. Then the music stopped and she would shake herself and laugh a little and slip away, her arm through Tim's if he was there, in search of him if he was not. Victoria always left before the end. Another record would go on, but the party was over once she had left, and it would be midweek before time and routine had stilled the eddies of envy and thwarted lust.

I had three boyfriends during the time Victoria was going out with Tim. Charlie Bassett was not one of them. I passed him in a corridor on the first day of the Lent term, after my bed-bound Christmas holiday, and he flushed that horrible plum colour that made him look as if he was going to burst and made a noise that could have been 'Hi' or could have been just a clearing of the throat. I didn't say anything. It was only a couple of weeks before he started going out with someone called Antonia, who might as well have been blonde Annabel's mouse-haired sister. He left that summer, after his A levels, and I don't think I ever spoke to him again.

I met the first of my three swains at the St Valentine's Day Social. His name was Martin Sloat. I knew him by sight, but I'd never spoken to him because he was doing all science subjects. He didn't look too bad. His hair was a bit sandy but he had nice hands and his skin was better than average. He didn't have much conversation but, as I said before, that wasn't a big problem at a Westaby Social. We spent the evening entwined amidst the gym-floor smell of feet and rubber, and the next day he sent me a late Valentine card, home-made, which said, 'Be My Valentine. P. S. I think you are a way-out snogger.' I thought by that stage that I really ought to have a boyfriend, so I stuck it out for three weeks, and then he said why didn't I wear make-up and why didn't I come to cheer him on in the cross-country relay, and I told him that I didn't feel ready for a committed relationship. Martin Sloat faded back into the closed world of the science block with no hard feelings on either side. With no feelings of any kind, really.

With Martin, our physical intimacy never progressed beyond the rather frantic display of the St Valentine's Day Social, so it came as something of a surprise when Jonah Gallagher asked me to sleep with him when we'd only been going out for a week. This was at the beginning of the Easter holidays. Jonah was in my year, in fact he took two of my three A-level subjects. I'd always been a little nervous of him. Most of the boys were hung about with great wads of ill-kempt hair, dry and brittle at the ends and darkly greasy in the middle, but Jonah's black hair was cropped as close as a moleskin. He had an interesting bump in his nose and he wore an earring, a broad gold gypsy band. He took it out for most lessons and for chapel, but he never forgot to reinsert it at breaktime and for other periods of public display. He kept it in for English, because Mr Bradshaw was cool about things like that.

Jonah and I became an item on an end-of-term trip to Stratford-upon-Avon. We all went by coach to see *The Winter's Tale* with one of those famous actresses who's now a Dame playing Hermione, and I was amazed to find, in Jonah, someone who was as exhilarated by the play as I was. Most people fell asleep on the journey back, but Jonah and I, having discarded our original seating partners, just talked and talked, and as the coach swung off the motorway into the inky woodland lanes that led to the College, he kissed me. There were only a couple of days of term left, but we spent them almost exclusively in each other's company, quoting things and holding hands and kissing. Jonah cradled my pudgy, freckled hand as if it were a fragile treasure – a thrush's egg, or a fine seashell. This is it, I thought. At last. As well as loving literature, Jonah wanted to be an artist. He wanted to draw me. He wanted to sleep with me.

The first weekend of the Easter holiday, I went to stay with him at his parents' cottage in Wales. I told my father that lots of other people from our year would be there, too, which was a wholly unnecessary lie because Dad wasn't remotely interested. But I couldn't bear the tiniest possibility that I would be stopped from going. Dad just said 'Splendid' and which part of Wales was it? Oh yes, the Eddw Valley. He remembered, once, with my mother . . . it was a magnificent part of the world, and did I need a lift to the station? Tim and Victoria were away that weekend, on a CND rally, of all things. I expect my father relished the prospect of having a weekend almost to himself.

The Welsh cottage had thick white walls and small windows with greenish panes, slubbed like raw silk. It crouched between a mountain and a rushing white river. The Gallagher parents were there, but they didn't pay much attention. They were media people who lived and worked in London; the cottage was for holidays only. They had friends with them, a loud-voiced couple who smoked and laughed and drank lots of red wine. Jonah and his fourteen-year-old sister Auriel led their own lives, unmolested.

I'd brought my sleeping-bag, and I assumed that I'd be unrolling it on the floor of Auriel's Indian-draped attic bedroom, but Jonah had other ideas. The first night, he whispered to me on the stairs, 'I've paid Auriel. She's sleeping in my room, and I'm coming in with you.' I cited his parents, my head swimming with longing and dread. 'They won't know. Auriel won't tell. And anyway, they wouldn't give a shit.'

Downstairs, I could hear his parents and their clattering, laughing friends. I thought of *The Eve of St Agnes*, the drunken revellers below, Madeline above so cool and self-enfolded in the honeyed middle of the night. Auriel's room smelled of cigarettes and joss sticks. Jonah held me, and we fell backwards together on to the narrow, creaky bed. His breath was hot and damp on my neck; there was a moment of struggle with a button or a belt, and then his jeans were round his ankles. I knew that this was it, though I tried to push him away. 'I don't want to get pregnant,' I whispered. He pushed his hands up under my shirt, his fingers chilly bars on my flesh. 'Oh for God's sake, Ruthie,' I heard him mutter, 'don't be so bloody bourgeois.'

I had expected it to hurt, but it didn't. I wasn't even sure when it was happening – I certainly wasn't sure when it had finished. Soon – very soon – Jonah stopped moving. His head lay hot and heavy on my fully clothed chest. I looked up at the rafters, and watched a daddy-long-legs make its fastidious progress through the dust-hung shadows.

Jonah raised his head. 'Ruthie, that was great. You were magnificent.' I was surprised. I hadn't been anything, except weakly there. I made a tiny crooning noise, and wafted a hand over the damp suede of his head. I longed for him to go, so that I could investigate the wetness that I could feel seeping out of me, which I was sure was blood.

It wasn't – not much of it, just enough to ruin the batik

skirt I was wearing. The only other garment I'd brought with me was a pair of jeans. The next day, terrified of some kind of haemorrhage, I lined my pants with folded lavatory paper, but could only find the hard kind in the Gallaghers' bathroom because that was all that was stocked in the minuscule village shop. All that day, I crackled when I walked.

On the Sunday evening the Gallaghers dropped me off at a station on their way back to London. 'Nice to meet you, Rachel, see you again,' said Jonah's father, shaking my hand, and no one corrected his mistake. Jonah waited on the platform with me, and when the time came to say goodbye, I cried. I cried because I wanted to make something happen. Jonah hugged me hard, and I willed him to say 'I love you' so that I could say it back to him, but he didn't. When the train pulled out I waved and waved, long after he was out of sight.

They must know, I thought, when I was back at home. You can tell, just by looking. There's an aura. But there didn't seem to be one, in my case. I mooched about for two days waiting for the telephone and plucking up the courage to ask my father if Jonah could stay with us the next week, but the moment never seemed right, so in the end I just announced it, gruffly. 'A friend of mine's coming on Wednesday. OK? Just for a few days.'

'That's fine, darling,' said my father, not lowering the *Church Times*. 'She'd better go in with you and Vicky because Marigold will be here by then.'

'Actually,' I said, 'it's a he.' I felt angry, suddenly, that I could do something as extreme as lose my virginity without anyone taking a blind bit of notice. 'Why do you always have to assume — '

My father put down the paper. He looked amused, puzzled, and rather old. 'I'm sorry I made an assumption, Ruthie. If your friend happens to be male, that's fine by me.'

'Of course it's fine,' I muttered.

'He can go in with Simon,' said my father.

'With *Simon*?' I was not prepared for that. 'Couldn't he go in your study? He could have a sleeping-bag?'

'My study? Well, if he must. Is it anyone I know?'

Was anybody else's father as obtuse as mine?

'Jonah Gallagher. You know. I stayed with him in Wales.' I felt furious with myself for blushing.

My father's eyebrows shot up. 'It was Jonah Gallagher in Wales, was it? I didn't quite take that in. The Eddw Valley, you said. Your mother and I . . . but young Jonah? He can't be Welsh with a name like that. Something of a firebrand, isn't he? No, perhaps *not* in with Simon. I do see.'

But do you, I thought, as I dialled the number of a family-planning clinic from a call-box opposite the school gates. Do you see anything, Dad, when it's a question of me?

At the family-planning clinic they didn't ask any questions at all. I'd taken along my passport, as proof of age, because people often thought I was younger than I was, but it stayed in the bottom of my tote bag. I was weighed, my blood pressure was taken, but Jonah wasn't mentioned. I left the clinic within twenty minutes, bearing a plain white bag containing three months' supply of the Pill, a handful of condoms to tide me over the first two weeks, and a leaflet about venereal disease. I sat on the top deck of the bus, at the back, and read the leaflet in glimpses, without pulling it right out of the bag. Then I read the instructions that went with the condoms. The diagrams were more explicit than anything I had yet seen in the flesh. I tried to imagine presenting the condom to Jonah; in my head I rehearsed various opening remarks. Should I sound jocular? Meaningful? Casual? I knew, really, that I would never have the nerve to say anything. When my stop came I waited until the bus was out of sight over the brow of the hill and then I shook the condoms out into the litter bin.

So we had two more weeks of unprotected sex before the Pill kicked in, but I didn't get pregnant. Which was more than just as well. Sex continued to be something which happened in a hurry; we never even took all our clothes off. I soon learned that there was a trade-off: our farmyard couplings were the price I paid for the luxury of deep conversations with Jonah about Art and Life. In theory, at least, Jonah was an iconoclast. He poured scorn on most of my sacred cows. 'We're living in a museum culture,' he scoffed. 'You've got to be prepared to destroy. Death is the mother of beauty, Ruthie.' I can't say, looking back, that I ever saw him put any of his ideas into practice, but it thrilled me to listen to him. Thrilled me far more than all that butting and shoving in the dark.

Victoria kept her distance. Uniquely, in my experience, Jonah didn't seem particularly taken with her. Perhaps the fact that she was rarely unaccompanied by Tim prevented him from seeing her clearly, I don't know, but whatever the reason for Jonah's indifference, it made him all the more precious to me. For precious he was. I was in love with him, or in love with the idea of being in love with him. In front of his friends he could be offhand with me, even dismissive, but it never occurred to me to challenge such behaviour. I was grateful; he sensed my gratitude, and basked in the flattery of it until it got on his nerves. Have I ever had a serious relationship that wasn't at least partly based on gratitude? I wonder.

Towards the end of the summer term, Jonah began to find me seriously irritating, but I was very slow on the uptake. When we went to the pub with his mates he all but ignored me, when I tried to initiate discussions about summer plans he was evasive. Once I even overheard his friends saying something about 'the limpet', and the conversation stopped at my approach. But somehow, limpet-like, I hung on. I renewed my supply of pills, stuffed a few T-shirts and a couple of Penguin Classics into my rucksack, and set off with Jonah and two of his friends to hitch-hike round Greece.

It was a miserable holiday for me, though I pretended that it wasn't. We took sleeping-bags but no tents; we slept on beaches, the roofs of pensions, garage floors. That was fine – that was great, in fact. I loved rinsing out my few clothes under one sputtering cold tap, passing round a bottle of Ouzo as we lounged by driftwood fires, living on bread and tomatoes and crumbly, salty cheese. I even liked the long waits by the side of the roads, squatting in the white dust, watching the scatter of lizards and playing every word game we could dredge up from memories of far-off family car journeys. I had importance, too, on the road. It was considered that a truck – it usually was a truck – was more likely to stop for a girl, so I would stand very much to the fore, my sun-peeled arm stuck out, the hot wind blowing my flimsy cotton garments flat against my body. Then, as the vehicle slowed, Jonah and Andy and Hutch would step out of the scrubby wayside bushes, and usually the driver would feel obliged to find room for us all, though I always had to sit up at the front, and sometimes I had to let him squeeze my knee with his square, hairy hand. But that seemed a small price to pay. They were generous, those Greeks. Not only did they often drive out of their way to take us to wherever we wanted to go, but they would rarely set us down completely empty handed. Lemons, still attached to twigs and leaves, hard bumpy sausages that only Andy would eat, cigarettes, watermelons . . . something or other was always thrust upon us.

No, it was not the ingredients of the holiday that were the problem. It was Jonah. He made no attempt to get near me. Hutch and Andy were tactful, and would regularly wander off on some sort of pretext so that we could have time by ourselves, but Jonah did not touch me. Mostly he'd say something like, 'Think I'll catch up on some kip. I couldn't sleep last night on that bloody concrete,' and then he'd unroll his sleeping-bag in the nearest shady place and close his eyes, and I would sit by his side picking at my sunburnt toes or meander into a village to buy postcards. And when we lay, all four, on a beach at night, he never kissed me goodnight, never even touched my hand. I lay on my back staring up at the stars, which looked thicker and smudgier than they ever looked in England, like golden freckles, and I thought how fond the Ancient Greeks were of rescuing people by turning them into constellations. And I could truly understand that. I could almost feel my soul rise out of my discarded body and spread itself, glittering, across the arc of the night. Some words from the play came back to me in Victoria's voice – 'Stella – Stella for star.'

Once, a stray dog picked its way across our four humped bodies. The others didn't stir – teenage boys sleep so soundly – but it stopped when it came to me and pushed its damp nose into the cup of my hand. It lay down by my side, wedging itself between my arm and my body, comforting like a hot-water bottle. Simon would have worried about whether there was rabies in its saliva, but I was too lonely to care.

Then one roasting afternoon, Jonah was sitting with me in the front of a pick-up truck that was taking us to Epidaurus, and Andy and Hutch were rolling about in the open back, and the driver, whose English was better than most, asked Jonah some question about his 'girlfriend'. Jonah, whose brows had beetled all day, growled, 'She's not my girlfriend.' The driver just shrugged and turned the conversation to the fortunes of Manchester United, but I felt the shock of rejection like a pulse through my body. I hardly noticed Epidaurus at all, though it had been me who petitioned to go there. I stumbled over the quiet bones of the past with the scent of wild thyme in my nostrils and the sky blindingly blue above me, but all I could think of was how to get a chance to press Jonah on exactly what he had meant by that remark. At last, Hutch and Andy set off in search of some bottles of Sparky. Jonah swung his dark head from side to side, like an animal sniffing for a means of escape. His eyes followed the tiers of the great theatre; he scowled up at the fierce azure. 'Think I'll climb to the top,' he said, not looking at me. 'See you in a minute.'

'Jonah,' I said, 'no.' I put a hand on his forearm.

He looked at my hand as if I'd wiped my nose on his skin. 'Now what?' he said.

'Now what? Now what?' I mimicked him. 'God, that's so unfair.'

He paused, considered, sighed. 'OK, Ruthie,' he said. 'Sit down.'

We sat. He held his head in his hands. 'Look,' he began, 'I don't – it's not – Oh, Jesus, this is so hard.'

I said nothing. I wasn't going to help him.

He scratched in the dust with a stick. 'Ruthie, you're a really nice girl and all that, and it's nothing you've done, but . . . Look, I know this holiday must've been pretty bad for you, but you can't say I haven't dropped enough hints. I mean, why the fuck do you hang on to me when I'm treating you like . . . like this?' And he stubbed the stick expressively into the dust.

'Because I love you,' I said. It wasn't something I had meant to say.

'Jesus!' Jonah almost spat. 'That's the ultimate guilt trip.'

'I'm sorry,' I said. 'I can't help it.'

We sat in silence. My body shook with the stifled sobs that surged, huge, through it. Tears rolled down my nose and formed little cushions in the dust. Of course, I hadn't meant to cry. I knew how ugly I looked, crying. But what I meant to do and what I ended up doing seemed destined to run on parallel tracks, never to meet.

Jonah put an arm round my shaking shoulders and gave me a squeeze. It's going to be all right, I allowed myself to think.

But it wasn't. 'Come on, Ruthie,' he coaxed. 'You're making me feel like a real bastard.'

What would Victoria do? I wondered. An empty speculation, since it was unimaginable that Victoria would ever find herself thus situated, but it gave me the courage to stand up and walk away. 'Don't worry,' I said. 'I know it's over. I'm not that thick. Tell the others whatever you like.' And I climbed, blind, to the top of the theatre and stood there, looking out at I don't know what, feeling nothing but the tug of the scorching wind.

That night, we camped under some pine trees, on soft sandy soil like pink sugar. Hutch and Andy had stocked up on ouzo as well as beer, and when it came to my turn with the bottle I just held on to it and drank and drank. The boys laughed at me at first, and I laughed back at them, and then they got worried and tried to snatch the bottle away from me. But I stumbled off, half-tripping over roots and rocks, until I found a little hollow where I slumped down and finished the lot. By the time they caught up with me, which wasn't long, I was already throwing up. I pressed my forehead against a pine trunk; I can still remember the touch of the warm, resiny bark. Hutch was the first to reach me; he sounded genuinely alarmed. 'It's all right,' I said blearily. 'I like throwing up. It's what I do best.' And then I don't remember any more after that.

Somehow, they got me to a small hotel − a taverna, with just a couple of rooms to let above the restaurant. When I woke Jonah was saying, 'Make her drink it,' and I struggled and screamed because the water they were trying to tip into my mouth tasted like neat ouzo. I think it was three days before

I became fully aware of my surroundings. When I did come to my senses, Hutch was sitting in a corner of the darkened room, trying to read by the thin stripes of light that were all the shutters let in. I remember what he was reading; it was *Crime and Punishment*, and it took me a few moments to sort out the impression that we were sharing some kind of prison cell.

I propped myself up on my elbows. 'How long have I been here?' Hutch jumped. 'Hey, you're better!'

'We can't afford all this,' I said. Hutch knew what I was talking about. In our many pre-holiday discussions, we'd all agreed that staying in hotels would be beyond our means. 'Ruthie,' said Hutch, 'it doesn't matter what it costs. Here,' – he filled a tumbler – 'water's the best thing.' He was a gentle person, open-faced, with big, broad hands. He gave me the water and sat at the foot of my bed, taking care not to jiggle it. 'Look,' he said, 'Jonah's one of my best mates, but he's been a real shit to you. He didn't know when he was lucky.' He swallowed, and blushed. 'I just wanted to tell you that.' I sat up properly and held out my arms despite the sour taste in my mouth and my three-days-unwashed body, and so it was that I made the transition from going out with Jonah Gallagher to going out with Chris Hutchins, because that was Hutch's real name, only in our year there were at least ten other people called Chris, so they all had nicknames. And he was very nice and kind and quite bright too, though not as intellectual as Jonah. I liked his wide, blunt-featured face and I liked the way he held me so that my head rested in the hollow of his shoulder, but I wasted most of the time we had left in Greece, which was only just over a week anyway, because I spent most of it watching Jonah out of the corner of my eye. I never caught Jonah watching me. He affected complete nonchalance, but there was one time, the night before we were due to leave, when he and Hutch had a fight. It wasn't a fight over me. It was supposed to be a play fight, but it went beyond that. Hutch was stronger than Jonah; he let the fight get to the point where he was winning, and then he stopped it. Jonah was rattled, and I exulted.

All the time we were in Greece Hutch never did more than kiss me, but when we were back in England and term had begun and we were still going out, he asked me to go to bed with him, and I couldn't see any reason not to. It was nicer than it had been with Jonah – friendlier, at any rate, though Hutch was a bit sweaty – but again I wasted it all, really, because I still thought I was in love with Jonah. We carried on as a couple until the autumn half-term. There was a big party in London that half our year was going to, Hutch and I included. But at the last minute I said I couldn't go because I had too much work to do, because I was taking my Oxford entrance exam in November, but actually my not going was a polite way of giving poor Hutch his freedom. Sure enough, he came back from London with a new girlfriend, one of the new sixth-form intake called Lucy Smallwood; she was little and sweet and I didn't feel any animosity towards her. Poor Hutch was desperately apologetic but I didn't blame him at all; I just felt thankful to be on my own again. It was only later that I thought about how nice he had been and how I'd allowed the whole relationship to pass me by.

Hutch and I had our final, sorting-out conversation by the banks of the river that curled through the grounds of Westaby College. The river, ringing by day with the shouts of the rowers, moved dark and silent now; smoke from bonfires of damp leaves struggled to rise through the still and clammy air. The gentle melancholy of the evening suited my mood; when Hutch kissed me a chaste goodbye, tears stood in his eyes as well as mine, but they didn't fall. I walked back to the lodge thinking about the way I'd been a year ago, starving and terrified, and I could hardly believe it was the same me. 'Rampling women are strong,' Aunt Marigold had once said; well, I felt strong now, strong and adult and alone.

Victoria was waiting for me, back at home. She knew where I'd gone and why, because we'd fallen back into the habit of telling each other things. She opened the door for me and held out her arms. 'Ruthie, welcome back,' she said.

19

Though none of my romantic experiments had been, to date, an unqualified success, put together they served some useful purposes. They had given me, and others, the impression that I had a life of my own, they had raised my standing at school at least into the 'normal' category, and they had stopped me from brooding too much about Tim and Victoria.

From Christmas time, when their relationship began, until the beginning of October, when Tim left Westaby to read Geography at Manchester, their coupleness had made them the fulcrum of our family life. It wasn't that they expected everything to revolve round them – Tim remained as helpful and unselfish as ever, and Victoria, following suit perhaps, rarely allowed us to dance attendance on her – but within weeks they became the reason why our household continued to function as an economic and social unit. Small as Lodge Cottage was, parts of it had withered or shut down since my mother's death. The living-room, for instance – it never seemed worth the effort of lighting the fire, and no one seemed to have the time or the inclination to watch television, particularly since, as an economy measure, we gave up taking the *Radio Times*. So the living-room became a twilight zone, a chilly, misnamed place into which one might sometimes creep to consult the ranked volumes of the *Encyclopaedia Britannica* for homework purposes. The little dining-room had never been much used, but my mother had always kept it bright, with clean window-panes and flowers on the table, and she'd insisted that we use it at least once a week, for Sunday lunch. But after her death, we had, in the mute complicity of mourners, blurred the pathos of its emptiness by allowing it to silt up with junk – cardboard boxes, old newspapers, broken lamps . . . even, for some reason, the hutch of the long-departed guinea pigs, which Simon was going to clean up and sell, one day. So the true function of both rooms was eroded. The little living and dining that went on happened in the kitchen. My father had his study, of course, and Simon was usually in his bedroom, but no one else set foot in these rooms from one week's end to the next.

Then, when Victoria and Tim paired off, a sort of thaw happened. From the start, they acted like a pair of newlyweds out of some 1950s *Woman's Own* fantasy. When Victoria made Tim a cup of tea she stirred the sugar in for him, and she would pick threads off his trousers and straighten his collar in a manner that made me itch with envy and irritation. They weren't always in the house – Tim's parents' house was warmer and less crowded – but when they were, they spread themselves. They were surprisingly languorous together. Tim started bringing in wood; they nestled on the living-room sofa with mugs of coffee and the Sunday papers. Victoria had some of Tim's photographs of churches enlarged and framed; they hammered in little hooks and twittered about hanging them straight. But at night, Victoria would return to the bedroom that we still shared, often long after I had switched the light off, and slip between the sheets without a word.

What they were doing was playing house, and some of the fun and warmth of their play spread out to the rest of us. One bright weekend in early spring, they got it into their heads to clear the dining-room. Tim made a bonfire of all the old boxes (and the guinea pigs' house, after a little negotiation with Simon), and Victoria announced, 'I'll do a proper Sunday lunch.' She invited Tim's parents over and, waiving my half-hearted offers of help, she roasted a lump of lamb fairly success-fully. 'Rosemary!' she said. 'That's what goes with roast lamb.' Tim cut a veritable branch off the rosemary bush that grew by the back door, but none of us was sure what to do with it. In the end she just stuck it into the lamb like the holly in a Christmas pudding; it had a certain gallant air. We all sat down, and there were sunbeams at the window and primroses on the table, and my father, a little dazed as he so often was these days, poured cider for the Bryants and beamed at Victoria. 'I feel I ought to propose a toast,' he said. 'But to whom? or to what?'

'To us,' suggested Victoria, her smile all-encompassing, but with the tiniest swivel of a glance in Tim's direction. We all raised our glasses, some of which were the remains of a Water-ford crystal wedding-present set, and some of which had been given away with a certain number of gallons of petrol.

Tim's father, Geoffrey Bryant, was a middle-aged version of Tim, just a little more socially assured. 'It's we who should be proposing the toast,' he said. 'Congratulations to you, Julian. Absolutely the right man for the job.' He raised his glass again. We looked at each other to see if any of us knew something the others didn't, and Tim's mother said, 'Geoff, I don't think this is public knowledge yet,' and Tim's father slapped his forehead with the ball of his hand and said in mock-tragic tones, 'Oh, Sheila, have I put my foot in it again?'

'Of course not. Of course not,' said my father. 'It's high time they were told. I don't know why I haven't already done so.' He took off his glasses, rubbed the bridge of his nose, and ran a hand through his hair so that it stood up straight on one side in a shape like a candle flame, before explaining that the deputy head of the school was to take early retirement because of his angina and that he, Dad, was to become the new deputy head. 'Officially from September,' he said, 'but in practice from after Easter, I expect, since poor Ron Shepherd is so very unwell.' We chorused our surprise and our congratulations. Victoria said, 'Papa, we're going to have to do something about your hair.' Simon folded his arms and moaned, 'Oh, *no*.'

Everyone said, 'What's the matter, Simon?' or words to that effect.

Simon raised his head. His fringe was growing out – or rather, it was never cut – and it was impossible to see his eyes. 'What do you mean, what's the matter?' he said, in his deepening new voice with its runaway squeak. 'What about Founder's Day?'

'What about it?'

'Dad'll have to wear – you know – a *dress*.'

We laughed, but I did fleetingly conjure up an image of plump little Mr Shepherd bobbing along behind the headmaster as the procession of Founder's Day dignitaries made its stately way through School Hall to the dais at the end. The deputy head, as far as I could remember, wore something purple and frock-like with furry bits on, in accordance with one of the

College's many semi-bogus traditions, and it had not suited Mr Shepherd, who looked as if he had strayed out of the Dick Emery Show. My father, who made a point of always taking Simon seriously, passed his hand over his mouth to conceal the twitch of a mastered smile. Then he said, 'But Simon, you've never objected to my chaplain's vestments. What's the difference?'

'I suppose I've got used to them.' Simon gloomily picked at his peas. He was still a vegetarian, so peas and carrots were all he was having, because the potatoes had been roasted in the fat round the joint.

'Dad will look a lot better in that outfit than Shepherd ever did,' I soothed. 'At least he's got the figure for it.'

'Thank you, dear heart,' said my father, 'but I wish you'd said *Mr* Shepherd. Or Ron, indeed.'

But Simon said, 'I don't think any man looks particularly good in a dress.'

Tim said, 'What about David Bowie?'

Victoria patted his hand, and said, 'Darling, that's not terribly helpful, because Papa doesn't look remotely like David Bowie.' Yes, she really did call Tim 'Darling', and she wasn't quite seventeen. 'In fact, I can't think of anyone who looks less like David Bowie.'

'I can,' I said. 'Mr Shepherd. Mr Ron Shepherd.'

'True,' said Victoria. 'But Simon, why do you care? It's not like you to get embarrassed. I thought you were above such banal reactions.'

'There are limits,' grumbled Simon. 'And I'm thirteen now, remember? Thirteen-year-olds are supposed to get embarrassed. Especially about their parents.'

Mrs Bryant seemed flustered, and I wondered whether she was reflecting that Victoria, Simon and I had less than our fair share of parents to shame us. She started to stack plates in the automatic way of women who have run homes and families for a couple of decades, and she said, 'Oh, you're quite right, Simon. Embarrassment is what being thirteen's all about.' I took the plates out of her hands and made her sit down, and I thought, yes, it will be embarrassing having a father who's deputy head, and I tried to imagine him putting any of us in detention. But it'll be good too, I thought, mainly for him. Victoria brought in an apple crumble which was stringy on top, a bit like Copydex, but all right underneath, and Tim followed her in with a tin jug with custard running down one side. He and Dad ate most of the custard because no one else was that keen. The Bryants were very pleasant and it was nice to feel that we were a family again, but it was strange that Victoria had suddenly become twenty years older than me. I looked at Simon, who had retreated behind his fringe and his glasses and was making a little rhythm by clicking his tongue and tapping the handle of his fork, and I wondered, not for the first time, what he really cared about. Were the flashes of eccentricity really him, or was there a great mass of ordinary teenage emotions submerged iceberg-like beneath the surface?

It was soon after that lunch party that I started going out with Jonah, and then it was as if I became the wild one, the teenager who flirted with danger but who always came home to touch base. Except that there wasn't any danger, apart from the retrospectively perceived danger of getting pregnant before the Pill took hold, and I didn't do anything very wild, though I accompanied those who did. And when I came home, it was Tim and Victoria I came home to, more than my father. You might have thought that once Jonah was well established we would go out as a foursome, but that never happened. Jonah was silent and surly in their presence, just as if they really did belong to another generation. I confronted him once about his lack of response to them. 'Separately they're OK,' he answered. 'But when they're together, Jesus, the way they fiddle! It drives me nuts.' I knew what he meant. They did fiddle – with each other's hair, or clothing. Victoria, especially, was always trying to put something right. She sewed a button back on to Tim's shirt, once, while he was still wearing it. And if Victoria wanted to look at something in the paper, Tim would fold it open and smooth it down for her. Her legs draped across his lap, his fingertips sketching patterns on her shin – yes, it drove me nuts too, if I thought about it. But perhaps that was because I wished that Jonah would be just a bit more fiddly with me.

We didn't lose contact, Victoria and I. We had some giggly conversations about Men and their funny little habits; the humorous tone was somewhat forced, but we both knew that such conversations were a means of keeping the door to intimacy open without having to talk about anything big. We knew, without discussing it, that our own relationship was on hold; the polite and careful manner with which we treated each other was a kind of apology for the fact that we had allowed men into our lives. So it was an easy time at home, a quiet time, and when Aunt Marigold periodically turned up to sort things out, she found there wasn't a lot of sorting out to do.

I don't really know how Victoria and Tim spent their summer, because I was in Greece for such a lot of it. I mean, I know where they went – they didn't go abroad except for a week's caravanning in Brittany with Tim's parents (they slept in the same caravan as Tim's parents! I could hardly believe it). They spent most of the rest of the time in the Dorset cottage with Dad and Marigold and Simon, so the cottage became even more Victoria's place and not mine. My father got going again on his research into our philanthropic forebear, and Victoria helped him, and took over my old role as assistant completely. But I couldn't blame her, because I wasn't there.

So, yes, I did know how they spent their summer in the literal sense, but I didn't know what was going on between them, that they made so little effort to be daring or original or even to be alone together. They said they didn't want to spend money; they were saving up so that when Tim was at Manchester University they could afford to visit each other every weekend, but that can't have been the whole reason, because they could have set off somewhere camping on their own and it would have cost virtually nothing. One thing that struck me when I got back from Greece was that they were both very proud of their sense of duty. They were always doing things for other people, and whenever anyone suggested doing something frivolous or indulgent they would say, 'That would be nice, but we really ought to . . .', or 'I'm afraid I promised . . .', or 'If I don't do this first, then it's not going to get done.' And when they made these pronouncements they looked all calm and smug.

Victoria had always been interested in the psychiatric hospital (prim face: 'It's not a loony bin, Simon, it's a psychiatric hospital') that she visited on the social-service afternoons when I visited Mrs Bishop, and this interest seemed to grow and grow. She took to spending time there in the evenings and at weekends and, once Tim had left for Manchester, she sometimes spent the whole night there, helping the nurses. She said that some of the patients wandered in the corridors and would go berserk if handled by anyone in uniform, but that she, Victoria, seemed to have the knack of coaxing them back into bed. Someone had even gone for one of the nurses with a pair of scissors, once, and Victoria had held out her hand and spoken gently and the scissors had been relinquished with no further fuss. 'I just pretended I was taming a wild horse,' she explained to us over supper. Simon said, 'It's amazing anyone survived at all before you came on the scene, Victoria,' but my father said, 'Simon, sarcasm is ungenerous. Victoria has been extremely brave.' My father never objected to her visits on grounds of danger – a dauntless spirit, like my mother's, was what he valued most – but he did worry that these sleep-free nights would interfere with Victoria's academic work. Like me, she was to sit for Oxford entrance in November. But she said, with a fine flexing of her nostrils, 'Papa, I learn so much more from these people,' and my father nodded earnestly; it was left to Simon to stick his finger down his throat and make sick noises.

Before he left Tim used to go along to the hospital too,

sometimes. There was an old man called Vince who they were both convinced was in the wrong place. Vince, an illegitimate orphan, had no visitors, so Tim and Victoria used to take him out. They took him to the cinema once because he hadn't been for thirty years. The only film showing at the Classic in Bullhampton (Westaby was too small to have a cinema of its own) was a Hollywood production about a disaster – an earthquake, I think, or maybe a huge fire – which was accompanied by a special effect called Sensurround which made the seats in the cinema vibrate. The effect, said Victoria, was not overwhelming, but they had to leave the film early because Vince complained that it made his false teeth rattle. A couple of times they brought Vince home for tea. He sat as close to the fire as he could, the heat releasing a miasma of urine and tobacco from his ill-fitting clothes, enjoying tea and Jaffa cakes and conversing pleasantly if indistinctly with anyone who came near him. I thought it was a good thing that Tim and Victoria brought Vince out – my feelings now would be rather more mixed – but I didn't understand why they thought he wasn't mad. He had a book that Cliff Richard had written about God, a creased paperback; at every lull he took it out of his pocket and read out a bit he'd underlined with a blotchy biro. I never had the patience to listen properly to his theory, but I gathered that all the underlined bits added up to proof of the Second Coming.

Tim set off at the beginning of October, his rucksack on his back and his acoustic guitar in his hand. His parents would have driven him, but at that stage he was opposed to private cars on ecological grounds and insisted on taking the coach.

Victoria visited him the second weekend. She didn't say much about it on her return and adopted a Greta Garbo hauteur that made it seem tactless to press her for details. A fortnight later it was Tim's turn to visit her. He hitched from Manchester and arrived at one in the morning, having walked the eight miles from the motorway exit. He had said he'd be with us by supper time. My father twittered about his non-appearance; Victoria remained serene, but she didn't wait up. It was I who let him in.

There were no more visits in either direction until after our Oxford exams, though letters addressed to Victoria in Tim's careful, ugly handwriting continued to appear two or three times a week, supplemented by the odd telephone call. I did wonder, though the decision to stay at home and work was so much in keeping with Victoria's new pose of sensible twenty-something maturity, that their keeping apart did not necessarily mean that the death-knell of their relationship had been rung. What about all that saving up? I thought. Victoria had always been mysterious about money. She had a much bigger allowance than I did, because she got the interest from some money her parents had left her, though the bulk of it was held in trust until she was twenty-one. She was not mean – in the pub she would always stand her round – but she never seemed to spend much. She had no more new clothes than I did; we combed Oxfam shops together, the difference being that when I wore a tatty old sack that cost ten pence it continued to look like a tatty old sack, whereas Victoria did things with belts and scarves that made people ask, 'Victoria, where did you get that? Have they any left?' But that all goes without saying.

So anyway, whatever was happening to Victoria's money – and I fancy that under Tim's influence quite a bit of it was going to Worthy Causes – it wasn't being spent on coach fares to Manchester. In the run-up to Oxford entrance both our lives contracted, mine to the bedroom and the library, hers to the bedroom, the library and the mental hospital.

Victoria was applying to read history, the family subject. That would have been my chosen subject too, only somehow she got in first. There was nothing to stop us both reading history, of course, only . . . I went for PPE instead, with more emphasis on the two Ps than on the E. The choice of college was a delicate issue. Very few of the colleges took both men and women in those days, so the range of choice was not wide. The difficult thing was whether or not either of us should apply to St Irmgard's, where Aunt Marigold held a position of some authority. St Irmgard's was the most respected of the all-female establishments, gabled, Victorian, high-minded and highly competitive. We had often visited Marigold there, and the familiar warm ugliness of its grey and purple brick attracted me. Unusually, we sought my father's advice.

'It had better be me,' said Victoria with a self-sacrificing sigh.

'It doesn't have to be either of you,' he said. 'I'm sure Marigold would understand – '

Victoria laid her little brown hand over his. 'It's all right, Papa. I'll do it. It'll be fine.'

I opted instead for one of the few mixed colleges, a sixties sprawl of low, flat roofs that lay outside the centre of the town and was unromantically named after its recently deceased businessman founder. My father called it a brave choice. 'I won't get in anyway,' I said, 'so my courage will go to waste.'

'Courage is never wasted,' said my father, who always took our remarks more seriously than we intended them.

But I did get in, and so did Victoria. We were the only girls from our year who did. Some people were quite jealous and muttered about us being the deputy head's daughters and strings being pulled, but I didn't care. The next few years of my life were now accounted for, and that felt superbly comfortable.

The results didn't come until the last day of term, which was also the day Tim came home. Victoria and I felt shy about our success and hung back, giggling; we left Simon to greet Tim at the door with the news. Tim, being opposed to privilege, didn't really approve of Oxford, but that didn't stop him from opening his arms wide. 'Hey!' he laughed, 'let's celebrate,' and the hug included both of us in almost equal measure.

That Christmas holiday was unusually cheery. Aunt Marigold and Dad were both cock-a-hoop about Oxford. Dad was loving being deputy head, too, and loving not having to be the chaplain any more, and the onset of adolescence seemed to have made Simon a little less vague – he got crosser about things, but that was better than just not noticing. He was growing fast, though most of his growth seemed to be going into his feet, his wrists and his nose. Victoria called Simon's feet his flippers, and claimed she was always tripping over them. She developed a teasing fantasy that he was half boy, half penguin – 'Look at you!' she would cry. 'Graceless on land, but cutting through icy Antarctic waters – what a mover!' It annoyed Simon when she overdid it, but it was jollier than being ignored.

Tim was in and out of the house, as usual, and on Christmas Day we combined forces with his parents – we cooked some things, but we took them over to the Bryants' to eat because they had a larger dining-table. Their Christmas was a reasonable approximation of Christmas as depicted in children's readers or situation comedies – paper hats, a tree with proper lights, new wrapping paper, a giant tin of Quality Street – all the things our family had never quite managed. Tim and Victoria had by this time decided to be vegetarians as well as Simon, so Victoria baked a hard, dark thing made of nuts, and there was an awful lot of turkey for the rest of us. The day hadn't begun too well; at breakfast Simon had announced that he was now a pantheist and would not be going to church, and my father didn't say much but he did look awfully pained. Aunt Marigold said, 'On Christmas Day, Simon, you can keep your ridiculous ideas to yourself. Church won't hurt.' Then Simon said, like a caricature of a sulky teenager, 'You can't boss me around. You're not my mother,' and slammed the kitchen door behind him. We were all astonished. Victoria said, 'The worm has turned,' and Marigold said, 'That's not a very nice thing to say.'

We fell silent. 'He should be made to go,' said Marigold, screwing lids back on jars, 'for politeness' sake. Julian?'

My father shook his head. 'I'm not going to force him. He has a right to decide that for himself. But he has no right to speak to you like that, Marigold. He must apologize for that.'

'Heavens, I don't want an apology,' said Marigold. 'All I

want is a show of respect for the traditions of this family.' And she made a little scoop out of one hand and swept the crumbs off the table into it with the other.

Church was at ten, and at a quarter to Simon appeared, his raw, bony wrists sticking out of the sleeves of his duffle-coat. 'I'll come,' he said. 'I'll be there in body but not in spirit.' So we all went, as usual, only Simon neither stood nor knelt, and kept his lips firmly sealed throughout every carol (which was just as well, given the vagaries of his still-breaking voice) except for 'The Holly and the Ivy', which I suppose he regarded as suitably pagan.

We took our presents with us to the Bryants' house and opened them all over their fitted carpet. I can't remember what I got, except that Simon gave me a Save the Whale coffee mug, which he said would be useful when I went to Oxford, but I do remember that Tim gave Victoria a feminist health manual called *Our Bodies Ourselves*, and Victoria didn't look as if it was absolutely what she had always most wanted. I remember, too, that someone – Sheila Bryant, perhaps – gave my father a soap-on-a-rope, and I found him, later, in the bathroom at home, carefully snipping the rope off. But he made appreciative noises at the time and everyone was cheery and the Bryants were most hospitable, and I remember thinking that Tim and Victoria would probably get married and go on having quietly civilized Christmases for the rest of their lives.

But it was only a month later that Victoria blew the whole thing apart.

20

'Ruthie,' said Victoria, 'meet Steve.'

Steve raised two fingers and tapped his forehead in a form of salute. I had never seen such thick, round fingers in my life. His hand looked like a boxer's glove.

'Pleased to meet you, Ruthie.' He didn't stir from his chosen position, where he filled the corner between the cooker and the sink. Steve was enormous – broad and tall and quite fat, too. He loomed, in our cluttered kitchen. Victoria was perched on the draining board, swinging her legs; beside Steve, she looked like a ventriloquist's puppet.

'Er . . . hi,' I said. It was past midnight on a Saturday night. I had spent the evening playing backgammon with Simon, and we had both gone to bed at half past ten, but I'd just finished my book (*Gormenghast*) and I couldn't sleep. Victoria had been at the mental hospital since six. I assumed that Steve was one of the inmates, someone Victoria had taken pity on, like smelly old Vince. I was surprised that Steve was allowed out so late. Perhaps he had escaped? I shot a glance at Victoria to see if she needed help, but she avoided my eyes. I had been going to make tea, but the kettle was behind Steve's wide back, so I just hovered.

There was plenty about Steve's appearance to support my assumption. He had that look that I've noticed in mental patients of being outside of his time, of having no connection with fashion or social trends. His age was hard to guess – late thirties, I thought, but he could have been older. His square-jawed face looked weather-beaten, and it was brown not as if he'd just been in the sun but as if it always had been and always would be brown. There were lines of grey in the oily black ringlets that fell to his shoulders. It was a cold night, but he was wearing a sleeveless T-shirt – black, with the faded logo of a heavy-metal band on the front – that didn't quite stretch over the hump of his belly. His jeans were cross-hatched in dirt, as were his hands. He had a letter tattooed on each knuckle; the bitten nails, sunk in pads of flesh, were outlined with grime. He wore big silver rings, and a copper-coloured chain bracelet, and something round his neck that I later saw was a St Christopher medallion. When he smiled, which he did readily, his teeth showed surprisingly white and even. It only occurred to me later that they might not be originals. He was smoking. No one ever smoked in our kitchen, not even Aunt Marigold. The cigarette looked tiny, like a thorn sticking out of his huge round paw.

Victoria made no attempt to open a conversation. I wondered if he'd followed her back, but I couldn't scan her for any signal because Steve was looking at me, sucking smoke through his fist and grinning. 'Cold night,' he remarked, sanely enough. 'You been out, Ruth? Anywhere nice?' The letters on his right knuckles spelled LOVE, those on his left, HATE.

'Er . . . no, actually.' I sounded like an elocution mistress. 'Just a quiet night in. Um . . . what . . . what about you?'

'Me? I'm on me holidays.' I made an enquiring noise. Steve was clearly given to wax loquacious at the flick of a switch. 'I work the rigs. Two weeks on, two weeks off. They give you good money, but not much of it gets further south than Aberdeen. The fellows blow it all on boozing and whoring. Me, I'm the one that got away.'

Seeking verification, I gave Victoria the quickest possible glance, and saw it in her shining eyes. 'Oh,' I said. 'Well. It must be a hard life.'

Steve shrugged; his muscles churned under his thin T-shirt. 'It's the boredom that gets to you,' he said. 'Cooped up on that rig with nowhere to go, nothing to look at except the frigging sea and the sky, 'scuse my French. Nothing to do but play cards and fight. And gamble. There's fellows on that rig'll lay bets on which raindrop's going to land first. It's worse than doing time. Except for the money.' When he smiled, his blue eyes almost disappeared into their creased pouches. The blueness of them was extraordinary against the gypsy skin and black hair. It was if his real eyes had been stolen and replaced by fakes.

'So if you work on an oil rig, what are you doing in Westaby?' That was what I wanted to ask, but I didn't want him to think that I doubted his credentials. And besides, I was beginning to feel self-conscious, standing there in my dressing-gown and socks. So I said, 'I only came down to get a drink, actually. Nice to meet you, Steve.' And I filled a tumbler from the tap and bore it up to my room.

I wasn't going to allow myself to fall asleep before Steve had gone and I knew that Victoria was alone and safe. So I propped

217

myself up in bed and started *Titus Alone*. It was over an hour before I heard any movement downstairs. I expected to hear the creak of the front door, but instead I heard whisperings and the bat-squeak of the airing cupboard being opened, and then a couple of thumps from the living-room. And then, at last, Victoria's light tread on the stairs.

'Still awake?' She was taken aback.

'Has he gone?' I asked. I was pretty sure he hadn't.

Victoria had her nightdress over her head. 'Nope. He's sleeping on the sofa.'

'Vicky!'

'What?' She was snappish.

'Does Dad know he's here?'

'Of course not. How could he? I'll tell him in the morning.'

'But what if he sees him first?'

'Ruthie, I don't need to be nannied. Steve's just a friend, all right? We've had friends on our sofa before.'

'Yes, but – '

'But nothing. Good night.' She pulled the covers over her head.

But there was no need, after all, to say anything to Dad, because there was no sign of Steve the next morning, save for the sleeping-bag which he'd rolled up neatly and slipped back into its nylon sack. Victoria replaced it in the bottom of the airing cupboard and then opened the kitchen windows to get rid of the smell of Steve's cigarettes. White January mist curled into the room, thicker than smoke. I laid the table and set water on to boil for Dad's egg; he had gone to early Communion.

On Sundays breakfast was later than usual, and a little more ceremonious.

'I knew he'd be gone,' said Victoria, measuring out coffee grounds. 'He's got to get back to Scotland by tonight.'

'How's he getting there? Train?'

'Hitching.'

'He'll never make it.'

'He will. He's done it before. Lots of times.'

'What's he doing down here, anyway?' I tried to sound casual, not suspicious.

'Oh, didn't I tell you?' Victoria knew perfectly well that she had told me nothing. 'He's going out with one of the nurses at Littlecote. Jackie. I must have mentioned him.'

'You've mentioned Jackie. But then why – '

'Oh, they had a row.' Her tone was lightly dismissive, but before she turned her head away I saw the shadow of a smile. Something inside was rubbing itself against that quiet ego of hers, making sparks.

I sliced the bread. 'He'll be back on the rig for ages, then?'

'Oh, ages. Weeks.' Victoria hoped to sound vague. 'Do you think we should wake Simon? It's incredible how much he sleeps these days.'

'Let's not bother. He's pretty foul when he's just woken up. Here's Dad.' I slid two eggs into the singing water.

Steve was back in less than a fortnight. It was a Thursday evening, and Victoria was washing her hair – she was going to Manchester the next day, to pay Tim one of her rare weekend visits. When the doorbell rang my father called from his study,

'Could you see to it, darlings? I'm on the telephone.' So I went, and when I opened the door I took a jump back because Steve was standing very, very close.

'Hello, gorgeous,' he said, so I assumed he didn't remember my name. 'Is Vicks about?'

'Is she expecting you?' I hadn't meant to sound so frosty. Steve dropped one crinkled eyelid in a slow wink. 'No, but she'll want to see me.'

'I'll go and see.' I left him standing in the cold. Victoria was in our bedroom, towelling her hair. 'It's Steve,' I hissed. 'Shall I tell him to go away?'

'No, no. I'll be down in a sec. Give him a cup of tea or something, will you, Ruth?'

I reluctantly complied. It wasn't that I had any grounds for disliking Steve, who was friendly and humorous. It was just that he wouldn't have been on the doorstep if Tim had been around.

Victoria took ages. I made Steve a sandwich as well as a pot of tea. I cast about, at first, for neutral conversational topics, but there was no problem. By the time Victoria appeared, her clean hair gleaming like a sheet of metal, I had heard about Steve's career as a minicab driver, a fairground manager, a bouncer at a nightclub ('Sod that for a game of soldiers'); about his spell in prison – nine months in Wormwood Scrubs, crime as yet undivulged; about his early, short-lived marriage to 'a Dutch bird – left me for a sailor', and about his later liaison with Trudy, who lived in South London with their son, Junior. Or at least, Steve had always believed Junior to be his, until one day Trudy had turned round and told him he wasn't.

I was gripped. Steve was a person who spent his life caught up in adventure, and no one within my small circle was like that. I was quite sorry when, at Victoria's entrance, he rose, hooked up his sheepskin jacket with his thumb, and said, 'All right, Vicks? Let's go. See you later, sweetheart.' I didn't know where they were going. To the hospital, I supposed. But what would Jackie the nurse make of Steve turning up with Victoria? What, indeed, was I to make of it? Victoria was leading a life for which my frame of reference was no longer adequate.

I dreaded the telephone ringing and it being Tim, but my father kept the line busy all evening because some sixth-form boys who had been found selling amphetamines to thirteen-year-olds had been suspended, so I suppose Tim didn't get a chance to call. Victoria came back very late. I heard the clack of the latch on the garden gate; I'd left our window open a crack, so that I would hear. I peeped out. Steve and Victoria stood in the dark garden together, talking, talking, and then he folded her in his arms. My head span; I couldn't bear to look. I eased the window shut and crept back to bed where I lay breathing rhythmically to still my jumping heart.

Steve didn't stay that night. I don't know where he stayed; I wouldn't have thought poor old Jackie would have given him house room. Victoria tiptoed up the stairs – I knew she would have slipped her boots off – and then climbed on to my bed. 'Ruthie, are you awake?'

I grunted, pretending I hadn't been. 'What's up?'

'Ruth, listen.' Victoria's hair swung over my face. It smelled of smoke. 'Will you do me a favour? A big favour?'

'Probably. Depends.'

'Tomorrow, I want you to ring Tim, and tell him I'm not coming to Manchester.'

'I can't!'

'You can. You must. I just can't see him again. I'll get off the bus and he'll be standing there looking all eager, and . . . I just can't do it. I've tried to tell him that it's all over, but he won't listen. He's so obtuse – well, you know what he's like. You tell him, Ruthie. He respects you.'

I said, 'It's you he respects.'

'Oh, God. You know what I mean. Please, please, Ruthie. You don't have to tell him about Steve. Steve isn't the reason. It would have happened anyway. Tell him I'm ill, tell him whatever you like. But I'm just not going.'

'I really, really think it should be you who tells him.'

'Oh, I'll write. But Ruth – oh, Ruth! It's the one favour I've ever asked of you . . .' Her voice cracked, diverting me from the untruth of this claim. A pair of tears ran down her cheeks, perfectly shaped, as if they had been painted. Victoria was crying! Victoria never cried. I held her in my arms; she felt little and thin to me, like a puppet. How much tinier she must have seemed in Steve's embrace. 'I'll do it,' I said, rocking her. 'Of course I will. But what about your ticket? You've already got your coach ticket, haven't you?'

'Oh, yes, but that doesn't matter. Hey, Ruthie, I've got an idea. Why don't you go instead of me?' Victoria shot up, sleek as an otter, her tears quite gone.

'Me?'

'Yes. Do go. Don't even ring – you'll only get the hall of residence anyway, not Tim. Just go. Then you can tell him properly. It would be much better that way. You know, kinder.'

'I'll think about it,' I said. Victoria rewarded me with one of her rare kisses. For what was left of that night she slept in my bed, like she used to when we were children. I lay with her dark hair between my fingers, breathing in the warm smokiness of it, thinking about Manchester and Tim. 'I'll go,' I said aloud to the quiet house. 'I'll do it.' Victoria didn't stir, though it seemed to me that she smiled in her sleep.

'Look,' I said, 'if you want me to catch the next bus back, I will.' Tim lifted his eyes from his coffee cup, the silent contemplation of which had occupied him for the last ten minutes. 'No, stay,' he said. 'I'm sorry. I'm glad you came.' He pushed spilt sugar grains into an orderly line with his forefinger. 'I'm really sorry.'

'Tim, stop apologizing. Why are you sorry? It's Victoria who should be sorry.' I said that because it was the kind of thing most other people would have said.

'Victoria? Oh, no. This was bound to happen, Ruthie. I was just kidding myself.' He counted some coins out on to the café table. 'Shall we go?'

I rose, and put on my duffle-coat. I had no idea what destination Tim had in mind. I'd skipped the last two lessons of that afternoon, feigning illness, but the coach journey had taken longer than I expected, and it was already gone nine. The last coach home left in half an hour. If I missed that then there would be nowhere for me to stay, except Tim's room. I hadn't brought luggage, that had seemed presumptuous, but at the bottom of my shoulder-bag, underneath *One Hundred*

Years of Solitude and my history prep, I'd stowed a spare pair of knickers and a toothbrush.

'Let's just walk,' said Tim. So we walked – along low brick terraces, their monotonous rows punctuated by pubs and bookmakers and late-opening Asian-run corner shops. Tim, still silent, walked quickly. I had to trot to keep up.

'So – this is Manchester,' I said, for something to say.

Tim stopped. 'Sorry. This is very boring for you.'

'The only thing that's boring is hearing you say sorry.'

'Sorry.' He made a noise between a laugh and a cough. 'Oh, God. We'd better sit down somewhere, I suppose.'

We found a bench on some sort of towpath, but whether by a river or a canal I couldn't tell in the foggy February night. We sat huddled quite close together, and I wondered whether any passer-by – and there were none – would have taken us for lovers, or a pair of old drunks, sunk in our shapeless coats. My teeth began to chatter. I could see Tim's watch, which had a luminous face. 'If I hurry,' I said, my words coiling out on the solid air like dragon's breath, 'I could still get that last coach.' I hadn't yet told Tim about Steve, but I knew that if I stayed the night, I would.

'Don't go,' said Tim. His voice had a croak in it. 'Unless you particularly want to, of course. Sorry.' He scanned my face, struggling to read my expression in the poor light, perhaps.

'I don't want to,' I said.

'You're cold,' he said, stretching out an arm. He put his arm round my shoulders, and I put mine across the small of his back, and we sat there feeling the dank vapour seep through us, sniffing in the air that smelled of yeast and soot and made our noses run. And Tim began to talk about Victoria, how good she was, how clever, how perfect, how he'd never been up to her standard and never would be, how lucky he was to have had a year with her. On and on and on. In my mind's eye was the picture of his face when he had seen me stepping off the coach, not her; of the undisguised mixture of disappointment and tenderness and alarm, and at last I could bear it no longer and I said, my voice high and bell-like, 'Tim, she's seeing someone else.'

His whole body jerked as if he'd been struck. 'She's not,' he said, as if I'd told him an outrageous joke.

'She didn't want me to tell you. She said she'd write.' I realized that starting to tell him had set me off on a complicated board-game in which I would inevitably become entangled in a dreary maze of false moves.

'Who is it?' said Tim, but then, as I opened my mouth to reply, 'No, don't tell me. She'll tell me herself if it's true.'

'Tim, do you think I would lie to you?'

'No, no, but . . . you might have got it wrong. It's possible. Oh, Ruthie, I'm sorry, I know you wouldn't lie on purpose.'

'That's a tautology,' I said, 'isn't it?' I meant to stop there, to leave the proper telling to Victoria, but for once I had some power, and I couldn't resist pressing the button. 'I've seen him,' I continued. I had the sense to say 'seen', not 'met'. 'Met' would have made me into a conspirator.

Tim swallowed. 'Has he been to the house?'

'Um, yes. I think just once.'

He got up and strode off up the towpath. I followed, almost jogging. When I reached him I tucked my hand under his elbow but he shook me off. I fell into step a few paces behind him and thus we made our way towards the centre of town, as if he were a proud chieftain and I his new slave-bride.

After twenty minutes in this mournful procession I asked, 'Where are we going?' I was cold and hungry, and the coach was long gone. We'd passed dozens of little take-away shops, each haloed by the hot, moist smell of frying, but there would have been something particularly heartless about buying chips. I would have to wait until Tim realized.

At last he stopped. 'You should have told me straight away,' he said.

'I wasn't meant to tell you at all.'

He took off his glasses and rubbed his eyes, an action of his that I had come to associate with anxiety. I knew him, I knew his ways. I really did.

'Back to my room, I suppose,' he said, in answer to my earlier question. 'It's quite a long way. Will you be OK to walk?'

'Of course I will.'

It took another half hour to reach the hall of residence, which was dissected by concrete walkways like a multi-storey car park. Tim's room was the one over the porter's lodge. Until late into the night, as I was to discover, the gate clanged shut and the arched gateway rang with the yells of drunken partings. The room itself was so narrow that all the furniture stood in one row. The slatted wooden bed was also narrow. 'I'll sleep on the floor,' said Tim, pulling down the blind to shut out the sodium glare. 'I've got a sleeping-bag.' He made coffee, but the milk had curdled, so we drank it black, no sugar. There was a packet of muesli on top of his bookcase. I asked for some and ate handfuls of it dry.

'I could go out for something,' Tim offered. 'Chips?'

'This is fine. Really.'

We talked about other things, in snatches. Books, films, Manchester. It was Tim who had lent me the *Gormenghast* Trilogy. I was surprised, and said so. 'I didn't think you'd be into anything so fantastical.'

'I wasn't, really,' said Tim, 'but I thought you would be.'

How were we to decide when it was time for bed? The question had been preying on Tim's mind, too, for on the stroke of midnight he shot to his feet and said, 'I'll go and, um, wash.' There was a basin in his room, last in the procession of bed, chair, desk and wardrobe, but I took his meaning. 'Can I have a T-shirt?' I asked. 'To sleep in?' The very word 'sleep' was embarrassing. 'Oh, sure, sure,' Tim mumbled, rummaging. The garment he came up with probably had been washed, but still it smelled of him.

When he was out of the room I put it on. It was the souvenir of an open-air rock concert that I remembered he'd been to with Victoria. It was very large, as I had hoped it would be. It covered the worst two-thirds of my thighs. I kept my knickers on, brushed my teeth in haste, and climbed into bed so that I could pretend to be ready for sleep. It was only after Tim had returned and unwound his sleeping-bag that I remembered I had forgotten to go to the lavatory.

It's all right, I told myself. You haven't drunk much. You'll last the night. But then a little voice said to me, *There was the coffee.* And then it added, *And there was that water you swallowed when you were brushing your teeth.* I lay with my face to the wall, my knees pulled up to my chest, trying to ignore the tight drum of my bladder. 'Mind if I turn this off?' asked Tim, reaching for the light, and I grunted sleepy assent. But I knew that sleep was out of the question.

I stayed quite still until Tim's breathing convinced me that he was unconscious, and then I rolled over in as creak-free a manner as I could. Tim had laid his luminous watch on the tiny bedside table, along with his spectacles and a glass of water. He was such a careful person, in many ways. The watch said ten to one. I crawled to the end of the bed so that I didn't have to step over him, then lowered myself to the floor. It was warm; there was underfloor heating. Poor Tim, sweating in his sleeping-bag.

The lavatory was right at the end of the corridor, and there was someone in it. Someone who took for ever. A big student with a ginger beard, it turned out, who left behind a smell like cooking cabbage. Was this a men-only residence, I wondered, loitering in the shadows. I knew nothing about the way these places worked, and hadn't thought to ask. But the bearded one looked bleary, and didn't challenge me. I don't think he even saw me.

When I got back, Tim was sitting up. Enough light seeped round the margins of the blind for me to see him in silhouette, bare-torsoed and with his hair sticking out like rays, almost like a figure Blake would have drawn. Instinctively I tugged down the hem of the T-shirt. 'Ruth,' he said, 'what's he like?'

I knelt at the foot of his sleeping-bag, mainly to hide my legs. 'Older,' I said. 'Quite old.'

'That makes sense. What else?'

'He's different. I don't know, Tim, I've only seen him once. Out of the window.' It seemed so much more brutal to say I'd talked to Steve in our kitchen, that kitchen where for so long Tim had talked and made toast and held Victoria's hand. 'He's not good-looking,' I added.

'Oh?'

'Quite fat.'

'Fat? You're kidding!'

'Well, big.' I had assumed it would feel better to be replaced by an ugly rival, but as I spoke it occurred to me that perhaps the reverse was true. If I had said that Steve was gloriously attractive, then maybe it would have been easier for Tim to accept his ascendancy as part of the inevitable scheme of things.

'Do you think it's serious, Ruthie?'

'I've told you, I don't know him. How can I – '

'But you know her. You know her best.'

It was probably contemptible that I was warmed by this remark. I said, 'She might think it's serious, but I don't. He's not the kind of man who'll stick around.'

Tim sat in silence for a while, hugging his knees. Then he said, 'I've always considered myself a pacifist, but you know, I'd like to kill him.'

I said, 'How?' I surprised myself.

'Just with my bare hands. Nothing subtle. Just so that he could see it was me doing it.'

'I don't blame you,' I said.

He hid his face. 'Oh, Ruthie, have I really lost her?'

I shuffled round till I was kneeling next to him. I put my

229

arms round his naked shoulders – I saw now that he had discarded his T-shirt because of the heat under the floor – and I felt the warm waxiness of his skin and smelt the old-teddy-bear smell of his wiry hair. I just held him for a while and then I said, 'It's so hot on this floor. Do you want to go on the bed?' I had meant to add, 'And I'll take a turn on the floor,' but somehow we had both rolled on to the bed together before I had time.

I'd like to think that I can spend a night in close proximity with a man without having sex with him, but when I look at the story of my life I realize that that's never, ever happened. The only way I've ever said no and stuck to it is just by avoiding it. And on this winter's night, at just before two o'clock (as I saw as that luminous green dial flashed before my eyes in the scramble on to the bed), yes, I did have sex with Victoria's freshly discarded boyfriend, and avoiding it was not an issue. I didn't think I could get pregnant, because my period was only a couple of days away, but I almost hoped that I would, because then he would be far more mine than he had ever been Victoria's.

But I didn't, and he wasn't, and I went back on the Pill, and got into the routine of visiting him in Manchester every other weekend.

The first couple of months were like a period of mourning for us. Tim was mourning, simply and frankly, for the loss of Victoria, now beyond his reach for ever. It was the same for me, too, in a way. I hardly ever saw her. Steve had abandoned the rig and Jackie and was living in a caravan about five miles from Westaby. He was looking for work, Victoria said, and living off his savings. Most evenings, Steve picked Victoria up straight after school and drove her off somewhere, presumably to the caravan, I don't know. Steve had acquired a very old pick-up truck for sixty pounds; they rattled off in that.

As far as I know, Victoria never spent the night in the caravan. Steve always delivered her home by eleven, except on Saturday nights; that way, my vague and busy father did not complain. Victoria and I developed an avoidance routine. The evenings she was out, I went to bed at ten, read for half an hour, then slept or feigned sleep in time for her return. In the morning I rose early, before she was awake. I set out breakfast for everyone else, chatted to my father about schooly things, bullied Simon into doing everything he would never do on his own like brushing his hair and remembering his gym kit, and left for school early to work in the library. Every other weekend I spent in Manchester, returning on Sunday night on the last possible bus. I would have gone every single weekend if funds had allowed, but they didn't, so on my non-Manchester weekends I spent nearly all the time in the library. And Victoria – well, she did whatever it was that she and Steve did together, all weekend. My father, who hadn't cottoned on about Steve, thought that she was up at the hospital. And perhaps she was. Nobody intervened. Dad may have worried that her A-level work would suffer, but he had spent many hours of his youth giving evening classes to the slum dwellers of Colborough; he would never have interfered with Victoria's Good Works.

So she and I skirted round each other by mutual, silent assent. There was no animosity. I had not told her, formally, about Tim, but I knew she knew, because the night I got back from that first weekend with him she'd sat on my bed and said, 'How did he take it?', and I'd tried to be truthful about his reaction but my answers came out all jerky and confusing, and she'd leaned forward and kissed me on the forehead as if she was giving me her blessing, and said, 'I'm really, really glad he's in a safe pair of hands.' That was the last time we had anything resembling a proper conversation. After that we withdrew into our separate, startlingly new lives, and performed our dance of avoidance with care and courtesy.

So, like Tim, I mourned the loss of Victoria, because I couldn't get near her, and I grieved, too, for the fact that I was glad she couldn't get near me. Tim and I had long conversations about her, not especially revelatory, just descriptive, really, as two railway enthusiasts might find satisfaction in recounting every detail of the journey from, say, Exeter to King's Lynn, just to let the pleasure of it linger in the telling. I ought to have found the whole thing insufferable. I ought to have minded that Tim wanted to talk about her, not me, that I had become his girlfriend because I was the only person to whom he could talk about her in such a way, but I didn't object. Not outwardly. I object now, hotly, on my own behalf, but things were very different then. I wanted to hear what he had to say, because I was quite as much in love with Victoria as he was, then, even though some latent instinct of self-preservation was causing me to put as much space between us as possible.

The Easter holidays loomed. Tim said, 'I can't come home,' but nor was he allowed to stay in his hall of residence, which was commandeered for a conference. We decided to camp, for the first week at least. We hitchhiked to the Lake District. Tim, a seasoned camper, knew how to keep out the wind and rain that were twisting the sheets of daffodils in a dance that was more possessed than sprightly. We pitched camp, made all ready for the night, found a pub with a decent jukebox, made our halves of bitter last. Our sleeping-bags zipped together to make a snuggish nest. One night, lying, almost warm, in his arms, I asked, 'Tim, how long was it before you slept with Victoria?'

Tim jerked away. He sat up, careless of the heat that escaped with him like air from a deflating balloon. 'I never slept with Victoria,' he said. 'I mean, Christ, what do you take her for?'

I said nothing. I rolled over and squeezed my eyes shut, trying to think of nothing but the surge of the windy lake and the sound of the rain that was flung at the tent in rhythmic, pattering attacks. Tim lay down too, eventually, and patted my shoulder. But I didn't respond. I couldn't, because I hadn't quite managed to stifle my hot weeping. So he turned away from me and we lay, not touching, staring at the walls of the tent, because there wasn't anywhere else that we could go.

21

My father, wilfully blind or astonishingly naïve, insisted on regarding Steve as a stray sheep, Victoria as a gentle shepherdess leading him back to some kind of fold. This view seemed to suit Victoria, who kept him fed with tales of Steve's chequered past. The divorce, the motorbike accident, the jail sentence (for driving a getaway car, it transpired) – accounts of these were released to us at strategic intervals, and were all recounted, in Steve's absence, in such a way as to present him in the light of a victim of circumstances. Because Victoria had first met Steve at the hospital, it took a long while for my father to dispel the impression that he had some kind of psychiatric illness, which of course enhanced his view that this was a man who needed to be helped.

After our week in the Lake District, Tim went away with his parents to visit some relations of theirs, and I joined the rest of the family in Dorset. Victoria was there without Steve. The weather was wet and wild, and we spent a lot of time indoors, playing Cluedo and Monopoly with Simon, who kept mourning the absence of Tim and chess, and testing each other on bits of A-level revision. It was a cosy, companionable, unthreatening time. Aunt Marigold was there, doing every-thing for us. She was in a state of almost unseemly excitement about our A levels. Aunt Marigold loved exams. Our stock with her had risen hugely since Oxford had accepted us, and now, with only months to go, the whiff of warm ink and manila envelopes was already in her nostrils and she positively spoiled us. So we sprawled on the shabby sofa with the brown Draylon cover that my father and Uncle Jeremy had once hauled out of a skip, and we draped our feet across each other's laps and learned our quotations from *Paradise Lost*, and Aunt Marigold brought us tea and toast and took a somewhat claustrophobic interest in our progress. We only stirred ourselves when sparks shot out of the driftwood fire on to the hearthrug; then we would spring up and swat them with our A4 pads.

It was Aunt Marigold who answered the door when Steve turned up. She had never met him before, and though she must have heard him talked of she had certainly not registered his significance in her niece's life. The wind was loud that evening, and neither of us had heard his truck approach. The first thing we heard was our aunt's voice, not gruff as it could be, but with a high, strained quality to it. There followed the rumble of a male voice, the words indistinguishable, the tone urgent. 'There's somebody there,' I said, thinking it must be a rambler who had lost his way, but Victoria sat up, her slender neck taut, her chin raised, her eyes bright. She looked like a racehorse, sniffing the air, alert to danger and excitement. A hand shot out and grabbed my wrist. 'It's him!' she whispered, and never before or since have I seen eyes shine like that. 'He's come for me.' Then we heard the scrape of the living-room door where it always got stuck on the carpet, and my wrist was dropped, Victoria's shoulders were hunched, and her head was bowed over her book just in time for Aunt Marigold to enter and find her the picture of demure studiousness.

'Victoria, my dear,' said Marigold, 'could you come here a moment?'

She uncurled herself with a show of reluctance. They left the door open, and I could hear the conversation in the hall – Victoria's modest greeting of Steve, her airy assurances to Aunt Marigold, our aunt's calmer but still suspicious, 'Well, I suppose so.' Then Victoria shot back into the living-room to get her shoes, which lay on the hearthrug like two faithful dogs. She flashed me an elfin grin. 'We're off out,' she said aloud, and then to me in a whisper, 'Talk to Marigold, will you, Ruthie? Like, he's just a friend and all that stuff?'

I nodded. 'I'll wait up,' I said. 'I'll tell her to go to bed.' Victoria ruffled my curls with a grateful hand, and was swallowed deep into the night, a great gust of wind banging the door shut behind her.

I did wait up for her. I waited and waited. Over supper I soothed Marigold's anxious breast with questions about the political aspects of *Paradise Lost*, and afterwards we played whist, at Simon's request, while my father read a biography of Dr Arnold of Rugby. My father was unperturbed by Victoria's absence. Steve's unannounced appearance didn't strike him as odd. I packed them all off to bed by half past ten, and then I sat and dozed and dreamed by the dying fire.

By midnight the wind had dropped, and the clouds rolled back to reveal a crescent moon, clear edged, like a silver slash in purple velvet. Victoria was out, on a wild night, with a man twice her age with a drink problem and a criminal record. Was

I mad not to worry? But then I thought of his voice as I'd heard it at the door, and I knew he was in love with her, in a way that no one had ever been in love with me. And being in love, or being loved, I thought, was like the glowing line that surrounded those children in the ReadyBrek advertisement: it protected you from all harm.

By the time Victoria returned I had fallen asleep, my head on my revision file. She shook me awake; what my eyes saw, before they could make sense of anything, was the face of a child, transfigured with Christmassy delight. I struggled upright. 'What happened?'

'This.' Victoria held out her left hand. The ring was small, a little chip of a diamond in a nest of seed pearls. 'He asked me to marry him, Ruthie.'

'And you said – '

'Yes. Because he wants me more than he's ever wanted anything else in his whole life.'

I blinked stupidly, and just said, 'Wow.' There didn't seem to be anything else in the world that I could say.

I didn't know anybody who was engaged. The term itself was redolent of a far-off time, the time of black-and-white photographs and men with shiny hair and women hardly ever wearing trousers. At school it just wasn't heard of. The most couply of the school couples used to have lovey-dovey conversations, sometimes, about how many children they would have (usually four – two of each) and what their names would be and how they would never smack them or let them have runny noses, but all this was just whimsy. Most sixth-form romances were conducted on an unspoken till-A-levels-do-us-part basis. Getting engaged belonged to the as yet unenviable world of adulthood.

So Victoria wore her ring from the beginning of the summer term, and nobody seemed to notice, just as no one at home had noticed, not even Aunt Marigold. I hadn't told anyone – least of all Tim – because I felt almost superstitious about it, as if saying the words out loud would make it come true. And I desperately didn't want it to come true. Not because Steve was so obviously unsuitable – I was idealistic enough to reject such notions as snobbish – but because marriage was a journey which, once undertaken, would carry Victoria to a far shore, where I could never reach her.

One warm afternoon I was spending my free period in the school library, as was my wont. One of my A-level set texts was *Emma*, and I was lying face down, on the high-backed green sofa that divided the fiction from the reference section, re-reading it. The large windows stood open; the sweetpea scent of wisteria drifted in on shafts of May sunshine, and the sofa cushions were soft and deep. There are more arduous kinds of revision than re-reading Jane Austen; all felt well with the world. And then my sluggish consciousness was tickled by an awareness of the conversation that was happening in the window recess at the end of the room.

Three girls from my year were sitting at the table where the newspapers were spread, the broadsheets attached like flags to their dignified poles, the *Daily Mail* allowed to wander free. Penny, Amanda and Claire; I hadn't noticed them, and they certainly hadn't noticed me, but though I didn't know them particularly well I could recognize them by their voices. Their murmured chat floated in the soft air as inconsequential as an insect's hum until my cousin's name leapt into my aural focus. I stayed where I was, deep in the sofa, straining to hear.

'She is,' said Penny. 'She's wearing an engagement ring.'

'How do you know? It could be just any old ring.'

'It's on her wedding finger. And it looks like an engagement ring. You know, a diamond in the middle.'

'I like opals,' mused Claire, 'but my grandmother says "Opal for tears". I suppose a sapphire would do.'

'You should ask her, Penny.'

'I wouldn't dare!'

'Are you scared of Victoria Rampling?'

'Of course. Aren't you?'

There was some laughter, as Amanda tried to assert that she feared no one. 'You ask her about the ring then,' said Claire.

'Who? Me? I couldn't. I don't know her well enough.'

'You see?' I guessed that Penny was spreading her hands in a comic gesture of resignation, 'you're scared too. Admit it.'

'Admit it, or I'll tell Mr Bradshaw you fancy him.' More laughter.

'If she is engaged,' said Amanda, 'who's she engaged to? Tim Bryant?'

'Hardly,' replied Penny, the sharpest of the three. 'Didn't you know he's going out with Ruthie now? I thought everyone knew that.'

'Of course I knew, but I thought he might have gone back to Victoria. I mean, who wouldn't, given the choice?'

'I shouldn't think he was given the choice,' said Amanda. 'It would be Victoria who did the choosing.'

'I'd rather go out with Ruthie,' said Claire. I couldn't see her, but I knew she would be drawing strands of her long fair hair over her head and scrutinizing them for split ends. 'Ruthie's really sweet.'

'Maybe, but Victoria is so bloody attractive.'

'Do you really think she's that attractive? She looks like a cat to me.'

'Well, cats are attractive. You've got to hand it to her, Victoria Rampling may be a stuck-up cow, but she is incredibly good-looking. There's no one in the school to touch her.'

'What about Fiona?'

'Fi Mac*Pherson*?'

'No, you dork, Fi Glenconner.'

'Oh . . . well, nice hair and everything – '

' – and nice legs – '

'OK, nice legs. But she's not a beauty. Victoria is. When you're a beauty, everything's different. You make the rules. Everything revolves round you.'

'Maybe you're right, but I don't think Ruthie looks too bad,' put in Claire, my hidden ally.

'Oh, come on, Claire. She's a bit of a pud. That frizzy hair, and those droopy cardigans . . .'

'She went out with Jonah Gallagher, remember.'

'That was just because she's brainy, and he's an intellectual snob. He soon got sick of her. I mean, I agree Ruth Rampling's quite sweet, but no one could seriously call her good-looking.'

'Except Tim Bryant.'

'Except Tim Bryant. She's just exactly his type.'

'It's a bit gross, isn't it, to go out with your sister's ex-boyfriend? I mean, do you think they compare notes about what he's like in bed?'

'Vice is nice,' said Amanda, 'but incest is best.'

The other two greeted this sally with squeals of mirth. From the far end of the room the librarian issued a warning cough. They lowered their voices, and I strained to hear. Claire said, 'I shouldn't think they sleep with him. Either of them. Tim Bryant is the virginal type.'

'Saving himself for marriage? Hey, maybe it is his ring.'

'Maybe Victoria nicked it off Ruthie. That would be typical.'

'Maybe he'll marry both of them. He could, if they all became Mormons.'

'Like the Osmonds, you mean?'

'Did the Osmonds marry lots of different people? I thought there were just loads of kids.'

'Oh . . . well, I can't remember. I thought Mormons could marry as many people as they wanted. Only the men, of course. As usual.'

'What do you mean, as usual?'

The lowered voices had crept up the register. The librarian strode towards them across the parquet with a notebook in her hand and a gleam of professional satisfaction in her eye. Penny said, in her most butter-wouldn't-melt kind of voice, 'Oh, Miss Ladkin, we were just having a discussion about the origins of the Mormon faith. I wonder if you could tell us . . .'

I stopped listening. I turned over the pages of *Emma*, my mind racing. What I had just heard was no more spiteful or inaccurate than hundreds of similar conversations I had taken part in myself. The difference was that those conversations had all been about other people. Up to that point, it had never truly dawned on me that people might discuss me at all, let alone compare me favourably to Victoria. Never before had I heard such direct criticism of Victoria, save for the odd jibe from Simon, and he didn't really count.

I swelled and ached with anger. I had assumed that the whole world shared my view of my cousin, and I was angry with myself for being wrong. I was angry with those girls, too, for opening a little hole into my mind through which a mouse of doubt could creep. 'Maybe Victoria nicked it off Ruthie. That would be typical.' That was the comment which, more than any of the others, was nibbling away inside me.

Part of me wanted to rise up from my sofa refuge and shame them, but another part – cowardly, or wise – ducked out. I knew that if I stayed put, face down, they would be unlikely to spot me – they didn't need to pass close to the sofa in order to reach the door. So I tamed my very recognizable hair as best I could by twisting it into impromptu braids, and stayed where I was, staring at *Emma*. And sure enough, when the bell rang at the end of the period, the three of them rose as one and sailed past with a flicker of hair and skirts, oblivious of my prone presence.

The truth took its time to inch up on my father. It was as if he was unwittingly playing a child's game, like Grandmother's Footsteps; for months he stood with his face covered, and then all of a sudden there it was, and his daughter, his niece, the only child of his dead twin, was snatched from him the minute he turned his head. One couldn't blame Victoria. Steve visited regularly; he often ate supper with us before they trundled off in his pick-up truck to who-knew-where. Steve was jolly and affable; when he laughed, which was often, his belly shook. He was courteous to my father, and even tried to be matey with Simon, who, still smarting on Tim's behalf, rebuffed him. As for me, I was in a fair way of becoming Steve's confidante. Victoria would leave me alone with him sometimes – probably deliberately – and he would switch effortlessly from the cheerful, bantering style he used in public to an earnest heart-to-heart mode which I found, I admit, flattering. But I never once saw him outside our house. Whatever it was they did together, I was never invited to join in.

No, Victoria could not be accused of concealing the true nature of their relationship from anyone. She wore her ring every day; it's true (I think) that she mentioned it to no one except me, but then it was our A-level term and rocking the boat would have been unwise and unfair. The truth was that my father failed to recognize Steve as Victoria's boyfriend because of his age, his looks, his lack of education, his social class. Steve was still her protégé, as far as Dad was concerned; he would have no more expected her to be engaged to him than to a woman, or an ape.

We had a quiet summer holiday. In August Tim and I went to the Dorset cottage with my father and Simon; Aunt Marigold picked up the reins at Westaby where Victoria, who now had some semi-official position at the mental hospital, had decided to stay. One evening, when Tim was playing chess with Simon, my father suggested that he and I walk along the shore together. We sat on rocks that still held the heat of the day and watched as the last scuba divers staggered ashore, bandy-legged in their streaming wetsuits. 'How strange these people would have seemed even a hundred years ago,' mused my father. 'Not like humans, but like creatures from the deep. The slimy things that crawled with legs upon a slimy sea, perhaps.' Then he said, 'Do you know, Ruth, I sometimes worry that our friend Stephen my be growing a little too fond of Victoria?'

I stared at the inky sheets of seaweed that draped the rock in front of me, the discarded veils of underworld brides. Clearly, I was expected to reply. I said, 'Would it matter very much if he was?'

'Were,' corrected my father out of long habit. 'If he were. Well, yes, dear, I think it would matter. His feelings could be very badly hurt. It is not as if she could ever return his affection.'

I felt my face burn, though I knew my father would never notice. 'Why couldn't she?' I asked, still not looking.

He gave a proud little grunt. 'Victoria is an extremely sensible young woman. Wise beyond her years. I sometimes think that the . . . what happened to her, propelled her into a maturity that is quite exceptional. She would recognize the unsuitability of such a – I believe we're meant to call it a relationship. She has been very generous in extending her friendship, but she would never allow it to go beyond that, I'm sure.'

'Then', said I, feeling like Judas Iscariat, 'what is there to worry about?'

My father clapped an affectionate hand on my shoulder.

'Perhaps nothing. But men are unruly beasts, darling. My concern is that Stephen's feelings may be stronger than Victoria has realized.' He rose, and brushed sand from the seat of his trousers. 'Shall we walk to the point? It's such a marvellous evening.'

In the latter part of August, we returned to Westaby in time for the A-level results. Victoria and I had identical grades: two As and a B. Aunt Marigold was a little sniffy about the Bs, but my father was delighted. He bought a bottle of champagne and we drank it, as a family, round the kitchen table; just us, no Tim, no Steve.

We toasted each other, and our future, and as many other things as we could think of. And then Victoria said, 'Champagne's rather appropriate, really. Because I've got something to tell you all.' She looked my father straight in the eye and said, 'Papa, don't fuss. Steve and I got married last week.'

22

My father paced the room, running his hands through his hair in a manner that would have been reminiscent of the most amateurish kind of amateur theatricals if it hadn't been so heart-felt. 'What can we do?' he wailed. 'There's nothing, nothing.'

'That's nonsense, Julian. Sit down, you're giving me the jitters. There's heaps we can do. Our priority must be to make sure that Victoria finishes her education.'

My father failed to sit down. 'How can she go to Oxford,' he demanded, 'with a husband of a few weeks' standing who is twenty years her senior?'

'Easily,' proclaimed Aunt Marigold. She brought the palms of her hands down on to the kitchen table with a slap. 'Julian, for pity's sake, sit *down*. I can't talk to you while you're behaving like a caged animal.' My father drew out a chair, and obeyed. 'Good. Now, first things first. Victoria's not going to want to part from him, not yet. And she can't live with him in a college room. So I shall take it upon myself to find acceptable married accommodation. There are dozens of flats in Oxford. The situation is by no means unique. The most important thing is that she should feel supported.'

'Don't all freshers have to live in? In my day – '

'Oh, one can plead exceptional circumstances. That won't be a problem, though I must say it's just as well she applied to

St Irmgard's. Leave all that side of things to me, Julian. Your job is to reassure her that you approve of the decision she has made.'

'But Marigold, you know perfectly well that I don't approve. I disapprove most strongly.'

'Then you must dissemble. Not your strong suit, I know, but needs must when the devil drives.'

'That's not a saying that I've ever liked, Marigold.'

'It has its uses. Listen, Julian, this is a temporary emergency. This marriage won't last. It can't. She's got to be able to feel we're on her side, so that when the crash comes, we're there to pick up the pieces.'

I was sitting on the stairs while this conversation was going on. I was, frankly, eavesdropping, but the kitchen door was ajar; little effort had been made to ensure privacy. From where I was sitting I could see them, and they could have seen me if they'd cared to look, but they were too absorbed. After a while Simon joined me. I put my finger to my lips and made space for him next to me. He sat down, unusually close.

My father said, 'So am I to understand that the thing I should hope for – which means the thing I should pray for – is the collapse of Victoria's marriage? I hardly think – '

'I never mentioned hoping, or praying. No, it's the thing we're *waiting* for. Simply because that's what is going to happen.'

'And if it doesn't happen?'

'As long as the marriage continues, we have to assume that they are both happy. And we must continue to offer our support, not least to any children that may – '

'Children!' My father tugged at his hair.

Simon hissed in my ear, 'Do you think they'll have children? If they do, Vicky will have to – you know – '

'Have to what?'

'Do it with him.'

A squashed smile made my mouth twitch. 'She'll have to do that anyway,' I hissed back. 'Obviously.' Simon pulled a face like a gargoyle's, and retreated into his own thoughts.

'So that's that,' declared my aunt, rising. 'I'll sort out married quarters, and you let Victoria believe that you think Stephen's a wonderful choice. Whatever else happens, I'm going to get that girl through Oxford. Now, don't mope. Chin up. Spilt milk, and all that.'

'Thank you, Marigold. I expect you're right.' Many people in my father's position would have been reluctant to place so much faith in my aunt's pronouncements, since it was during the period of her chaperonage that Victoria had made her ill-starred match, but it had never been part of my father's nature to apportion blame. He shuffled to his feet, and Simon and I slipped hastily away.

Victoria had moved out of our house the day she broke the news to us. She'd carted all her possessions off to Steve's caravan, which she had taken to calling home. I found the speed of her actions shocking. The gaps left in our shared bedroom throbbed like wounds. Our dressing-gowns had hung for years on the back of the door, side by side in silent woolly companionship; a framed print of a Fra Angelico Annunciation which a god-mother had given Victoria at her confirmation left a pale oblong above her bed, like a blind window. Even the books – we'd always used each other's books, but now Victoria had winnowed through them with an unerring recall of exact ownership, and the survivors leaned drunkenly against each other or collapsed on their sides, sickly and sad. Our – my – room looked so forlorn that I considered asking Simon if he would do a swap, but then I heard Aunt Marigold's kitchen conversation with my father and resolved to keep Victoria's space empty, awaiting her return. 'They also serve who only stand and wait,' I told my reflection with portentous misapplication, and my eyes brimmed with noble tears.

Tim was not as shocked by the marriage as I had feared he might be. A key part of his ideology was that one should not stand in the way of individual choice, unless someone had chosen to build a nuclear-power station or harpoon a whale, and he doggedly defended Victoria's right to lead her own life. By this time he had met Steve on several fleeting occasions, and he refused to breathe a word of criticism of him. That was his pride; after those first few weeks of rage and grief he covered his pain, even from me, with a coat of mature reasonableness. No, Steve was fine, an interesting bloke; he couldn't see what all the fuss was about, and my father was just being a snob. Marriage itself was a pointless, anachronistic institution, but if it made Victoria happy – well, that was up to her. If he thought to himself – as he must have done – *She's sleeping with him. She never slept with me*, he didn't divulge. To me he continued to be interested, considerate, quietly affectionate, as he had been all summer; to Victoria he was breezy and affable, though they never talked about anything much.

A week after her wedding, Victoria rang from the telephone

box by the gate of the caravan park. Steve had gone away, she explained, on a one-off driving job, and she was lonely; would I come and visit her? On my own? Of course I would. I scribbled down instructions on the back of an envelope and set out on my bicycle.

It was a warm day, one of those end-of-summer days when the blue and green and white are overlaid by the merest haze of coppery autumn. Spiders had trailed their lines from one blade of grass to another; these were hung with dewdrops like fairy washing. Swallows and martins circled low in the fields, as if trying to dodge the faint oppression that freighted the air. Their beaks opened in fierce scissor shapes. Soon they would all be gone.

The caravan park seemed almost deserted, though tubs of pink geraniums stood by some of the doors, valiant little voices proclaiming, 'This is home. Honest.' Victoria stood at her own front door, watching for me. She was wearing an apron – yes, really – and I could tell from her face that she was longing to see me. She showed me round with cheery pride. The caravan was spotless, except for a full ashtray on the little fold-away table. Victoria smoked five Number Six the first hour I was there. 'Numbies?' I said, expressing surprise at the brand instead of at the quantity smoked. She shrugged. 'They're cheap,' she said.

I admired everything there was to admire, all the toy furniture and the clever contrivances, and then we sat down at the table and had a cup of tea. 'So,' I said, sipping, 'is it any different, being married?'

Victoria lit another cigarette. 'Not really,' she said, and then, suddenly, 'Yes, very. It's very different. I don't think – ' her voice faltered, 'I don't think I'm very good at it.'

It was an important moment, and one that I failed to seize. I said, 'Which bit aren't you very good at?'

'You know,' said Victoria, and then suddenly she was crying. Howling, weeping, her face jagged and torn apart like Picasso's crying woman. Never in my life had I seen her cry like that. It possessed her.

'Has he hurt you?' I asked, moving to her side, but she shook her head. 'No, no. Other way round. Oh, Ruthie, I just don't know if I can do it.'

I said, 'You can always come home.'

The crying eased, and for a moment I thought she might agree. Then she sniffed, and pushed her hair back, and said, 'This is my home now. I'll be all right.' She got up, and wiped her face on her apron. 'Steve will be back at seven,' she said, 'and I've got to get him his supper. Will you come to the shop with me to buy something? I have to shop nearly every day. The problem with the caravan is, there isn't much storage space. The fridge is so tiny, you see.' She unfastened her apron and hung it on a plastic stick-on hook, and off we went to the shop where she bought two frozen fish fillets, a tin of sweetcorn, and a packet of white sliced. It was clear that the subject, whatever it was, that had come so perilously close to being opened was now back in its box and tightly sealed.

23

True to her word, Aunt Marigold installed the newly-weds in an Oxford flat. It was a basement flat in a quiet street off the Cowley Road, a long way from St Irmgard's; Victoria disdained bicycles, so Steve drove her to lectures and tutorials. The flat consisted of a large, dark front-room, carpeted in burgundy swirls; a small bedroom almost filled by a double divan – you had to climb over it to reach the chest of drawers; a kitchen, looking out on to a concrete garden, which wasn't big enough to sit down in; and I suppose there was a bathroom, though I don't remember the bathroom. What I remember very clearly was the smell – a soupy smell of fungus and frying and cigarette smoke. The walls, covered in peeling woodchip, were speckled with damp. There was little furniture except for a three-piece suite covered in tan-coloured fake leather with buttons that looked like chocolates punched into the back. Fra Angelico's Annunciation looked odd on the empty wall, but we were young, and a flat of any kind was something wonderful.

That first term, Victoria led a very domesticated life. Work and Steve – that was all, and she applied herself diligently to both. Apart from a few little cash-in-hand jobs, Steve was unemployed, so there wasn't, in my view, any reason why Victoria should have done everything, but she did. She seemed to want to. Whenever I visited, Steve would be lying on that faintly sticky sofa, smoking and watching television, a plate of food or its remains near him on the floor, while Victoria wiped the kitchen surfaces or unpacked bags of shopping or handwashed his huge jeans. He called her 'my princess' but he didn't seem to treat her like one. Driving her about in his truck seemed to be his sole practical contribution, though he was very affectionate and was forever giving her squeezes or pawing her sleek hair.

In spite of the smell and the smoke and the television that was never switched off, that flat was something of a refuge for me at first. I did have a bit of a social life; I met my friends Katie and Maddy in the first couple of weeks, and of course I still had Tim every other weekend. But I wasn't so sought after that there weren't times when the heart of Oxford seemed a great whirling top, humming and spinning and casting off weaklings like me who foolishly tried to climb aboard. I worked quite hard and I liked my work, but still there were many afternoons when to leave the Radcliffe Camera and whizz away from studenty Bridesheady golden-stone Oxford down the gritty shabbiness of the Cowley Road for Nescafé with Victoria, drunk out of the 'Love Is . . .' mugs that Steve had given her, seemed a consoling option.

I wasn't their only visitor. Victoria didn't spend much time away from the flat, but that didn't prevent her from making several new acquaintances who soon became devotees. They were all male. I suppose she met them at lectures. It was hard to categorize them, but certainly they were nothing like Westaby boys. They were mainly from grammar schools, rural or suburban; they seemed bewildered, and solitary. One, I remember, had an abnormal interest in weaving. They were not friends with each other, and if their visits to the basement flat overlapped they stared at each other with pale, baleful eyes. Victoria's married state seemed an added attraction, if anything. She dispensed tea and Wagon Wheels (expensive, but Steve's favourite biscuit) and doled out small but equal measures of flattering attention, interspersed with spells of enigmatic, dreamy silence, like a Pre-Raphaelite model. There was something chivalric about these colourless young men and their inert and unrequited adoration.

Steve didn't object to their presence, in fact he seemed to welcome it. He must have – correctly – perceived that they posed no threat, that their mute esteem only enhanced Victoria's value. He liked to tease them, quite genially, in ways they didn't fully understand. Steve's behaviour became noticeably more earthy in their presence. He would belch and scratch his belly and stub his cigarettes out on the plates that bore the remains of his meals, which were usually something-and-chips with lots of ketchup. And he would fill Victoria's Pre-Raphaelite silences with the same tales of his adventures which had once enthralled Victoria and me. The stories became a little more embroidered with each retelling, but I noticed that the core of them remained intact.

So a pattern of life was established, and it continued with little disruption for the first term and a half. But then one of Victoria's camp followers cottoned on to the idea that pursuing me might be a good way of getting closer to her. His name was Stuart, and he was reading Old Norse. He tracked me down to my room in college one damp afternoon, and stayed so long that I was obliged to give him tea. After three hours of sporadic conversation he still showed no signs of shifting, and I was about to concoct a lie when I was saved by a knock at the door from Maddy. She bustled in, as usual, with hair flying and cheeks blazing, full of excited chat, and Stuart looked aghast. He shuffled off, thanking me carefully for 'the biscuits and the two cups of tea'. I assumed that he had found the afternoon as laborious as I had done, but no, he was not deterred. His calls became far too frequent; if he found me out he left notes on the door of the 'Where were you?' variety. Something had to be done. Quite out of character, I took the bull by the horns and told him that my boyfriend was very jealous and possessive. In readiness for this conversation I had stuck a photograph of Tim – looking, I have to say, exceedingly mild – in a prominent place above my bed. This did the trick. Stuart was not the confrontational type. But just to make doubly sure I stopped calling on Victoria for a while, and so for the rest of term saw very little of her. Somehow it was taken for granted that, as a married woman, she would not come and visit me.

She didn't come home for the holidays, either, or at least only for Easter weekend. They stayed in the Oxford flat, she working and Steve watching television, I imagine. So it wasn't until her birthday, which was May 1st – how well it had suited her, as a child, to be Queen of the May! – that I began to feel uneasy on her account.

She held a tea party with proper invitations. 'Victoria Cruttenden invites . . .' I still did a double-take on the rare occasions when I saw her married name. 'Cake provided. Bring champagne.' Champagne? Bring a bottle, fine. But asking people to bring champagne seemed to border on the presumptuous.

I excused myself from champagne, and turned up with a birthday present – a volume of Emily Dickinson, who was my new discovery, and a bunch of pure white tulips. Victoria had always loved white flowers. I had only seen her once since Easter – I was no longer avoiding Stuart, but with the advance of spring my own social life had blossomed, and I had been involved in a fair amount of textbook undergraduate revelling – in fact I was feeling sandy-eyed from having drunkenly ushered in May Day at a series of breakfast parties that very morning. The day was unseasonably cold. Sheets of stinging rain slapped at me as I cycled down the Cowley Road, and I arrived with my hair smeared across my face and my jeans clinging to my thighs. Steve, who was on door duty, greeted me with a bear hug and an unwelcome kiss on the lips. It was only four o'clock, but he was already drunk.

Quite a lot of people came. The pale young men were there, of course, and two or three Old Westabians, harmless, unglamorous boys who enjoyed team games. There were some girls, too – Victoria must have been spending more time getting to know people at St Irmgard's than I realized. Some of these girls had brought boyfriends; the front room became quite crowded, and the smell of wet wool and wet hair overlaid the usual muggy smokiness. Steve switched on an electric fire which gave out a toasty smell of burning dust that was almost appetizing.

Victoria sat, her legs tucked under her, in one of the plastic armchairs, over which she had thrown a swathe of crimson velvet. In the dim basement light it looked sumptuous, but I recognized it as part of an old curtain, thrown out when the music room at Westaby was refurbished. Victoria wore black. Against the glowing background of colour her skin looked milky white, and her eyes burned like a consumptive's. The tendons in her neck stood out like ridges carved in marble. As each new arrival proffered a bottle she bestowed thanks with a kiss, directed them towards the cakes which were laid out on two suitcases that, draped with a sheet, served as a low table, scrutinized the bottle, and either handed it to Steve to be passed round or slid it under her chair where the folds of drapery concealed it. After a couple of minutes' observation I understood that she was hoarding the bottles of real champagne and distributing for public consumption the Asti Spumante or the various forms of méthode champenoise.

The cakes bothered me, too. They seemed entirely uncharacteristic. There were six of them – great big gâteaux like Edwardian hats, cloaked in various shades of pale brown and bedecked with rosettes of coloured creams and curly shavings of chocolate. As the heat in the room intensified the icing began to gleam and glisten; as each fresh slice was cut the cakes collapsed further in on themselves like Toulouse-Lautrec's ageing showgirls. To me they bore no relation to eating or appetite, but there was nothing else to eat at all.

I toyed with a slice, cutting it into small crumbly columns and posting each one into my mouth. A circle of admirers formed itself round Victoria's chair and she conversed with bright-eyed animation, her frail fingers pleating and plucking the red velvet. She ate and drank nothing, but she smoked endlessly through a long black cigarette holder – an affectation I had not seen since *Streetcar*. The animation brought twin stripes of colour to her white cheeks, but she looked thinner than I had ever seen her. She did not once stir from her velvet throne. I thought of her dancing days, of the energy that used to spiral out of her. If she tried to dance now, I thought, she would buckle and snap.

I kept away from her. I was sure she wanted me to. I tried to keep away from Steve as well, but he would keep grabbing me and holding me against him with more than fraternal closeness. That would have bothered me more, except that other females were receiving the same kind of treatment. I told myself, snobbishly no doubt, that someone like Steve regarded such behaviour as *de rigueur* at all parties, even parties where the only other form of entertainment was cake and fizzy wine.

I laughed and wriggled out from under my brother-in-law's arm and made pleasant, insipid conversation with some of the St Irmgard's girls, most of whom seemed to be of the variety who joined the Christian Union and shuffled along in fluffy slippers to the pay phones at the end of college corridors to make long telephone calls to their mothers. They certainly knew how to put away cake. Doubtless they knew how to make it, too. I sipped my wine and talked about my course. My mouth was prickling with longing for olives or gherkins or hard, salty cheese.

The girls started to leave after an hour or so – I even heard one of them express concern about missing dinner in hall, cake or no cake – and with their departure the mood of the afternoon changed. Steve put on some music – some unfashionable kind of heavy metal with a hard, driving beat. Nobody danced, but people started to sway a little, and the Old Westabians' eyes glazed over and their mouths set in foolish, nostalgic grins. Stuart the Norseman lurched over to me and said in a voice that was unnaturally loud, 'You thought I was in love with you, didn't you? What made you think I was in love with you? Bloody women, you're all the same.' I shrugged and turned away. When, several minutes later, I looked back, Stuart was slumped in a corner of the sofa, his head hanging to one side.

I wanted to slip away, but Victoria noticed – those glittering eyes missed nothing – and she called out, 'Ruthie, don't go! I haven't had a chance to talk to you yet.' So I hovered on the edge of the all-male circle that surrounded her, feeling angry and faintly sick. I could see no way that this party was ever going to end, but then all of a sudden Victoria tipped some kind of a wink to Steve, who made a few valedictory comments and gestures, and the whole gang of them shuffled away as if he were a stern ward sister announcing the end of visiting hours. So that left just me and Victoria and Stuart, now insensible on the sofa.

'Darling, I'd love a cup of tea,' cooed Victoria, stroking the great slab of a hand that rested on her shoulder, and Steve lurched off into the kitchen to do as he was bid. To me she hissed, 'Don't go. Please. Just stay until – ' but then he was back in the room, asking, 'Tea for you too, Ruthie?' so she just fixed me with a look and I gave her a tiny answering nod. The thought came over me in a rush that perhaps he hit her when he was drunk, and the idea seemed at first corny and then obviously true.

I thought, at first, that Victoria must be courting disaster, because when Steve came back with the slopping mugs of tea she drew out one of the hidden bottles of champagne and handed it to him. It was a magnum of Moët, the gift of the hearty Westabians. 'I saved this for us,' she said, with a glassy smile for her husband. 'It's the real thing.' Steve smirked as his thick fingers fumbled with the gold foil seal. 'The real thing!' he chuckled. 'Like you and me, eh, Vicks?'

The cork hit the low ceiling so hard that the light shook. It landed on the shoulder of the unconscious Stuart, who shuddered as a horse does when bitten by a fly, but didn't wake. We all laughed, and the foam cascaded over Steve's hands and wrists. 'Here, Ruthie,' he said, winking. 'Lick it off. Don't waste it.'

Smiling, I declined the invitation, and fetched glasses. I didn't in the least want any more, but I pretended to drink, because Victoria wanted me to. I held a sip in my mouth, where it buzzed against my tongue like a trapped insect. Steve drained his glass in one swallow, refilled it, and did the same again. He rolled over to change the music, and I whispered to Victoria, 'Shouldn't we take it away from him?' and Victoria shook her head and whispered back, 'I want him to drink the lot. Don't go until he has.' Steve put on a tape of what he called ballads. He stumbled back to his place by Victoria's side. 'What's going on?' he asked, still grinning. 'What are you two gossiping about?' Victoria stroked his cheek. 'Girl talk,' she said, playfully. 'Here. Time for a refill. We haven't drunk any birthday toasts, yet.'

And Steve did drink the lot. He gave up on his glass, but lay on his back, his head propped up by the cushion off the other armchair, tipping the bottle straight into his mouth. His eyes closed; I thought he was unconscious, and wanted to take away the bottle in case he choked, but Victoria restrained me. 'He knows what he's doing,' she said. Sure enough, it wasn't until every last drop had been drained that he allowed the bottle to roll away from him. Then he turned on his side and began to snore. He looked pitiable, lying hunched like that, with his belly spilling sideways over the top of his belt. I said, 'What are we going to do with him? We can't just leave him like that,' but Victoria said, 'He'll be all right. You know, Ruthie, sometimes they're better that way. Husbands.' I could, and perhaps should, have asked more, but my head was throbbing because I had had no sleep the night before, and I had an essay due in the next day that I hadn't even started, and I felt angry, angry about Victoria's cigarette holder and porcelain skin and crimson throne, so I just said, 'Well, I wouldn't know about that, would I?' and I climbed up out of that soupy flat and cycled back to sane, clean college in the soft and drizzling dusk.

24

'Well, if it isn't Stella! Stella-for-Star!'

I was in Blackwell's, pondering the purchase of a textbook which was several pounds more expensive than I had expected it to be, but which I knew would transform my life. I knew who that dry, drawling voice belonged to before I turned my head.

'Sholto de Grey!' I said. He stood by my shoulder, as close as a shadow, enfolded, despite the warm October afternoon, in that same dark greatcoat that had been his trademark at Westaby. I looked him up and down, quite rudely I suppose, but he had always seemed to me more of an exhibit than a person. He was, if anything, thinner than ever; his legs still looked eighteen inches longer than they had any right to be, but his foxy ringlets had been cropped so close that he looked even more cadaverous. He wore suede pixie boots, one purple, the other pink, but otherwise identical. 'What are you doing here?' I asked, unimaginatively.

'Here in Blackwell's, specifically, or here amidst the dreaming spires? I'm here in Blackwell's to steal some books, and I'm here in Oxford to sit out the second act of the farce they call a classics degree.'

'But I didn't know — I never saw you — '

'Ah! You're in your second year, I suppose? They don't call

me the human calculator for nothing. Well, a little local difficulty meant that I had to spend quite a lot of last year elsewhere. So they've put me back a year. Good of them to let me return at all, some would say. One is bound to live aimlessly, so one might as well do it in pleasant surroundings.'

Sholto was more amiably loquacious than I'd ever known him, but still I didn't dare ask him all the obvious, eager, uncool questions – what college was he at, why had he been rusticated, was he still in touch with Rick Emerson? I picked up the worthy textbook, with its ugly cover of wavy orange and brown stripes, and said, awkwardly, 'I was just going to buy this.'

'Do you have to? You poor darling! But no, little Stella. Allow me. This horrid orange book would eat such a hole in your poor little grant. No cocoa parties for weeks – terms – years! You must let me relieve you of it.'

I understood that he intended to steal it for me. I wavered; it was his way of being friendly, and it really was very expensive. But my upbringing held firm and I took it out of his hand.

'No? Ah well. Ever the chaplain's daughter. You see, I remember you very well, Stella-for-Star. If you won't let me do you that favour, then do me one instead. Join me in my rooms for a little smackerel of something. I long to hear all the news.'

He swept me across Broad Street and through the Covered Market, pausing to buy a tin of anchovies – 'We'll have anchovy toast' – on the way. When he paid for the anchovies I saw that the lining of his coat was bulging with stolen volumes. He was at Christ Church, it turned out, sharing a fine set of rooms in

263

Peckwater Quad with someone he introduced to me as 'Trevor'. Trevor, who wore a rugby shirt and training shoes, as labouring at a desk with an A4 pad; he looked up and grinned through his shaggy hair like a dog.

'Trevor, this is Stella Kowalski, an old and valued friend of mine,' Sholto declared. 'Bye for now, Trev.' Still grinning, Trevor shuffled to his feet and left. 'He's most obliging,' said Sholto, before the door had finished closing. 'His name's not really Trevor, of course, but I can never remember what it is. He always makes himself scarce when I've got visitors. I'd do the same for him, of course, but he never has any.' He pulled the haul of books from his coat and arranged them in a fan shape on the central table.

'What's his subject?' I asked, for no good reason.

Sholto stared. 'I've absolutely no idea.'

I could feel myself blushing. 'Tea! Tea!' cried my host, and then, after some rummaging around, 'Tea seems a little complicated. Let's keep it simple.' He extracted a slim, long-necked green bottle from a fridge, which stood in a corner covered with a tiger skin. The tiger skin was moth-eaten enough to be real. Sholto drew the cork. 'When the fridge growls, it gives one a pleasing frisson to fancy that the growl comes from the tiger.'

I studied the room, which was, decoratively speaking, divided strictly down the middle. On Trevor's side there was his neatly ordered desk, a green anglepoise lamp, a Newcastle United banner and a poster of a girl in tennis whites rubbing a ball against her bare buttock. All the rest of the furniture had migrated to Sholto's side. White cyclamen stood in blue and white Chinese bowls along the top of the well-stocked bookcase; a delicate pencil study of a languid youth, handsomely framed, was flanked by two watercolours of what I took to be Venice. 'An ancestor of mine was a close associate of Bonington's,' said Sholto, following my gaze. 'Rather insipid, but I find them restful.'

I had never heard of Bonington. I sipped my wine, which was ambrosial – the colour of weak sunlight, tasting of honey and the scent of flowers. 'This must be what it's like to be a bee,' I said, nuzzling my glass.

Sholto laughed. He sat down, extended his scissor legs in front of him, folded his long hands behind his head, and said, 'And now. Tell me all about your delicious little sister-cousin, my exquisite Blanche du Bois.'

I said, 'Well, she's married,' but even as I said it I wondered if she really was. Steve was working on the oil rig again, ostensibly because they needed the money. But he seemed to have been away for most of the summer, and Victoria had been with us in Dorset and at Westaby, reading, helping my father with his research, chopping things in the kitchen with Aunt Marigold. She had slipped effortlessly back into her pre-marriage ways.

'Ah yes. I did hear that from someone or other. What an extraordinary thing to do. But she didn't marry that dreadful boyfriend of hers, did she – that bespectacled person? Little Timothy Bryant?'

I was still going out with Tim, though seeing less of him as his third-year work mounted up. I knew that my silence to Sholto on this point was a true betrayal, but I failed to bring myself to put the record straight. 'No, no,' I said, 'Steve's very different. He's – ' I couldn't quite think how to put it – 'He's got tattoos.'

Sholto shrieked with laughter. 'A man's man! And a pleb, to boot! Oh, I do understand. Now, I insist you tell me all about him. A full, photofit description, please.'

I obliged. I'd never talked about Steve so much before, and as I described him, I realized how ambivalent my feelings towards him were. I told Sholto about his clothes, his drinking, his taste in music, his police record, but I didn't attempt to convey the sense of vulnerability that I saw in his slow-moving bulk, or how my heart ached when he held Victoria's increasingly reluctant hand between his great hairy paws.

'Well!' exclaimed Sholto when I ran out of steam. 'It sounds as if our little Blanche needs rescuing from the lair of this ogre.' He refilled my glass.

'Oh no,' I cried, 'it's not like that at all.' But then I thought, perhaps it is like that, actually. Sholto must have caught my hesitation, because he said, 'I don't believe you. Operation Bail Out Blanche begins forthwith. Bring her to tea, Stella darling – how's Thursday for you? No excuses. If you don't, then I shall just have to hunt her out myself. You have been warned.'

'I'll bring her.' I drained my glass. 'Four o'clock, Thursday? And now I really must go home, for an evening with my horrible orange book.'

'You call it home? Your college room? How touching.'

'Oh, I live out,' I said. 'In Jericho. With a couple of friends.'

266

'Of course you do. Of course you do. Underwear dripping over the bath, lentils with everything. Lovely. You must invite me to supper some time.'

'I will,' I said, and fled, back to the sweet little terraced house that felt like mine, although of course it wasn't. It was my turn to cook for Katie and Maddy that evening, and as I stirred the sauce for the cauliflower cheese I reflected that the virtue of refusing to have a book stolen for me was more than cancelled out by my craven failure to correct Sholto's view of dear, faithful, truth-telling, unpretentious Tim.

Victoria showed little reaction when I told her about the proposed tea with Sholto, but I could tell she was excited. She had tired of her pale young men and their Christian Union female equivalent; she still let them in when Steve was at home, to act as some kind of buffer, I suppose, but when he was away working – which was more often than not – she just drew the curtains and sat, smoking, in the dark, not answering the doorbell. I knew this because I'd visited a couple of times and assumed she was out, and as I'd turned away to unlock my bike she'd opened the door and called me back. She seemed terribly glad to see me. I don't know what she did with her time – the television was never, ever on when Steve wasn't there, and she didn't seem to work much any more. The wind and rain had set in early that autumn, and the walls of the flat now shone with damp. Victoria was always coughing. She seemed to live off tea and cigarettes, and I did wonder whether I should tell Aunt Marigold. But no, I reasoned, Aunt Marigold must see her in college, several times a week. What I didn't realize was that, without Steve to drive her, Victoria went in to college less and less.

That Thursday, I called for her at her flat on foot, so that we could walk to Christ Church together. I was afraid that if I didn't escort her, she would fail to turn up. But I need not have worried. From her appearance I could tell that she had prepared herself most thoroughly. She was wearing one of her junk-shop treasures, a kind of tunic made of ragged black lace that looked as if it had strayed from some acting cupboard; this she wore as a short dress, with footless black dance tights and little black ballet pumps. Unusually, she was wearing make-up – a smudge of kohl round the eyes, a vermilion mouth to make the pallor of her skin look almost luminous. Her hair, still long, hung over her face, carefully unwashed. She smelled of musk and cigarettes. I'd never seen her look remotely like this when Steve was around. I was wearing jeans and Kickers and a baggy sweatshirt. I must have stared; she gave a self-conscious little laugh. 'One needs to be a little theatrical,' she said, 'for Sholto.'

'You'll freeze,' I said. She shrugged on a black leather jacket rejected by Steve as too tatty. The sleeves hung down over her hands so that only her fingertips showed. We set off up the Cowley Road, past shop windows full of saris and suitcases and secondhand bicycles. On Magdalen Bridge she paused, ostensibly to look at a pair of swans whose whiteness flared on the dark water, and I realized that she was quite seriously out of breath.

Sholto's room was full of white lilies. I had never seen anything like it. Their fragrance seemed to coat every surface, dissolving hard edges. The luckless Trevor had been roped in as a kind of batman; he handed us plates of delicacies (the anchovy toast, forgotten on my previous visit, made its appearance) and cups of china tea, but he said nothing unless he was spoken to. Sholto was wearing an embroidered kimono, dark green silk with frayed cuffs. He greeted Victoria with extravagant delight, fingering her clothing. 'Leather and lace! My dear, how perverse!' And then later, after the anchovy toast and the tiny chocolate eclairs, the *mille-feuilles* and the Muscat grapes, all of which I wolfed down but which Victoria hardly touched, he said, 'It's such a relief to me, little Blanche, to find you don't look married at all.' It was then that I looked at her hands and saw that she wasn't wearing any rings, except, on her little finger, the finger that was missing the top joint, a silver ring shaped like a skull.

Dusk gathered. Wine was opened. Trevor melted away without a sound. Sholto talked, in a continuous stream, of art and books and clothes and people and Oxford, but though he was apparently so much more forthcoming than he had ever been at school, it occurred to me that about his private life he had revealed not a single thing. As for Victoria, she sparkled. She said little compared to Sholto, but when she did speak she was pithy, stinging, brilliant. When the room was quite dark but for the glow of the lilies, Sholto lit candles. In their flickering light her eyes shot fire.

I heard Great Tom strike seven, and stood up, galvanized by a sense of my superfluousness. 'I must go,' I said. Only the most cursory efforts were made to detain me. On the long cold tramp back to Jericho I wondered if it was right to leave

Victoria to make her way back, alone in the dark, to her empty basement, but then I reflected that perhaps she wouldn't be going anywhere that night. 'It could be over,' I said aloud. 'Her marriage could be over,' and I hugged myself with anxiety and glee.

The next time I saw Victoria, she had cut all her hair off. She called on me, unexpectedly and uncharacteristically, in my little house one mizzly Saturday afternoon. The gas fire was on in my bedroom; I was wearing a poncho and slipper socks, and I was eating chocolate digestives from the packet and writing to Tim. My room was on the ground floor, next to the street. When I heard the tap on the window I looked up, but failed for a moment to recognize the crop-haired young boy outside.

I shuffled to the front door. 'Oh no! What have you done?'

'What does it look like?' She ran a hand through her half-inch of black bristle, dislodging a scatter of raindrops. It did suit her, in a way. It accentuated, as a fashion magazine would say, her high cheekbones and slanting eyes, the neat turn of her slender neck. She looked as if she was in some avant-garde French film, standing out there in the rain.

'Aren't you going to let me in?' she complained. 'I've come for some cosiness.' I stood aside, and she took off her shiny black PVC mac with the pointed sticking-up collar and hung it, dripping, over Maddy's bicycle. Then she pushed open the door of my room. 'A fire! And chocolate biscuits! This is perfect.' I saw her eyes stray to my writing pad, lying exposed on the bed. 'Dear old Tim,' the letter began. She made no comment. Under the pretext of straightening the bedcovers, I turned the pad face down.

'Well?' she enquired, spiking her hair up in the mirror. 'What's your verdict?'

I didn't reply immediately, and then I said, 'I loved your hair.'

She looked a little taken aback. 'You never said so.'

I just shrugged.

'It was Sholto's idea. All that excess growth! It was like I had something to hide. You should do it too, Ruthie. It feels great.' She gathered up my mousy frizz and scraped it back from my face. 'Really, you should. It would put years on you.'

'No, thanks,' I said, wriggling free. 'I need my hair, for warmth.' I stood back and examined her from all angles. 'I suppose I'll get used to it. What will Steve think?'

A little colour rose to Victoria's face. 'He can think whatever he likes,' she said.

Steve returned, on leave from the rig, and with him came an early burst of winter. It was only mid November, but the wind tore sackfuls of leaves from the trees, and the colour drained out of the city. I wore three sweaters and it wasn't enough. I wrapped my scarf round my head but still the deep cores of my ears sang with pain. Katie and Maddy and I stuffed newspaper in the gaps where the windows didn't fit properly and cursed our landlord because we had no radiators. At mealtimes in our steamy little kitchen we hunched our shoulders over our plates and punctuated every conversation with the lament, 'It's just so bloody cold!'

I had intended to keep my distance from Victoria while Steve was about, but one morning, surprisingly early, I heard the pick-up truck grind to a halt outside my bedroom window, and there was Steve on my doorstep, stamping his feet and blowing on his hands. He didn't greet me with his usual embrace, but said, 'I'm worried, Ruthie. Can I come in?' And he really was worried. His face was grey with lack of sleep. I remembered then what I'd always known – that Steve truly loved Victoria.

I brought him into the kitchen and made him coffee to warm his hands. His eyes were almost invisible in folds of loose skin. 'She's not well,' he said. 'It's the cold. And that flat's a hole – it's running with damp. And she smokes like a bloody chimney – that don't do her no good.' He lit a cigarette himself; the action was too automatic for irony.

I made a sympathetic murmur. I couldn't quite see why Victoria's being ill had brought him to my doorstep at what felt like dawn.

'She was coughing all night,' Steve continued. 'I tell you, Ruthie, she was coughing all bloody night. I don't know what I'm supposed to do. I laid down on the settee. She wouldn't let me near her. She never lets me near her.' He fixed me with an imploring look. I feared anything confessional, so I rubbed my hand over my face, to break the beam of his gaze, and said, with a prim little clearing of the throat, 'Have you called a doctor?'

He hung his head. 'She won't let me. I've told her and told her, but she says there's nothing wrong. It's like, I'm not allowed to do nothing for her. She'd listen to you, Ruthie. You get her to see a doctor. You was always her best friend.'

Such a remark still had the power to warm me. I said, 'Of course I'll try, if you think it'll do any good. I'll come over this afternoon and – '

'Come now,' he said. 'I'll drive you.'

'Now? I'm not even dressed.' I had lashed on my dressing-gown as tightly as I could when I had realized who was calling, but underneath I had nothing but a shortish nightshirt.

'Go and dress, then. I won't look.' And Steve gave me a grin and a wink, a weak reminder of his usual line of humour.

I withdrew to my room and dressed. Before I took off my dressing-gown I folded a tissue and stuffed it into the keyhole. I don't quite know what made me do that.

I put on my layers – thick tights under my dungarees, two T-shirts and a sweater and over it all a saggy Peruvian cardigan with fuzzy brown llamas on it, and then Steve and I climbed into the truck and bumped our way south through the clammy morning streets. The truck had no seat-belts, which made it impossible not to fall against Steve's shoulder. That didn't really matter, though. I wanted him to feel that I was friendly towards him, even through such involuntary gestures of closeness.

Victoria was sitting up in bed when we arrived, coughing and trying to smoke, but she wasn't getting far because her teeth were chattering too much. The electric fire was on, but it only managed to create a bubble of warmth; the corners of the room were as cold as if the house had no walls or roof. Her face was white, apart from two flaming patches on her cheeks. Her short, short hair was flattened on one side where she had lain on it. Her nightdress had a white lacy collar; she looked like a clown who had just taken off his wig. I recognized that

273

nightdress with a pang. It had been sent by her London grandmother, Aunt Angela's mother; it was from Harrods and was made of the most beautiful embroidered lawn. Victoria had laughed at it when she opened the box, as she laughed at most of her grandmother's exquisite, inappropriate gifts. I had no idea she ever wore it.

When she saw it was me her face flooded with relief, but her greeting was lost in a surge of coughing. 'Vicky,' I said, patting her uselessly on the back, 'we've got to get you a doctor.'

She shook her head. 'It's only a cold,' she said, between splutters. 'Anyone would think no one had ever had a cold before.' She shot a glance at Steve, his large frame hesitant in the doorway. 'Get me some Marlboro, would you?' she said. 'I'm almost out. Oh, and some more of that Benylin. That's good stuff.' She didn't use his name, as if she couldn't be bothered. He turned and left without a word.

I started to say something, but she held up her hand for silence, and kept it that way, head cocked, until she heard the door click shut behind him. Then she grabbed my wrist and said, 'Ruthie, you've got to get me out of here.' I didn't need to ask. I knew what she meant – out of the flat, out of the marriage, out of everything. Her grip was tight on my wrist. For once I was able to think fast.

'I'll ask Aunt Marigold,' I said. 'I don't need to say much. Just that you're ill, and this flat is too damp for you. There must be a sick room in college, or something, and then Steve can think . . . well . . .' I faltered, unsure of what she wanted Steve to think.

Victoria's face was stretched into a tight smile. 'He can think I'm coming back,' she whispered. 'He'll go back to the rig at the end of next week, and he'll think I'm coming back, but I'll pay off the landlord and move the stuff out and that'll be that.' She released me and hugged her knees, rocking with fierce delight.

'Vicky,' I ventured, 'has he . . . done anything? I mean – '

She didn't look at me. 'What hasn't he done?' she murmured in a faraway sing-song. 'Oh, what hasn't he done?'

I heard him at the front door, whistling, and stabbing at the lock with clumsy, frozen fingers. 'He's back,' I whispered. 'I'll go and see Marigold right away. Don't worry any more, Vicky. I'll sort everything out for you.'

She stroked my cheek with her little finger. 'I know you will,' she said. Her voice was soft, and the corners of my mouth twitched with pride.

Aunt Marigold was in. She was sitting in her usual chair, the one with the stretchy dark-green cover and bare wooden arms, marking papers, a large glass of sherry on the little table by her side. I saw my aunt about once a month – we met for a walk in the University Parks, or I gave her lunch in my shabby little kitchen – but our meetings were always by arrangement. I never dropped in on her. I had felt a little fearful as I climbed the stairs to her flat – suppose I caught her doing something entirely uncharacteristic, like dancing or doing yoga or entertaining a man? But there she was, with her marking and her sherry and her long flat shins, with the gas fire bubbling in that cocoa-coloured room, and everything was just as it should be.

I was direct. I said, 'I've come about Victoria,' and she said, 'Ah! I might have known. It couldn't possibly last.' I had a choice, then; I could have said, 'No, no. Everything's fine with Steve. It's just that she's not very well.' That was what I was supposed to say. But Aunt Marigold's eyes, keen under their hooded eagle lids, were fixed on me, and I blurted, 'She's got to get away from him. But the thing is he mustn't know.' And then I told her the whole story – or at least, as much of the story as I knew, which I realized half way through my narration wasn't very much. I didn't know, though I could guess, what Steve had actually done, and I had enough control to realize that airing my guesses would not be at all a fair thing to do. But Aunt Marigold didn't seem to need any details. She nodded at everything I said, her face set.

'This had to happen sooner or later,' she said, pouring sherry for me, 'and sooner is better than later. Victoria still has all her life before her. We must do everything in our power to keep her path clear.' Now it was my turn to nod, thrilled with the sense of a secret mission.

She made me lunch – tinned oxtail soup, and liver sausage spread on toast, and big hard tomatoes the colour of the gummy bit of false teeth – and she talked about Victoria in a way that I had never heard her talk before. 'An early marriage was inevitable, or nearly so,' she pronounced, finishing her toast in neat tortoise-like bites. 'She was looking for love, poor child. Love and security. To replace all she'd lost.' From so unexpected a quarter, such platitudes rang true. It was a long time since I'd thought about Victoria in terms of her having lost anything. 'Why Steve, though?' I asked, unable to make any kind of link between clever, sophisticated Uncle Jeremy and dainty Aunt Angela on the one hand, and dirty, shambolic, rumbustious Steve on the other. 'Why, indeed?' replied Marigold, slicing an orange round its equator. 'He must have seemed safe to her. So big, and so much older. Like a big, safe house.'

We sat on either side of the gas fire to drink our Nescafé, and Aunt Marigold unfolded her plan. 'She'll come here,' she said, 'to this flat. She can have my bed, and I'll sleep on the put-you-up. No, don't raise objections' – holding up a hand to still my protest – 'I can sleep anywhere. Always have been able to. Must have been all that camping with the Guides. Stephen can visit, and I'll be hovering, and I'll get rid of him when she can bear it no longer. Then once he's away I'll get her into a proper college room, and when he comes back he'll find a *fait accompli*.' She glanced at me as if to check my reaction. 'Not the least duplicitous way of acting, I know, but it's imperative that we support her by whatever means are available to us.'

The morning fog had vanished now, giving way to blades of sleety rain that sliced at the window-panes. I had to agree with everything Aunt Marigold said, but I thought of Steve's grey, tired face, and inwardly I sighed.

It didn't occur to me, then, that Victoria wasn't the only one who had lost a mother. I never thought to ask Aunt Marigold or anyone else why Victoria's loss should lead her to make such dramatic and daring and, frankly, ill-judged decisions, whereas I had hardly deviated from the quiet path my education and upbringing had mapped out for me. Heaven knows, I was introspective enough, yet I never dwelt on my half-orphaned condition, and nor, it seemed, did anyone else. With Victoria, though ... I suppose I was just so used to Victoria writing her own rules. Resentment didn't come into it. Victoria was different; there was nothing to resent.

25

So Victoria lay in Aunt Marigold's bed for a week, propped up with cushions. The college doctor prescribed antibiotics and asked her whether she smoked, to which Victoria replied, 'Just socially.' Aunt Marigold spent as much time as she could in the flat, heating soup and encouraging Victoria to listen to plays on Radio Four, and while Marigold was there Victoria was very polite and quietly grateful and didn't smoke at all, but once she had gone out Victoria would jab the radio off and fling open the window and smoke with her head and shoulders leaning right out into the sticky winter air. I know, because I was there a lot. Marigold asked me to call whenever I could. She wanted to minimize the amount of time Steve and Victoria were alone together. Steve visited assiduously for the remaining days of his leave, and he always brought something with him – a box of Black Magic, or a bunch of carnations dyed in circus colours. Victoria accepted everything with a finely judged display of enthusiasm muted by physical frailty; she always became much iller when she heard Steve's heavy tread on the stairs. She let him pet her, too, without wincing, let him tousle her cropped head or stroke her blue-veined hand. One afternoon, though, she whispered to me, when she heard his wheezy breathing outside the front door, 'Oh Jesus, not again. I just can't face him this time. Tell him

I'm asleep,' and she pulled the blanket over her shoulder and rolled over to face the wall. I answered the door, and added another lie to the catalogue I had already told for her. Steve laid his paper cone of yellow chrysanthemums to one side. 'She needs her sleep,' he said. He and I sat by the gas fire with our mugs of tea. His face looked more creased and worn than ever, but try as I might I could see nothing in those lines that betrayed brutality. I could see nothing, really, except for a kind of bewildered concern. The hand that wasn't holding the tea hung slack, and I yearned to reach out and touch it as if my touch could restore it to life. But then in my head I heard Victoria's voice, 'Oh, what hasn't he done?', and I resurrected my guard.

'The trouble is,' Steve was saying, 'the trouble is, Ruthie, she can't trust a man. You know them wild horses she used to ride, out in Africa? She told you about those? That's what she's like, I reckon. She won't let a man's hand come near her. You think you're getting close, and then – she's off, and you're back where you started. Which is nowhere.'

I nodded. I didn't want to say much, but I knew what he meant.

'I can talk to you, Ruthie.' He leaned forward. 'I always know you'll understand.'

Just then there was a stirring from the bedroom, an elaborate noise of yawning and stretching. Victoria had steeled herself to receive him and was pretending to wake up. Steve jumped to his feet with an agility quite startling in so heavy a man. He took the chrysanthemums in to her. 'Hello, sweetheart,' I heard him say, 'I've brought some daffodils for you.'

★

So the play was played out until the end of his leave, and at that point Victoria recovered enough to convince Steve that it was all right to leave her. He went back to the rig, Aunt Marigold found Victoria a college room, and the landlord of the Cowley Road flat was paid off. My father was apprised of the situation ('Leave that to me,' said Marigold), and the end of term happened before Steve's next shore leave, so Victoria and I were ensconced at Westaby by the time he returned to find the flat empty and Victoria's letter of explanation Sellotaped to the kitchen work-surface. Tim was with us at Westaby; like my father, he sprang almost eagerly on the idea that Victoria – or perhaps both of us – would need to be protected from Steve, so he stayed the night with us, instead of going to his parents. Simon's was the only dissenting voice. He had been told not to open the door to Steve, unless my father or Tim were there.

'Why not?' demanded Simon. 'What's he done?'

Truthfulness and natural reticence combined to make it impossible for my father to give a satisfactory answer to that question. 'His behaviour towards Victoria has . . . upset her,' he replied, tight-lipped.

'Diddums,' said Simon. 'I bet she's upset him too, in her time.'

'Simon, this has to be taken seriously. Their marriage is going through a difficult patch, and – '

'What if he calls round to say he's sorry? One must always give people scope for repentance.' Simon mimicked my father's patient, reasonable tone.

'That's quite true, Simon, but under the circumstances it really would be better . . . I must insist . . .'

'If he comes round,' Simon declared, 'I'm going to ask him what he's done.'

My father tugged at his wings of hair, but he could extract no promise from Simon that Steve would not be granted admittance.

In the event, when Steve did turn up, Simon was the only one who was out. Steve had rung from a call-box, hot from finding the letter in the Oxford flat; Victoria put the phone down on him. My heart sank, because I knew that would only be a spur to him, and sure enough barely two hours later there he was, hammering on our front door. We had rehearsed this scene. My father let him in, and the rest of us gathered in the living-room to form a closed circle round Victoria. I hated my part in this; it tasted of treachery. But to refuse to participate would have been treacherous to Victoria, and that would have been far, far worse.

He stood there in front of us, swaying slightly, his head turning from side to side in a way that made me think of a bull. He had lost weight, even in the couple of weeks since I'd last seen him, and the folds of his face were furred with the beginning of a dark beard that made him look more gypsy-like than ever. He looked at each of us in turn – I hung my head – and then he said, 'Victoria, I need to see you on your own.'

My father, who was standing, his arm draped protectively along the mantelpiece, said, 'That's not possible, I'm afraid.' His voice was shrill, schoolmasterly. Then he added, more gently, 'I'm sorry.'

Steve ignored him. 'Victoria,' he said, 'you're a grown

woman, and you're my wife. If you was old enough to marry me, then you're old enough to tell me what's going on. In your own words.'

Aunt Marigold spoke. 'That was the trouble, Stephen. She wasn't old enough to marry you. In law, perhaps, but not in any other way. I blame myself – ' but he cut across her as if she had not spoken. He took two strides towards Victoria and seized her by the shoulders. The movement caused a couple of the Christmas cards on the mantelpiece to flutter down into the fire. They twisted and writhed on the hot coals, and no one rescued them. Tim and my father sprang across the room and prised Steve away from Victoria. He could have flattened them, I'm sure, but he didn't resist. He shook them aside, and walked towards the door alone. There he paused, and surveyed us once again. 'You too, Ruthie?' he said. I shrank into my chair. To my father he said, 'I always had you down for a decent man, but it turns out you're the worst snob of the lot.' He spat on the carpet – he could spit a long way. 'Nest of vipers,' he said, and was gone.

Nobody said a word until we heard the revving of the pick-up truck. Then Marigold went over to Victoria and said, 'My dear, are you all right?' and there was a general convergence on Victoria, in the process of which Tim ground the white mound of spit into the carpet with his toe. Victoria, bolt upright and smiling serenely as if she were a hostess receiving compliments, murmured, 'Oh yes, I'm quite all right.' Aunt Marigold said, 'So are we to assume that that is that?' but Victoria said, 'No, no. He'll be back. You don't know Steve.'

'Ah,' said my father, pondering a course of action. Marigold said, 'The Wintles.' The Wintles were my Cumbrian cousins, my mother's sister and her family. We didn't see very much of them, but they borrowed our cottage sometimes and stopped to visit us *en route*, and about every other year some of us – usually Simon and I, sometimes Victoria – would make the long train journey north to visit them. They were good, solid, dependable people, definitely a port in a storm.

At that moment Simon bumped his bicycle into the hall, and came in to find us all standing round Victoria as if she were in a hospital bed. 'I saw Steve driving off,' said Simon. 'What's up?' He looked as though he was asking Victoria, but she left my father to answer for her.

'Victoria has had a very difficult time,' he said, patting her arm. 'Stephen's behaviour has been . . . dishonourable. It will be best if they live apart, for the foreseeable future.'

'Why?' asked Simon. 'What's he done?'

There was a little silence. Then Marigold said, 'Simon, you shouldn't need to ask.'

Simon ignored her. 'Ruthie,' he said, 'do you know what he's done?' I swallowed and shook my head.

'A man's innocent until proved guilty,' said Simon.

My father stepped forward. 'Simon, that's enough. Your sister has been through – '

Simon said, 'She's not my sister.'

'Go to your room,' said my father, his tone as icy as I had ever heard it.

'Just a statement of fact,' said Simon, shrugging. Tim, hitherto silent, laid a hand on his shoulder. 'Go on, Si. Give her a break.' His voice was firm, not unfriendly, and Simon obeyed him. He left the room without another word. We heard him banging up the stairs, whistling, and we were left with Victoria who still sat in our midst as cool and unblinking as a snow maiden.

There was a need for words and action, which Aunt Marigold supplied. 'Julian, do ring the Wintles. We'll go there for Christmas. I can always put up in a B & B if they haven't enough room.'

'It's very short notice,' I ventured. 'Won't they mind?'

'Mind? This is an emergency. They don't have the option of minding. Now – supper. Come on, Victoria, and you too, Ruth. There's plenty to do. Sprouts and potatoes, and table laying. Timothy, I hope you're staying for supper?'

We spent ten days in Cumbria, and Steve didn't track us down. My Aunt Sarah, a primary-school teacher and a squatter, more prosaic version of my mother, cooked and bustled and fussed in a reassuring and space-occupying way; her three big boys, all still living at home, chopped wood and had snowball fights, and we all, except Aunt Sarah, avoided asking questions. Victoria spoke very little, that whole holiday. She glided about being quietly helpful, a distant smile glued to her lips, but she did not join the rest of us on our bracing tramps over the empty, ice-gripped landscape. We would leave her curled in the window seat of the long, low-ceilinged living-room, a detective novel or a newspaper to hand and the fat marmalade cat vibrating like a beehive on her lap; she would wave until we were out of sight, and a couple of hours later, when we returned red-cheeked and blowing, there she would still be sitting. She never looked as if she had stirred at all.

Aunt Sarah had my mother's honesty without my mother's tact. She believed herself to be everyone's natural confidante, and certainly she appeared to have an open and cheerful relationship with her three sons. Dispensing advice came to her as naturally as making all the beds straight after breakfast or cooking large meaty meals to satisfy male appetites. At the beginning of our stay, her calm smile and knowing exclamation of 'Ah!' whenever the subject of Victoria's marriage was approached indicated her certainty that she would be the one to coax out the truth. However, she soon discovered that Victoria's reserve was like a glass mountain in which no foothold could be found. Victoria managed to deflect each advance so swiftly that not the least offence could be taken. She was like a skater spinning on her heel.

After a while, Aunt Sarah gave up and turned to me instead. It was the day after Boxing Day and I was tailing Brussels sprouts – there was a dauntingly large sack of them on the scullery floor – while Aunt Sarah stripped the turkey carcass with a practised hand. 'Turkey and rice today,' she remarked, 'turkey soup tomorrow, and then we'll call it a day. I like to start the New Year turkey-free.' She glanced across the broad pine table at what I was doing. 'Ah! You cut a cross in them. Just like your mother. I only cut them across once. Life's too short for crosses.'

This wasn't intended as a rebuke, and I didn't take it as one. I examined the sprout I was holding. 'Mum had some little

286

story', I said, 'about why you had to make a cross. Something about letting the Devil out. I can't remember it now.'

Aunt Sarah laughed. 'I'm sure she did. Frances had a story about everything. Though why the Devil should take up residence in a Brussels sprout I can't imagine.' She pushed a twist of hair back from her face with the inside of her wrist, the only part of her hand that was free of turkey grease, and the gesture brought my mother back to me with an immediacy that was literally breathtaking; it made me gulp. I hung my head so that my own hair would fall over my face; I dreaded a rush of tears.

'You are very like your dear mother in some ways,' continued Aunt Sarah, 'and Victoria is very like hers. Though of course I only met Angela once or twice. Wouldn't you say they were alike, though?'

I could see no resemblance between respectable, limited, well-intentioned Aunt Angela and my bewitching, elusive sister-cousin. My Victoria wasn't to be compared with anyone. I didn't say so, though. All I said was, 'She does look rather like her, I suppose. Same hair.' Though even that wasn't true . . . Aunt Angela's hair was always neatly confined, arranged in keeping with whatever outfit she was wearing. Victoria's hair was an expression of herself, not of her wardrobe.

'I can't imagine Angela getting herself into the kind of pickle Victoria has made for herself, though,' reflected my living aunt. 'Poor child, she's had to grow up too quickly. What is it that this dreadful Steve has been up to, Ruth? Rape, is it? You must know all about it.'

Rape, is it? The phrase exploded between us as if somebody

287

had thrown down a rotten egg. Rarely had I felt so much at a loss. I had been trained to speak the truth, but how could I, when I didn't know how much of the truth I really knew? And my pride in being Victoria's secret twin prevented me from saying that I knew nothing, that she didn't confide in me. 'I . . . I think so,' I stammered, not sure who I was betraying. 'Something like that.' And then two of the big boy cousins burst in with the dogs, and Aunt Sarah lost her moment, and I avoided being alone with her for the rest of the time we were there.

When the snow melted, the return to Westaby had to be faced. There was a drift of letters on the front doormat, addressed to Victoria in Steve's big blocky handwriting in which upper and lower case were freely mixed. Victoria scooped them up without a word and shoved them all, unopened, into the Rayburn. She tamped them down hard with a poker, and as she did so she was almost smiling. But, of course, the burning of the letters didn't solve anything. The telephone calls were incessant. Usually my father answered; he was polite but firm. 'I'm afraid she doesn't want to speak to you. I think it would be very much better if you could resist ringing, at least for the time being.' When Aunt Marigold picked up the phone she was brisk. 'No, there's nothing anyone can do about it, least of all you. My advice is to leave well alone.' He got Simon, once. 'Oh, hi there, Steve. Did you have a happy Christmas?' Simon was the only person in the world who could have said that without the faintest tint of irony. I avoided answering, but once it rang at exactly the time I was expecting a call from Tim. When I heard Steve's voice, I froze. There was a tape, at that time, that someone had sent anonymously to the police which purported to be a message from the Yorkshire Ripper. It later turned out to be a hoax, but when I first heard it on the radio I remember telling myself, 'You are listening to the voice of pure evil.' Now Steve's voice sounded weirdly similar, growling and slow. 'Ruthie,' he pleaded, 'don't hang up on me. You're my last hope.' I hung up on him.

He didn't turn up, because he knew, I suppose, that there were so many of us protecting her like a princess in a tower, but once we were back at Oxford he haunted her. The first time, she was caught out. It was quite early in the morning, and she came back from the bathroom to find him in her college room, standing at the window, blocking out the light. I think he did hit her, that time, or at least shook her; she showed me the marks the pressure of his fingers had made on her thin yellow arms. After that she always locked her door, whether she was in or out. And she was often out. Sholto de Grey's rooms became her perfumed sanctuary. She never came to my house, because that was an obvious place for Steve to look.

There were the fortnightly respites, of course, when Steve went back to the rig. Victoria lived in terror of him chucking the job in, but so far this hadn't happened. We were young, and a fortnight was a long time; Victoria and I went out and about together, and laughed a lot and had what most girls of our age would recognize as fun. She dyed her already dark hair an even deeper shade of black and had her ears pierced, three holes in each. Round her neck she wore a little china skull on a thin black ribbon – some funny little thing she found on a market stall. She never seemed remotely ashamed to be seen with someone as firmly wedded to corduroy and hairy wool as I was, though she did suggest that there were other colours I could wear apart from brown.

The contents of my college pigeon hole were rarely interesting, but one morning I found an invitation in there amongst the Christian Union notices and the leaflets offering contraceptive advice. It was a proper engraved party invitation, very different from the folded sheets of wonky photocopying which heralded the parties of most of my friends. (Actually, getting invited to parties at all was a step up from the first term, when Katie, Maddy and I, at Katie's instigation, would loiter in the King's Arms on a Saturday night until somebody came in with a bottle under his arm, whereupon we would trail him at a discreet distance and gatecrash whichever party he was heading for.) No, this stiff piece of card was the real thing, and needless to say it came from Sholto. I was bidden to a 'Schoolmasters and Schoolgirls' party in his rooms on the following Saturday.

I felt a pang of guilt at the relief I felt when I realized that I was not expecting Tim that weekend. Tim was now in his final year, and his extra workload was the reason given for the decreasing frequency of our visits, but at the back of my mind I knew that, in the time we did spend together, a sense of duty was quietly overtaking simple pleasure in each other's company. I loved and respected Tim, and I didn't imagine at that stage that I would ever part from him, so intimately entangled had he become with the most important aspects of my life. But as for the fact that I would be free to go alone to Sholto's party – well, I was glad.

I enjoyed planning my schoolgirl's costume. I had a black pinafore dress that reached to midcalf, which resembled an old-fashioned gymslip; underneath it I wore a high-necked white blouse and thick grey tights. I had some flat leather sandals that I wore in the summer which made my feet look like plates, and a grey cardigan with a hole in one elbow. I parted my hair down the middle and screwed it into two little bunches above my ears. I wanted a felt hat, or a beret, but the only hat in the house was Maddy's, and that was a pink satin pillbox affair with a little veil. So I sallied forth hatless, and of course make-up-less, the image of a bun-faced schoolgirl. I stopped on the way for a bottle of wine. Our corner shop sold something pinkish called El Sol which cost 99p and which was what we usually took to parties, but somehow I didn't think I could take El Sol to Sholto's. I opted for a bottle of Valpolicella.

I didn't set out until half past nine; on foot, because my bicycle needed repair. I didn't want to be the first to arrive. It was a chilly night in early March, the wind like clear cold water, with a half-moon racing across a cloud-littered sky. In Cornmarket, town girls leaned against bus stops or stood in pairs in the doorways of shuttered shops, their denim skirts short, their bare thighs mottled. They folded their arms across their chests and laughed at the cold, and as I passed them I caught the gleam of their teeth and the whites of their eyes, polished by the wind. You didn't see undergraduates in Cornmarket on a Saturday night, except for a few lone males, donkey-jacketed, queuing for burgers. Feeling conspicuous in the sodium glow, I quickened my pace, making for the relative darkness of St Aldate's, uncomfortably aware of the foolish slap of my sandals and the sad jauntiness of my purple-wrapped bottle. I wished I'd arranged to meet Victoria beforehand, so I could have slipped in under the shadow of her grand entrance.

There was no one to notice me in the splendid space of Tom Quad. A group of roaring young men were busy throwing someone into the fountain; I skirted through the shadows to Peckwater. I could hear the noise of Sholto's party as I climbed the stairs – the familiar rising whine of frenetic hilarity – but unusually for an undergraduate party there was no music.

The door was opened for me. Trevor stood there, dressed like a butler in a costume drama, trying to dampen a grin of childish excitement. 'Your coat, madam?' he said, removing it. 'And a little refreshment?' He brought out a tray on which was a mirror arranged with neat lines of white powder. This he balanced with some skill on the flat of his hand, while with his other hand he held out a rolled-up ten-pound note. 'Er . . . no thanks, Trev,' I said, apologetically. 'Just a drink, please.' Pink champagne, in a proper flute, appeared from somewhere behind the door.

I sipped, and took stock. The room was seething. There seemed to be people piled on top of other people. In my memory of it, afterwards, I saw people stacked as high as the ceiling, like acrobats, but of course they can't have been. There were few men, as far as I could see, just piles of incredible girls, none of whom I recognized. They wore black stockings – fishnet, some of them – and suspenders, and spike-heeled black shoes, and tiny little tunics with pleated skirts and no blouse on underneath. The girl nearest me wheeled round and bumped into me, spilling my champagne, some of which rolled into her cleavage. She stuck a finger down, licked it, and giggled. Most of the rest of the champagne landed on my wrist, soaking my buttoned cuff.

'Sorry,' I said to the girl, which turned out to be the only word I said to anyone at that party, apart from Trevor. I saw Sholto in the middle of the room, rook-like in flowing gown and mortarboard; I saw him flex a cane across the palm of his hand, and I saw his long teeth bared as his mouth stretched in laughter. And next to him, reclining, somehow, along the back of his sofa, I saw Victoria, dressed like the other girls, only more so. She had on an undergraduate gown, pinned together, but only just; from beneath it her stockinged legs uncoiled like black wires. She'd had her hair cut again; her eyes were black slashes, and her mouth a crimson one. As I watched, Sholto bent over her and gave her earlobe the tiniest possible bite.

She hadn't seen me. I had hardly moved three feet in from the door. I was hot in my high-necked blouse and my knitted tights, but still I felt my skin tighten. I took a step or two forward, knocking into someone, a girl with arched eyebrows and a sheet of white-blonde hair. 'Oh, for God's sake,' she said. I turned, and fled.

I had reached the top of the stairs when I remembered my coat. I hesitated, hating to go back, but dreading still more the need to return to retrieve it the next day. There was a shout of 'Hey!' and Trevor appeared, holding it out, my beloved brown duffle-coat. He helped me on with it. 'Not your scene,' he said, to the back of my head. 'Never mind.' My throat ached as if I was going to cry, so I didn't reply, just patted his arm, and scooted out into the welcome night.

I walked the long way back through dim side-streets, careless of drunks or rapists. I walked as hard and as fast as I could, trying to dissolve the lump of obdurate shame that lodged in my breast, uncomfortable and unmanageable, like a boiled sweet swallowed before you've sucked it enough. The shame was all for myself, for my silly schoolgirl costume that showed me up for what I really was. The whole party had been a sophisticated game, and I had only the shadowiest under-standing of its rules. But Victoria had known. She had been there, right in the centre, the star of the circus act. But how? What instinct did she have that I so humiliatingly lacked?

By the time I turned the corner into the flat-fronted brick terrace where I lived, I was comforting myself with jokes. For Maddy and Katie's benefit I formulated a humorous description of the evening in my head; I did hope they would be in. But as I turned the key in the lock I remembered that they would not. They had gone to hear a band play in an unglamorous club in Headington. I could have gone with them. I would have had much more fun.

Oh, well, I thought as I filled the kettle, there's much to be said for an early night with a good book. I made myself a peanut-butter sandwich and snatched bites from it as I got ready for bed. I turned my gas fire up as high as it would go and curled up in my armchair in my dressing-gown and slipper socks, a Margaret Atwood to hand.

The knock was at my window, not at the door. Katie and Maddy must have forgotten their keys, I thought. Or perhaps Victoria had had enough of schoolgirls and schoolmasters. So certain was I that the knocker was female that I answered the door with my dressing-gown hanging open. My nightshirt was short, and haphazardly buttoned.

I wasn't prepared for Steve. He looked ill and unsmiling; he barely greeted me, and he was in my bedroom before I could divert him to the kitchen. 'No, no tea,' he said. 'None of that crap. Where is she, Ruthie? I've got to know.'

'I don't know,' I said. 'Out. It's Saturday night, remember.'

'You're lying,' he said. 'You do know.' He fixed his eyes on my face, but I saw a flicker of a glance run up and down my body, first.

'All right,' I said, 'I do know. She's at a party. But no, I'm not telling you where. She's got a right to go out, Steve. She's not living with you any more.'

He flumped down on the edge of my bed and rubbed his unshaven chin with his hands. With the deep sigh that escaped him I felt my old urge of sympathy return. I sat down next to him. It would have seemed rude not to. 'Steve,' I said, softly, 'you have to accept it. The marriage is over.'

His head jerked up. 'Marriage? What marriage? There never was no marriage. Let me tell you something, young lady, even though this ain't the kind of thing that's fit for a vicar's daughter to hear. That precious sister of yours wouldn't let me touch her. I'm talking about non-consummation here.'

My head span. I cleared my throat for a suitably bland response, but none seemed called for. Steve was still talking, the weight of his shoulder resting against mine.

'At first it was all, "Wait till we're married. I'm saving myself for marriage." And I believed it, seeing as she was young, and what with your dad and everything. Oh, she was a tease; she'd let me go so far and no further, and I was desperate, I can tell you that. I never wanted no one like I wanted her. So then we got married because I thought that was what she wanted, and we had a few tries, but she'd always pull away from me. She said it was like a serrated knife.'

I thought of Victoria, sobbing in the caravan, 'I just don't know if I can do it.' Still I said nothing. Steve was too heavy against me, but I didn't move.

'Then she stopped trying, and there was always reasons. "I'm not feeling well, I'm nervous about Oxford, it's the wrong time of the month." All that kind of rubbish. Then there was all these deadlines! "We'll do it at Christmas, it'll be your Christmas present. We'll do it on Valentine's Day. We'll do it on my birthday, I promise."'

I nodded. Now Victoria's birthday tea party made more sense to me. All that champagne. All those cakes. Steve passing out on the floor.

'Since then, nothing. She can't stand the sight of me, I know that. When she cut her hair, that's when I knew. I always told her I loved her hair.'

I said, in a whisper, 'I loved it too.'

He put his arms round me, held my head against his shoulder. He said, 'I swear to God, Ruthie, I've done nothing wrong,' and I said, 'I know. I know.' Then he twisted round, and his hot sour mouth was on mine, and his hands were on my breasts. I tried to pull free, but he was very strong. He said, 'Ruthie. Just this once. Let me, and I'll leave her alone.' He pushed me backwards, tugging at his belt. 'Oh Jesus,' he said, 'this is something I've got to do.'

So I let him. I wasn't sure whether I had any choice. When his face, red and puffing, loomed over mine, I scrunched my eyes shut, and forced my mind to fly out of my body and hover in a corner of the ceiling where the lamplight couldn't reach. So I made love to Victoria's husband, and he held me afterwards, more tenderly than anyone else had ever done. I lay there immobile, trying not to breathe in his stale smokiness, willing him to go, but when he dressed and slipped out into the night I found slow tears sliding down on to my pillow and it seemed that, after all, I had wanted him to stay.

26

Steve's visit had one immediate effect: it made me certain that the time had come to break with Tim. I didn't have to tell Tim about Steve – I couldn't possibly tell him about Steve – but I did have to finish with him because I wasn't any longer the sort of person he thought I was. Steve was gone, and none of us would be seeing him again. I knew he would keep his word to me, and leave Victoria alone. Soon, very soon, poor Tim would be gone too. When I imagined my manless future I saw a pale, quiet landscape; I saw a lemony sunrise reflected on still water, and I felt clean and lonely and at peace.

It was important to make the break with Tim as soon as possible, partly to minimize the occasions for dishonesty, partly because it was already nearly the end of term and Tim had to revise for his finals – it was only fair to give him as much time as possible to get over me (two to three weeks, I reckoned modestly) so that it didn't interfere too much with his revision. I was terribly considerate. There was no reason not to be. I felt no animosity towards Tim, only pity and respect and an eye-pricking nostalgia for our shared past.

Telling him by letter would be easiest, but I knew Tim would see that as cowardly, and I did want to keep what was left of my integrity intact. He was due to visit me in Oxford the following weekend, the last weekend of the Lent term. I often wrote to him on Sunday evenings, long, friendly letters about books I'd read, films I'd seen, essays I'd got stuck on. Such a letter, this time, would be a kind of lie in itself, this rainy Sunday when I could still smell Steve in my room, in my hair, in my bed. So I just sent Tim a postcard. It was of Piero di Cosimo's 'Forest Fire', which was one of my favourite pictures in the Ashmolean. It was highly coloured, like a child's dream of danger, and it didn't seem to carry any hidden meanings that could worry Tim. I filled most of the space up with comments about the picture, and then I put 'V. busy. No time for more,' which wasn't true. Last of all I put 'See you next Friday,' and I made my handwriting larger than usual so that there was no room for my customary signing off which was 'All my love dear Tim.' Instead I just put 'R' and a couple of kisses.

All week the calculations went round in my head. He usually arrived at about eight in the evening. I met him from the bus station, and we ate pasties in a pub near Walton Street where some Irish fiddlers played. Tim's taste, not mine. Then we went back to my house, and if Katie or Maddy were about we talked to them for a bit, and then – well, then we went to bed. So I had got to tell him before that point, because going to bed with him when he hadn't been told would be a wretched thing to do. It wouldn't be fair or easy to tell him in the pub, either, with the noise and the people who always greeted us, so I would have to start talking almost as soon as he got off the coach. He always looked so eager to see me as he unfurled himself after his long journey, and I hated to crush that eagerness, but that was what I resolved to do.

I didn't, of course. Luck wasn't with me. Tim stepped off the coach in a mood that was not only eager but exceptionally loving. He swept me into his arms and told me I was looking great – perhaps I was, anxiety sometimes makes my eyes glitter and my face look less comfortable and well fed – and almost immediately he started talking about the Easter holidays and how he was going to take a long weekend off and devote it totally to me, and maybe we could go to Dublin because that was somewhere which had caught both our fancies. I said, 'Tim, I don't feel like the pub tonight. Shall we go for a walk?' And he said, 'Sure. It's a beautiful night.' And it was. We walked across Port Meadow and watched the lavender dusk deepen into night; we prowled round the outside of the little church that nestled down fatly in the darkness like a mother hen. When we turned back, our Kickers squelching in unseen mud, the moon, now just past full, threw our Giacometti shadows down on the turf. We leaned against a gate and Tim kissed me a lot, and I let him, and still I hadn't told him.

Back in Jericho we made a detour for fried rice and spring rolls. We took the sweaty carrier bag home and ate in my kitchen, and still I didn't tell him. Maddy was out with Ned, her glamorous new OUDS boyfriend. Katie joined us in the kitchen and picked the hard little prawns out of our rice as she told Tim about how much she fancied her Middle English lecturer. Katie will always tell anybody anything. He was about fifty, Katie admitted, but she loved the way he swung his legs when he got down from his bicycle, and the languorous way he pronounced 'Sir Gawaine', it sent shivers down her spine. Tim laughed at her in a friendly way and then washed out the greasy aluminium boxes left over from our meal because he always recycled everything, and then we went to bed, and still I hadn't told him.

I lay in bed with my face to the wall. I knew what Tim was doing – he was fumbling in his knapsack for his condoms. I'd stopped taking the Pill since our encounters had become less frequent. This was Tim's suggestion. He said he didn't like the thought of what those chemicals might be doing to my body. I thought, I've still time to say something, but I didn't. He switched the light off and climbed into bed, and I let him roll me over towards him. When I heard the sticky stretch of the rubber I did think, just fleetingly, that Steve and I hadn't used anything, but then I just thought, oh well, I'm probably infertile anyway. And I reached out to Tim and put my arms round his neck.

Afterwards he said, 'You didn't enjoy that much. I'm sorry.' I opened my mouth to say it was nothing, I was just tired, but then I thought, No, no, just tell him, for Christ's sake. So I told him, lying there in the dark, and he was completely and utterly baffled. I tried, 'I just don't think it's working,' and 'We've been together for too long,' and 'We're too young to tie ourselves down,' but he rebuffed all of these with arguments of solid sense and logic. At last I said, 'Tim, believe me. I mean it.' He said, in a very small voice, 'There's somebody else, isn't there?' And I said, in a voice that sounded cold and harsh, 'Yes there is. But it's no one you know.' Which was not what I had meant to say at all.

Tim pulled his arm out from behind my head, where it had somehow stayed. He got out of bed and then sat on the edge, his shoulders hunched, just as Steve had done less than a week before. He clasped and unclasped his hand and said, 'I can't believe that you let me . . . just now. I just can't believe that you let me go through with that.' I couldn't believe it either.

He pulled his clothes on, retrieved his ex-army coat from where he'd bundled it in a corner. I said, 'Tim, don't go. You can't. Where will you go to?' I clung on to him, naked, and his big metal buttons pressed into my flesh. He shook me off. He said, 'First Victoria, now you. I just can't bloody believe it.' I said, 'We're not the same. We're not.' His face was grim, set. He said, 'You are. You might as well be.' And he left, slamming the door. I called out to the vibrating house, 'I'm not, I'm not. I'm not the same as her,' but when I thought about it – which I did, all night – it didn't seem clear to me what the real differences were.

I never found out where Tim went that night. I knew he was all right – I mean, all right-ish – because I came across him at Westaby a couple of times during the Easter holidays and we had short, civil, strained conversations which at least assured me that he was in no danger of going off the rails. The last time we met was in the village post office. I said, 'Maybe we should meet for a drink,' and he said, 'I don't think there would be much point.' I fiddled with the string on the parcel I was posting for my father. 'Oh. Well, good luck with your finals,' I said, and Tim said, 'Yeah. Thanks,' and turned away.

I didn't see much of Victoria that holiday. First she went off with Sholto to a house party in some West Country mansion, and then I stayed with Katie in her parents' snug Janet-and-

John house in Thames Ditton, so we didn't overlap much. Katie's house had a green-painted garden gate and crazy paving the colour of old skin. I liked it; I liked the stained-glass panels in the front door and the seedlings in the greenhouse and the round, humming tortoiseshell cat. I tried my hardest not to think about Steve or Tim; I just wanted to have a simple girlie time, reading and talking and looking at the places that had mattered to Katie in her girlhood. I felt vaguely carsick all the time except when I was eating, so I ate, though I only fancied dry, crispy, salty food. The wetness of salad made me feel worse. The first missed period I put down to emotional upheaval; Katie's kind, bosomy mother told me I was looking peaky, and said perhaps I was anaemic. She made me drink Ovaltine; I pulled down my lower eyelids in front of the mirror and imagined that the pink rim looked pale. I thought yes, perhaps anaemic was right. Anaemic, and still a bit upset underneath.

In the end, I only had two days of knowing I was pregnant. The queasiness hadn't lessened once I was back at Oxford, but I still would never have thought of it for myself, if one day Maddy hadn't come crashing into the kitchen shouting with rather exaggerated relief because her period had started. The first time with Ned, she declared, the condom had split, and then, 'Jesus, I felt so *sick*! But it must have been the vodka after all, because I'm not, I'm not!' I was sitting at the table sipping tea and trying to think myself out of my nausea, but with Maddy's announcement I just knew. I said nothing, but after that morning's tutorial I slipped off to the Family Planning Clinic and they took a urine sample. When the result came through positive they weighed me and took my blood pressure, and sat me down with a little dial thing and said my baby was due at the end of November. I was perfectly calm, because I had a powerful sense that this wasn't happening to me, that the real me was watching from quite a long way off. And then they said, 'Is this a wanted baby?' and I said, 'I don't really know.'

I was told to come back for counselling and discussion, and was given an appointment for the following week. 'Don't worry,' they said, 'you're only nine weeks. There's plenty of time.' They sent me away with some leaflets; I remember a drawing of a pregnant woman with a transparent stomach, with wholesome things like a loaf of brown bread, a bottle of milk, some oranges, and a fish fanned out round her and her coiled baby. I sat on the edge of my bed, where Steve had sat, where Tim had sat, and I read the leaflets and tried to imagine that my own stomach was transparent, tried to see through to where Steve's child lay, because if I could see it, I thought, then I would know what to do.

I spent the next two days walking. The weather was the kind they use when they set costume dramas in Oxford, the sweet, rustling, dancing weather of full spring. I walked along the banks of the Cherwell, past punts full of laughing lovers and other people's friends. I reached a field that was washed emerald with new shoots of wheat, and I ran all the way round the edge of it. I ran and ran and ran, close to the hedge, like a horse that has gone mad.

On the evening of the second day of walking the pains began. My abdomen felt at once tight and heavy, as if something

304

was dragging at me from below. As I picked at my supper — Maddy's vegetarian chilli, which was the best thing she made, but which I just couldn't eat — I told the others that it was the beginning of a really bad period, and they put me to bed with a hot-water bottle and the bottle of gin that Katie's lovely mother equipped her with for just such occasions. They were both going out, thank goodness; it was the day before May Day, and they were going to parties that were meant to last all night. I said no, I couldn't face coming, and yes, of course I'd be fine, and yes, if I felt better I'd join them later. I held the hot-water bottle to my stomach and sipped the gin, and that did take the edge off it. I spread towels over my bottom sheet, because I didn't quite know what to expect, but I thought there might well be blood.

There was, though not much at first. At about midnight I crawled to the lavatory, bent double with pain. I sat there for ages with my head in my hands and then something happened which was like a letting go, and I slid off the seat and knelt on the floor, shivering and retching. When I dared I looked into the lavatory bowl, and there I saw dark clots, and grey skeins, and something small and pale, not much bigger than a thumbnail, humped like a new moon. I took a toothmug and scooped it out, and carried it back to my room. There I set it on my dressing-table. I could see the bump of its brow, the dark bulge of its eye. It reminded me of the trout alevins we used to hatch in the biology lab at school. 'Little thing,' I said aloud, 'you were never meant to happen.' I searched my drawer for a suitable container, and drew out the narrow box that held the mourning band Aunt Marigold had given me for my sixteenth birthday, the last birthday before my mother died. It was my one precious thing. I took it out, the diamond-heavy band, and held it up to catch its winking glitter.

I laid the band back in my drawer and covered it with socks and tights. Then I tipped my inch of baby on to a folded handkerchief and laid it in its coffin, on its sumptuous velvet bed of midnight blue. I was about to close the box, but I knew that once I did I would never be able to open it again. I sat on the bed for a few minutes, waiting for the moment to come that would tell me what to do. I took a towel and wiped at the trickles of blood that were snaking down my legs.

I found my writing paper and a pen. In my most careful italics I wrote 'Thomas Stephen Cruttenden. First of May 1979.' Thomas because it had always been my favourite boy's name, Stephen for his father. No, of course I couldn't see whether that little luminous semi-circle was in fact a boy, but it never occurred to me that it wasn't. I folded the paper over and over, and as I did so I remembered that it was Victoria's twentieth birthday.

I put the paper into the jewellery box, snapped shut the two brass hooks. Then I lay down on my bloody towels and closed my eyes. I was pretty certain of being alone all night. I could bleed to death, I thought, cradling my aching stomach. It never occurred to me to call a doctor. I can face death if I have to, I told myself, my mind calm. I've got all night to prepare for it. The thought was almost luxurious.

I did sleep, though, and woke to May sunlight striking through the chinks in the curtains. I flexed my muscles, cautiously; stretched out one limb and then another. I pushed myself up to see if I could sit. I felt trembly, but no longer sick, and definitely alive.

I dressed, put wads of cotton wool inside my knickers, and picked up the little box. At the back of the house was a garden of sorts, where Katie grew a few herbs in buckets, and an old apple tree corkscrewed up out of the blowing grass. Some daffodils, withered now, grew at its foot. I dug a hole with Katie's trowel. I dug as deep as my strength would allow, and then I buried the little box. On top I put back the daffodil bulbs I had displaced; next spring, I thought, they'll bloom again. From the apple tree I snapped off one blossoming twig and laid it on top of all. Brown was already staining the pink and white of the pearly flowers.

Then I cleaned up the bathroom, and gathered up all the clothes and sheets and towels that bore the evidence of last night's loss. I carried them to the launderette in Walton Street and sat there for the whole cycle, doing nothing, thinking nothing, just watching the clothes spin round and round. I'm thirty-seven now (well, just), but that's the only time I've ever been pregnant. It's funny, really, I suppose.

27

Victoria lived a high-speed, hectically coloured, Sholto-centred life that summer term, and then quite suddenly it all crashed. For the first four weeks I saw very little of her. Every so often I dragged myself to her room – going anywhere in that lost-baby time was a drag, a physical and mental effort spurred only by force of habit and a respect for force of habit – but she was usually out, and for me that was something of a relief. The notepad stuck to the outside of her door was covered with cryptic scrawls from people I could not identify. I would add my own more mundane message, and feel satisfied; I had maintained contact without danger of exposure. When I reminded myself that I had slept with Victoria's husband and miscarried his baby, all without a word to her, the sense of betrayal made my head spin. Much easier to leave a friendly note and slink off home to my books and my dressing-gown and my cheery, busy friends who were so wholly unaware.

We met for lunch, once, in a narrow, healthy place near Little Clarendon Street, where spider plants in macramé baskets swung overhead, and Victoria yawned and yawned and picked the bamboo shoots out of her salad. Lunchtime, I gathered, had become for her what five in the morning would be for most of us. Between yawns, a picture of her life pieced itself together, of parties and yet more parties and punting by moonlight, of spur-of-the-moment sorties in sports cars to London and Scotland, of champagne and old lace in the crumbling ballrooms of aristocrats, and beer and gobs of spit in punk clubs in Soho basements. Adventure was what she craved, just as I shunned it in equal measure. 'And what about you?' she asked as our coffees arrived. 'I've never really heard about why you split up with Tim.' But I was spared a reply by the noisy entrance of a couple of acquaintances of hers, who shrieked where the fuck could you get cocktails at this time of day? Not here, that was obvious. They towed Victoria off with them; I declined the extended invitation, and stayed behind to pay the modest bill, and that was the last I saw of her for some weeks.

And then, right at the end of that term – such a quiet, melancholy term for me – came an urgent summons from Aunt Marigold, and the beginning of Victoria's long retreat. It looked like a suicide attempt, but it couldn't possibly have been. Both Marigold and I were agreed on that, as we stood by Victoria's sleeping figure in the John Radcliffe Infirmary. She had swallowed too much of something, or of several things, but there was no note, no sense of a cry for help, no visible despair. Her scout had found her, and would have thought she was only sleeping had she not been lying, fully dressed – or as fully dressed as Victoria ever was in those days, which wasn't very – on the floor. Medically it was all quite easy. Her stomach was pumped, she was kept in for observation for a couple of days, during which time Marigold and I reiterated to each other that, while Victoria might enjoy sailing close to the edge, there was something tightly woven inside her that was never going to unravel; then we packed up her things – no clues amongst them, all anonymous and orderly – and my father drove her home to Westaby, where she lay on the sofa like a nineteenth-century heroine, with hot lemon and honey and a little bell beside her, and thin hands fluttering moth-like on the counterpane.

Aunt Marigold convinced herself, and therefore convinced my father, that Victoria must have been slipped something 'at one of these parties. Her drink must have been spiked,' she said, using what she imagined to be the language of a world of which she had no knowledge. I could not connect my sister-cousin with so haphazard a disaster. I kept my opinions to myself, but I felt sure that whatever Victoria had done she had done deliberately, as a dramatic and final escape from a situation which, for reasons unknown to me, had ceased to suit her. It soon became clear that Sholto was a thing of the past. If he made any attempt to contact her, I was not aware of it. He certainly made no attempt to contact me.

Victoria spun out her invalid status for as long as she reasonably could, and I think the whole family enjoyed it. My father's attempts at waiting on her were irritating and endearing in equal measure. He was endlessly solicitous; was she warm enough? Too warm? The sunlight must be striking her full in the face – should he draw the curtain? (Victoria was never so weak that she could not turn her head to avoid a sunbeam.) Would it tire her to read the newspaper, was the wireless too loud? He would not contemplate leaving her alone in the house, so he organized a rota of well-meaning women, the wives of housemasters and of local clergy, to sit with her during the times when none of us was in. I think these women were the only reason that Victoria ever decided to end her illness. Nothing short of Mrs Pedlow and her crochet work and her unedited anecdotal style – 'I was saying to your father on Tuesday – or was it Wednesday? No, it must have been Tuesday because it was after I picked up my repeat prescription and they only have afternoon surgery on a Wednesday' – nothing less could have dislodged Victoria from her comfortable and advantageous position on the living-room sofa.

Simon, still furious with me because of Tim's departure, got on better with Victoria during her convalescence than he had ever done before. Simon was in the sixth-form at Westaby now, and struggling – or rather, not struggling; it was the school that was struggling to hang on to him. His attendance at lessons was erratic, the handing in of his preps even more so, and yet nobody could ever quite write him off as lazy or disobedient. He forgot things. He forgot where things were kept, or why certain tasks had to be completed. When challenged, he simply explained that he had forgotten, and the look on his face was more puzzled than stricken. Everyone believed him. As a child, Simon had been very slow to grasp the principle of lying; he said he didn't see the point. 'Lies are boring,' he said. 'They're just hot air.' Now, at the age of sixteen, his ruling passion was Third World politics; he was especially interested in ex-colonial Africa. On Saturday he worked for no pay in a shop-cum-warehouse organized on fair-trade principles. He subscribed to several slender magazines, printed on paper so thin it almost felt wet, and he had amassed a great deal of knowledge about self-help irrigation projects. He took advantage of Victoria's prostration to explain these to her in some detail. To my surprise, her responses were placid and unsarcastic. I wondered at Simon's change of heart; he, alone in the family, had always seemed impervious to, if not suspicious of, Victoria's charms. I suppose he just needed someone, and he wasn't spoilt for choice. Poor Simon, there weren't many people in his life, and the ones he had weren't much use to him. The new, softened Victoria offered him something that he needed as even the thorniest plant needs water.

It occurred to me that Victoria's unwavering niceness to those around her – including Mrs Pedlow – was all part of a long-term settling-in plan. My aunt and father harboured the illusion that she would return to Oxford and complete her degree, if not this coming Michaelmas, then after just one year off for recovering her full strength. Victoria said nothing to dispel this notion, but every day that passed saw her settled down more rootedly at Westaby. She had decided, for undivulged reasons, to make herself indispensable.

When I followed Victoria home, about a week after her collapse, I found her already established in a kind of consultative role. My father had taken to showing her essays written by his pupils, on which Victoria would write marginal notes in faint pencil. Each morning she would talk Simon through his day – school term carried on for several weeks after Oxford had finished – making him show her the contents of his school bag, ticking off work completed and underlining tasks still to be undertaken in a little yellow notebook. Other people, myself included, had tried to organize Simon in the past, but to none had he submitted with so good a grace. Mrs Pedlow, in conjunction with her friend Mrs Flaherty, had volunteered to make us some new curtains for the living-room. (The existing ones had come with us from Gadham, and doubtless from the Lincolnshire rectory before that. They were made of a coarse open-weave fabric and had once been blue, but where age and sunlight had worked on the folds they were now striped a dirty moss green. They had never really fitted; when you tried to close them there was a depressing gap.) Now these two excellent women brought swatches of fabric samples to show Victoria, and knelt by her side discussing chintzy merits and demerits with enormous concentration.

And I, too, found myself drawn to her once again. I sat on an old beanbag with my back against her sofa, and this way, with our faces half averted, we told each other confidences. I don't think they were real confidences. I talked about finishing with Tim, but I was careful; I didn't say anything that she couldn't have inferred for herself. She said, 'And how do you feel about him now?' I replied, 'Just sorry for him. And a bit embarrassed.' 'That's how I felt, too,' cried Victoria. 'That's the trouble. That way of feeling is not very . . . lust-making, is it?' We both laughed, and the subject was dropped, and that was the closest we ever came to talking about having sex with, or not having sex with, poor Tim.

In return, Victoria told me a beautiful story about a party that lasted a whole weekend. It was in a ruined castle ('Well, a bit of a castle, with a house built on the side') owned by a cousin of Sholto's called Tancred (the name made me suspect her of making it all up, but there are people called Tancred in the world, and it stands to reason that they should be related to people called Sholto). Sholto had set up a poker game, she said, with her, Victoria, as the prize. She had thought it was a joke and had gone along with it, but Tancred, who was six foot five and had had the bridge of his nose reconstructed because he snorted so much cocaine, had won, and had claimed his reward. He took a fur coat out of a cupboard and held it out to her – an enormous coat, floor length, of Arctic fox, she thought. 'Come to my room,' he ordered. 'Wear this, and nothing else, I'll be waiting.' Still half laughing, Victoria had turned to appeal to Sholto, but one glance at his face had shown her that no help would be forthcoming. 'Go ahead,' he said, 'I'll be watching.' Victoria shuddered at the memory. 'His face was terrible,' she said. 'Kind of all slack and staring. He looked like a gargoyle.'

'So what did you do?'

'I pretended I was going outside to change, and I climbed out of a window and dropped down like they show you how to in fire practices at school. Then I walked and walked until I found a main road. A lorry gave me a lift back to Oxford. I was back in my room at six in the morning, and still felt lousy so I took a load of paracetamol. Too many, obviously, but I didn't know. That was all it was – paracetamol. Hey, Ruthie, you won't tell anyone, will you?'

'Of course not,' I said, and meant it. I would never have told anyone this story, partly because I was good at keeping confidences, and partly because I knew it wasn't true. The top layer of my mind accepted it, because I'd always found it difficult not to believe Victoria, but below that, the story put down no roots.

She didn't talk about Steve. We didn't always talk about anything, much. Sometimes I read to her – despite her private claim to me that all she'd done was swallow a few paracetamol, she still chose to behave as if she was suffering from a lingering illness, and I chose to play along with her – and sometimes I just read to myself while she dozed. Once, I was in danger of telling her about the miscarriage. It was a dim, cloudy afternoon, chilly for July, and the fully clothed trees crowded motionless round the house, their clotted darkness pressing at the windows and pushing the two of us still closer together. I wanted to tell her something that would make an impact; I wanted to matter. There was no one else in the house, and I could so easily just say it. I felt dizzy with the power I had, the power to make her take notice. But then Simon, whistling nothing recognizable, bumped his bike into the hall, and the moment passed.

Victoria's month on the sofa brought us together as a family; it gave a new shape to our lives. At the end of July she announced that she was well enough to travel, so we packed up and set off for Dorset and Aunt Marigold joined us there. In quiet, homey hours that summer wore away. Victoria relinquished her illness only in stages. Throughout August the quality and quantity of her sleep, the danger of her becoming over-tired on her short walks, the size and nature of her appetite, remained fit subjects for daily discussion amongst the rest of us. Even Simon, famously oblivious to the needs of other people, opined that she should not go out in the middle of the day when the sun was at its hottest, and he fetched and carried for her without having to be asked.

I was mesmerized, lulled by an age-old rhythm of walks and talks and family meals. There had been a plan that I should join a group of my college friends in Edinburgh for the fringe festival; I quietly forgot it. I wrote no letters, made no telephone calls. Any part of the outside world seemed intrusive; all I wanted to listen to was the murmur of the summer garden, the slow swing of the sea. The days were washed away like wave-licked sand. By the time we returned to Westaby it had been tacitly accepted by all of us, even Aunt Marigold, that in October I would be returning to Oxford alone. There had been a shift, somewhere, and Victoria's place was now at home.

I went back cheerfully and calmly, back to the Jericho house which Katie and Maddy and I had agreed to rent for another year, back to my work and my friends feeling soothed and fed and whole, and if I thought about the little box buried beneath the apple tree my thoughts did not rise up and haunt me. Marigold, in consultation with her college authorities, had arranged a year off for Victoria; on health grounds, she was to spend a quiet year at home. Then she would arise, invigorated, and sweep back to Oxford, and scoop up the glittering prizes that were hers by right. That, at any rate, was the adults' idea. For my part, I sensed that her departure from Oxford had been final. Victoria never revised things, never retraced her tracks. I settled down to enjoy my last year. Her absence made the place more ordinary, but also easier. Broad daylight had replaced a world of flickerings and halftones.

She wrote to me, often. Her long letters, scribbled in biro

316

on lined A4, described every detail of Westaby society. She gathered up scraps of College gossip and intrigue and rearranged them in a way that was as entertaining as any novel. Though incidents and characters were coloured and distorted for my amusement, I recognized the essential accuracy of the picture, and I recognized, too, as time went on, that Victoria had infiltrated at every level. She was no longer the ex-sixth former, the master's daughter who had moved on, as they all do, to start her own life. She became my father's right hand, secretary, prop and stay, a mother substitute for Simon and a fittingly reliable and intelligent partner for the deputy head of Westaby College. When I came home for Christmas her hair had grown back almost to shoulder length; the black dye had long since grown out. She wore it bobbed, with a neat fringe. She had on a high-necked woollen dress, dark green with a maroon paisley pattern, and she was in the middle of inviting masters and their wives to end-of-term sherry and mince pies.

I didn't stay at home for long, that holiday, because just a couple of weeks earlier I had met Daniel. Daniel was in the same year as me, reading the same subject, though at a different college; I suppose I had known him by sight, through lectures, for a long time, but it was only – I realized in retrospect – once Victoria's eclipsing presence had been removed that I could allow myself to look squarely at the glory that Daniel was. Because he really was glorious to me. He was a public-school boy who was anxious to shake off the fetters of his class. He wanted to make a career as a left-wing journalist – the reason I first met him properly was because he came to our house for a meeting with Maddy, who was on the editorial committee of the radical student magazine he had helped to launch. He espoused many of the causes that Tim and Simon considered important, but unlike either of them he had a lightness of touch, an iconoclastic humour, and a sense of self-ease that gave grace to his reforming energy. He was utterly at home inside his tall, well-knit body. His movements were fluent and confident; his voice, though not especially loud, was the voice you always noticed first at any gathering. He wore his curly hair cut very short, as most young men did that year; he had a hooked, bony nose and a strong jaw, usually dusted with a couple of days' growth of stubble, which in my opinion made him look manly and distinguished. He was warm, he was tender, he took to me at once. Oh, he was lovely, my Daniel.

I didn't take him home for ages and ages. I needed to be sure of him first. I knew he would disapprove, and probably mock, the two institutions that shaped the life of my family – Westaby College and the Anglican Church – and I didn't want him to see how much a part of this life I still was, until I knew that he would stick with me come what may. And I felt a bit shy about him meeting Victoria, because I thought he would take against her in her new, middle-aged guise, and it was still important to me to have everybody love her. During the holidays, Christmas and Easter, we stayed in Oxford for much of the time – Daniel more or less lived in the Jericho house, which Maddy and Katie were very good about – and I paid fleeting visits home, where my absences were readily accepted as a need to work for finals undisturbed. It was not that I kept Daniel secret. I mentioned him in my letters, in an 'Oh, by-the-way' manner. I told them about his politics, his journalistic ambitions, his background. (He was a Londoner; his mother worked in opera administration, his father was a QC. Daniel was inclined to be dismissive of both.) I didn't tell them about the shadowy corners of his eyes where his skin was soft as silk, about the curved downy dove-grey hollow of the small of his back. I didn't mention that the sight of his dark hair tapering to a little twist at the nape of his neck could move me to inward tears of delight, or that the sound of his voice when he said my name made me feel as if no one had ever spoken it before, as if I was Eve in Eden, awakening by his side. I let my family know the facts of his existence, but I didn't tell them that it had become central to my own.

At some point in the spring a new character joined the cast list of the increasingly elaborate Westaby drama that Victoria's letters half created, half described. This was Gerald Hepburne, a Cambridge academic turned author who had taken up residence at Westaby for a few weeks for the purposes of his research – he was writing a history of the English public schools established in the nineteenth century. ('Well, somebody's got to,' wrote Victoria.) He seemed to have struck up an instant friendship with my father – an unprecedented occurrence, within my memory at least – and his visits to Lodge Cottage soon became frequent. 'Must stop writing now, because Gerald Herringbone-Tweed is at the door, and I've got to go and be nice to him until Papa gets back – he's rather sweetly boring and incurably earnest.' She satirized his scholarliness, his receding hairline, his stoop, but I noticed that she was soon mentioning him more often than anyone else. 'Gerald in the chapel was an amazing sight. He went into a swoon of ecstasy, like St

Theresa, when he saw all those fake coats of arms. I thought I was going to have to whip the gladis out of their vase and dash the water over him to bring him round,' she wrote, but I did wonder what she was doing with him in the chapel at all, if she found him so negligible. But as the weeks went by the tone softened, the nickname was dropped. Gerald, it seemed, was in no hurry to leave Westaby. 'He's in the middle of a very messy divorce. His wife (greedy bitch – ran off with their lodger) is claiming that their child isn't his. Poor man. He's going to fight it.' A blood test revealed all; the child, now about a year old, had indeed been sired by the lodger. 'Gerald is bowing out gracefully, but the shock – can you imagine?' And in the next letter, 'Gerald has decided to rent a room in the Master's lodge for the whole of the summer, so you'll meet him. I wonder what you'll make of him. I know he'll like you.'

My finals were upon me, so I didn't give the unseen Gerald much thought. After eight three-hour exams in the space of a week, Daniel and I tumbled out of Schools into the waiting arms of a dozen friends, to be carried off to a protracted and drunken picnic on the banks of the Cherwell. We hung our caps and gowns on the trees and left them there; when the evening grew chilly we lurched back into town and took possession of the back bar of the King's Arms. At closing time we all went back to my house and stayed up talking for what was left of the night, high on love and youth and relief. We had a huge fried breakfast in a greasy spoon café round the corner, and at gone nine in the morning the others peeled away and Daniel and I went to bed and lay all day in each other's arms.

There followed a few bitty, unsatisfactory days with our university life breaking up like melting ice floes, days spent stowing books into cardboard boxes and trying to remove the Blu-Tack marks from my bedroom wall so the landlord wouldn't charge us. At last we parted, after a prolonged embrace at the coach station, Daniel for London, I for Westaby. Daniel was going to spend a month in Nicaragua on what was grandly termed a 'fact-finding mission'; I was to stay at home to catch up with my long-neglected family. Then, reunited, we would look for jobs and accommodation in London. Daniel was confident. He knew, he said, of lots of decent squats.

Back at home, I found Victoria at the humming centre of a busy little world. The house, though not exactly transformed, looked cleaner and brighter than it had ever been since my mother's time. Mrs Pedlow's curtains were long since completed. I had been prepared to scoff at their fussy swirls of pink and pale green, but I had to admit that with the sun filtering through them they did make the living-room look soft and fresh. Victoria (who, I discovered, had got my father to set up a housekeeping account for her complete with cheque book) had bought a rug to match them, large enough to cover most of the scorch marks and coffee stains that punctuated the old grey carpet beneath. Corners of junk had been cleared, pictures had been cleaned and rehung, the dear old Formica table in the kitchen had been covered by a smart terracotta oil cloth. Vases of flowers stood everywhere. Victoria was artful in making the most of what little bloomed in our dark and jungly garden. White roses and grey-blue catmint freshened the bathroom window-sill, and the narrow, gloomy hall was lit up by fat, floppy peonies that spilled their crimson richness out on to the telephone table.

Into this new-established prettiness came an organized succession of visitors. Westaby Wives Club came for coffee every other Tuesday, bringing baked offerings on paper plates covered with foil. The Charity Committee, a subset of the Wives, came to a regular soup–and–salad lunch at which they discussed fundraising plans. There was a weekly tea for sixth-form girls, attendance voluntary, 'to give them a bolt hole when they've had enough of the boys,' as Victoria explained. 'Bolt hole' was a very Westaby Wives sort of expression. And, to my amazement, there was a supper party every single Friday evening. Victoria was working her way through the list of College staff. Matrons, lab technicians and the like were invited as well as teachers, six at a time, and Victoria did all the cooking. 'It's easy,' she said carelessly. 'If you can read you can cook.' But if I, who could also read, tried to help, she always said things like, 'Quick, stir it, Ruthie, that's going to curdle,' or 'You really don't need that much salt, I promise you,' so I usually ended up just laying the table.

I tried to poke fun at Victoria the hostess, calling her Westaby's answer to Fanny Craddock, but she would have none of it. 'These are the things that the deputy head should do,' she said, floating pansy heads in finger bowls, 'but of course poor old Papa would never think of anything on his own. A community's only as good as the people in it, Ruthie.' I said nothing. In the old days I would have responded with sick noises, but in the old days Victoria would never have said such things. She wore her smooth hair pushed back, now, by a velvet Alice band; a Liberty print skirt and a well-ironed white blouse were her usual attire. She had put on a little weight, not in a lumpy way, but in a smooth firm layer all over. Most people said it suited her.

Gerald Hepburne clearly thought so. I hadn't been in the house for twenty-four hours before he made his appearance. His pretext for calling was to return a book about Prince Albert that my father had lent him, but I noticed that he called at a time when my father was very unlikely to be in. Victoria withdrew to make tea, leaving me perched next to him on the living-room sofa. He asked me grave and courteous questions about Oxford, and I made a few further clueless enquiries about his research. I liked him. I thought he was about forty. I wasn't good at guessing ages above twenty-one, so I could have been several years out either way – lean, a little faded, with kind blue eyes and not a great deal of gingery hair. He had a slight stammer – a kind of pause, and then the words came out in a rush. I was interested in the stammer. Victoria hadn't mentioned it.

Gerald came to the supper party the first Friday I was at home. People were supposed to be invited in strict rotation, but it soon became clear that Gerald was a regular. 'He's so lonely,' said Victoria. 'He's left the whole of his past life behind him.' Lonely or not, he made himself very useful, doing the things my father was absent-minded about, like helping people to drinks, and initiating conversation with everybody with the same hesitant courtesy. 'Everybody', on this occasion, consisted of the head of chemistry and his wife, who'd been at the school for ever, a nervous young classicist called Ian

Riddle who'd only been out of university for a year, and Moira Brice, the headmaster's secretary, a divorced mother of two teenaged sons who was, it was widely assumed, looking for a second father for them. The numbers were made up by my father, Gerald and myself. Simon was out. He went to a Fair Trade Society meeting every Friday night. 'That's why I do this on a Friday,' explained Victoria. 'It wouldn't do to have Simon around.' I could see that it wouldn't, but still I found her remark a little chilling. Simon did, after all, live here. In recognition of this, Victoria set aside portions of food for him, neatly covered, with a note.

Moira Brice had brought the first course. She had insisted on making a contribution. 'That's a pudding,' I whispered to Victoria as I unveiled it in the kitchen. 'She must have got it wrong.' But no, the round pink jellied thing that looked like a cheesecake was in fact flavoured with prawns. 'Prawns and toothpaste,' said Victoria, grimacing as she licked a finger. 'No point in saving any of this for Simon. It'll be boiled horses' hooves that's making this stick together.' Moira had also provided a bag of chopped-up lettuce, with instructions for its arrangement. 'I might have known Moira would be a garnisher,' Victoria commented as we made a frilly green bed for each wobbly pink slab.

Victoria had placed Moira between my father and Gerald. I was opposite, so I had ample opportunity to observe her. She had that kind of gold-tinted hair that seems to hover, all of a piece, above the scalp; it all held together, a bit like a shower cap. Her skin was what I would now recognize as good for her age – which was early forties, Victoria said. It was soft and pink, and free of blotches. She was solid, but not fat; a chasm of powdered cleavage, two or three inches of it, surged above the V-neck of her otherwise demure navy-blue dress. Her jewellery, which all matched, was made of thick gold links, her navy shoes were ornamented with flattened bows. I would guess her aim had been to look highly presentable, with just a trace of hidden sensual depths. She gave off no whiff of straitened circumstances.

I had to talk to old Mr Chemistry Sharpe on my right and poor nervous Ian Riddle on my left, as well as helping Victoria to clear plates and serve, so I couldn't listen to as much of Moira's conversation as I would have liked, but I could tell that she was keen to impress Gerald Hepburne with the strength of her opinions. I caught a snatch of her praising Margaret Thatcher – the influence on the hair style was made clear – and I suppressed a smile, because I thought that with Gerald that particular seed would fall on stony ground. I barely knew him, but in manner and interests he seemed so similar to my father that I had assumed he would take a gently ineffectual left-of-centre stance. But I was wrong. Gerald replied with approbation, saying that it was high time someone took the unions in hand. My father, never one to sacrifice truth for the sake of politeness, abruptly abandoned Mrs Chemistry Sharpe and took up the issue with some vigour. 'A heartless philistine,' I heard him say of the new prime minister, 'and possessed of the most appalling potential for destruction.' That must be that, I thought, time for a change of subject. But no, Moira rose to the bait, and a lively discussion ensued. Gerald must have been functioning far below his true intellectual capacity, but he didn't seem to mind. His face was mobile, his smile was ready, his gestures vigorous. He's enjoying talking to her, I thought. She's a woman, and she's got a bit of spirit, and she's paying him lots of attention. Could it be that Victoria will have a run for her money?

I had a few moments of contemplation, because Mr Sharpe was engaged with Victoria who was on the other side of him, and Ian Riddle, who was terribly tall and hungry, was busy with his second helping of chicken Marengo. It surprised me to find how quickly I had fallen into thinking of Victoria and Gerald Hepburne as a couple. Now it seemed that perhaps the assumption was absurd. Why would Victoria want him, a nervous middle-aged academic? Why would she want any man, when she had my father, my brother, my home to run? Stealing quick glances at her, I could detect no sign of jealousy at Moira's monopoly, only a kind of suppressed excitement for which I couldn't quite account.

Next it was profiteroles. Victoria had spent all afternoon scraping out their soft insides. There were three each; Victoria took only one. I could see Moira eyeing hers with greedy concentration; when Gerald's head was turned away she shot out a plump pink hand and ladled on an extra dollop of chocolate sauce. I knew Victoria would have noticed. I looked; she had. We each risked a tiny smile.

Afterwards, we cleared up together and listened to Simon talk about his meeting as he finished the profiteroles at the kitchen table. 'What do you reckon, then?' I said to Victoria. 'Is she after Gerald, do you think?'

'Oh, yes,' said Victoria, wiping surfaces. 'She's after him all right. But she's not going to get him.'

'Why not?' asked Simon, but Victoria did not reply, and he soon lost interest. I thought about it for a while as I lay in bed waiting for Victoria to come back from the bathroom, but soon my thoughts drifted back to their most usual course. I thought of Daniel, of his skin, his hands, his whereabouts . . . was he safe, was he happy, was he thinking of me?

28

Daniel and I started our life together in a Housing Association flat in Primrose Hill. The flat took up the first floor of a semi-derelict house. It was large, shabby, unheated, cheap, and I loved it. There were no carpets, no curtains, and very little furniture. We sat in two deck-chairs; Daniel's hi-fi stood on an orange box; we made a bookcase out of bricks and planks. We slept in the same room that we lived in, because it was the nicest room – high-ceilinged, with two tall fly-speckled windows. It stretched across the width of the house. There was a big, dirty kitchen overlooking a strip of untended garden, and a smaller room at the back with a mattress in it for our friends to sleep on. We kept our bikes in there, too. There was a lavatory, but no bath; we washed in the kitchen sink, for baths we went round to Daniel's friends Paddy and Maria, who had a flat of their own in Camden Town, and once a week we went swimming and used the showers at the pool. If we were dirty in between times it didn't matter; we liked each other's dirt.

We slept on a futon under the windows in the front room. The futon had been provided by Daniel's parents, and was virtually the only thing in the house that hadn't come out of a skip. I remember lying there, with Daniel asleep in my arms, watching the car headlights swing across our high white ceiling, listening to Daniel's quiet breathing and to shouts and catcalls and the sound of an overturning dustbin from the street below, and thinking that I had never been so happy in my entire life.

Daniel found a job very quickly, working as a research assistant for a Labour MP. The MP was in cahoots with Ken Livingstone, the leader of the GLC, which was under threat from the new Conservative government; there was a lot of talk about subsidizing housing and public transport, and Daniel threw himself in wholeheartedly. He had ferocious energy. His working hours were long, but that didn't stop him from firing off articles about Nicaragua to various left-wing publications, going on anti-apartheid demonstrations, organizing benefit concerts for assorted victims of social injustice, and going out with me and our friends, to hear bands, to dance, to watch fringe theatre and alternative cabaret, to argue loudly over pints in pubs.

The daily miracle was that Daniel loved me. He really did. Every morning he got up first – so far I had only found a part-time waitressing job, and that didn't start until noon – and I would watch him stride across the bare splintery floor in all his marvellous proud nakedness, and my stomach would clench with the excitement of possession. He made us mugs of tea and brought them back to bed, and then he would dress and shave reluctantly, breaking off at intervals to stroke my hair or drop kisses on my naked shoulders. When it was time for him to go he held me close and said, 'I'm going to miss you,' even though we would only be apart for a few hours, and then off he would go, bumping his bike down the stairs, and I would just lie there exulting. I didn't know why he loved me. Compared to him – and compared to Ella, his former girlfriend, a slender Polish girl who wore dark red lipstick and never smiled, whose existence I could never contemplate with even a show of equanimity – I was so dull, so naïve, and besides, I had freckles and lumpy thighs. But after a while I worried less, and relaxed, and just accepted that love me he did. People spend so much of their lives not paying enough attention to the phase they're in, just marking time while they wait for the next bit to start. Well, that was not true of me when I was living in Primrose Hill with Daniel. I was young and in love, and I knew that life was rich and sweet.

My waitressing job was at a café round the corner, and it left me with plenty of time on my hands. Through a friend of Daniel's older sister, I started writing short reviews for a listings magazine, little notices about plays and films. I didn't think my comments were particularly pithy or interesting, but somebody must have liked them because soon I was asked for longer pieces. So I wrote up the political events that Daniel took me along to, and soon my name began to appear at the bottom of my articles. I kept up the waitressing; despite the cheapness of the flat we never had enough money, and when the lunch-time stint at the café finished we menials were allowed to help ourselves to whatever food was left over. So Daniel and I lived on cold quiche and coleslaw and croissants that had lost their lustre, and the money we saved on food we spent on bottled Guinness and rough red wine. In my letters to Victoria I regaled her with all these details of my new life, though I didn't say much about Daniel himself. Our correspondence continued to flourish. There was no telephone in the flat, and besides, those letters had developed a life of their own which entertained both of us. For Victoria's benefit I made verbal caricatures of the customers at the café, and for me she provided sketches of the Westaby social network with especial reference to the machinations of Moira. Moira, it seemed, was hedging her bets. 'Gerald is her number-one target,' Victoria wrote, 'but the trouble is, he hasn't really noticed – he can be a bit vague about anything post 1900 – so she has had to resort to the Bursar.' It was no surprise to me to find that, come the autumn term, Gerald Hepburne was still there. The school seemed more than willing to accommodate him. He had been provided with some sixth-form history teaching and a small staff flat.

'In some ways,' Victoria continued, 'Moira would be ideal for Gerald. She's about his age, and she's super-organized – which he's not, poor lamb. Trouble is, I don't think he's remotely interested.' I can well believe it, I thought to myself. Who could be interested in plump, powdery Moira when my lovely slant-eyed Victoria was there for their delectation, with her sideways smile and her air of mystery and her slim quick hands?

Victoria didn't meet Daniel properly until well into October. He'd called at Westaby briefly on his return from Nicaragua, when he'd helped me to transfer my few belongings to London, but Victoria had been on her way out somewhere and they had exchanged no more than the briefest of greetings. But now my father's birthday approached. Victoria wrote to fetch me down for the weekend – 'And do please make Daniel

come. You must know that we are all consumed with curiosity.'
I did not take this literally. 'All' just meant Victoria; Simon
had never manifested curiosity about any other human being,
and my father was almost as bad. But I felt sure enough of
Daniel, now, to take this step. I had met his family many times;
we often had supper with them on Sunday evenings. Daniel
was scornful of their affluence and often described them as
'morally bankrupt'; he said that the metropolitan upper-
middle class to which they belonged was 'fossilized' and 'politically inert'. However, when he was in their company his scorn
softened into an affectionate impatience. Though he always
refused their offers of money, he was not above accepting
presents like the futon, and we hardly ever left their house
without some small item designed to make our lives a little less
spartan. I was nervous of them at first – they were so well
dressed, and so knowledgeable, and so charming, but soon I
found myself enjoying our evenings in their warm South
Kensington house. I revelled, a little guiltily, in their carpeted
floors and soft lavatory paper (Daniel stole ours from the
lavatory at the Commons; the quality was surprisingly poor),
and we both ate our fill of Miriam Bolt's delicious food.
Miriam used ingredients that I had never come across before
– wild rice and pimentos and fresh coriander; she would
often parcel up leftovers for us to take home, which made a
welcome change from all that quiche. She was dark and
manicured, elegant in proper jewellery and black cashmere;
he – Anthony – was tall and silver-haired, running to fat
which he tried to keep at bay at his expensive tennis club.
They had famous friends and grand dinner parties. They were

bright, warm, expansive people, and they were unfailingly kind to me.

So it was fitting and natural that I should tell Daniel about Victoria's invitation. He said, 'Ah! So you think I'm good enough for your folks, at last!' and rumpled my hair when I protested, and said, 'Only kidding.' He insisted on buying my father a birthday present which was separate from mine, which touched me. It was a volume of short stories by Jorge Luis Borges, and my father was pleased and appreciative.

The weekend was a typical Westaby entertainment, new-Victoria-style. Various College people had been bidden to join us for the birthday meal on Saturday night. I noted that Moira was not one of them. The food was laid out on the dining-room table and we carried it back into the living-room and balanced it on our knees. I heard Victoria describe it as a 'fork supper', which made me wince. When Daniel found himself standing in the middle of a circle of tweedy geography masters and their faded wives, a plate of chilli con carne inaccessible in one hand, a glass of red wine in the other, his face was a picture. As soon as I could I steered him towards Simon, with instructions to talk to him about the Third World. I was happy to see that they soon retreated to the kitchen together, where they could eat as much as they liked and where their conversation was animated and apparently mutually satisfactory.

I hadn't said anything about sleeping arrangements. Victoria forestalled me. 'It's all right,' she said, when we had shooed my father off to bed and were tidying up in the kitchen, 'I'll sleep in Aunt Marigold's room.' So Daniel and I spent the night together in my high narrow childhood bed, snug as two

333

spoons. He slept with his head on my shoulder and I lay awake, breathing in the smokiness of his dark hair, just as I used to lie with Victoria.

The next morning, a crisp blue-and-gold Sunday, the ever-present Gerald took Daniel, and therefore me, on an unsought-for tour of the school – the chapel, the dining hall, the vast library that had been carted in wholesale from a demolished country house. Gerald talked about everything with great knowledge and even greater enthusiasm, and he had a store of small anecdotes that anyone with even a glimmering of interest in and respect for English public schools would have found genuinely amusing, but in Daniel there was no such glimmering. The only way Daniel could contain himself was by saying nothing. I asked a few polite questions, even though it was I who was on home territory, and when Gerald walked in front of us Daniel nudged me or took my hand and squeezed it behind my back. I squeezed his in return, but I didn't want to laugh at Gerald. I felt quite fondly towards his bald patch and his thin corduroy-covered shoulders. He really was rather like my father.

The College looked its best in the clear autumn sunshine, its wedding-cake architecture hard-edged against the clean blue sky. Recent wind and rain had swept away all that remained of the dusts of late summer, the horse-chestnut leaves were rimmed with coppery gold as fine as the hair of saints on early Renaissance panels, but Daniel's silent sarcasm gave me a tightness in my throat. I longed for the day to be over. The longer we stayed at Westaby, the more closely he would associate me with what he despised as irrelevant, outdated privilege, and then, I thought, he would have no option but to turn against me. Better to risk nothing. Better to keep him safe in London with me, in our new-established world of alternative this and radical that, circumscribed, no doubt, but well understood.

At one o'clock we walked back to Lodge Cottage, where Victoria had prepared yet another meal, not last night's leftovers reorganized, either, but a proper Sunday lunch of roast pork and apple sauce and some separate cheesy thing for Simon. We helped wash up – I insisted that my father sit down with the paper, largely because he tended to sing hymns while washing up, and that was something I couldn't bear Daniel to witness. Then we said we must set off before it got dark, so Dad drove us to the beginning of the motorway. We stuck out our thumbs and waited for a lift back to London, and I didn't know whether I was glad or sorry that I hadn't had one minute alone with Victoria to find out what she thought about Daniel.

The afternoon had turned grey and chilly, as if dirty water had been spilt over all the bright colours. A lift was slow in coming. I complained of cold ears. Daniel wound his scarf round my head; he tucked the ends into my collar and kissed me on the nose. I put my spare hand into his big coat pocket and started to feel happy again. 'Well,' I ventured, 'what did you think of Victoria?'

Daniel said, 'I thought you said she was the same age as you.'

'She is. Four months younger.'

'I'd have thought she was four years older. At least.'

I smiled. 'You mean I look like a kid.'

335

'No, I mean she looks like . . . well, a wifey.'

'She was a wifey,' I said, 'though she didn't look like one then. I told you about that, didn't I?'

'Yeah. That's just such a weird story. I mean, she had the rest of her life to do that in, for Christ's sake.'

We stood in silence for a little while, and then I said, 'Don't you think she's pretty, though?'

'Well, not really. She would be, I suppose, if – '

'Oh, Daniel, she *is*! Everybody thinks she is.'

'If you say so.'

'Admit it, she's much prettier than me. If you say she isn't, I won't believe you.'

Daniel cupped my scarf-swaddled face in his hand. 'You're not giving me much choice, Ruthie. But I know what I like. You've got an intelligent face.' And, careless of any missed lifts, he kissed me for a long time.

We didn't get back to Primrose Hill until nearly nine. The flat was dark and freezing, and there was nothing to eat at all. Daniel went out for chips, and to keep warm we ate them in bed. We put some music on – the Clash, or some reggae, I expect – and finished a half-empty bottle of wine that we'd forgotten about. It was too cold to undress properly, and when I slipped my hands up under his shirt he rolled over and said, 'Sorry, Ruthie. I'm just too bloody knackered,' even though it wasn't at all late. I said, 'OK, that's fine,' and turned to face the other way, but it wasn't really fine, because that was the first time he ever turned away from me.

29

Nobody was very surprised when Gerald and Victoria announced their engagement just before Christmas. Aunt Marigold harumphed a bit, because it meant that she had to relinquish her dream of Victoria ever returning to Oxford, but she couldn't find much to complain about in Gerald himself. 'Not many girls of her age would find him exciting, I wouldn't have thought,' she remarked to me the day after the announcement. 'But then, I'm no expert. And perhaps Victoria feels she's had enough excitement.' My father was enthusiastic. 'Gerald really is a most interesting person,' he said with some fervour, 'and a very able historian.' If I had a feeling that being a very able historian didn't automatically prepare you for marrying an orphaned girl half your age who'd already been married once, I didn't voice it. I liked Gerald, and I had long since resigned myself to Victoria's habit of making decisions about her life that were only partly explicable to me.

Simon said, 'Gerald's OK, but I don't know why she has to go and marry every man she meets.' 'For security, I suppose,' I replied, and Simon said, 'What's so great about security?' I didn't elaborate, because what I meant by security was actually rather the reverse. Victoria might play the part of a free spirit, but in reality she was stuck. She still, I believed, fastened her hopes on marriage as something big enough to free her, to push her over the edge. She hadn't slept with Tim, she hadn't slept with Steve. I was pretty sure she hadn't slept with Sholto or any of his friends. And as for Gerald – well, Gerald was quaint. I couldn't see him pressing the issue before the wedding night. It was as if Victoria was hanging from the window-ledge of a burning building, waiting for someone to stamp on her fingers and force her to let go.

I didn't explain any of this to Simon, of course. There wasn't anyone in the world with whom I could possibly have discussed Victoria in such terms, because my overwhelming instinct where she was concerned was still a protective one. To Simon I said, 'Do you think it's funny that she should turn out to be the one who's so keen to settle down?' and Simon said, 'Yes. Anyone would have thought it would be you.' I was touched, sort of, to find that Simon had ever thought about me in that way and to that extent. I said, 'Well, I suppose I am settled now, though we've got no intention of getting married.'

Simon looked puzzled, and then he said, 'Oh, you mean with Daniel? Maybe you and Victoria should do a swap.'

I was startled. 'What on earth are you talking about?'

'Well, Gerald would be more suitable for you, and Daniel would be more suitable for Victoria.'

I sighed. 'Oh, Simon, for heaven's sake.' I might have thought I had been detecting signs of maturity in my overgrown little brother, but in many ways he was just as obtuse as ever.

The happy couple visited us in London one fresh, cold day in early spring. Theirs was to be a proper wedding, or as proper as it could be given that by then both parties would be divorced.

Certainly, Victoria intended to do the shopping bit properly. Expeditions to London were to be a regular occurrence.

The plan was that the ceremony itself should take place in the registry office in the morning, with no guests except the necessary witnesses; then a service of blessing which was as similar to the real thing as was decently possible would take place that afternoon in Westaby Chapel, with flowers and trumpet voluntaries and a cast of thousands. 'I want to remember it,' she said. 'I mean, really remember it. Ruthie, do you understand?' The date was fixed for mid July; by then, the divorce should long have been finalized. This procedure had been made easier by the appearance, out of the blue, of a Christmas card addressed to me. It had a cheery picture of a drunken robin in a night-cap clinging to a candle, and Steve had written a message inside. 'I'm back with Trudy now,' it said, 'trying to keep straight this time. If I never said it before, thank you Ruthie for what you done.' There was also an address, Something Mansions in Southwark. This was passed on to the solicitors, who wrote the necessary letters, and no objections from Southwark were forthcoming. There had been no point in my concealing the card. Victoria was always up before me, these days; she had handed it to me when I at last came down to breakfast. I had to show her. 'Oh?' she said. 'And what is it you're being thanked for?' Her tone was humorous, but with an edge.

'I don't really know. Just for talking, or listening, I suppose.' My surprise at receiving the card was genuine, and was enough to mask my evasion. If Victoria's face darkened, it was not for long. On her finger was Gerald's pretty Victorian engagement ring, garnets in a setting of chased silver. And the address on the card made the problem of the divorce brilliantly solvable.

By the time Victoria and Gerald arrived on our Primrose Hill doorstep that windy blue-and-white Saturday, arrangements were well underway. The bridal dress was being made by someone in Chelsea known to and trusted by Pamela Brooke, Victoria's maternal grandmother, with whom they were staying; Victoria had had a fitting that morning, to which Gerald, following tradition, had not been allowed to come. He had put in three useful hours, he said, in the Reading Room of the British Museum. Three hours! Daniel and I had been up for less than one. I had done my best to make the flat look welcoming. I had moved the hi-fi on to the floor and spread our lunch (yesterday's bean salad from the café; bread and fancy cheese bought by Daniel from the pretentious delicatessen in the next street) on the orange box, but the pale spring sunshine seemed determined to show up nothing but smears and dust.

Victoria was undeterred. 'It's wonderful! It's perfect!' she exclaimed, embracing me with an uncharacteristic effusion that belonged to her newish, bridey-hostessy self. 'Don't you think so, Gerald? It's just exactly how I imagined.' She had obviously loved her fitting. The same sunlight that made me and my few belongings look worn and dishevelled made Victoria glow and dance. Daniel seemed pleased by her praise. 'It's not much,' he said, in a self-satirizing, Uriah Heep voice, 'but it's home. Don't take your coats off, though. It's still bloody cold.' It was. Our one fan heater could not quite penetrate the great depth of cold that had built up, layer upon layer, over the winter months. Already the tip of Gerald's long, sharp-tipped nose looked pink and moist.

Victoria's animation carried us through the meal. Every detail was overhauled. At first I hesitated to join in the debate about which hymns to choose, because of what Daniel might think, but then I asked myself, why hold back? He had to know, ultimately, that there was a side of me that quite liked talking about hymns. It was this aspect of the wedding that seemed to excite Gerald the most. He revealed an astonishing knowledge of hymns, their authors and their origins. A couple of old favourites were dismissed as 'too Wesleyan'; he revealed a taste for mid-Victorian melodrama. He knew the names of all the different musical settings, too. In the middle of a detailed comparison of the various settings of the twenty-third psalm, I sneaked a glance at Daniel, who, not surprisingly, had contributed little. He was leaning back in his deck-chair, one ankle balanced on the other knee, rolling a cigarette and grinning. 'What about Kum-by-a?' he asked suddenly. Victoria giggled, but it took Gerald a few seconds to identify the remark as a joke.

Only a couple of weeks earlier, Prince Charles had announced his intention of marrying Lady Diana Spencer, and ever since the newspapers and street-corner conversations had been full of little else. The official engagement photographs had shown the prince with his straight side-parting like a white zip, Diana in bright blue, all buttoned up to the chin, her stomach thrust forward and her mouth skewed to one side. In some of the pictures Charles's hands were splayed on her shoulders in a pose intended to imply proud possession, but

Diana's shoulders were hunched as if he were playing a tiresome practical joke on her, like dropping an ice cube down her back. Daniel and I had laughed at these pictures, then given the matter little further thought. Victoria brought it up now.

'I hope they don't fix the royal wedding for the same date as ours,' she said.

Daniel lit the straggly twisted end of his cigarette. 'Would it make any difference if they did?'

'Of course it would! Lots of people would be longing to go and watch it,' said Victoria. 'Including me, actually.'

'You'd hardly be bothered about watching it on your own wedding day,' I suggested.

'Oh,' replied Victoria, 'I'd hate to miss it. So would Gerald. He loves that kind of thing.'

I remembered the last royal wedding, that of Princess Anne and Captain Mark Phillips. The commentators always stressed '*Captain* Mark Phillips,' almost as if that were his Christian name. Victoria and I had been about twelve at the time. We had drawn a series of cruel and – probably unconsciously – suggestive cartoons depicting the bride as a horse being ridden by her wooden soldier of a groom. Captain Phillips' groomsman was someone called Captain Eric Grounds; for some reason his name struck us as funny. Most things did in those days. For a whole day, Victoria had pretended to be desperately in love with Mark Phillips, I with the blameless Captain Grounds. We told our parents that we would form a suicide pact if our love remained unrequited. I assumed that Victoria, and therefore by association Gerald, would approach the Charles and Diana show in a similar spirit. I was wrong.

'I must admit, I do love it,' said Gerald, almost simpering. 'I think it's splendid. There's such a marvellously rich tradition of – '

'Of what?' interjected Daniel. 'Virgin sacrifice?'

This seemed to touch a sore point. The rest of Gerald's face turned as pink as the tip of his nose. 'There's nothing wrong with saving oneself for marriage,' he bristled.

'Nothing wrong,' snorted Daniel, 'except that it's completely pointless.'

'I think there's something very special about it,' countered Victoria. 'Lady Diana makes me feel very – well, yes, very proud.'

'Proud to be British,' chimed Gerald. I couldn't believe my ears.

It was too much for Daniel. He rose and paced the room, fiddling. 'Proud? What the hell is there to be proud of? Some jug-eared twit who soaks up other people's money for sitting on his arse and grinning all day long – '

'Actually, everyone says Prince Charles works jolly hard – '

' – who's reached the age of forty or fifty – '

'Thirty-two – '

'Thirty-two, then, knocking on a bit anyway, without managing to make a proper relationship with a woman, finally decides for the sake of decency to buy himself a soft young pudding of a girl who hasn't had a sexual experience since she left Pony Club – '

'Daniel,' I said, 'do shut up.' I turned apologetically to Gerald. 'Sorry. We'll just have to agree to differ on this one. Would you like some tea, or coffee?'

But Victoria said, 'Oh Ruthie, don't make him stop. I'm enjoying this.' And she was.

Gerald helped me carry the dirty plates out to the icy kitchen, while Victoria and Daniel carried on the debate in ever more exaggerated terms. I couldn't find a spoon, so I shook Nescafé into mugs. Gerald said, 'One of the many admirable things about your entirely admirable sister is that she's not afraid of a good argument.'

I smiled. 'Well, I've certainly never beaten her in one. Come to think of it, I've never beaten her in anything.'

'I'm surprised you've ever tried.'

'Oh, why?'

'Because I didn't think you two had a competitive relationship.'

'No, I suppose we don't.' I considered. 'It's funny, I've never really thought about it.'

Gerald's face was suddenly suffused with earnestness. 'It's one of the things she most values about you,' he said.

'What, that I never win anything?'

'No, that you don't try. You mean a lot to her, Ruthie. She's always saying that you're her bedrock. But you must know that.'

I mumbled something that wasn't as gracious as I meant it to be and carried the mugs back to the other room. Daniel and Victoria were standing together at the window. Daniel was gesticulating, the movements of his long hands unconsciously elegant, and Victoria was tossing back her hair. 'You see that old man down there?' Daniel was saying, and I knew he was making some political point.

344

They left about an hour later. 'Come again,' offered Daniel genially, 'any time.'

'Thank you,' said Victoria, flashing one of her uninterpretable looks at him. 'We'll be back soon, because we'll need a dress for Ruthie. You will be my bridesmaid, won't you, Ruthie?' She laid a light hand on my arm.

'I didn't think you were having any.'

'Only you. Of course we must have you.'

Daniel and I stood at the window and watched them as they trotted off down the street, Victoria with her hand tucked in the crook of Gerald's arm. 'It's incredible,' he said. 'I can't believe she means it when she talks all that land-of-hope-and-glory crap.'

'Perhaps she doesn't. She's a bit of a chameleon, sometimes.'

'That's the first negative thing I've heard you say about her.'

'Oh, I didn't really mean it to be negative. But Dan, you were a bit tactless.'

'Was I?'

'About Prince Charles being so much older, for a start.'

'Well, he is.'

'And so's Gerald. And about all that virginity stuff.'

'Come off it. Victoria and Gerald are hardly virginal. They've both been married before.'

'Yes, I know, but still . . . she's sensitive, you know.'

'Is she? She always seems rock hard to me.'

'That's just her way of coping. She's not hard underneath.' Even as I said this, I felt unsure. 'She's had a lot to cope with, Daniel.'

Daniel put his hands on my shoulders, not awkwardly like Prince Charles, but in a tender, massaging kind of way. 'Ruthie,' he said, 'you make so many allowances for her. Yes, I know she's had a hard time, with her parents and all that, but she's not the only one.'

'Oh, I know everyone has problems in their lives, but – '

'I didn't mean everyone,' he said, 'I meant you.'

'Me? I'm all right.'

He pulled me closer. 'I think you're incredibly strong,' he murmured into my hair. 'In fact, I think you're absolutely amazing. People should have much, much more respect for you than they have for Victoria.'

I revelled in his admiration, but still I couldn't hear Victoria slighted. I kissed him, but then I wriggled free. 'You know, Dan, I feel really grimy. Shall we go over to Paddy and Maria's and cadge a bath?'

Throughout that spring and early summer of 1981 Victoria made frequent visits to London, sometimes with Gerald, sometimes alone. Her appetite for shopping seemed boundless. There was, after all, to be a second bridesmaid, a small niece of Gerald's who would have been put out at being excluded, and the three of us spent several long, dusty, and to my mind rather boring days trawling Harrods and Laura Ashley and Harvey Nichols. The niece, whose name was Alice, was a pert, pretty eight-year-old who bore no resemblance to her unworldly uncle except in the colour of her hair, though where Gerald had definite gingery edges little Alice could be fairly described as strawberry blonde. She would perch on high stools in the sandwich bars where we made frequent stops, her blue eyes bright above the rim of her milkshake, discussing the merits of damask over taffeta, artificial flowers in the head-dresses over real, with far more stamina than I could manage.

I suppose many girls in my position would have been envious of Victoria. I wasn't. I didn't have the slightest desire to marry Daniel. To stay with him for ever and ever, yes. To be loved by him to the exclusion of all others, certainly. To bear his children – probably, yes, in the fullness of time. It was certainly a pleasing fantasy, though one I was not yet ready to share with him. But to put an official stamp on the whole thing, to draw up lists of guests and choose china for people to give us – no, that was all alien, unimaginable. 'When are you and Daniel going to get married?' demanded young Alice, swinging her legs in the café. I smiled with adult indulgence at her eight-year-old directness.

'We're not,' I replied.

Alice was disappointed. 'Doesn't he love you, then?'

'People don't have to get married just because they love each other.'

'But Ruthie,' put in Victoria, 'don't you want him to ask you? Admit it, everyone wants to be asked.'

I pulled a face. 'I'd hate it,' I said. 'It would be so out of character.' My reply was quite sincere. I relished it when Daniel told me that he loved me – which he still did, sometimes, though perhaps not quite as often as he used to. But a proposal – well, that just wouldn't be the Daniel I knew. I would have to treat it as a joke.

★

347

We visited Westaby more often as the year wore on. Daniel became quite keen to go. He liked my father, with whom he had long philosophical talks usually ending with the borrowing of books, and he listened patiently to Simon's diatribes. I was grateful for this. Simon had never taken his A levels, declaring that they, and university, were just part of an establishment conspiracy to steer young people away from the Real World, but he showed little sign of joining this real world, wherever it might be, or of helping to solve its problems. He had been mooching about at home for a year now, doing little except writing long and usually unpublished letters to radical journals. He claimed to be writing a novel about the evils of British colonialism, but I don't think it ever got beyond the planning stage. It seemed unlikely to me that Simon would be able to write a novel, since he never read any, and in the past had often declared that he couldn't see the difference between fiction and lies. He'd even given up working in the Fair Trade shop, since he'd fallen out with the manager 'on a point of principle'. I gathered that their incompatible views on Robert Mugabe had led to a vehement argument.

So little by little Daniel came to seem like a fixture in my family, which both pleased me and worried me, the worry being that their assumptions about his permanence would make him feel twitchy and claustrophobic. But so far there was no sign of that. His relations with Victoria were a little less genial, a little edgier, than with the others. He found her wedding obsession hilarious, and when his teasing went too far her dark eyes would snap and flash a warning. But after that first Diana argument he was careful to curb his remarks in front of Gerald. Daniel was a young man in his pride, strong and graceful, deserving of the status he had always effortlessly achieved as leader of the pack. He had natural magnanimity, and no desire to humiliate the gentle, guileless Gerald.

The College authorities had promised to provide the newly-weds with accommodation in the shape of a small house on the opposite side of the grounds from Lodge Cottage. Several similar houses had been built at the same time, in the 1960s, in recognition of the growing trend for married schoolmasters. The houses were three up, three down, with proper central heating and picture windows framing a reasonably good view of the playing fields, but the back windows overlooked only a dull stretch of the road to Bullhampton. Each house had a garden, divided from the next by a Leylandii hedge. Victoria seemed more than happy with the arrangement, and planned soft furnishings with enthusiasm. They were to be a thoroughly Westabian couple. From September, Gerald was to become a full-time member of the teaching staff. He would carry on with his research in the holidays, Victoria explained, and she would help him. She might even do a little teaching herself. She didn't consider her lack of a degree to be a drawback.

'That would fit in well, I suppose,' I said, trying to enter into the spirit, 'if you had a baby.'

This conversation took place on a Saturday afternoon. We were wandering round Harris's, a glorified ironmongers in Bullhampton, which was the town's nearest equivalent to a department store. Victoria replaced the stainless-steel salad-servers she had been inspecting.

'There won't be a baby,' she announced. 'It's not going to

be that kind of marriage.' And before I could reply she took me by the elbow and steered me towards a low flat metal thing with a flex. 'Look,' she said, 'what do you think of that?'

'I don't think anything of it,' I replied, 'because I don't know what it is.'

'Oh yes, you do. It's one of those things that heats up, so you can keep the vegetables warm on it while the meat's being carved.'

'Oh,' I said vaguely, 'good.'

'I hope someone gives us one for a wedding present,' said Victoria. 'It would be really useful.'

'Don't look at me,' I said. 'I'd rather give you something more – more – '

'Not more expensive, I hope.'

'No, more meaningful.'

'What could be more meaningful than warm vegetables?' asked Victoria, with something like her old laugh. She checked her watch. 'Come on, let's go upstairs. I want to have a look at their bathroom cabinets before the bus goes.'

A fortnight before the wedding, Victoria and I spent a few days alone together at the Dorset cottage. Victoria was insistent that there should be no one else. 'I'm getting jittery,' she said. 'I don't want any men around. I need a rest from men.' So I arranged to take time off work, kissed Daniel goodbye, and set off for Waterloo with all I needed in a small backpack. I met Victoria at the station. She was waiting at the ticket barrier wearing a crisp pink sun-dress and a straw hat, and for a moment she could have been Aunt Angela.

The train sauntered westwards. We rolled past suburban gardens bright with paddling pools and begonias and clots of roses nodding against brick walls. We opened the windows of the carriage as wide as they would go, and the air was warm and sweet. Victoria kicked off her shoes, stretched out her bare brown legs. Her narrow, high-arched feet rested beside me on the seat. 'This feels like the beginning of an adventure,' she said, 'though I don't suppose it is.' She closed her eyes, turned her blissful face to the sun.

They were extraordinary, those four or five days, a bright bubble that escaped from time. We had no transport, so we ate only what we could carry from the village shop, which was a mile and a half from the cottage and which was more interested in selling stamps and postcards than food. We lived off cheese and bacon and chocolate. We'd hoped to find some fruit in the garden, but nothing was ripe yet, though we tried stewing some small, hard plums. We did everything together. I hung back, at first, thinking Victoria might want to go on thoughtful premarital walks alone, but she didn't. By day we scrambled over the cliffs and the shore or read our books side by side in deck-chairs under the cherry tree; by night we carried our bacon sandwiches outside and lay in the long grass and watched the stars winking on through the dusk. On the third night, when the full moon was brimming over like a pail of milk, we picked our way down to the beach at midnight and swam in the blood-warm sea. Afterwards, without saying a word to each other, we made our way to our old Throne Stones and sat on them, wringing out our hair. The moonlight caught the turn of Victoria's shoulder and changed it to smooth pewter. She twisted her hair with both hands; it was once again long enough to make a dark rope.

'Do you miss Daniel?' she asked.

'Yes, of course,' I said. 'It's the longest I've been without him since Nicaragua.' But then I looked at the completeness of it all, at the moon and the shining sea, and Victoria's dark shape at one with the humped Throne Stone, and I changed my mind. 'No, I don't. I miss him in theory, but – well, he's never been here, has he?'

'Why hasn't he?' Victoria asked. 'Why do you want to keep him separate?' She looked straight at me. Her face, sharp-planed in the pale moonlight, seemed detached from the rest of her body. She shone it at me like a searchlight.

'I . . . I don't think . . .'

'I think you're afraid.'

She was right. I was afraid. I was afraid of losing Daniel, and at that moment I was afraid of her. I said, 'No, I'm not. I just don't think he'd fit in,' but my voice sounded shrill and weak. Victoria utterly disregarded my remark. She said, 'You don't need to worry, Ruthie. You're strong. You've got your own life. You always will have your own life.'

I wasn't quite sure what she was getting at, but her notice was still, even then, such an honour to me that I swallowed her comments like a potent drink, and said nothing. We sat silent for a while, relishing the creeping tautness of our fast-cooling skin. Then Victoria said, 'Do you remember, Ruth? Remember what we said?'

I knew she meant here, on the Throne Stones, twelve summers ago. I said, 'I remember everything.'

'We said we'd always give up anything for the other,' said Victoria, 'and we said we'd always try to understand.'

I didn't remember that bit, exactly, but I murmured assent.

'We are a divided self, you and I,' she said, 'so there can be no holding back. There's nothing you'd hold back from me, Ruthie. I know that.'

But there was. There was the night with Steve, and there was the nine-week baby. I could tell her those things now, offer them up as sacrifices to our kinship. But I didn't. I just said, 'I'll always be there if you need me, Vicky. I'll always be your last resort.'

'Last resort? First, you mean. First and last. Perhaps that should be our new vow. To be each other's first and last resort.' She stretched out her hand to me across the chasm between the Throne Stones, her little finger crooked. I curled my finger round hers.

'There'll never be another time like this.' Victoria withdrew her hand and sighed. 'Why does something that ought to be a beginning feel like an end?' I cleared my throat. I couldn't think of anything to say that wouldn't sound like a criticism of Gerald, but Victoria said, 'No, that's not a question that needs an answer.'

We wrapped our arms round ourselves and our teeth began to chatter. 'Come on,' cried Victoria, switching moods, 'this is silly. I can't afford to catch pneumonia two weeks before my wedding day.'

Back at the cottage, we scraped out the bottom of an ancient tin of Ovaltine and managed to chip off enough to make two mugfuls. We drank it side by side on the brown draylon sofa, wrapped in an old tartan rug. I said, 'I wonder . . . if your real twin had lived, how things would have been for me.'

Victoria gave the tiniest jerk, and slopped some of the Ovaltine on to her hand. 'You are my real twin,' she said. 'The only one.' And she rested her head, just briefly, on my shoulder.

There were four bedrooms in the cottage, but we had chosen to share our old room with the bunks. This night, like the nights before it, we murmured things to each other before we fell asleep, dreamy disconnected things, but now was the first time that I wasn't glad we were together, because absurd as it may seem, I'd reached the age of twenty-two believing in that dead twin, and only now was I able to understand that there had been no such being. And I felt foolish, but also bereft. There was a loss; something else was lost that night beside Eleanora, the baby who never was.

30

The last few days before the wedding were fun. Even I began to enter into the spirit of things. The reception was to be held in a rose-and-ribbon-bedecked marquee on the College's largest lawn, and there was plenty to be done to get that organized, in addition to which our house had to be prepared for an influx of guests. Our Wintle cousins were coming down from Cumberland, and Paul, the oldest of the three big boys, was bringing a girlfriend. More alarmingly, Victoria's maternal grandparents had invited themselves to stay. I had visited their Chelsea flat only rarely, but on each occasion I had been struck by its cleanliness, order, and suffocating warmth. It could hardly have been more different from Lodge Cottage.

Even Victoria could not manage all this on her own, so Aunt Marigold and I had agreed to stay at Westaby from the Tuesday onwards. I braced myself for another parting from Daniel. The original plan had been that he should take time off work and join me at Westaby, but at the last minute he changed his mind. 'It's just a terrible time,' he said. 'We've got a mountain of stuff to get through in the office. I'm sorry, Ru, but anyway I think it'll be better without me. You need to spend as much time as you can with Victoria.' He spoke her name with reverence, almost.

'You make it sound as if she's got some terminal disease,' I said, 'not as if she's approaching the happiest day of her life.'

'Well, she isn't, is she?' said Daniel bluntly. 'I don't see how anyone can think that she is. But it's your job to help her pretend.'

So, for the second time in a fortnight, we prepared to part. 'We're getting quite good at this, aren't we?' I said as I kissed him goodbye at Paddington. He patted my cheeks. 'I'll ring you from work,' he said. 'Love you.' Then he turned and walked quickly away.

The bustle of moving mattresses and airing sheets and planning meals took my mind off Daniel. Sleeping arrangements were going to be very complicated, not least because Lady Brooke, Victoria's grandmother, did not find stairs easy any more, so she and Sir Ronald, recently knighted for his services to industry, were going to have to sleep in my father's study. We weren't supposed to call them Sir and Lady, of course, but we had never managed to get our tongues round Ronald and Pamela, so we tried to avoid calling them anything. There was no downstairs bathroom, just a lavatory with a small handbasin. I did not imagine that Lady Brooke would be overjoyed by this discovery. Victoria shrugged. 'Too bad. If she can't live without a bath, I'll get Gerald to sweep her upstairs in his arms.' The idea made us giggle. The cousins were all to sleep hugger-mugger on the living-room floor; it was quite a relief when Aunt Sarah rang to say that she thought the journey would be too much for their three labradors.

Number Two Woodland Walk, the little red-brick house with its rotary washing line and newly cleaned double-glazing, stood empty, waiting for Victoria and Gerald to return from their honeymoon. (Two weeks in Burgundy, looking at churches.) In all our planning and contriving as to how to shoehorn eight more people — nine, actually, since Daniel would be there for the wedding itself — into our already crowded house, no one suggested that any use of it should be made. As a viable dwelling place, it just hadn't penetrated anyone's consciousness. It sat there, neat and silent, waiting for Victoria to make it come alive.

That week, Victoria was too nervous to eat or sleep much. Her eyes glittered, and the flesh seemed to fall away from her face, leaving a taut arrangement of angles and slanting planes. 'You'd better be careful,' I said, as I watched her tilt her head from side to side in front of our bedroom mirror, 'or you'll have to have the dress altered.' The dress was too flouncy to fit in our wardrobe, so it hung, swathed in plastic, on the back of the bedroom door. I had been taken aback when I first saw it. There were a lot of bows, a lot of stitched-on seed pearls — pretend ones, anyway — a big sash, and several net petticoats. Victoria hadn't let anyone see her try it on, but I imagined the effect would be somewhere between Cinderella and Little Bo Peep. Little Alice and I were to wear powder-blue. I privately thought the colour rather babyish, but it was said to match my eyes.

'I won't have it altered,' said Victoria, 'I'll just tie the sash tighter.' She scooped up her hair above her head and slowly let it fall. 'I still can't decide what to do with my hair.'

'Plait cornflowers into it,' I said, 'like Aunt Ange used to, when we played those games. Do you remember?' I was lying on my bed, half reading, so it was easy to keep my face averted as I spoke.

'I certainly do,' said Victoria. She picked up one of her white satin bridal shoes and held it against her cheek. 'Poor Mummy. She would have loved all this.'

'Does it make you think of her?' I asked. 'I mean, more than usual?'

Victoria considered. 'No. Not really. I suppose she never was much of a mother to me.' She set the shoe down. 'Mummy would have been marvellous at ordering the flowers and the food and all that, but it's your mother who could truly have helped me.'

A lump swelled in my throat. 'She was your mother, too.'

'No. She wasn't.' Victoria moved round the room, tidying up things that didn't need to be tidied. 'It wasn't her fault. She tried to be, but I wouldn't let her. I wouldn't have let anybody. No one could have done any better than her.'

I tried to pretend that I wasn't wiping my eyes. I said nothing for a bit, and then, 'What did you mean, when you said she could have helped you?'

Victoria's reply, when it came, was small and tight. 'I don't know. Told me what to do, I suppose.'

'But you don't need anyone to tell you what to do! You always – just do it.'

'Perhaps you're right.' She plumped her pillow, smoothed her eiderdown, tucked in the loose fall of her top sheet with care. 'I sometimes wonder,' she said, 'would my life have been very different if I'd ever had a proper mother?'

'You make it sound as if your life's already over.'

'Well, it is. I mean, one phase of it.' She arranged her ancient teddy and rag doll in the centre of her pillow, as if she were a nurse preparing a bed to welcome a sick child. 'It's all right for you, Ruthie. You've got that stability, you see. That means you'll always be all right, whatever happens to you. But I – ' She turned her back to me to gaze out of the window, one thin cheek cradled in the hollow of her hand. She must have been well aware of the dramatic impact of her pose as she stood silhouetted against the lavender light of the summer dusk, but the sight moved me, just the same. 'That's why I'll never have children,' she said, her voice low and clear. 'That's one reason, anyway.'

'You can always change your mind,' I said, feebly. 'You've got lots and lots of time. I think you should. If you had a daughter, you would know how to make it all right for her.'

She was silent for a while. Then she came over to my bed and rested her hands on the brass rail. 'Ruthie,' she said, 'if I ever do have a child, you're going to have to be the one to give it what it needs.'

'Me?'

'Do you promise?'

'Of course I promise. But – '

'Whatever happens? Whatever happens between us?'

'Yes, of course. But Vicky, nothing's going to happen. What are you talking about?'

Her face relaxed, and she gave a fluttery little laugh. 'Oh, nothing. Just nonsense. Just pre-wedding nerves, I suppose. After all, my experience of weddings hasn't been that great so far.'

'This one is going to be very, very different,' I said, perhaps with more conviction than I felt.

'You're right. Of course you're right. Listen, Ruthie. I'm going to London tomorrow.'

'Tomorrow? On the day before the wedding? Why?'

'I just need to get away. I'm getting jumpy. I need . . . well, my last little taste of freedom. Keep the others calm about it, will you, even if I'm late back?'

'All right,' I said, 'I will. And I'm not to worry. Right?'

'Right. There's absolutely no point in worrying. There never, ever, is.'

'That's true,' I said, and the conversation came to an end.

'She says her shoes don't fit properly.' That was how I explained Victoria's departure to my father and Aunt Marigold. 'She's got to take them back to Harrods. She'll be back later. It's no big deal.'

'It's rather awkward, with her grandparents coming,' said my father. 'They're arriving in time for lunch, so that they can see something of her before the wedding.'

'Well, they'll see her this evening. It's not the end of the world, Dad. I'll be nice to them.'

'I'm sure you will, darling. But I can't understand why she just slipped off like that.'

'Because she was in a hurry to catch the bus to the station. I told you that already.'

'Yes, yes, but I could so easily have dropped her off in the car.'

'She wanted to go on her own. She's nervous, Dad. She

doesn't want to have to bother with talking to anyone today.'

'That's perfectly understandable,' put in Aunt Marigold, folding towels. 'She'll have to do a great deal of talking tomorrow. Don't make a mountain out of a molehill, Julian. She'll be all the better for spending some time alone.'

Simon looked up from his newspaper. 'Except she won't be alone,' he said, his voice free of expression, 'because she's meeting Daniel.'

'No she's not!' I cried. 'She's going to see if she can change her shoes. What on earth made you think she was going to meet Daniel?'

'Because I heard her say so,' said Simon levelly, 'on the telephone.'

'But he hasn't rung.' This was a sore point with me. He'd said he'd ring from work, but he hadn't.

'Yes he has,' said Simon. 'You were out.'

I was dumbstruck. My brain twisted the information this way and that, but the only sense I could make of it was to assume that Simon had got it completely wrong. 'She can't be meeting Daniel,' I said. 'She would have told me.'

Simon just looked at me.

'She must be planning a surprise,' suggested my aunt. 'A bridesmaid present for you. Something like that. I wouldn't inquire too closely if I were you, Ruth.'

A surprise present. That did seem plausible. I resisted the temptation of ringing Daniel at work, and set about washing lettuces for our ham-and-salad lunch.

All day, people kept arriving. First came Ronald and Pamela Brooke, with their monogrammed leather suitcases and the air they carried with them that they alone knew how to do things properly. It was plain that they were taken aback by their granddaughter's absence but they were too well-bred to be openly critical. Lunch passed off without too much strain, but when Aunt Sarah and Uncle Roger and the three big – grown-up – boys and Paul's girlfriend Jenny who he'd met through Young Farmers all bounced in, dumping sleeping-bag rolls and knapsacks and embracing everyone in sight, Lady Brooke looked a little shaky and, at her husband's insistence, retired to her makeshift bedroom for a rest.

Aunt Sarah and her family took up an awful lot of space, but they did jolly us all up, and in their company the day passed too quickly for any of us to give much thought to Victoria. At about six, Gerald's sister and brother-in-law turned up, with Alice, the little bridesmaid. Not Gerald, though – Victoria had insisted that he keep his distance for a whole week, to make Saturday, as she put it, seem even more important. Alice, who was entranced by Victoria, was loud in her disappointment at not seeing her. 'I really would have thought – ' murmured my father to no one in particular. 'We're expecting her to ring from the station at any time,' said Aunt Marigold. 'Do stay as long as you like.' But Alice and family were engaged to dine with Gerald at the hotel where they had put up, and after two hours of sherry and peanuts they made their excuses. 'Do you think', asked my father as the door closed behind them, 'that we should start worrying yet?'

'Well,' said Aunt Sarah, 'She is twenty-two. And it's only eight o'clock and still broad daylight.'

'I suppose you're right,' said my father, without conviction.

362

Aunt Sarah had brought supper with her, as her contribution – three vast trays of lasagne, wedged into the back of their Landrover under sheets of silver foil. But there was still plenty to do, like finding enough cutlery and making more salad and sawing up sticks of French bread, and it wasn't until after the meal, at nearly ten, that I ran upstairs to my room to get a cardigan, as the last warmth of the July day faded. By this stage my father had telephoned the station and found that trains from London were not subject to delays, and yes the public telephone at the station was fully operational, thank you very much. The Brooke grandparents had been twittering for some time now, and despite what Victoria had said to me the night before I was finding it hard to suppress my own uneasiness. So when, as I pulled my cardigan out of my drawer, I noticed the white envelope stuck into the frame of the mirror, I knew what it was at once. Everything inside me jolted, as it does when you put your hand on an electric fence. I didn't touch the letter at first. I believe I sat on the edge of my bed, even that I read a couple of paragraphs of my book, as if I was clinging on to the last little fragments of normal life that remained to me. When at last I opened the envelope, drawing out the letter was as difficult as putting your hand into a hole or a hollow tree, when you don't know what's inside but you think it might be something alive.

Ruthie,

I don't know where we'll be by the time you read this. Don't try to stop us. It won't do any good. And please don't blame Daniel. Blame me. You know I always have to take what I want.

Please, Ruthie, look after Gerald for me. He's a good man, and
he doesn't deserve to suffer. I know you can provide him with the
kind of comfort he'll need.

I'm not going to apologize, because I know that what I've done
goes beyond any kind of apology.

V.

I read it through, dry-eyed, my brain ticking like an over-
wound clock. It was only on about the third reading that I
could make sense of it. From downstairs drifted talk and clatter
and intermittent laughter. The boy cousins, undismayed by
the Victoria drama, were working their way through a crate
of beer.

I stood in the middle of the room, just holding the letter. I
didn't know which way to turn. All I knew was that I didn't
dare catch sight of my reflection, because I felt sure that the
face that looked out at me would be very, very old.

There were footsteps on the stairs. I held my breath. No
one, surely, would come in. But the door creaked open, and
there was Simon.

'She's gone,' I said.

'She's not coming back?'

I shook my head, and handed him the letter. When he'd
read it, he said, 'Good. I'm glad. I never want her to come
back.'

'But I do,' I said, 'I do, I do,' and then I began to cry.

Simon took me in his arms, which I don't think he'd ever
done in his life before. 'You'll see,' he said, 'it'll be better.
You'll come to realize, Ruthie.'

For a few luxurious moments I wept into his T-shirt. Then I pulled myself away. 'I'll have to tell the others,' I whispered, wiping my nose with my hand.

'I'll get someone,' said Simon. 'Aunt Marigold?'

I shook my head. 'Aunt Sarah.'

'She's more like Mum, isn't she?' said Simon. 'Good idea.'

It was too late to contact many of the wedding guests, though Aunt Sarah and Uncle Roger did their best. I remember very little of the day, though I do have an image of a few stragglers calling to see if there was anything they could do to help, forlorn in tails and frocks and hats. How Gerald spent the day I've no idea. I do know that I had no intention of comforting him. Not then, not ever.

Maddy and Katie sorted out my life for me. They arrived, because they'd been invited to the wedding; I think they were in my room that afternoon, and I know they both spent the night there. They pulled the mattresses and the bedding down off the two high beds, and we slept there in a row on the floor, with me in the middle. I did sleep, too, because I was given something, something to swallow out of Granny Brooke's travelling medicine chest.

Maddy and Katie took me back to London with them, eventually, and set me up in Katie's flat, Maddy having already established a quasi-marital arrangement with handsome, actorish Ned. I resigned my job at the café, because Katie's flat was in Clapham, which was too far away to make it worthwhile, but I soon found another job in one of the new wine bars that were springing up almost daily as the first wave of Thatcher's children discovered a taste for champagne and cocktails and fancy foreign beers. I found a huge burst of energy from somewhere, and I tarted up my CV and fired it off to every newspaper I'd ever heard of. It wasn't long before I got a staff job on one of the South London papers. But I still kept on at the wine bar, partly because I needed the money, and partly because incessant work, day and night, was the best way to keep the spectres of Victoria and Daniel at bay.

I never went back to Primrose Hill. Maddy and Katie went over and sorted out my things. They reported that all Daniel's stuff had gone, and there was no note, nothing. The Housing Association weren't bothered. They had a long waiting-list of prospective tenants. I should think our lovely, dusty, icy flat was reoccupied within days.

So work and London became my life, and one newspaper job led to another, and I think I've done pretty well, really. I've always had a social life, and there have been men, too, not a constant supply, but respectable. Some have lasted weeks, some months, one or two a couple of years, but no one has ever come close to replacing Daniel. Until now.

I would have expected Gerald Hepburne to leave Westaby, but Moira Brice got in first. Gerald had stayed put in his bachelor flat; Number Two Woodland Walk remained empty until it could be bestowed upon some deserving young Westaby couple. As time passed and other parts of life grew up to cushion the pain, I thought that I ought to go back and visit Gerald. I had no intention of adopting the role at which Victoria's letter had hinted, but not ever to speak to him again would make me a coward. So one lightless winter day about six months after the wedding that never was, when I was paying one of my rare and unaccompanied weekend visits to what remained of my family, I buttoned my coat under my chin, crammed a woolly hat of no great glamour on to my head, and trudged off in the direction of Gerald's flat.

He was out. The relief was considerable. I dithered about leaving a note, but then – with a fresh surge of relief – I realized that I had on me neither pencil nor paper. I almost skipped back down the path and whistled and kicked up leaves. And then who should round the corner in the chill half-light of early afternoon but Gerald and Moira, bearing shopping. I greeted them, but in the split second before I did so I could see that they were quite prepared to pretend not to notice me. We chatted for a little, without mentioning Victoria. I didn't say that I had been to call. They both looked pink, Moira evenly, softly pink like a marshmallow, Gerald pink at the edges, ears and nostrils and the rims of his eyes. The neck of a wine bottle was sticking out of one of their carrier bags, but they didn't ask me in.

We parted cordially, with best wishes for the coming year. When I reached the next corner I looked back. They had paused at the door of the building which contained Gerald's flat, and they had put down their bags while he groped for his keys. There was no embrace, but Moira reached up and brushed something, real or imaginary, off Gerald's shoulder with her mittened hand.

31

Victoria's leaving blasted the landscape of our family life; all that remained were twisted distortions and charred stumps. For a long time, going home was awful. Everything felt unfinished and half-hearted. Sentences trailed off midway; conversations flickered and died. Without Victoria, the interior of Lodge Cottage came to look like a series of auction rooms. Household objects seemed to gather in unlikely clusters on surfaces, where they drooped, drained of any function, forlorn repositories for dust. It wasn't possible to look at something ordinary − an egg whisk, say, or a magazine rack − and see what it was actually for. Everything just seemed to be a study in pointlessness.

Marigold spent as much time as she could with my father, but I don't think she did much good. As of old, she tried to pull things together, but she no longer had the energy or, perhaps, the conviction. Marigold, like all of us with the possible exception of Simon, had been so wrong about Victoria; she had never felt truly wrong about anything in her entire life and really the experience came too late. When my father had his stroke and had to stop work it was almost a blessing for Aunt Marigold, who promptly made my father and his health the centre of her life.

I only glimpsed the ashy desolation of the months that

followed Victoria's departure because I spent as much time in London as I decently could, fully occupied with blocking everything out, but I imagine Simon was the least affected. It had always been hard to tell, with Simon, how much family mattered – he gave the feeling that it was either everything or nothing. Whichever, once Victoria had gone, Simon seemed to grow up overnight, later than everyone else but more emphatically. He never did take his A levels, always maintained his scorn of university education, but he did amass a surprising amount of practical experience through a series of menial, poorly paid jobs on farms, in hospitals, on building sites. After a couple of years, he was off on aid-work projects, mainly in Eastern Africa, working six months here, a year there. He's been in the Sudan for the last four years and we're all terribly proud of him, though we have to be proud from a distance because he's only been home once in that time and there can be no question of Dad or Aunt Marigold travelling to see him. The centre of Oxford is beyond them now.

Simon is in charge of a major irrigation programme and he's made himself fluent in the local dialect. His letters are rare and brief, but they express a terrific sense of certainty and purpose. I'm always pleased to get them, of course, though they bear so little connection to the awkward, dusty-haired brother who was once always on the periphery of my vision. The letters are holy tracts in the Boar's Hill flat where my father has lived with Aunt Marigold ever since his second stroke. Marigold, herself diminished by osteoporosis, took early retirement from St Irmgard's. As soon as my father was well enough to come out of hospital, which wasn't for many months, she set him up in this ground-floor flat where everything is specially adapted. She can't lift him; these days she can hardly lift a kettle. A home help calls twice a day and washes and changes him, and once a week he's lowered into the bath with the special handles that are really more use for Aunt Marigold because my father doesn't have much grip. He spends a lot of his time parked by the living-room window, which has a view. I set up a bird table in front of it, because he's always liked watching birds, even the dullish ones that venture into an Oxford suburb. If the representative of any remotely unusual species turns up he lets out a kind of gasp – he has some speech left, but it's an effort – and Aunt Marigold hobbles over and notes it down in the little book that's kept for that purpose alone. Marigold is by far the best at working out what he's trying to say. The pain of her crumbling bones seems, if anything, to have sharpened her other senses.

Dad is still working on his life of Gilbert Wenham Rampling, even though he can no longer turn a page or hold a pen. Every day, Aunt Marigold spends two hours sitting with him, reading bits out to him and translating his grunts on to paper. The book inches forward, but completion is not in prospect. I suspect that Aunt Marigold sees to that. I think that, like me, she sees the book as the kind of task that might be set in a fairy tale. As long as you're toiling at it, you stay alive, but the moment it's finished, you die.

Except, of course, in the fairy tale you don't die. You don't because the hero comes along and releases you from the spell. I don't know whether my father is waiting for such a rescuer, and I don't know who that rescuer could be. Not me. Aunt

Marigold won't let me visit more than once every six weeks. 'You've got a life to lead,' she insists. So I do take trouble to write letters, and I know that all my articles are cut out and pasted into scrap-books, and pored over again and again in that too-warm fawn-coloured flat. The flat was bought and equipped, partly, with the proceeds of the sale of the Dorset cottage. I agreed to the sale – indeed, I initiated it after that second, catastrophic stroke – but still it felt like the saddest thing that had ever happened to me.

I'd told Alex Malone about most of this, over the last few months. We'd talked a lot about our backgrounds, the way you do when you're establishing whether a new relationship is important or not, so what remained of my family was closer than usual to the forefront of my mind, I suppose. Naturally we'd talked about past affairs too, and I'd mentioned Daniel, but only as one of a (not very long) list. I'd given little substantial detail. The recent end of Alex's marriage (her instigation – drifting apart cited as the main reason, but he'd later uncovered an affair) got a lot more airplay. I'd also heard a good deal about his large and jolly family who were scattered here and there but who all congregated for noisy Christmases and cheerful weddings. He had three sisters and was very fond of them all, and he had sounded a little sad on my behalf when he'd asked me, 'So it's just you and your brother, then? That's all?' But I hadn't found it so very hard to say yes, that's all, I haven't got a sister. Because I hadn't any more, and often I felt as if I never had.

The evening at Maddy's drew to its natural conclusion. We

bowed out with presents, embraces, and mutual promises of telephone contact. I played my part well, I thought. How strange it seemed that I could sit for several hours with some of the people who are closest and dearest to me, and not one of them could possibly have guessed that I had a new fiancé, a soon-to-be-adopted daughter and a sister who was dying. We are all so closed from each other, and all our social behaviour, even our giving and taking of love, is so clumsy and ignorant and blind.

The thought made me forlorn. 'How do you feel?' asked Alex when we were on our way home on the second taxi ride of our engagement. I replied, 'That was a great evening,' or something equally evasive. Alex, who was sitting very close to me, said, 'Is something wrong, my darling? You're very quiet.' I smiled and patted his hand and said no, I was fine, I just had a lot to think about.

'No second thoughts, then?'

'Absolutely not.'

'Thank goodness for that.' He put his arm round my shoulders; it took a real effort of will to resist the urge to wriggle free.

Back at the flat I rushed to rescue the flowers from the sink. I tried arranging them in a bucket, but that looked terrible, so I had to divide them between my three vases, which ruined the effect. At thirty-seven I was no better at arranging flowers than I had been in Victoria's day. Perhaps I was no better at arranging anything. Alex said, 'I don't think they should be divided,' and I said, 'OK. You do it then,' in a tone that was almost snappish.

While he fiddled with them I drank three glasses of mineral water to help the evening's excesses through my system, and tidied away a few things and checked the answerphone – there were no more messages – and braced myself for the moment, which was imminent, when he would suggest bed.

'There,' he said, propping the flowers – back in the bucket – on what the landlord called the breakfast bar, 'that's the best I can do. I'll buy you a vase tomorrow. I should have thought of it.' He took my left hand and stroked it. 'I didn't buy a ring. I thought that would be presumptuous.'

'You can presume whatever you like,' I said, smiling at him, 'but I don't need a ring.'

'We'll choose one together,' he said, 'on Saturday. OK?' and he pulled me towards him. He fumbled with the buttons on my jacket. 'I did want to make love to you on the day we got engaged, but look, it's already tomorrow.'

'Tomorrow will do nicely,' I said, and we made our way to the bedroom. Once more I felt the crush of Victoria's letter in my pocket, and for the first time ever with Alex I had to fake it. Afterwards we lay cuddled up in bed murmuring things to each other, and it should have been simply perfect. Alex took ages to fall asleep.

When I was sure he really was unconscious I eased my numbed arm out from under his chest and slithered to the floor. I put on my father's dressing-gown and a pair of downtrodden slippers which, like the dressing-gown, were not normally in use or evidence when Alex was in the flat. I drew the letter out of my rumpled jacket and bore it into the kitchen at arm's length. To reopen it took an immense physical effort; my fingers felt as if they had been frozen.

I read it through again, and all at once I was seized by a passionate anger. Who was this child? Was she Daniel's daughter? What had Victoria done with Daniel – my man, whom I had loved so much, far more intensely than I loved this gentle, patient Alex Malone who was keeping my bed warm for me? Dropped him by the wayside, no doubt, as she had done with everybody in her life. As she was now preparing to do with her own daughter.

I didn't believe in her cancer. The knowledge came to me suddenly. It was exactly like my own mother's – she was playing all the notes that she thought would move me most. Well, she was wrong. I was no naïve young girl any longer. I didn't need to let her lies into my life.

And yet even as I told myself this, a voice was saying, what if? It could be true. Lots of women do get breast cancer and then it spreads. If she was lying, why was she being so unoriginal? Victoria was always original.

I looked at the letter again, whispered the words aloud into the silence. 'Do you remember, the things we said by the sea, all those years ago?'

I remembered. Memory was like a pair of hands reaching out for me, pulling me away from my lover and my flat and everything about my life that was decent and orderly and properly understood. Memory tugged at the yearning in me; I saw and heard and tasted the beauty and the danger that were Victoria. For so many years Victoria had stood like a statue in a corner of my mind – like one of those statues that unsettle

Watteau's landscapes, marble and yet living, beckoning without motion. With a huge and constant effort of will I had kept my eyes turned away from that enchantment, had concentrated my attention on the sunlit ordinariness in the foreground of the picture. But now the statue had wriggled into warm life, and I could ignore it no longer. I wanted to surrender, wanted to follow Victoria down the shadowy path into the magic realm where she would guide me, take me over, live my life for me. For that is what Victoria had always done. Victoria was damaged, and she tried to repair the damage by stealing things from other people. And as she stole, she spoiled and plundered and destroyed.

I knew this. I had known it so deeply, so long. I clenched my mind like a muscle, made the statue change into a grinning gargoyle, turned the mermaid into a stinking harpy with talons that would rend flesh. There was no response I could make to her letter that would not give her access to me, to the core of me, to what I had trained myself to believe was most precious. There was only one option open to me, if 'me' was what I was to remain.

My eyes swam. My tears were for the lost past, for the thin dark girl-child with the caramel skin who had once so dazzled me. I let them run down my cheeks until they had begun to soften the smarting of my wounded heart. Then aloud I said, 'No, Victoria, I won't do it. I'm not going to let you back into my life.' I replaced the letter in its envelope and twisted it into a tight spiral, and then lit it on the gas hob. When not one legible word remained I swept the silky ash into the palm of my hand and, late and cold as it was, I unlocked the French window and stepped out into the frozen garden. All was hushed, even the traffic. I made my way round the dark rectangle of frosty grass, sprinkling until not one whisper of ash remained. 'Victoria,' I said, my voice firm and clear, 'at last you've given me a chance to say goodbye to you. Thank you for that.'

Then I stepped back into the flat and bolted the window and washed my hands clean of the last traces of Victoria. I took my diary out of my handbag, turned to next Saturday's date, and wrote, 'a.m. – Shopping for ring with A', though it was hardly likely I'd forget. I checked the time. It was nearly three. 'That's that,' I said to my reflection in the window. 'Time for bed.' But I didn't go to bed. I sat in my armchair, hands folded in my lap, staring at the child's face that flickered across the empty wall.